Yesterday's Bread

The story of one Priest, from boyhood to Priesthood and beyond

M.P Burns

Email: mpaulburns@hotmail.co.uk

Yesterday's Bread © M.P. Burns, 2008

ISBN 978-1-4092-1182-2

OTHER WORKS BY THE SAME AUTHOR:

Jesus and Mary Magdalene: a Love Story
In this book, the author attempts to tell the story of Jesus in the first person, hoping thereby to enter his mind to some degree. Jesus is seen as being completely human, "like us in all things except sin" as St Paul puts it. The implication is that besides experiencing weakness, limitation and even ignorance, he must have been a fully integrated sexual being, with his sexuality playing a decisive part in his psychology. Mary is seen as the mysterious "disciple whom Jesus loved" who features prominently in the fourth Gospel. Their relationship is explored with what is hoped is openness and honesty. The work is itself fictional, but follows closely the Gospel narratives.

Credo: One Catholic's view of his Church.
The Catholic Church is seen by the author in this book with deep love and affection, but also with not a little exasperation. It sets out to show Christianity in general and Catholicism in particular, as a deeply satisfying and exciting vision. Problems are outlined and faced, and hopefully imaginative solutions proposed.

Essentials: A basic handbook of the Catholic Faith for ordinary people
Most supermarkets produce a range of basic necessities at a bargain price. This explains the title: the book is a no-nonsense look at what being a Catholic involves, with the stress on the wonder of it all.

Published by Lulu.Com
Set in Book Antiqua 10pt

INTRODUCTION

One of the many reasons for writing this book is an admiration for, and a wish to emulate the achievement of the sixteenth century goldsmith, sculptor and (at least in his own estimation) general genius Benvenuto Cellini. His autobiography is to say the least an extraordinary document, covering as it does every aspect of his life from the sublime to the profanest of the profane.

So often, books tend to be one-sided, dealing with limited aspects of a person's life. Religious biographies in particular seem curiously devoid of any idea that the human beings they write about do other things besides preaching, praying, and being all-round Good Sorts. The joy of Benvenuto's book is that he can pass from a description of how he seduced his serving girl to a profound account of a vision of Christ he claims to have had, and back again.

This surely reflects more accurately the true nature of human life. We are not cardboard cut-outs, but deeply and richly varied composites, with elements of sin and grace inextricably intermingled. To put it perhaps a little crudely, we can be making the sign of the cross with one hand, while scratching our behinds with the other.

This is the spirit in which I approached the writing of this book. It has many purposes, the chief of which I shall now attempt to outline.

It is an autobiographical work, though cast in a fictional mould. It is an 'Apologia pro vita sua' on my part as I attempt to share with the reader the joys and sorrows, the happiness and despair, the faith and doubt, the love and resentment that all went into the making of a priest, his subsequent career and at least partial disillusionment. The book is at least an attempt to describe honestly and frankly the thoughts and feelings, the desires, fears, sin and grace that are part of human living. It was painful to write in parts, but it is hoped that the attempt at frankness will assist in the achieving of the aims and purposes of the writer in approaching his task. It is his view that the story is worth telling, and any element that assists in the realistic narration of the tale should therefore be included.

It is meant to be a fairly accurate picture of life in a Roman Catholic seminary and religious order in the fifties and sixties, continuing into the late seventies, with the attitudes common at the times mirrored with reasonably accurate fidelity. Though the work inevitably reflects the experience of only one man, it is hoped that the reader will be helped to understand more fully that fascinating and enigmatic being, the Catholic priest.

The book also seeks to propound the author's own vision of Christianity: not that he claims to have lived up to this vision, but he saw it then and sees it now as a deeply satisfying understanding of God's dealings with man, and how the Church could possibly seek to play a more integrated role in the world in which she finds herself.

Christianity has always stressed the dichotomy between sin and grace, and secular and sacred. Perhaps the greatest heresy in Church history has been the tendency to remove the 'and' between the two pairs in that statement, thus identifying grace and sacred, and sin and secular. Thus the former become the good, the latter the evil.

From this error flow most of the problems besetting the Church today, as in former ages. She has persistently found it difficult to find goodness in the secular, the temporal, the material, and so in spite of regarding marriage as a Sacrament, she has always had to struggle to delete from her own consciousness the notion that sex is something sinful. It is hardly surprising, therefore, that she constantly has to struggle to maintain the faith and devotion of her children, secular beings as they are, immersed in a material world.

And yet the answer lies in her own precious storehouse of truth. "The Word was made flesh and dwelt amongst us." The Body of Christ is an object of worship for the Christian, yet this body is a body like ours, and that is the point. It is a body which delights in pleasure, is prone to weakness and suffering, and yet is beautiful, warm and tender, possessing all the qualities that make up humanity.

Through the Incarnation, God has called the secular, the material, and the temporal to partake in eternity. In Christ, the gulf has been bridged. To the world at large, Jesus Christ is at worst an expletive, and at best an historical figure who has had a profound if varying influence on the development of human civilisation as we now know it. To the Christian, he is a living reality, someone to be encountered now in faith, who makes us alive through a sharing in his life. For many Christians, however, he is a prisoner, locked in the trappings of formalised religion as surely as the host is locked in the tabernacle, or the Divine guest kept securely within the recesses of the individual heart and mind. It is part of the vision of the author that Jesus Christ, the Word, be made flesh in this day and age as truly as he was when he walked the hills of Judea and died on his cross. This is surely what is meant by Incarnation. We the Christians are to be the flesh, blood and bones of Jesus Christ, so that he is just as truly and visibly alive now as he was then.

The sacred and the secular are worlds apart; if this book can assist the process of the continued Incarnation of the one into the other, then it will have succeeded to an extent only hoped and prayed for by the author.

The characters depicted in the book are fictitious; the central character is to all intents and purposes myself, though not exclusively and entirely so. The other characters are drawn from many intermingled sources, most real, but some imaginary. But though the work is a fiction, its elements are not. All the events and attitudes are based on reality, so it is hoped that the work cannot be accused in any way of being biased or unreal.

The work is also meant to be an entertaining story; what is sometimes referred to as a 'good read'. It is hoped that this end, too, has been achieved.

To sum up, the book is intended to be a reflection of the rich variety of human life as it is in reality, embracing as it does the sacred and the profane, mirroring the nobility and the crudity, the mirth and the tragedy, the grind of the daily routine and the excitement of the heights and depths achieved by human beings in their pilgrimage through life. To what extent this is realised must be left to the judgement of the reader.

Finally, a word about the title. It was suggested to me by a chance remark of my wife, and its aptness seemed immediately apparent. "Yesterday's bread" has formed and moulded us the way we are today, for better or worse, but new bread must be the food of today, to make us the men and women we will be tomorrow. Yet the new bread we eat today is the product of yesterday's rain and sunshine. So while acknowledging the irreplaceable part played by yesterday's bread, we must move confidently forward to the future, nourished by the Bread of life who is the same, yesterday, today and for ever.

PROLOGUE

It was a beautiful day, a day for long walks along country lanes, the fresh young growth showing a vivid green among the darker twiggy growth of last year. A day of hope and joy, when everything was new and the future bright with promise. On this day, the slanting rays of the sun came down through the lambent air and broke into a thousand shades of red, green, azure and indigo as they passed through the stained glass of St Augustine's collegiate church, and fell on the recumbent bodies of four young men, chastely dressed in white. Ordination day was the culmination of a journey that had taken thirteen years and more, and henceforth it would direct the remainder of the four lives which were about to be consecrated.

Mark was sweating slightly; he could feel the floor beneath him vibrating as the organ crashed out the opening chords of the 'Veni, Creator Spiritus.' The air was warm and incense-laden, the atmosphere electric. A moment of panic suddenly induced a feeling of nausea in him.

"What am I doing here?" He shivered in spite of himself. "Keep calm, Mark" he told himself sternly. "This is the Big Day. Dear Lord, this is for you. From now on, every breath I breathe will be your breath; I shall be your living presence among men. Is that blasphemy? No, it is you who said it when you told us that he who hears us, hears you: or as St Paul put it, we are the body of Christ. What a responsibility! But no more than that of any Christian. We are all the body of Christ, so he who sees us, sees Christ, or at least that's the general idea. My God, a pretty poor shower we are," he muttered to himself. "We don't make much impression on the world at large."

He pressed his nose into the carpet; the rich warm smell of wool soothed his anxieties, the dust tickled him and he knew a momentary desire to sneeze.

Next to him, Peter clenched his fists fiercely. "I've made it," he whispered exultantly. "I'll show the bastards." He'd never been very bright at his studies; philosophy had baffled him: crap, he had often called it. Bloody nonsense about matter and form: cogito ergo sum. Church history was boring, theology and scripture things to be learned by heart, hoping he'd picked the right horses when examination time came round. The superiors in the Seminary had often hinted that perhaps his vocation lay elsewhere, but he had developed a thick skin, and such half-hearted efforts to dissuade him counted for little when set against his grim determination to succeed.

Third in line was David. He gritted his teeth together to stop them chattering. "Just remember what your father confessor told you" he desperately reminded himself. "You have a vocation; this is the will of God. But Oh God, did I explain properly about those thoughts? It is a mortal sin to receive the Sacraments in sin, and if I didn't explain properly...maybe I didn't let him see that they could have been deliberate." His mind was in torment, whirling round and round. Suddenly a voice seemed to say to him, "David, you've got to get a grip of yourself; you'll go out of your mind, and then you'll be no good to anyone, man or God." In an agony of terror that sickened the pit of his stomach, he clung to the words his confessor had used. "You must trust me, David: there can be no question of sin. These thoughts are obsessions, not wilful, lustful desires."

Obedience to one's confessor, absolute, unquestioning obedience: this was the only cure for scruples. Gradually, calmness came again, and soothed by the majestic smoothness of the organ, and the ancient mellow phrases of the "Veni, Creator Spiritus" as they echoed round the warm, dusty air, he breathed a prayer of thanks. "Oh God, you are so good to me, much more than I could ever deserve. Mary, mother of Jesus, help me through this day. I give my life to you."

Ken had noticed David shivering slightly out of the corner of his eye. "Poor bugger" he said to himself. "You'll be OK, David." But what a way to run a Church. What the hell was the Church doing to the poor sods who gave their lives to her?

His thoughts drifted away from David. Ken had been in his twenties when he had decided that the priesthood was the life to which he would dedicate himself. Now, six years or so later, lying on the sanctuary floor, his mind was filled with images of the past flashing before him. National Service in the Army, the square bashing and the seemingly endless meals of sausages and baked beans. And bloody hell, how those boots pinched on that first route march!

His brother's wedding; he could still feel the soft warm cheek of the bridesmaid as he kissed her; what was her name? Iris or Dierdre or something. The sickly, slightly warm sparkling wine and too much beer afterwards. The pride he had felt at being Godfather to the twins a couple of years later. Those little imps would be fidgeting now five or six rows back behind him on the right hand side. Uncle Ken was their favourite, and they weren't going to miss his big day.

Proud parents and families, they'd all be there, he mused. He'd noticed Peter's lot a bit nearer the front than his own; the ladies all in their best new coats and funny hats. A woman wearing one of those small, tight rather smart hats was likely to be a bit narrow-minded; like her hat, small and tight...steady! Get behind me, Satan. Whereas the ones with the big, wide-brimmed floppy hats so often had bottoms to match.

Bloody hell, stop it! You're supposed to be thinking holy, elevated thoughts on a day like this, but if you go on in this way, it'll not be your thoughts that'll be elevated.

Sanity returned. The 'Veni Creator' was finally at an end. The Master of Ceremonies stepped forward. The moment had come.

ONE

Mark couldn't remember ever not wanting to be a priest. He thought back to his early childhood; he could only just remember his father, who had died when Mark was five, yet well into adulthood, he would occasionally dream that his father had not died after all, and he had found him with a joy that always gently evaporated on his waking once again to reality. His mother was a good Catholic without being ultra pious, and the family had simply made its faith as ordinary a part of life as the Sunday dinner or Monday's washing.

Mark smiled to himself as he remembered the games of dressing up; the best table cloth draped round his shoulders as he solemnly dispensed mint imperials to his younger brother as Holy Communion. He and his brother had become altar boys at St Margaret's at the age of seven; how proudly those little boys walked out in procession as torch bearers at Sunday evening Benediction. The joyful, sorrowful and glorious mysteries of the Rosary mirrored the changing seasons of the year; the sermons that had young eyes inexorably closing, or young feet inevitably shuffling, and the grand finale of the solemn blessing by the priest holding aloft the magnificent jewel-encrusted monstrance.

He could still hear the ker-ching ker-ching of the thurible as the thurifer performed his office at that sacred moment. Then the soft rumble through the church as the congregation took up the 'Divine praises', and then the 'Adoremus' as the priest put the Blessed Sacrament back into the tabernacle. Finally the last hymn, always something rousing, but solemn, such as 'Crown him with many crowns' as they all left the altar and returned to the sacristy, a room somehow always redolent with the smell of old candle-grease, incense and slightly sweaty cassocks.

But the Church had not been his only love in those days; like many another boy he had come home filthy after a long hard campaign in the trenches, or a tough day's tracking in the jungle. Many a time he had come home reeking of fish with his hands salt-chapped after a day spent supporting the family by his toils as a fisherman off the end of the pier in the little seaside town where the family was spending its annual holiday.

He had been no stranger, too, to the softer emotions. Julie was his first love; he could still remember the way her soft, fair hair curled away from the nape of her neck, and the utter joy he had felt when with apparent nonchalance he had managed to end up sitting next to her in the Art lesson. His infatuation was complete; he had lived and breathed for that girl, there was nothing he would not have done to serve her. Too shy to walk home with her after school, he would go home by a circuitous route which included her street, even though it meant making a considerable detour. He became quite expert at the little white lies needed to cover up when answering his mother's questions.

"Late for your tea again, Mark." "Oh, Billy owed me some marbles, so I called at his house to collect them." He knew they'd laugh at him if he told them the real reason.

The funny thing was, he could remember loving Julie and quite a few others after her for longer or shorter periods, each one as though it were yesterday, but he could never remember what caused him to change those youthful, fickle affections. But as the reality of his desire for the priesthood grew, he gradually began to realise that the love of woman was to be an avenue closed to him. He still recalled the many sighs of resignation and renunciation which accompanied his farewells to the latest inamorata on his departure for the Junior Seminary. She had tearfully declared her firm intention of becoming a nun. He often wondered what became of her; their paths never seemed to cross in subsequent holidays.

Another strange thing was that sexual desire had already made itself felt in his young life, but he had not yet linked this with his various idealised loves. From the age of eight or nine he could remember waking up occasionally with the most desperately sweet sensation in his genitals. He felt that this was what heaven must be like. Already he had a vague idea that he must not try to make it happen; sexual morality was inculcated from the tenderest age. Talking about wee-wees and bottoms and jokes about lavatories and girls' knickers were very definitely taboo, though somehow this was different. This pleasure was a noble thing; he had not yet been taught to see it as something shameful or disgusting.

His life changed almost beyond recognition when he went to the Junior Seminary. A year or so previously, a couple of priests had come to the parish to give a Mission, which was a fortnight of spiritual renewal. Each evening, a special sermon would be preached; but these were no ordinary sermons. They were not the sort that had the old ladies nodding off to sleep, and the children shuffling and pinching one another. These were sermons which had the church ringing; you could hear a pin drop one moment, and then the preacher, with a hushed whisper, would start to denounce sin with a majestic deliberation which climaxed in a thundering and comprehensive damnation for those who dared defy the all-embracing mercy of God. The two priests had a presence that was magnetic, and a way with words that was almost witchcraft. The congregation was close to tears at the description of the suffering of the dying Jesus, and yet unheard of ripples of laughter would run through the church at the witticisms which punctuated the proceedings at suitable moments. Every emotion was made to contribute to the renewal of faith and deepening of commitment.

It was towards the end of the fortnight that the knock came to the door of Mark's home. The priest seemed to fill the house. Having made sure that the family were attending the Mission, he then asked the row of little faces looking up at him if any of them wanted to be priests. Mark immediately said yes, he did. The priest then explained that the Order to which he belonged ran a Junior Seminary for boys aspiring to the priesthood, and if the family agreed, he could arrange for Mark to go there.

From then, everything had seemed to move swiftly and easily to the day when he had bidden a tearful goodbye to his family as he climbed onto the train, tugging the heavy suitcase that could have told a hundred stories of the ups and downs of the family history over the past forty years. Now, it was full of the neatly arranged clothes faithfully assembled and packed by his mother, together with his writing case and a few treasured possessions; photos from the family album and a couple of his favourite books. In his pocket he had half a crown for expenses on the journey, and safely inside his writing case was a crisp ten shilling note, his term's pocket money. He found a seat, and his mind a whirl of mixed emotions, settled down for the journey.

TWO

The taxi from the station finally drew up before a large red brick building which seemed enormous to Mark. As the driver lifted out his case and counted out his change, the little boy stared solemnly upwards at the grimy facade. He wondered nervously what he would find inside; well, all would be revealed soon enough. The taxi pulled away as he climbed the steps to the front door. A tentative finger pressed the bell-push, and after a short pause, the door slowly swung open.

A brother with a kindly enough face looked down at the little boy.

"You must be one of the new boys."

"Yes, Father" said Mark.

"No, I'm brother. Brother David." he smiled. "It's rather confusing at first, but you'll soon get used to it. The fathers have white collars on their habits, the brothers black. Right. I'll take you through to the Junior Seminary."

He picked up the suitcase as if it were a feather, and strode off down the corridor, Mark half walking, half running to keep up. Along passages, up stairs and more passages. The walls were lined with the dark, solemn portraits of clerics of yesterday, whose faces seemed to suggest that the drains were in need of attention. Everything however smelled of polish, with the faintest whiff of cabbage. Finally, they came to a door which led into a separate part of the establishment.

"This is it" the brother announced, and knocked at a door half glazed with frosted glass.

"Come in" called a voice. Brother David led Mark into a book-lined office.

"Good afternoon, Father. This is one of the new boys."

"Thank you, brother," replied the priest. He rose from his desk and came forward. Glancing at the label on the battered suitcase, he said "Ah, Mark - Kennedy, is it?"

"Yes, father."

"Well, Mark, welcome to St Saviour's. You'll soon settle in, and I know you'll be happy here. Have you had anything to eat? No, I'm sure you're starving. Come with me, and we'll sort out something for you."

He led the little boy along the corridor to a large spacious room with high windows and beams across the ceiling. Another brother brought in a cup of tea which had already been sweetened, and a plate of biscuits.

"Our evening meal is in an hour, Mark, so that should keep you going until then." He bustled busily about, making sure that Mark had all he needed, then added: "Your case will be taken up to the dormitory, so after your tea, the brother will show you where that is. I'll see you later to sort out a few more details."

With that, the priest left the refectory, and Mark began nervously sipping the hot tea.

"That was Father Director. I'm brother Thomas, by the way. You'll be one of the new boys. What's your name?"

The boy told him, and as he drank his tea and munched the biscuits, brother Thomas began to talk. He quickly put the little boy at ease, and very soon Mark realised he had a friend in this place. Brother Thomas was an endless fund of stories and good advice, as Mark would discover. A simple goodness and holiness seemed to shine from the gentle face as he talked.

When Mark had finished the tea and there were no more biscuits on the plate, his mother's lesson of never clearing a plate somehow forgotten, brother Thomas took him to the dormitory.

As they reached the door, it became apparent that all was not well. A couple of small bodies were locked in mortal combat on the floor, gasps and thumps punctuated by cries of "you did," "I didn't," "yes, you did." Brother Thomas hurried forward.

"Now, Peter, John, what's all this?"

"Just playing, brother."

The two combatants hurriedly stood up, brushing themselves down.

"Well, make sure it *is* just playing."

He then led Mark to his bed, on which his case lay ready.

"Peter and John will show you the way back to the refectory: remember, it's supper in half an hour."

Without more ado, Brother Thomas slipped away, and Mark was left staring at the other two boys.

"Are you one of the new boys?" asked Peter.

"No, he's the man in the moon" John scoffed. "Of course he is. You haven't seen him around before, have you? Elementary, my dear Watson."

Peter chose to ignore this sally.

"We're old hands" he remarked in an offhand manner. "We both started last term. I'm Peter Clark - welcome to the dump."

Mark introduced himself and soon the boys were quickly making friends. Football teams were supported and derided, details of preferred hobbies exchanged, and Mark was given a rapid worm's eye view of life at St Saviour's. The half hour to supper time quickly passed.

As they walked down the corridor, Peter asked "What did you think of the 'D'?"

"The 'D'?" answered Mark. "Who's that?"

"The Director, cloth-head. That's what the boss is called. Haven't you seen him yet?"

"I saw a priest when I first arrived..."

"Shh – that's him", whispered Peter as they neared the refectory, and Mark saw once again the priest he had met on his arrival.

"He seems very nice."

"He's OK, great if you're worried about anything, but he can be a right terror if you get on the wrong side of him."

The boys joined the throng lining up outside the refectory door.

"Settle down now, and less noise" said the Director sharply.

The whispering and shuffling ceased immediately.

"Now boys, you are back at St Saviour's for another term, another year. You are here to work, remember. The holidays are over, so the sooner we get into the term the better. Right, lead off."

So the long line of boys, starting with the eleven year olds at the front, filed into the large room in silence, and after a little confusion caused by the new boys being uncertain where to go, soon all were standing quietly at their places.

The tables lined the walls, and as Mark was quickly to discover, a rigid hierarchy reigned. The oldest boys were at the top on one side, and then the height of the rank gradually declined as the eye moved down the school, with the occasional pimply exception, until one reached the boys in the middle of the school who were at the bottom of the room. Crossing over past the great entrance door, the line resumed on the other side with more of the boys in the middle of the school, until it reached the top of the room once again, where Mark and the other new boys stood.

Mark found himself next to Peter, and would find himself next to Peter for the next thirteen years of his life. On such firm foundations are established the friendships of a lifetime.

The seating arrangements in the refectory were one of the most important factors in charting progress at St Saviour's; to cross the refectory from the top of the Junior side to the bottom of the senior side was as important a moment in life as the donning of one's first pair of long trousers, or passing one's "O" levels.

Grace was said, and with much scraping of chairs, the assembled diners took their seats. In the top corner of the room stood an ornate Gothic pulpit, and the deep tones of the head boy's voice filled the room with the words of Scripture, easily making itself heard above the clatter of knives in butter dishes and spoons in cups and saucers.

Then in came the first of the trays, each with six plates on it. The second and third senior boys with swift efficiency soon had the assembled throng fully served. Boiled ham with a tomato was the menu, a meal which would become as familiar to Mark as bread and butter.

"We'll probably get a 'Tu autem'" whispered Peter. "It's our first night back." The Latin phrase was pronounced as 'twowtem.'

"What's a 'twowtem'?" Mark whispered back.

"Shh" Peter replied. "I'll tell you in a minute."

Sure enough, the Director after a few moments longer gave two rings on a little hand bell, and at the end of the sentence he was reading, the lector chanted "Tu autem Domine, miserere nobis."

"Deo gratias" the boys responded gladly, and immediately the noise rose to a crescendo as seventy voices broke into the holiday reminiscences of the past six weeks.

"Normally we get reading right through the meal" explained Peter. "But on special occasions and feast days, we are allowed to talk after the Scripture reading. If the 'D' only gives one bell, the reader starts the book. But if he gives two, it means a "tu autem", and we can talk."

Such was Mark's initiation into monastic traditions which could be traced back to the fourth century Egyptian desert and beyond. It was all rather overwhelming, but Mark felt a deep pride and joy in belonging. There was so much to learn, but with so many teachers, he would soon get into the way of things.

Next to him, Peter was busily engaged in spreading butter on bread, making a furtive ham sandwich. A small, stocky boy, he came from somewhere in the Manchester area. Not too happy with life at home, the chance to go to St Saviour's had come as a Godsend. Already at twelve, he was wise beyond his years, with a wisdom learned in the streets and school playground. But he was a warm hearted boy, and had impulsively decided to take Mark, an innocent abroad, under his wing.

"The big thing is, Mark," he was saying earnestly, his mouth full of ham sandwich, "keep out of trouble. Don't get found out, and life here is pretty good."

It had been pretty good to him so far, he thought to himself. He had been glad to get back to St Saviour's after the holiday. Mum and Dad's bickering and rowing made him unhappy; at least here he was away from that, and could put it out of his mind. Here he was with a new term ahead. He could look forward to the treats: fairly regular visits to the local cinema, popularly known as the 'bug hut', where the boys were marched crocodile-fashion when suitable films were showing, and the swimming baths and football matches.

Of course, there was work to be done, but that needn't be too much of a bind, as long as enough was done to avoid the strap, that was all that mattered. He had a good supply of comics; reading them in class wasn't too easy, but the evening study period was a different matter. One of the older boys sat at the top of the junior study hall, keeping an eye on things, and the 'D' paid an occasional visit. But his visits were predictable, and whenever he came round, Peter always seemed to be virtuously immersed in Latin irregular verbs, or the intricacies of Algebra.

The meal was coming to an end. The boys detailed to the washing up that week were busily clearing away the debris, and eyes were turning expectantly to the top table. The little bell tinkled, and silence immediately descended. After a moment, it rang again, and with much scraping and scuffling, the sated partakers of the meal rose, pushing chairs back under tables, standing behind them. After Grace, the Director announced:

"Right, boys, it is your first night back, so you will all be tired. Half an hour's break, then assemble for night prayers."

The boys immediately scattered to the four winds; some to the common rooms for a quick game of billiards or table tennis; the more athletic running down to the football pitch for a kick-around. Others strolled around the grounds in the fast fading evening light, gossiping and planning the coming term's events. Among these were Mark and Peter, who joined a larger group of the junior boys who quickly and naturally accepted the newcomer to their ranks.

That night as he lay in bed, Mark reflected on the day's events. The long rows of beds lay quiet, apart from the creak of springs as an uneasy sleeper turned over. Moonlight streamed in through the slightly parted curtains, giving the room a somewhat ghostly appearance.

The small boy shivered slightly. So much had happened in so short a time. Only this morning he had been having breakfast with his family. He and his Mum, his sister Brenda and his little brother Tony had eaten the meal as on any other day. But then things had started to happen with alarming swiftness and inevitability. The upshot was he had left one world, and entered another. He wondered what was happening at home now, and suddenly a longing and yearning awoke in his heart. Everything around him suddenly seemed too big and strange; the warmth of his mother's arms was far away; it would be an age, thirteen weeks or more, until he saw her again. The embryonic monk was once again the child, silently weeping for his mother and the warm, familiar things of home.

But eventually a kind of peace came to the small, tearstained face as sleep took its inevitable toll of the weary little boy. Tomorrow would be another day.

THREE

The next few weeks passed with gathering swiftness; Mark was soon immersed in the strange new world of Grammar school subjects. "We are learning Mathaletics" he proudly informed his family in an early letter. But he was an intelligent boy, and quickly grasped the ground rules of the new subjects to which he was being introduced. The primary school lessons in sums, spelling and writing had given way to geometry, history, Latin and French. He revelled in Latin and history particularly, his vivid imagination enthralled by the life and customs of Classical Rome and the chivalry of mediaeval England.

His world was now the classroom with its ancient desks, marked with the initials of a hundred predecessors, its atmosphere pungent with the smell of chalk dust and sweaty football gear stuffed into leather satchels. His teachers were a mixture of laymen and priests, the Director himself taking the daily Religious knowledge class.

Discipline was strict, as was the norm in those days, but not unduly oppressive. Misbehaviour in class or obvious neglect of work were punished with the strap; inevitably it was Peter who was its first and most frequent customer that term. Years later, Mark could still vividly remember the first occasion on which he had seen it being employed. Peter's Maths homework had been a hurried scrawl of blots and mistakes, and he had been summoned to the front of the class. The book had been exhibited to the rest of the boys with dire warnings about the consequences of such work.

Mark had watched with a kind of horrified fascination as the thick black supple instrument of punishment was brought out. Following the teacher's sharply spoken command, Peter had slowly held out his hand. The lethal looking strap was raised over the teacher's shoulder, and then with a sudden forceful swing, brought down with a sharp crack on the outstretched palm. The noise as the strap made contact caused Peter to flinch slightly, while the other boys winced. He then held out his other hand, and the performance was repeated. He then returned to his place, hugging his stinging reddened hands to his sides.

Afterwards at break, he had shown them to Mark with nonchalant bravado, and Mark had felt a reluctant admiration for his courage.

"I'd rather have the strap than detention" remarked Peter, who was not short of physical bravery. Mark replied that given the choice, he would do the detention. But as no choice was given, Mark too along with nearly all the other boys found himself on the receiving end on occasion. The first time was an ordeal as with thumping heart he had gone forward with several other boys following some fairly minor misdemeanour. It was not so difficult as the other boys seemed to bolster his courage, but the short agony was enough to ensure his good behaviour in general for the future.

He soon became accustomed too, to the new and at first strangely intensified spiritual life of St Saviour's. Morning prayers and Mass at seven o'clock every day, Rosary after tea, night prayers after evening recreation. The hurried Confession each Saturday night as the boys strove to be the first to the common room to guarantee a good seat for the weekly treat of an hour's television viewing. The highlight of the term was, however, the Retreat.

For three days in November, all normal activities ceased, and the time was given over exclusively to matters of the soul. Peter was looking forward to it, which surprised Mark at first.

"It's great" he enthused; "no class for three days, and lots of free time." Mark suddenly realised that Peter would probably not be doing much praying during the free time.

"Who's giving the retreat this year, I wonder?" another boy asked.

"I think it's Father O'Dowd" someone else answered.

"Father O'Dowd" exclaimed Peter with a low whistle. "During his Missions he's supposed to scare folks half to death."

Mark thought back to the Mission he had attended at home the previous year. His mother had not let him go the night the sermon was on Hell. In fact, no children other than a core of older, though trembling, altar boys were allowed that night. He began to wonder nervously what was in store during the forthcoming retreat.

That year in November, it rained as though the skies were the sea. In the college chapel, the boys sat awaiting the entrance of the retreat master. Somehow it was fitting that the skies were dark with scudding clouds and the rain was beating furiously against the lancet windows. The chapel was warm, however, as the ancient central heating system was already doing its winter stint, and in those days before the world had heard of fuel crises, it gave out plenty of heat though it consumed mountains of coke. As juniors, Peter and Mark were near the front. Just inside the Communion rails, a small table had been prepared, with a crucifix and two candles. A chair, ready for the retreat master, had been placed behind the table.

The clock on the wall ticked slowly away. It had a large, clearly etched face, and if one studied it closely, the hands could be seen slowly creeping round. The silence grew oppressive, and yet the boys sat tense, expectant.

At last, footsteps could be heard, but no-one looked round. Father O'Dowd paced solemnly up the centre aisle, and finally reached the steps at the foot of the altar. A large man, he was big in every way. Over six feet tall, broadly built, he had a magnificent physique and a voice like a cup final football crowd. He knelt at the bottom step, and with bowed head, invoked God's blessing on the proceedings with the words of the 'Veni, Sancte Spiritus.'

The retreat consisted of three talks each day, with common sessions of prayer and plenty of free time for private prayer and personal reflection. But the talks were the highlight. An expert in his field, the retreat master took his young listeners on a tour which encompassed the whole of the Christian life; though the main emphasis was on the negative aspects of sin, death and the need to avoid eternal damnation.

With widened eyes and pale face, Mark listened to the thundering denunciations of sin; how perilously easy it seemed to be to fall into it; the slightest impure thought consented to could negate a lifetime of moral effort, and if death suddenly intervened, then the unthinkable torment of hell for all eternity was the consequence.

The preacher spared the boys nothing. Death, normally so remote from healthy young minds, suddenly seemed to loom with terrifying nearness; the stench of the grave seemed to fill the musty chapel. The Christian life seemed to be like an obstacle course; a journey through a minefield. But there were redeeming features, charms almost which ensured safe passage through all these dangers. Devotion to Our Lady was put forward as the infallible protection. Love her and pray to her, and nothing ultimately could go wrong.

But terror was not the only emotion aroused in the retreatants. Tears sprang to Mark's eyes as he listened to the story of the gentle Christ, betrayed by his friends in the garden of Gethsemane, scourged so cruelly and crowned with thorns. He seemed to feel every spasm of his Master's pain; he saw every drop of sweat and blood shed by the suffering Jesus on that terrible day of his crucifixion and death. The little boy's heart filled with love and gratitude as the preacher's words went home.

Between the talks, Mark wandered around the school buildings and grounds, when breaks in the almost constant rain allowed. In the common room, books had been laid out, the approved reading matter for the retreat. Most of them seemed incomprehensible to the young boy; they smelled of dust and of the years they had spent in monastic libraries. Some of the books, however, were more suited to younger minds. Mark found one which told the story of the English martyrs of the Reformation; the men and women who laid down their lives for the Faith under King Henry the Eighth and Elizabeth. With growing fascination he devoured the book, which read like a thriller: the stories of courageous men who stole in from abroad, foiling the government spies and secret agents, risking all to bring the Mass to the embattled faithful. The bravery with which they defied their captors and gave their lives, hanged drawn and quartered, moved him deeply and stirred in him the desire to emulate their sacrifice.

Mark was deep in this book when Peter found him and nudged him.

"Come for a walk, Mark."

"No", Mark whispered back. "We've got to keep silence, Peter. Why don't you find a book? I've got this one; it's terrific."

"They're all so boring, a load of crap" grumbled Peter as he trudged sulkily away. The retreat had not had much effect on him: certainly, the histrionics of the preacher had made him sit on the edge of the bench in chapel, his heart thumping as he listened to the terrible threats; but Peter was made of sterner stuff than Mark. Already he had developed a thicker layer of skin; once the talk had ended, its impact was over.

He brightened up as he noticed that the downpour outside had slackened. He slipped out, and was soon far away from the buildings, bringing cascades of water from the rain-heavy privet and laurel bushes as he valiantly drove back the combined attack of Cardinal Richlieu's guard with his rapier, just cut from another bush with his trusty penknife. There was an hour to go until the next talk; buried treasure could be found, or continents discovered in an hour.

FOUR

The retreat was over, and the term was slowly drawing towards its close. The class work went on much as usual, but soon the masters began to wind up their programmes, and to start revising the term's work in preparation for the examinations. A gradual increase in the application of the boys to their studies could be noticed as the examinations drew closer, some even beginning to study in their free time, a practice that Peter found mind-boggling. The really desperate ones tried to salvage a term's slacking by surreptitious study sessions under the blankets by the flickering light of a torch.

Mark, naturally a conscientious if not industrious pupil, found the revision not too demanding. He was even slightly looking forward to the challenge of the examinations. Peter was an academic ostrich; exams were not to be thought about or worried over until he sat with pen in hand, his name carefully written at the top of the sheet, wondering why he hadn't the slightest idea what the questions were about. In most of the subjects he managed a page or two, and so avoided the ultimate catastrophe of zero marks, but only in one or two subjects did he manage to succeed in scraping a pass.

It was about three days after the last of the examinations that the results were pinned up on the notice board. Word flew round the school faster than gossip at a ladies' bingo session that the marks were posted, and the crowds quickly gathered around the notice board. There was much jostling and pushing, and of course the younger boys could not see the board until the seniors had drunk their fill and moved on, the successful ones modestly exclaiming that they had been positive that they had failed, and the less successful shaking their heads, muttering that they were sure they had done better than that.

Mark finally squeezed near enough to the front to see the first year lists. His heart leapt with excitement when he saw that in two or three subjects he had come first, and in most of the others he was in the top four or five. Even in his poorest result, he had managed a pass.

Peter too was consistent, but near the bottom of the list. Only in one or two disciplines had he kept his head above water; by and large, he came last, or in the last two or three.

"My dad'll murder me" he muttered, shaking his head slowly. The holidays were due to start in a few days' time, and Peter, though glad to see his family again, knew that high words would be spoken about his results, maybe he would be beaten. Still, that was a bridge he would cross when he came to it, and turning to Mark, he said:

"Come on, brain box, I'll race you down to the jungle."

The two friends ran off at top speed, careering down the garden paths and onto the sports field, at the far end of which lay the jungle, a small wooded area hidden behind a long embankment known as the Abbot's walk.

It was one of the school myths that on dark, moonlit nights, the ghostly figure of a monk could be seen pacing up and down the mound, but on this bright, sunny morning of early winter, the frost sparkling on the sedge coloured scrubby grass, such thoughts were far from the minds of the panting friends.

"Beat you" gasped Peter.

Mark was happy to let his friend enjoy his little victory, so contented himself with giving Peter a friendly push.

"Peter", he remarked pensively, "what will happen about your results?"

"Oh, nothing much, though I expect my dad will get mad with me, and I'll probably get shouted at. But here, I'll most likely just get a lecture from the 'D', and told to pull my socks up. Don't worry, I won't get expelled or anything."

The small freckled face with its pugnacious snub nose was set determinedly.

"They'll not get rid of me," he muttered, "I'll show them; I'm going to be a priest. The only person who can change that is me."

But boys had been expelled from St Saviour's in similar circumstances, and Peter knew he would have to watch his step. He duly received his lecture and was warned about the possibility of expulsion if he did not improve, but he lived to fight another day.

For Mark, the thought of the holidays was an excitement that was hard to bear. Though he had not wept since that first night, he had often felt the strain of being away from home and loved ones, grief sometimes causing an ache in his throat and bringing him close to tears. But now, with only a few days of the term left, he found that he was counting the hours and even working out how many minutes and seconds remained. He had always loved his home and family, but the separation had made this love grow almost into a passionate obsession.

The last night finally came. A sense of wild excitement pervaded the school. Cases came down from the box room, and the packing began. The dormitories looked like battlefields, everyone's belongings being heaped on his bed, spilling over onto the floor. Though one or two of the boys were neat, generally being mocked by the others because of it, most of them just crammed their clothes and assorted treasures, newly augmented by the term's acquisitions, into their suitcases. With impatient sighs, the authorities insisted on a semblance of order, and so most of the packing had to be undertaken two or three times, until the results passed muster.

During the day, the boys were allowed out in small groups to go and buy railway tickets; parents had been sending postal orders the previous week to their offspring for this purpose. At supper that night, the Director gave the boys his final holiday briefing.

"Remember boys, on holiday you are still St Saviour's boys, and you must behave as such."

"That means no kissing girls or anything like that" whispered Peter, ever irrepressible.

"Daily Mass is not of obligation as it is in term-time" continued the Director, "but a St Saviour's boy will not be content with only going on Sundays. Prayer, too, must be a part of your daily lives, just as it is here during the term. For the rest, enjoy your holidays and come back next term refreshed and ready for hard work and progress on your journey towards the priesthood. I would sum up the message like this: you are St Saviour's boys on holiday, not on holiday from being St Saviour's boys." This was a favourite aphorism that the Director always used on such occasions, and as he pronounced it, one or two of the senior boys silently mouthed the words with him, to the great amusement of their friends.

That night, with discipline somewhat relaxed, there were sporadic outbursts of pillow-fighting and unofficial feasts, provided by the change left when overgenerous parents had sent more than required for the train fare.

Finally, the patrolling Father Director had good naturedly but firmly ushered all the boys to their separate dormitories and beds, and such fitful sleep as the excitement and tension allowed eventually descended for a few short hours.

The cold morning air was mist-laden, and acrid with the smell of burning coal. The loud speaker droned out its incomprehensible messages of arriving and departing trains; whistles blasted and hooted; it seemed as if half of the population was visiting the other half for Christmas.

"My train is in twenty minutes on platform four" shivered Peter. "Here's yours now."

In the distance, the giant main line express crept relentlessly nearer, groaning and grating as though the slowness of the motion was frustrating its natural urgency for the excitement of speed. As it approached, the crush of expectant travellers pushed closer to the platform's edge.

"See you next term, kid; have a good Christmas."

"You too, Pete." Mark choked on the words as a sudden rush of affection for the friend who had taken care of him in his first term threatened to overwhelm him. There was suddenly so much to say, but no time to say it.

Mark's aching fingers tugged at the heavy suitcase as he struggled with the milling throng to join the train. He turned and glimpsed Peter's cheeky grin as his friend pushed him in the back.

"Go on, get on, you'll never get a seat if you don't hurry up."

A burly sailor took pity on the little boy's struggles, and shepherding Mark in front of him, soon had Mark's case and his own kit bag safely bestowed on the luggage rack of a crowded compartment. A grateful Mark sank into a corner seat and quickly rubbed the steamy glass to see if he could catch a glimpse of Peter. He thought he saw a red cap bobbing in the distance. Was it Peter? He couldn't tell; and with a grinding jolt the express slowly began to pull out of the station.

FIVE

Two or three years had passed; Mark and Peter were well established in the middle of the ranks at St Saviour's. The steady pattern of life had become a routine; though a routine shot through with moments of excitement and fear, laughter and tears as term-time and holidays alternated and the boys began to grow up.

Mark had swanked about in his first pair of long trousers, proud as Punch of the heavy grey flannel, with the turn-ups touching his shoes. His hair, no longer allowed to fall forward in a childish fringe, was swept back in a quiff.

Peter showed signs of adolescence. His favourite colours became the dark green and blue of the Woodbine and Capstan packets as the cigarette machine, with less discrimination than the shopkeeper, disgorged its exciting contents for the benefit of whoever had inserted the requisite shilling.

"Try one, Mark?" offered Peter one day as they walked, with the necessary permission to the nearby shops.

"Pete, you idiot, don't tell me you've taken up smoking" gasped a horrified Mark. "If anyone sees you, you could get reported."

On occasion, the local parish busybodies were not slow to report such infringements to the authorities. The red blazer was a dead give-away: a St Saviour's boy quickly learned what it meant to be a marked man.

"Maybe you're right. I'll keep it till later". For once, caution had prevailed, and Peter returned the offending packet to the relative security of his blazer pocket. Back at school, however, the boys still had ten minutes before the beginning of the afternoon lessons, and so in the suitably discreet environment of the jungle, the Woodbine was lit with due ceremony. The match rasped on sandpaper, and with a puff of pungent blue smoke, Peter exhaled luxuriously.

"How long have you been smoking?"

"Oh, let's see; I've had the occasional fag before; the first was years ago, before I came to St Saviour's, but I've only been a regular smoker since about the middle of last term."

Mark was amazed. How could you be someone's best friend, and not know that they smoked? There were obviously hidden depths to Peter that he had scarcely begun to guess at.

"Go on, Mark, have a drag".

In similar words, Eve must have persuaded Adam, and so after a hurried glance round, Mark accepted the proffered weed and tentatively took a puff. Drawing the smoke back into his lungs on Peter's instruction, the inevitable bout of spluttering and coughing followed. He hastily handed the cigarette back, but knew that another step on the road to manhood had been taken.

Sucking the statutory mints on the way back to class, the boys talked. Hobbies and interests were slowly changing. St Paul had obviously known the same experience: "When I was a child I thought like a child...but now I am a man, I have put away childish things."

That night after supper, an astute observer might have noticed two shadowy figures making their way down to the jungle. Fortunately there were no astute observers on duty that evening, so the friends went undetected. Mark declined the cigarette Peter casually tossed his way, and in the slowly gathering dusk, Peter's cigarette glowed brightly as he sucked in the fragrant smoke. At first, the boys chatted about this and that; the fortunes of the rival football teams they supported, and the possibilities arising from the imminence of a couple of days free from the regular routine. Then Mark casually changed the subject.

"How do you find life at St Saviour's, Pete?"

"What do you mean?"

"Well, are you happy here; do you really want to be a priest?"

Peter's casual approach to life and his somewhat bohemian lifestyle baffled Mark. According to the official line, Peter was definitely not framing well as future priest material.

"Yeah, it's OK at St Saviour's; I take the rules and regulations with a pinch of salt, I suppose; I don't see the point of a lot of them. But this I do know: I want to be a priest, or at least I think I do. If you were to ask me why, I'd be stuck for an answer. It's just the way I feel about things. What about you?"

Mark leaned against a tree, his hands in his pockets.

"I've always wanted to be a priest. Like you, I find it hard to explain the reasons. I suppose the faith is in our blood, it's so much a part of us. I'm happy enough here at St Saviour's; the priests seem to be a good bunch, and the thought of being one of them some day is all right by me."

He hesitated for a moment, then continued:

"But I don't know, it's not a very exciting life. I can't imagine myself, somehow, in fifty years time just living the same old routine, the "regular observance." I love God, or at least I think I do, but I find I get bored with all the praying, and even Mass bores me, too."

"My God, and here's me thinking of you as St Mark" laughed Peter. "Maybe we all get bored by religion. That's why I like my little outlets like the occasional fag, and reading thrillers in study." Peter had graduated from the 'Beano' to the works of Leslie Charteris.

"I'm sure religion shouldn't be boring" frowned Mark, concentrating hard. "When you think about the story of Christ's life and death it's all very inspiring. So why don't I feel inspired?"

The young minds had begun to grapple with the age-old questions; questions that perhaps never in their lives would find a satisfactory answer.

"When I was younger I suppose the glamour of the fine vestments and the incense, lights and music played its part. But it doesn't seem enough now."

Peter dropped the stub of his cigarette and ground it out with his heel.

"I see what you mean, but why do you have to dig and question so much? You'll go bonkers thinking about it all. Just take life one day at a time. I think there's even something in the Bible about that: 'sufficient for the day' and so on."

"There's something too about even the devil being able to quote Scripture when it suits him" laughed Mark.

"But you need to think about these things."

The friends were growing up, but they were still young enough to have a race back to the main buildings, the last one back to be generally stigmatised as inferior in every respect.

SIX

So the middle years at St Saviour's passed, the boys growing and developing as mind and body kept pace. But in some respects, development was muted, to say the least. Mark had always been quickly and deeply smitten by feminine beauty, but now he knew that such feelings had to be kept ruthlessly under control. Admiration had been joined by a more definitely recognised desire, and he could not restrain his eyes from roving along the ranks of the demure young girls of the Children of Mary, a parochial organisation which occupied the front two or three rows of the Parish church when assembled for their weekly meeting and prayers.

One in particular caught his eye and she filled his thoughts and dreams for more than a few weeks. By assiduous though discreet enquiry, he discovered that her name was Marie. Her long, fair hair and smooth, soft complexion made her a beautiful young girl, and he ached with longing for a word or even a glance. Saturday night devotions began to be eagerly anticipated, though he had to console himself with furtive glimpses and the ennobling of his desire through prayer for the adored one. This too salved his conscience, for how could prayer for anyone be wrong?

Lawful opportunities for meeting or speaking with girls were non-existent for the neophyte celibates, but one or two bolder spirits among the inmates of St Saviour's found a way. Mark confined his aspirations to the heart; Peter however was a man of action.

He proudly related his exploits to the scandalised Mark, who listened with a grudging admiration as he unfolded the tale of his conquests.

"She's called Elizabeth, a real smasher. Met her down at the shops. Actually, it was she who made the first move" said Peter, modestly. "She asked if I was from St Saviour's; the local girls call us the untouchables, apparently. I think getting a St Saviour's boy for a boyfriend is quite a feather in their caps. And I didn't mind being got for a boyfriend. Those kisses, wow!"

He showed Mark the love-letters, written in a small, neat hand, unlike the unruly scrawl that Mark and Peter called handwriting. Mark felt a stab of mixed emotions; desire, envy, admiration, as he gazed at the letters, but fear for the safety of his friend was uppermost.

"My God, Pete - a couple of lads were expelled last term for this sort of thing!"

"Don't worry, Mark", Peter replied casually. "In love affairs there's a saying, if you can't be good, be careful. I'm careful all right, I won't get caught."

But Mark was deeply troubled. For a few days he nursed his concern, watching anxiously as Peter unobtrusively slipped away at odd moments during the evenings, returning in time for night prayers. But his mind was in a whirl. How could Peter reconcile his chasing after girls with his position as a junior seminarian? The boys had been taught many things about their future lives and aspirations, but the point most strongly made from the very beginning had been that there had to be absolutely no contact with girls under any circumstances. Mark still blushed when he remembered a party he had been at during the holidays; the young people had been playing 'postman's knock' or some such game that young people play on such occasions. He had given and received the required pecks on the cheek, and had felt like King David after his seduction of Bathsheba in consequence. But this matter of Peter's philandering was altogether different, Mark recognised that.

"What's the matter, Mark? You've been mooching about for the last few days as though the weight of the world was on your shoulders."

Mark jumped as Brother Thomas' friendly voice cut into his gloomy thoughts one day.

"Nothing, Brother," he hastily replied.

But Brother Thomas was not to be put off. "Come on, Mark, tell me all about it. You know you can trust me."

And Mark knew that he could. He had often confided his childish troubles to Brother Thomas in the past; but of course his present worries dwarfed the petty problems of yesterday.

"Come on, Mark, I'll make us a cup of tea and we can have a chat." So with little choice in the matter, Mark followed Brother Thomas to his room, and was soon perched on the edge of the battered armchair while Brother Thomas sat on the bed.

"Now then, what's all this about? In this room, it's like the confessional; anything you say is in absolute confidence. Father Director or anyone else will never know what you confide in me."

Mark knew he could trust Brother Thomas, but still he hesitated. "It's not really my problem or my secret, Brother, but I would like to talk to someone about it."

So without mentioning names, he unburdened himself of the story of Peter's carryings-on.

"So that's what Peter is up to" mused Brother Thomas.

"It's all right Mark; it's obvious that it is Peter you're worried about. Talk about David and Jonathan - what surprises me is that two such opposites can be such good friends."

He smiled faintly and continued: "But I knew Peter was up to something; thank goodness the priests have their heads in the clouds so much, or maybe one of them would have noticed, and then it would have been goodbye Peter. I know he shouldn't be chasing the girls; but after all, it's what all the other young boys of your age outside are doing. Look at it this way, Mark. Boys are like young growing plants. You can train and gently prune a plant, and it will grow into a fine specimen; but if you twist and chop ruthlessly, it will grow into all sorts of weird and distorted shapes. I'm in favour of letting Peter sort this out in his own way. If it turns out that the priesthood is not for him, then it's as well that he finds that out now. But if in fact he has a vocation, then this experience won't do him any harm at all."

This was definitely not the official line, and Mark marvelled at how simple Brother Thomas made it all seem. Feeling happier and more relaxed, Mark began to confide some of his own worries to the brother, and soon the pair were deep in discussion of some of the problems concerning the linking of faith and everyday living. Mark had seen Brother Thomas praying in the chapel for hours on end:

"How do you stick it, Brother?" he asked wonderingly. "I find it hard to concentrate and enjoy the Mass, even for half an hour."

"Everyone keeps telling us that prayer is talking to God" replied the brother. "I think that's where we make our big mistake. Prayer *is* talking to God, but that's the less important part of it. Prayer is listening to God, first and foremost, and I'm sure that what God has to say to us is a lot more important than what we have to say to him. Our Lord once said 'Listen, you that have ears to hear with.' I often think he was being rather funny in a sharp sort of way, just as your teachers might say 'wash your ears out, Kennedy' if you aren't paying attention very well in class. He's saying 'you've got ears, so use them.' Listen to what God has to say."

Mark scratched his head as he tried to assimilate all this. "But how do you listen to God?"

"Your catechism tells you that God is everywhere; in other words, in every human being you meet, in the beautiful things all around you, in the things we usually call religious, like the Bible, the Mass and the Sacraments. So just relax and let the message God is trying to give you come through in everything, and I mean everything, that happens to you. That's the secret of prayer as I see it, Mark. Most of the time we tend to try so hard to talk to a God we cannot see and won't let ourselves hear; just try letting God get a word in edgeways, and start the conversation. We do talk to him, but our talk always has to be a reply. After all, it you were to meet the Queen, or someone else important, it would be rather rude of you to try and do all the talking. You let the important person take the lead."

Mark thought about this for a while. "So God is talking to Peter, even in these experiences I'm worrying about?"

"Of course he is" smiled Brother Thomas. "The pity is, though, that the authorities won't see it that way if young Peter gets caught. But don't get hold of the wrong end of the stick; I'm not saying that I think young boys in your position ought to be chasing girls; just that almighty God has his own way of guiding our lives, and it's not always via his official mouthpieces."

Mark rose from the armchair and stretched.

"Thanks, Brother, for what you've said; it's helped a lot."

"Off you go, Mark, and tell young Peter to be careful."

Mark left the room and went out into the garden, blinking in the strong sunshine and revelling in the warmth, suddenly realising how cold and damp it seemed indoors that day. He watched the bees as they busily went about their business among the green, gold and scarlet of the flower beds, marvelled at a pair of dancing butterflies, and basked in the feeling of being young, happy and at peace with God.

SEVEN

With relentless inevitability, the day came when Mark and Peter achieved the dignity of the top table in the refectory, a new generation of small boys occupying the lowlier places. The final exams would be over shortly, and they would then know the brief joys of life in the sixth form, which at St Saviour's was a gentleman's limbo between the G.C.E. 'O' levels and the Novitiate.

"How do you feel about the exams, Pete?"

There was a babble of voices as the sixty or so seminarians of assorted ages tackled the breakfast baked beans and fried bread.

"No wonder we keep farting all day" grumbled Peter. "I wish they'd give us bacon."

"What's bacon?" laughed Mark. "But the exams, Pete; are you going to be all right?"

Mark had good cause to be concerned about his friend, whose academic achievements had not improved over the years.

"Don't worry about it Mark. You'll be OK, and I'll survive; I've survived up till now, haven't I?"

He grinned broadly at his friend. "I've got staying power, you've got to admit that."

Peter's career through St Saviour's had been a chequered one to say the least, and on several occasions the threat of expulsion had hung over him, but somehow he had always avoided the ultimate catastrophe.

The exams were to be held at the nearby convent school, and there was a general flutter of excitement at the thought of mixing with the girls for the sitting of the papers.

"There are some very tasty morsels among that lot" observed Peter as the beginning of the examination period became imminent.

"I tell you, Mark, I know I haven't got a girlfriend now; I must be getting pious in my old age." He glanced sideways his friend, joining his hands and casting his eyes up to heaven. "But a flash of thigh and a glimpse of navy blue still just about sends me berserk."

"I know what you mean" agreed Mark. "It's funny how stirred up you can get just at the sight of a beautiful girl. The way they curve in at the waist and out again over the hips; my God, I don't know how the hell we'll be able to concentrate on the exam papers."

But when the day came, the importance of the occasion was such that even the attractions of the girls became no more than a temporary diversion, and the nail-biting tension mounted as the boys and girls waited outside the examination room in their segregated groups.

"Why the hell didn't I work harder?" groaned Peter, as the tension finally penetrated his customary sang froid.

"You know now what the foolish virgins felt like" grinned Mark.

But the Scriptural allusion was lost on Peter, who retorted: "How the hell do I know what the girls are feeling about the exams? I just know that if I'd worked harder I wouldn't be standing here shitting myself."

"Come on, Pete, you'll be OK" consoled his friend. "You have been working, and besides, all that class-work and homework can't have been going in one ear and out of the other completely."

"I just hope they ask the right things, that's all."

The doors opened, and the assembled youngsters moved forward, looking for the numbered desks. The two boys went their separate ways, Mark murmuring to himself an anxious 'Hail Mary' as he peered at the numbers on the desks, searching for his own. He found his place, and stood behind the desk.

"Dear Lord," he prayed silently with closed eyes, "help Pete and me to do well in these exams so that we can go on preparing to be your priests."

Peter too was muttering a prayer to himself. "I know I've not been boy wonder at St Saviour's, Lord, but I do want to serve you and I'll try harder in future, I promise. Help me today. And I'll try to be pure in mind and body" he added hastily, as his eye caught the flowing chestnut locks and creamy complexion of the beauty to whom had been assigned the desk next to him.

Some days later, the last exam safely out of the way, the two friends compared notes.

"Thank God they're over and done with" Peter sighed, as he sorted through the grubby last minute lists of history dates and Latin irregular verbs before consigning them to the waste paper basket, their function as aides-memoir completed for better or worse.

"Want a fag, Mark?" Though still in general a non-smoker, Mark allowed himself to bend the rules as far as an occasional cigarette.

"Thanks, Pete, I think we've earned it."

The two were strolling among the trees in the jungle a few minutes later, as smoking still required a great deal of circumspection.

"Just one more year in this dump, then it's off to the Nov. Looking forward to it, Mark?"

"I think so; it'll be a challenge, but I must admit I'm a bit scared about it. I suppose it is a step into the great unknown. A little bit like dying, in a way."

"There's a lot to give up" said Peter, reflectively. "I see what you mean about dying. Maybe it'll shrivel up and drop off," he added crudely. "But seriously, I think this talk about dying to the world seems a good way of putting it. The impression you get is that it's a different world that we'll be entering when we go to the Novitiate. It's some thought, though. No sex, ever; no booze, at least for the first couple of years; no money; do as you're told."

Mark shivered. "It sounds so stark when you put it like that. The thought that we'll never be able to take a girl in our arms and say 'I love you';" He paused for a moment. A couple of sparrows were chasing each other through the leafy glades, and the air felt crisp and fresh. "Life outside has a hell of a lot going for it," he continued. "Life inside seems so - well - unattractive, somehow. What makes us want to be priests, Pete?"

Trying to rationalise his wish to be a priest was a problem that Mark had endeavoured to solve on not a few occasions. He had no great or burning desire to convert the heathen in Africa, or in Britain too for that matter. Working in a parish seemed humdrum and ordinary; why did he want to be a priest? Yet he was certain that this was his allotted path; he wanted to be a priest. He had spoken to father Director about it on occasion, and also to his confessor in his weekly frequentation of the Sacrament on a Saturday night, but the best advice he had received was that a vocation was an inner summons, a call to be obeyed, whether one liked it or not, it would seem. The attractions of the world were temptations to be overcome; to give up one's vocation for them would be a contemptible cowardice and treachery. One priest had said:

"You become a priest not because *you* want to, but because *God* want you to." Mark thought of the passion and death of Christ; "Not my will, but Thine be done," Christ had prayed in the Garden of Gethsemane. Giving his life as a sacrifice for others in union with the crucified Christ made a kind of sense, Mark pondered; well, what this sacrifice entailed they would learn in the not too distant future.

Mark voiced some of these thoughts to Peter, who, true to form, tended to dismiss them rather lightly. The priesthood was still years in the future, and even the sacrifices entailed in entering the Novitiate were a year away. It was one thing to discuss them in a detached sort of way, but quite another to start worrying too much about them at this stage. The year of the sixth form still intervened, and the possibilities arising from that were distinctly interesting.

EIGHT

During their years at St Saviour's, Mark and Peter had often looked up enviously to the sixth formers; at last they had themselves achieved these dizzy heights. New privileges became theirs; a separate common room to enable them to escape from the vulgar herd; the occasional permission to stay up late for suitable programmes on the television, and even the occasional cigarette, officially permitted in strictly controlled circumstances. The curriculum was very free and easy; in most ordinary sixth forms, the G.C.E. 'A' levels were the goal after two gruelling years. At St Saviour's, the Novitiate followed a single year. In consequence, a little gentlemanly dabbling in Latin literature and basic Greek, together with some English literature, history and general social studies just about summed up the academic activities.

It was during this final year that the dirty picture scandal rocked St Saviour's. Some not particularly explicit glamour photographs had been found in the desk of one wretched boy from the fourth year. The whole school had been assembled after breakfast with the realisation that something Big was in the air. An atmosphere of hushed expectancy hung over the assembled throng, and though it was a full five minutes before the Director strode in before them, there was no impatient shuffling as there would normally have been.

Tight lipped, he quietly announced that one of the boys had that morning been expelled. "This is the reason" he added, his voice gradually rising in volume. "These disgusting pictures were found in his desk." The voice rose to a deafening crescendo. "Pictures like these stink of hell; hell and eternal damnation!" In shocked silence, the rows of white faces stared up at the Director, whose seething anger was gradually being brought back under control. In quieter tones, but with a voice full of determined menace, he continued:

"If any more of this filth is ever discovered here at St Saviour's, the instigators will be publicly expelled before the whole school. If necessary, I would close down the whole establishment; expel you all, to purge this evil from our midst. It would be better to close the school and make a fresh start than to allow such a risk of sin and pollution to flourish among us. Consider this as a solemn warning."

With that, he turned on his heel and left the room. After a few minutes waiting in uneasy silence, the boys were dismissed. Mark walked alone in the garden, his mind in a turmoil. The possibility of sin in sexual matters, or rather the near-inevitability of sin seemed to strike him with particular force. He had often been told that the slightest thought in these areas, willingly consented to, was mortally sinful. He had long known this in theory, but now it seemed to come home to him with a dreadful urgency and reality. The world, which had seemed innocent and desirable, suddenly became the haunt of demonic beasts, lurking and lying in wait to entrap him with their disgustingly cloying webs of sensuality. How could one go through life with in-built sexual desires never far beneath the surface, waiting to be roused by the random thoughts and images that existed all around? To open a newspaper or to walk down the street was to be confronted with the occasions of sin. The more he thought about it, the greater grew the sickening sense of despair.

He said nothing about this to Peter or to anybody else, though his friend knew almost at once that something was troubling him. The more he worried, the more sexual thoughts rose to pester him. Desperately wielding prayer like a battle-axe, he drove back the threatening throng, clinging to the thought that as long as he prayed, he could not give full consent to the temptations.

One week, he tried to talk about his worries to the priest in the confessional. "These thoughts are filthy" replied the priest. "Try to think of them in that way; as disgusting rather than attractive. One of the Latin authors had a saying: 'Inter faeces et urinas nascimur omnes'. Just think that sexuality is concerned with those parts of the body that we think of as dirty, unclean. That will make it seem much less attractive. Then your mind will want to turn to more wholesome, cleaner matters." He paused for a moment, then continued in the same vein: "The Scripture tells us that the sinner goes back to his sin like a dog to its vomit. So we must be pure and noble, above the filth of sin."

Needless to say, this advice did nothing to help. "Am I a dirty, disgusting wretch" wondered Mark. "Maybe I'm depraved, a pervert; this is perhaps what is meant by being a dirty old man; the only difference being that I'm still young."

Fortunately, Mark's dismal mooching about did not escape the eye of brother Thomas for long, and it did not take much persuasion for Mark to join the brother in his room, sipping the obligatory mug of hot tea. After much blushing and stammering, and after a few false starts, the story emerged. Once set upon the theme, the inhibitions gave way, and Mark, in tears, poured out his heart and soul to his friend.

Brother Thomas let him continue, the burden lifting as the words tumbled out. "Ought I to leave, brother? I'm not fit to be a priest, I know. Maybe I should look for a proper outlet for these feelings in marriage?"

The brother smiled. "The way you make it sound, Mark, it's a wonder you don't feel that you couldn't inflict such a beast as yourself on some poor girl!" "I'm only joking," he added hastily, "to help you to see how silly it all can look. Not that it is silly; I know you've been through hell the last few weeks. But it is so easy to get things out of proportion, and that's what has happened."

"Let's take things from the beginning. And in the beginning, God made man and woman. The desire of man and woman for each other is a holy thing, Mark, a God-established thing. There is nothing unclean about it, or about the human body, for that matter. Don't ever let anyone persuade you otherwise. We insult God's wisdom and creation when we despise the human body, and unfortunately, there has been a tendency in the Church to fall into this heresy for centuries. When you get to the Novitiate, you'll find lots of this in the old ascetical books. Always remember to take it with a pinch of salt, and you won't go far wrong."

Mark looked at him and smiled tentatively over the steaming tea, and brother Thomas continued:

"Don't be afraid of your desires, Mark; they are good and they are there for a purpose. Talking about bad thoughts; it's a good thing that someone thinks such thoughts on occasion, or there wouldn't be many people around in the world! About mortal sin, too: remember it's not so much a deed done, as an attitude of heart. To be mortal sin, something you do has to be an expression of an evil heart. It takes a lot of wicked determination to commit one; it's not something easily fallen into on the spur of the moment. In fact my own feeling is that very few people ever actually do commit such a sin."

Mark smiled at the brother.

"Brother Thomas, you make everything seem so good, so simple."

"It is simple, Mark; that's how Our Lord made it. 'You shall love the Lord your God with your whole heart, and your neighbour as yourself.' Just think of that and you won't go far wrong. As long as you are trying honestly and sincerely to love God and everyone else, then you can't be far from where God wants you to be. Now off you go, and start smiling again."

Mark left the brother's room, and on a sudden impulse, went along the corridor to the chapel. Inside, he knelt down and prayed: "Thank you Lord for the gift of Brother Thomas as a true friend to help and guide me."

He sat down, and was content to enjoy the peace which once again filled his heart. Later, he went looking for Peter.

"Hi there, misery guts, how's it going?"

Peter grinned at his friend. "You've been walking around like a wet weekend for the past while now; I knew something was up, but you seem different again today. Maybe you've been constipated, and have just managed a good shit" he added crudely.

"That's true, in a way."

Mark was happy enough to let it rest at that, and Peter, relieved at Mark's obvious change of mood, forbore to pester his friend for all the details of his recent crisis.

NINE

The year slowly passed; winter gave way to the tentative early days of Spring, and the Novitiate began to loom closer.

One day, Peter suddenly grabbed Mark by the shoulder. "What are we going to do in the summer holidays? It's the last taste of freedom before the Nov. Let's do something as a sort of last fling."

"What do you have in mind?"

"Oh, I don't know. A holiday abroad, maybe; something like that."

The practical Mark pondered. "Sounds great; there's only one problem, apart from getting our parents to agree. What about cash?"

This seemingly insoluble problem put a temporary end to the speculation, but the seed had been sown. With two fertile minds bent to the problem, an answer was certain to emerge. It was Mark who came up with the solution.

"I've got it, Pete; why not make our holiday a trip to Lourdes? It's somewhere I've often felt I'd like to visit, and who knows? It might be our last chance, at least for the next ten years or so."

Peter tugged his lower lip dubiously.

"I don't know about Lourdes; wouldn't it be all prayer and so on? Besides how does that solve the money problem?"

Mark waved a deprecatory hand. "Don't worry, the genius has got it all weighed up. First of all, it wouldn't be all praying at Lourdes, not by a long chalk. It's supposed to be a beautiful place in itself, at the foothills of the Pyrenees, snow-capped mountains, crystal-clear streams tinkling through rocky valleys, with little alpine meadows dotted about."

"OK, Thomas Cook, you've sold it to me. But the cash, doubloons, coin of the realm?" he asked, clicking his fingers like a spiv demanding payment for his black market contraband.

"Here's the sheer brilliance of the scheme" replied Mark, modestly. "Parents and grandparents; we've a few of them between the two of us; work out how much at the very least we'll need, and then we'll put our cards on the table. Two young men, about to give their lives to the service of the Church, want to make a pilgrimage to Lourdes to obtain God's blessing and help for the future, and all that sort of thing. They wouldn't shell out for a week in Blackpool for us, maybe, but this is different."

And so it proved. The selling point was irresistible, and with return rail fares calculated, together with a modest amount of spending money, and accommodation arranged at the 'Cite Secours', where pilgrims could stay and simply pay what they could afford, the final hurdles were easily overcome. The families agreed to support the venture, and so the holiday-cum-pilgrimage was arranged.

Mark and Peter's last term at St Saviour's finally drew to its close, and the day of departure from St Saviour's duly arrived.

"Your time at St Saviour's is over" father Director remarked at supper on the eve of departure. "These years have been important, but what lies ahead is of vastly greater moment. You have four weeks holiday before you are due at the Novitiate; use the time well to prepare for what lies in front of you. Your childhood is over; manhood now beckons. May God bless and guide you to the great goal of the priesthood."

The speech was greeted with a cheer by the assembled junior seminarians, who clapped their hands and stamped their feet to speed the departing seniors on their way.

Next morning, after bidding farewell to brother Thomas and promising to keep in touch, and after many slaps on the back and thumps on the arm from all and sundry, Mark and Peter found themselves on the platform of the main line station once again.

"I remember saying goodbye to you for the first time on this very platform, Pete" said Mark. "It seems like a lifetime ago."

Well, it's six years or so, kid; maybe the best six of our lives, if what some of the rumours say about our future lives are true." He groaned and shrugged his shoulders. "Gather ye rosebuds while ye may."

But Mark was in no mood for gloomy prognostications.

"It's an adventure, Pete - see it like that."

"Blood, sweat and tears, more like; still, I suppose it's the price of the priesthood."

"Just make sure you're at Victoria Station next Thursday at 9.00 a.m. sharp. I'll see you there," laughed Mark, leaning out of the window as his train pulled out.

With a laconic wave of the hand, Peter grinned, and turned away to look for his own train.

TEN

Precisely seven minutes late, the boat train pulled out from Victoria station the following Thursday with the two intrepid travellers lounging at their ease in corner seats, luggage safely bestowed on the rack above. The lighter clicked, and the blue smoke from the Senior Service cigarettes curled lazily towards the roof. The grimy London suburbs quickly slipped away, and soon the train was racketing along through the Kent countryside, the great adventure of foreign travel now well and truly under way.

"I hope your French is up to this lark" remarked Peter. "I'm bloody useless at it, so you'll have to be chief interpreter."

"As long as we can get directions we'll be fine" his friend reassured him.

"How do you say 'where is the nearest pub?', or 'you have gorgeous legs, baby'?"

Mark smiled at his friend. "If the occasion arises, I'll find the right words somehow; trouble is, I'd be speaking for you, but it would be me who'd get my face slapped."

With the good natured banter, the journey was over almost before they realised it, and within a remarkably short time, the train was drawing up within sight of the cross-channel ferry.

"That must be it!" exclaimed Peter, boyish excitement bubbling over, dispelling for a moment the air of maturity he was usually at pains to cultivate.

Passport control safely negotiated, the moment of embarkation arrived. The oily, salty sickly smell of the ship hit them as they boarded.

"God, I hope I won't be sick" groaned Peter.

"Here, take one of these." Mark's mother had made sure her son was well provided with such essentials as seasickness pills, and so suitably fortified, the two friends went on a tour of exploration.

"We're moving" cried Mark, as he suddenly noticed through a window as the quay slipped past, the cranes dipping and swinging, and a hooter sounding mournfully in the distance. Up on deck, they watched the white cliffs recede. A curious sense of regret, almost, seemed to come over them.

"Bye-bye, Blighty" commented Peter, his years spent in the perusal of 'Wizard' and 'Hotspur' not entirely fruitless.

"Come on, Mark. Let's get a drink."

Downstairs in the bar, the atmosphere was warm and fuggy, the beer fizzy and expensive, but it tasted delicious as the ham sandwiches were hungrily wolfed down.

The sea crossing was short and calm; very soon Mark and Peter found themselves on French soil, the sights and sounds of a strange country a source of wonder and delight. Paris was a mad scramble as they crossed from the Gare du Nord to the Gare de Lyons for the journey south. Mark's French proved adequate to the task of seeking directions and ensuring that they boarded the correct train, and so exhausted, they sank into their seats as the express began the long journey across France.

The sky was a vision of gold, blue, scarlet and purple as the train hurtled south, gradually giving way to the darker shades of night. On and on through the long hours of night the express rattled and swayed, dimly lit towns and villages a vague and confused impression.

Eventually, weariness took over, and Peter slept. Mark walked in the corridor to stretch his legs, his mind turning to the experiences which lay ahead.

"Lord, make this pilgrimage a real experience of faith for me" he prayed, staring out into the darkness. "Teach me how to give myself generously to you."

Restlessly, he walked along to the toilet, and after relieving himself, quickly washed his sticky, grimy face. Try as he would, however, he could not rid himself of the acrid taste of travel in his dry mouth. Rejoining Peter, who nodded and lurched with the train as he slept, undisturbed by the motion, he too eventually dozed into a fitful sleep.

Several times he awoke, once to find a bedraggled Peter smoking a cigarette.

"God, I've got a mouth like a piece of shit in a sandpit" croaked Peter. "What time is it?"

Mark fumbled for his watch.

"Twenty past three; we're due in at Lourdes at half past nine."

Between alternate bouts of sleeping, desultory conversation, and staring out at the lightening French countryside, the seemingly endless journey finally drew to its conclusion.

"There's the basilica" exclaimed Mark, and slowly, the long train gradually came to a standstill. Not being one of the pilgrimage trains, only a few passengers descended. Mark and Peter, laden with baggage and feeling as if they hadn't slept for a week, pushed their way down through the crowded streets. Lourdes was already a mass of bustling pilgrims, hurrying back to their hotels for breakfast after the morning Masses. Further and further down they trudged, gazing in wonder at the unending souvenir shops, rosary beads, statues and illuminated grottoes piled high, plastic Lourdes water bottles hung up in bunches, rattling gently in the soft morning breeze.

Finally they came to the large open square in front of the basilica, with its two all-embracing arms surrounding them.

"The grotto's just through there, on the right" whispered Mark, a reverent and awed silence having fallen on the pair as they stood and stared.

"Let's have a look before we go searching for the Cite Secours."

So on past the huge racks of candles for sale, and the throngs of pilgrims queuing for Lourdes water, the two new pilgrims finally stood before the grotto, gazing up at the statue of Our Lady in the niche, the image occupying the very spot where the Blessed Virgin had appeared to Bernadette in what seemed the not too distant past. For a moment, they seemed to be transported back, the marvellous events had only happened yesterday. They sank to their knees onto the polished marble pavement, and bowed their heads. A sense of awe at the holiness of the place had come over them, and they both prayed in their own way, asking Our Lady to look after them and their families.

"Be my mother and guide in my journey to the priesthood," prayed Mark, while Peter groped for his rosary beads.

After a few minutes, the two quietly rose to their feet, and almost reluctantly retraced their steps to the gate at the edge of the Domaine. There, they felt free to talk normally again.

"It's some place, Pete, don't you think?"

For once, the usually irreverent Peter was quiet and thoughtful.

"It certainly is", he replied. "I'm glad you had the idea of coming here, Mark. I think it's going to be an experience we'll remember for the rest of our lives."

Then pressing human needs supervened, and so they quickly adjourned to a nearby cafe where pilgrims were enjoying huge steaming cups of cafe au lait and croissants.

"Let's get ourselves wrapped round a bit of that" said Peter enthusiastically. "Come on, Mark, get that parley-vous going, and sort us out some breakfast."

Half an hour later, rested and refreshed, the young men rose from the squeaking plastic chairs, and toiled up the nearby hill, following the directions Mark had managed to obtain from an official looking gentleman at the gates of the Domaine.

They found that the Cite Secours was a modern, well-appointed camp for communal living, which made an ideal base for their stay. After a good wash and midday meal, they felt sufficiently energetic to retrace their steps back into the centre of the town to explore. They missed the afternoon Blessed Sacrament procession, but joined in the evening torch light procession, their two candles lost in the twinkling mass of surging, singing humanity.

"It really brings home to you the fact that the Church is Catholic, or universal" observed Mark. "There must have been prayers and hymns in six languages at least."

They were walking back through the darkened streets afterwards.

"One in the eye for the Proddies, eh?" laughed Peter.

The first faint stirring of the Ecumenical movement had yet to touch the Catholic community in general, at least in the British Isles. The Catholic Church was the one, true Church, and all the other Christians were simply dabbling at the edge of the pool.

"It's a great family that we belong to; it makes you proud to feel we'll be serving it as priests one day."

They stopped at one of the cafes for a drink, and content, sat smoking and discussing the day's events. There was a lot to fit into the few days of their visit, and so they agreed to make an early start next day, but not too early, Peter amended hastily. Arriving back at the Cite Secours, they sank gratefully into the narrow bunk-beds, and soon were fast asleep, a sleep that was deep and long as nature took its toll of their exhausted frames.

It was nearly nine when they awoke, and scrambling out of bed, only just managed to make it to the dining room in time for breakfast.

"We'll have to do better than this, Pete" laughed Mark as he dipped the hard roll into the dark bitter coffee in the wide brimmed cup.

"Come on, let's get down to Lourdes again."

They gulped down the hot coffee, and munched the remains of the hard rolls with butter and apricot jam, then it was off down the hill, cameras slapping against their chests as they strode down the dusty road. Lizards basking in the hot, morning sun scampered away as their shadows passed, but before long they were back in the town, exploring the souvenir shops, buying postcards to send back home. Everywhere they went, the darkly beautiful face of the young peasant girl Bernadette gazed at them from a hundred postcards. Mark bought as many different ones as he could find; ever the romantic, he was unconsciously falling in love with the young girl Saint. He said nothing to Peter, fearing his friend's mockery, but he visited the houses and the convent connected with Bernadette with a new fervour. His favourite place was the Cachot, or prison cell which had served the Soubirous family as a home at the time of the apparitions, and to his great joy, an English-speaking priest asked him to serve his Mass there the following morning.

And so the days passed, with the constant round of visits to the Grotto, the processions and the ice-cold waters of the baths. They had heard all sorts of stories about being plunged into the dirty water in which countless diseased bodies before them had been bathed, but nothing daunted, found the water clear and pure when their turn to don the freezing, clammy loin cloths arrived.

One afternoon, they made the Stations of the Cross on the rocky hillside above the Grotto, Mark content to walk round in his shoes, but Peter, braver or more foolhardy, insisting on joining the tough penitents who made the journey barefoot. Unfortunately, the devotional aspects of the way of the cross were slightly marred when Peter, not watching where he was going, stubbed his toe painfully on a sharp rock.

"Fucking hell" he groaned as the blood oozed out, the old unredeemed Peter surfacing temporarily. But grace triumphed, and with emergency first-aid applied and shoes resumed, the exercise was successfully completed.

The pilgrimage drew to its close; with a last look back at the basilica and Grotto, the two friends settled back into their seats as the express slowly started the long journey back to the north. Many hours later, two dirty, scruffy and tired young men made their farewells as they travelled on the Underground from Victoria to the northbound stations of Euston and King's Cross, before journeying on to their respective homes. Mark sighed.

"Just over a week at home, then it's off to the Nov. Enjoy it, Pete - see you there."

"My God, it's some thought, Mark. The condemned man ate a hearty breakfast."

"Thanks for the past week or so, Pete; it's been a fantastic experience. Glad we did it?"

"Course I am, Mark. It was great. But don't let your enthusiasm carry you away. Keep your feet on the ground, or you're sure to come a cropper when some bugger kicks you up the arse."

"Always the cynic, Pete," laughed Mark. Then his mood suddenly changing, "Take care, Pete; you've always been a good friend to me. I'm glad we're facing the future together."

"Yeah, kid," replied Peter hastily, embarrassed by the threatened descent into sentimentality.

"Just enjoy your last few days of freedom, and then we'll sort out this Novitiate lark together."

"Lambs to the slaughter" he muttered enigmatically to himself as he left the underground train at Euston, leaving Mark to travel on to King's Cross, a couple of stops further on.

As his train drew into the station of his home town, Mark smiled to himself, and resolved to follow Peter's advice, and make the most of the next few days. Life was good, he felt; he was young, and life in its varied fascination lay before him. The Novitiate was something to be feared, up to a point; but in a way it held the fascination that any slightly fearful experience exercises. "Childe Harold to the dark tower came," he quoted to himself, shivering with a not altogether unpleasant sense of foreboding. But this was still some days away, and first, there was the joy of homecoming to be experienced.

At home, the family gave him its usual warm welcome; his mother had his favourite meal prepared for him when he came downstairs after a long hot soak in the bath; his sister Brenda made her boyfriend stay and listen to the adventures, while young Tony dug into his elder brother's luggage, hunting for the promised presents.

Mark had always enjoyed a warm and loving relationship with his family; Brenda had been an elder sister who worshipped her two younger brothers, but none the less kept them in order, while Mark and Tony had done everything together since they had been small children. In the early days before St Saviour's, they had shared a room with twin beds, but more often than not the two little boys had finished the night curled up together in the same bed.

During his years at St Saviour's, this warm family relationship had been a constant delight, with holidays looked forward to with longing, and the return to school an ache to be stoically endured.

Now he was starting his last short holiday with them before the Novitiate; he knew that it would be years before he saw his home again. The few remaining days were precious; but they passed all too quickly, and served merely to make Mark realise the depth of the love he felt for them, and so the pain of separation was all the greater when the day of departure for the Novitiate came. He managed to restrain the tears, though only just, but as he sat in the train, numb with grief, he knew that the family at home would be sharing the same pain.

ELEVEN

"Welcome to the Novitiate, brother."

The new title sounded strange in Mark's ears as he passed through the heavy wooden double doors into the stark, stone-floored corridor.

"The other postulants are in the common room, waiting for supper. Leave your cases in your room, and join them there for the time being."

The Novice Master was a gentle, elderly priest, totally unlike the novice Masters of myth and legend, who were first cousins to Torquemada if the stories handed down were true. Feeling a certain sense of reassurance, Mark followed the elderly priest up two flights of stairs and along another corridor. At last, they came to Mark's designated room. Already it bore the title "Brother Kennedy." Inside, it was severely simple, with a bed, table and chair, washstand with jug and basin, and curtained-off clothes cupboard. The floor was of bare wood, highly polished. A crucifix and picture of Our Lady were the only adornments on the wall.

"I hope you'll be comfortable" smiled the priest. "So freshen up, then join the others in the common room until supper time. Do you think you will be able to find your way there? It's along this corridor, down the stairs at the end, then first door on the left."

With that, he left Mark to his thoughts. It didn't seem too bad after all, he pondered with a certain sense of relief. The Novice Master seemed to be approachable, and though life was obviously going to be Spartan, he felt that it would probably be bearable.

After a quick wash, he followed the directions he had been given, and found the common room without difficulty. Opening the door, he found a small group of young men, talking quietly. He recognised Peter and the three other classmates who made up that year's contribution from St Saviour's.

"Hello, Mark," one of them laughed. "Good to see you made it."

Mark looked round.

"Where's Chris?"

"Chickened out, I think," replied Peter. "I'm beginning to wonder whether he hadn't the best idea."

He then added casually:

"Have a look in that cupboard."

Wonderingly, Mark opened the cupboard door. Inside was a row of pegs, on which hung some small five-thonged whips, and some spiked bracelets. Goggle-eyed, Mark stood and stared.

"What the hell are those?" he gasped.

"I'm told they're called disciplines" replied Peter. "Apparently, we've got to whip ourselves with them, for penance. Bloody crazy, if you ask me. Still, shut that door; I don't know whether we're supposed to know about it yet."

Mark did as he was told, wondering to himself what further surprises the future held.

A few minutes later, a bell sounded and Mark followed the others down another flight of stairs to the refectory, where the small group of young men, feeling somewhat conspicuous in their civilian attire, waited patiently, whispering among themselves.

Suddenly, a distant clatter of footsteps could be heard, and along the corridor in an orderly line processed the novices and community, soberly attired in their black habits. The novices were the previous year's intake who would shortly be professed; there were four of them, two of whom Mark recognised as being the year ahead of him at St Saviour's. They were immediately recognisable, though they looked thinner; gaunt even, with hair cut short, almost to the bone.

With eyes cast down they waited at the door; the Novice Master then ushered Mark and the other postulants into the refectory, indicating their places. Then the novices and community followed. After a Latin grace, the meal commenced and as expected, the father Superior allowed conversation after a little reading.

Later, the Novice Master assembled the novices and postulants in the Novitiate common room, and addressed them.

"Today we welcome the postulants, the young men who have come to begin their religious lives in the Order. You have a great deal to learn, but that is why you are here. Everything may seem rather strange at first, but you'll be surprised at how quickly the Regular Observance becomes second nature to you. You will learn to base your lives on this."

As he spoke, he held aloft a small black book.

"This is the Holy Rule. You will each be given a copy, and it is to be carefully studied. But it is not simply a list of regulations; you must look upon it as a way of life. You must learn to love the Holy Rule. Keep the Rule, and the Rule will keep you."

A shiver ran down Mark's spine, and he glanced at Peter, who winked back.

"Your lives are to be based on three great principles, which are enshrined in the vows you will take at the end of your year here; vows that the Novices are due to take at their profession in a few weeks' time. These are the vows of Poverty, Chastity, and Obedience. The Rule explains these, and if you follow the Rule faithfully, then the vows will automatically fall into place."

He then paused before continuing, while his audience looked on expectantly.

"And now a few practical pointers. I am your superior in all matters, so any questions or problems, come to me. You will find me, I hope, approachable and ready to help. My job is to teach you the Religious Life; submit to my guidance, and all will be plain sailing. We shall shortly be having night prayers; after night prayers, the Great Silence begins; from then until breakfast there is to be strict silence. Is that understood?"

He then briefly outlined a few more matters of immediate application, then left the common room to join the community for recreation, leaving the novices and postulants to become acquainted during what remained of the recreation period.

There were seven postulants in the year; besides Mark and Peter, there were their three classmates from St Saviour's, Martin, Eric and Tony, and two 'outsiders'; David, who had come straight from school but had completed his 'A' levels and so was a year older than the St Saviour's boys, and finally Ken, an older man in his late twenties, who was known as a 'late vocation'.

The novices took the lead and introduced themselves to the newcomers, and soon the whole group was chatting happily together, the novices trying to answer the questions fired at them machine-gun fashion by the curious beginners.

Naturally enough, the instruments of penance seen earlier were the subject of much questioning, not to say a little ribaldry, though one of the novices portentously announced that they would not find these things quite so funny when they started to use them. They were not used by postulants, but they would be issued with the full complement of discipline and cilice, or spiked bracelet, on receiving the habit after about three weeks.

Peter was muttering something under his breath about 'crackpots' when a bell sounded, and immediately the whole group retired to the church for night prayers.

Later, lying in bed, Mark pondered fearfully on what lay ahead. He had heard of the ascetical idea of being dead to the world, or mortifying the flesh, and wondered whether this dying business was going to be a painful experience.

Just then, a gentle tap sounded at the door, and on his call of 'come in', Peter slipped quietly into the room.

"Just popped in for a chat and a smoke" he announced. "We haven't had a chance to have a gab since you got here."

"Pete," whispered Mark urgently, "What about this Great Silence business?"

"Ah, balls" replied his friend cheerfully. "We'll keep it low, and no-one will know."

He took out his cigarettes, and tossed one over to Mark.

"Should we, Pete?" he asked. "We might get thrown out if we're caught."

"If they throw us out for that, then God help us when something serious happens."

So talking in whispers, sitting by the open window, they compared notes, swapping details of their last few days at home, and first impressions of the Novitiate. They agreed that the regime seemed to be almost unbelievably strict, and wondered a little disconsolately about their chances of survival. It was well known that a reasonably high dropout rate was to be expected.

However, the next few days proved that human beings can adapt to almost any situation. The routine was quickly established, and the constant round of prayer, work, recreation and rest became second nature to them. Small treats became highlights almost childishly anticipated.

The novices quickly and skilfully taught the postulants the ground rules, and so by the time they entered their pre-profession retreat, the newcomers, on their own for the first time since their arrival, felt more or less at home.

The day before the profession, the postulants were solemnly invested with the habit, and for the first time stood admiring themselves in their unfamiliar, but thrilling garb. The same evening, they were presented with a copy of the Rule, to be learned and thoroughly assimilated, and also with their instruments of penance. As they sat in the common room at evening recreation, nervously examining the wire spikes of the cilices and the sinister looking waxed thongs of the disciplines, differing emotions ran through their minds; a sort of nervous fear, tinged with a little excitement and distaste; looking back years later, Mark thought just like Victorian brides on their wedding night.

Next morning, when talking was allowed after breakfast, they compared notes, all admitting to having tried them out tentatively, but not with any degree of severity.

The profession day passed in a whirl of activity, and the next day, the newly professed religious departed for the major seminary, leaving their recently established successors in sole occupancy of the Novitiate quarters.

TWELVE

The following day was a Wednesday, a day which in many ways summed up Novitiate life.

At six o'clock the main bell sounded, and a brother came round knocking on every door to rouse the sleeper within.

Wearily, Mark stretched and tumbled out of bed onto the hard boards. Shivering slightly, he quickly washed in the ice-cold water and shaved, a not too difficult task as his beard had not yet attained the density of full manhood. He then knelt down by his bed and said his morning prayers. Once again the bell rang, and knowing it was time he got himself down to the church for morning meditation, he rolled up his left sleeve, and clumsily tried to fasten the cilice onto his arm. After two or three attempts he finally succeeded, and gingerly rolled his sleeve back down over his arm, wincing slightly as the spiked wire nipped his flesh.

As he emerged from his room the other doors were opening, and he joined the group that silently made its way down the stairs to the church. There, on the stroke of half past six, the half hour's meditation began.

After a short prayer, one of the novices appointed for the purpose read out a passage from the designated book of meditation themes, and then silence once more fell over the assembled community. Trying to keep his throbbing arm off the bench, Mark endeavoured to think about the words he had just heard, but nothing seemed to strike a chord, and soon his mind was wandering freely over all sorts of topics.

"Distractions" he commented silently to himself, and again tried to drag his mind back to the subject matter. Next to him, Peter, his hair shorn in the traditional Novitiate haircut, was making similar valiant efforts. He did not notice the cilice, as he had fastened it just tightly enough to avoid its falling off. His knees, aching at the hardness of the kneeler, suddenly demanded relief, and so he leaned with his forearms on the bench to shift his position. A sharp stab of pain quickly reminded him of the cilice, and so carefully shifting his weight onto his right arm, he managed to make himself a little more comfortable.

"I hate meditation" he muttered to himself, and doggedly tried to think elevated thoughts. At a quarter to seven, the reader once again rose to his feet, and read the second point which was of as little use to the struggling prayers as the first. The battle of concentration lasted a further quarter of an hour, and then thankfully the appointed priest emerged from the sacristy for Mass. As this brought them back to more familiar ground, most of the novices sighed with relief, and found themselves strangely more able than normal to concentrate on the ageless liturgy in which they were sharing.

Afterwards, however, there was the effort of thanksgiving, which like meditation was a struggle in concentration, without even the help of a point being read out. But after what seemed an age, they heard the raps on the bench which signalled the end of the exercise, and hungrily, they processed to the refectory for breakfast.

Hot coffee, porridge, and as much brown bread and butter as they liked; the young men rapidly demolished all before them. As talking was permitted for a short time after breakfast, there was no temptation to linger too long over the coffee, and so in a short time Mark and Peter found themselves in the garden, where the first task was to roll up the sleeve and remove the cilice, the prescribed period of wear being over.

"Phew, that's a relief" gasped Mark, as he tucked the wire instrument into the front of his habit and examined the weals left by it with a sense of pride and achievement.

"How did you find it, brother?"

"Brother?" exclaimed Peter, "What do you mean, brother? I'm not calling you brother after sitting next to you day in, day out for the past six years."

"But we're supposed to, Pete," cried Mark, ever the law-abiding citizen.

"Save it for when you might be overheard. It's barmy, if you ask me, like this penance business. What would your family say if they knew about that?"

"I shudder to think" grinned Mark.

Just then, some of the others strolled up.

"String band tonight, then" remarked Ken. "That's what some of the blokes call the discipline, apparently."

The humour of the situation, coupled with some understandable nerves, had the whole group quickly convulsed with laughter.

David, however, had stayed apart from the main group, his absence not at first noticed. But already, David had begun to stand out from the group. He was a young man who seemed to prefer his own company, and as the months of the Novitiate wore on, it would become apparent that all was not as it should be with him. But that morning, he simply declined the invitation to join the group, smiling slightly as he turned away, and so the others left him to his own devices.

The group quickly broke up, returning indoors for the chores of bed making and room tidying, after which the inevitable bell signalled the start of the morning's activities; ascetical reading, during which the novices read in turn from one of the old classics of monastic spirituality

In general, it made mournful enough reading, though some of the stories and examples quoted to illustrate a truth again had the brethren in stitches. Making the point that it was wrong, or even dangerous to disregard the prohibition of eating between meals, one story related the sad tale of the nun who incautiously ate a lettuce leaf on which a devil was sitting, who promptly took possession of the unfortunate consumer. When commanded to leave by the exorcist, the devil complained that he had simply been innocently sitting on the lettuce leaf enjoying the sun, when along comes this greedy nun...

Other classes in the study of the Rule, elocution, Latin studies and the like followed, which together with a period of manual labour in the gardens, brought the community to lunch time. After particular examen, an exercise in which the brethren examined their consciences on the morning's observance of the Rule in general and the special monthly virtue in particular, the religious processed to the refectory.

On a given signal, they filed into the room, carefully stepping over the prostrate body of one of their number, who as tradition demanded, was performing a public act of self-humiliation as a penance. Inside, during the initial reading from Scripture, all the brethren performed similar acts of penance; some holding their arms outstretched in the form of a cross, others kneeling on their hands, and others making crosses on the stone floor with their tongues. Mark, entering into the spirit of the occasion, felt at one with the Church Militant and the suffering Christ; Peter merely felt a fool, and was relieved when the exercise was over.

After lunch and the post-prandial period of recreation, the novices retired to their rooms for the afternoon exercises of spiritual reading and meditation, at each of which half an hour was to be spent. The warm September sun combined with the gravity of the tome he was perusing soon had Mark nodding, struggling manfully to keep his eyes open. The problem worsened when meditation took over half an hour later. Eventually succumbing to human nature, he knelt by his bed, and it wasn't long before he was slumped over it, still in a kneeling position.

The bell signalling the end of the exercise found him with a throbbing head and a nasty taste in the mouth, but the afternoon manual labour which followed soon cleared his head.

So the day wore on; evening classes followed tea, then evening meditation, supper and recreation. After supper, it was the novices' task to prepare the corridors for the exercise of the discipline by closing shutters over the windows.

With mixed emotions, the novices performed their task; this was the first time that they would be using the discipline in earnest. Night prayers followed, and then the community hastened each to his room to prepare.

Mark quickly grabbed his scourge and joined the others in the darkened corridor, each one standing outside his own room. Following previously given instructions, he folded his habit round his waist and dropped his trousers. Shivering, he slipped his right hand through the loop attached to the handle of the instrument, then grasped the discipline in his sweaty palm, waiting tensely for the start of the psalm 'Miserere'. As he trembled, he could hear the lashes of his scourge rattling slightly together, and fearfully wondered what the pain would be like.

The introductory prayers were over, and the psalm was intoned. Gritting his teeth, Mark slowly began the regular whipping swings to left and right, not too hard at first, but increasing the pressure as he found the pain sharp but bearable. All round the monastery the swishing, slapping sounds filled the air. Mark turned his thoughts to the suffering Jesus, picturing him being scourged, crowned with thorns and crucified. A kind of exaltation took hold of him as he found himself identifying closely with the sufferings of Christ;

somehow, at that moment the pain seemed to bring a nearness to his Saviour that he had never before experienced.

Along the corridor, David lashed viciously at himself as he recalled the statements in his current ascetical reading that the body was prone to evil desires and required taming. The body must become the servant, it must know its place, and its rebellious nature must be broken.

Further down, Peter swished gently at his still trousered seat; some weeks later, he claimed to have misunderstood the instructions; no-one ever knew whether his mistake was genuine or not.

The psalm ended, the exercise was over. The young men thankfully resumed their clothing during the final prayers, and with the lights on once again, prepared for bed as usual. That night as he lay in bed, Mark prayed earnestly, thanking God for the experience of closeness to Christ that he had felt, particularly the exhilarating, almost mystical sense of being raised out of himself with Christ. The throbbing warmth that the penitential exercise had left was not unpleasant, too. He felt a sense of achievement; even excitement; maybe this discipline business would be something he could accept, and even look forward to, in a way: and with a feeling of joy and contentment, he quickly fell asleep.

Along the corridor, David wrestled with entirely different feelings. He had always been a quiet, earnest boy, whose inclinations to the priesthood had surfaced during his grammar school days. He had often been accused by his classmates of taking things too seriously, and he had entered on his Novitiate with the seriousness of total commitment. He was not prepared to compromise, and so even in these early days, grave problems were becoming apparent. He demanded of himself a scrupulously exact obedience to the Rule, and followed all the ascetical maxims with complete fidelity. If despising the world was what the religious life demanded, then despise it he would. He totally rejected its comforts, and looked for every opportunity to mortify his flesh, and avoided as far as possible the limited pleasures available to the novices. His God was a God of justice; certainly a God of mercy too, who forgave the lapses of his children, but with the imagined perfection standing before him with stark clarity, every failure seemed deliberate and magnified in its malice.

He now knelt in his room, trembling slightly, thinking about the penitential act that had just been completed. He wondered why

God, in his infinite Wisdom, had made man body and soul. So much trouble and complication could have been avoided if man were all spirit. Perhaps we were given bodies for the purpose of self-chastisement and penance, he thought. He resolved with more determination than ever to mortify the flesh, even crucify it, not granting himself any respite or particularly pleasure that could be avoided. Bodies were disgusting, dirty, prone to disease and death. He began to look forward to the release from this vale of tears that death would bring. He felt that he understood the longings of the Saints in this regard.

Ken was already fast asleep in his room, while Peter lay in bed, wishing he had a cigarette. The illicit supply he had brought with him had long since been depleted, and he stoically resigned himself to a tobacco-free life, at least in the short term. This Novitiate lark was bloody barmy, he reflected: people going round whipping themselves...my God, the Sunday papers would have a field day if they got hold of the true story of monastic life.

He saw his journey forward to the priesthood as a long hard road, and he wondered whether he would have the strength and determination to stick it out. Then he relaxed. Life is what you make it, and it needn't be too bad. This year was only a year after all, and within a few short months they would be professed and in the seminary, where life by all accounts was very different, and full of all sorts of possibilities. Any bridges he met would be crossed when he came to them, but for now sleep was the thing. It was going to be another early start in the morning; of course, it was the weekly recreation day too, when regular observance was much lighter. Life had brightened up already.

THIRTEEN

The months in the Novitiate began to slip by, and the hard routine became familiar, even Peter fitting in to it reasonably well. Mark knew a new kind of happiness as his love and knowledge grew, though he too, like David, had his moments of worry.

The Novitiate rules concerning custody of the eyes, which was the controlling of the eyes' freedom to gaze around at will, coupled with the strict teaching of the Church on sexual matters tended to produce in Mark a nervous scrupulosity in these areas.

On the infrequent trips into the nearby town that they were allowed to make, he found that his eyes always seemed to fall on sights that could trigger off sexual thoughts; the curve of a woman's body, displays of ladies' underwear in shop windows, or even the forking branches of the trees. He confided his worries to his confessor, who helped keep things in perspective; but for a time, he knew the real torment of scruples. He suffered the nagging doubts as to whether he had sinned, followed by persistent worries as to whether he had explained everything clearly to the priest, so that the advice given could be safely followed.

"It is a question of obedience, brother" the old priest patiently explained one day. Clearly, this was a problem he met in every batch of novices as year succeeded year.

"The only cure for scruples, and that is what you have, is to place yourself entirely in the hands of your confessor. You must follow his advice and guidance implicitly. Tell yourself that even if there were sin there, the greater duty is obedience to your confessor. If necessary, I'll take the sin on my own shoulders. Remember too that the scrupulous person makes God out to be a very strict and harsh Being, rather than the loving, forgiving Father that we know he is."

Fortunately the crisis was of relatively short duration in Mark's case, though clearly David was entering dark new worlds where the spirit could be crushed by the final enemy, despair.

In one area, however, Mark's worries were more persistent, and proved to be of greater substance. He suddenly realised one day that the frequent self-flagellation enjoined by their way of life produced in him a feeling of excitement that for a time he had confused with the experience of mystical elation (or so he had understood it) he had known on that first occasion on which they had undergone the use of the discipline. For a while he refused to acknowledge to himself the nature of these feelings, but eventually the bodily evidence of sexual arousal left him in no doubt. He realised that he had to discuss the matter with his confessor at the first possible opportunity.

The next morning after breakfast, Mark duly made his way to the room of the elderly priest who served as the Novitiate confessor. Twice, three times, he went up to the door, and was about to knock when his courage failed him. How could he mention such a shameful, degraded fascination? But needs must, and finally steeling himself, he knocked timidly on the door.

Too late to draw back now, he thought as the voice from within called on him to enter. Feeling sick with fear, he approached the desk and knelt. But the priest, seeing his state, smiled encouragingly and invited him to sit down.

"Now, brother, what seems to be the problem?" he asked gently.

Haltingly, Mark tried to explain his feelings, his face scarlet as the details emerged. The old priest nodded understandingly.

"Pain and pleasure are very close together" he commented. "I think this problem is possibly more common than we imagine. It's just that most people fortunately don't make the connection between the two. I often wonder whether we should discontinue some of these penitential practices, though of course we must remember that they have been sanctioned by centuries of use in the Church. However, in your case, always remember that intention is paramount. You intend the penitential aspect, so try to ignore other feelings. But if you find that you cannot, then we will have to think again."

Feeling somewhat relieved, Mark left the room, but soon afterwards began to wonder whether he had expressed himself clearly enough. But clinging to the advice he had been given that acts good in themselves performed with a good intention must be without sin, and recognising his duty to obey his confessor, he was prepared to let the matter rest there for the time being.

On another occasion, problems whose existence he never even suspected were suddenly thrust before him.

One morning after breakfast, the Father Master called Mark to his room. Wondering what it was all about, Mark dutifully made his way to the Novice Master's room, and hesitantly tapped on the door. Summoned to enter, he opened the door and went inside. Sitting at the invitation given, he waited for the Novice Master to begin.

"This is a rather delicate subject, brother Kennedy" he started. "But one or two members of the community have noticed your friendship with brother Clark."

"Yes, father" replied Mark. "We have been friends since we started at St Saviour's."

"This is a general word of caution" continued the priest. "Friendship is, ah, in general acceptable, but it must never be allowed to become a particular friendship; that is, one which chooses one member of the community before others, and especially to the exclusion of others. Firstly, such a friendship militates against community life, and secondly..."

He paused, and coughed, somewhat embarrassed. "There is always the danger that such a friendship can be soft, and unmanly."

After a few more general words of warning and a statement that brother Clark would be given the same general warning, Mark was dismissed.

Later, somewhat troubled, he mentioned this to Peter, who laughed.

"Yes", he replied. "I got the same jawing. They must think we're a couple of homo's. Bloody cheek. Still, I suppose we'll have to toe the line, and try not to be seen too much together. Don't pay too much attention to it" he insisted, seeing Mark's worried frown.

But Mark, the born worrier, was not content to let it rest. With Peter, such things were in one ear and out of the other. "But they do leave a tide mark" he once protested when taxed with this.

Mentioning it to his confessor, Mark received the same general advice as he had from the Novice Master. Fortunately at about that same time, his friend from St Saviour's, brother Thomas, was visiting the Novitiate community to make a few days' retreat. Remembering the brother's helpful advice in the past, Mark sought him out, and asked him for his advice on the problem.

"Peter says they think we're..." he hesitated. "I don't know how to say this, but 'homo's' was the word he used."

Brother Thomas laughed.

"I don't think so, Mark" he answered. "After all, we're friends too; there's no harm in that. No, there is nothing at all wrong with friendship. It is one of the greatest gifts that God has given us; and friend can love friend, with a love that is in no way homosexual. St Aelred of Rievaulx - that's Rievaulx Abbey in your part of the world - wrote a wonderful book on friendship. Read it, and you'll see that there is absolutely nothing wrong with a healthy friendship. Of course, the particular friendship thing does refer to homosexuality; that is something which has not been unknown in religious communities. Mercifully it is very rare, but I suppose the Church has so great a horror of such things that even genuine healthy friendship can cause a panic. Does that solve your problem?"

Mark relaxed. "I think so, even without the cup of tea."

The brother laughed. "Now tell me how you're getting on."

And so Mark regaled brother Thomas with his Novitiate impressions and adventures until it was time for him to hurry away to join in the next of the Novitiate exercises. He did not mention, however, his problems with the penitential exercises. In this area, he felt a natural reluctance to speak that only urgent and pressing needs could overcome; and for the moment he was still following the advice given him by his confessor.

FOURTEEN

Christmas that year was a feast that was celebrated with an enjoyment that was out of all proportion to the meagre indulgences offered.

Advent had slowly passed, and as Christmas drew near, the carols were practised and decorations prepared. On Christmas Eve, the church was decorated and the crib with its life-size figures assembled. As excited as children thrilled at the imminent arrival of Santa Claus, the Novices worked with a will. Garlands of holly were draped from pillar to pillar, lush greenery recklessly stripped from any available evergreen in the garden was piled high in the sanctuary, with tinsel and baubles festooned everywhere. A mixture of beer and sugar was concocted by an inventive member of the community in an attempt to add a frosty glitter to the paper and cardboard rocks which formed the crib.

"People will think we've been having a piss-up" whispered Peter to the easily scandalised Mark.

Midnight Mass and the carol service came, and with a heart too full for words, Mark contemplated the new-born Christ in his crib, the smell of beer now mercifully masked by incense.

Afterwards, the whole community repaired to the refectory, where all were regaled with cold pork pie and copious draughts of altar wine, a hitherto unheard of treat for the Novices. An hour later, the slightly tipsy young men staggered to their beds, with permission to sleep in until the 8.30 a.m. Mass next morning.

The unbridled merriment continued next day, with silence dispensed and unlimited free time allowed. A carefully chosen selection of reading material was permitted, and so the spiritual reading books were abandoned in favour of the novels of John Buchan, and the detective thrillers of Agatha Christie and Dorothy L. Sayers. After a cold lunch, the novices were sent for a long walk to prepare them for the evening festivities, the heart of which was the Christmas dinner. Recklessly ignoring recent homilies on the subject of particular friendship, Peter and Mark naturally found themselves together, and were soon deep in conversation, covering all topics from the weather to the re-establishing of right order in the world.

It was a crisp, clear and frosty day, and conversation turned to Novitiate affairs. Their feet crunching through the thin ice that bordered the road, they talked on.

"How would you say you are finding the Nov., Mark?"

"Hard going sometimes, but great. I sometimes feel that I could spend the rest of my life here, just following this routine. Somehow, it's so peaceful and trouble-free. I sometimes wonder if I'd make a good contemplative? Mind you, the Order is contemplative and active, though I think I prefer the contemplative side."

Peter laughed. "Staying here would drive me bonkers. I know what you mean about being trouble-free. All you have to do here is to do as you're told and keep your nose clean, and you're an ideal novice. No wonder you fit in so well, Mark; you're a dreamer, kid. Here, you're sheltered from the big bad world and all its problems."

"But we've retired for a time from the world so that later we can go back with some real spiritual strength behind us."

"It sounds fine in theory, but how much do you think that most of the priests and brothers we know are in touch with the real world? I sometimes think that we get stuck with our heads in the clouds in this hothouse atmosphere" he continued, recklessly mixing his metaphors, "and we never get back down again. What have our priests and brothers got to say to Joe Bloggs who gets his hands dirty and spends all his spare time wiping his kids' bums and snotty noses, then boozing down the pub?"

"I'm sure the major seminary will prepare us for all that", insisted Mark, with what Peter perceived as touching confidence. "You've got to trust the Order, Pete; they know what they're doing; after all, they've been doing it long enough."

Ken and his companion came alongside and joined them. He quickly grasped the general trend, and to Mark's surprise, came into the conversation on Peter's side.

"He's got a point, Mark, but of course being our Pete, he does exaggerate. But I've seen a bit of life; after all, you have just come from the sheltered atmosphere of St Saviour's straight to the Nov. You haven't had the chance to see anything of the real world."

Mark walked on, a frown creasing his brow.

"I have seen something of the world; we did have holidays from St Saviour's."

But he recognised the general truth of what the others were saying, and realised that there was much of life that was very much a closed book to him. But for the moment he was content to bask in the security offered by the little world in which they lived, and so the conversation soon drifted back to present joys, and the happy anticipation of the Christmas dinner, and the evening revelries which lay ahead.

David meanwhile walked along with eyes cast down, answering with monosyllables the attempts at conversation made by his companion. On walks, it was quickly recognised that David was hard work, and so the others tended to leave him in his isolation, pairing off until some unfortunate member of the group was left with no alternative partner. Or if numbers allowed and all had paired off leaving David alone, then a twosome charitably but reluctantly admitted him to their ranks.

Christmas was a baffling time for him; he thanked God fervently for the gift of Christ to the world, but found the community's forsaking of the ascetical ideals to savour worldly flesh pots disturbing. He resolved to himself to enjoy them as little as possible, using the abundant free time to pray all the more, offering up his self-denial for the conversion of sinners, including some of the brethren. His view of the Faith saw vast numbers of mankind falling like leaves in autumn into the eternal fires of Hell, just as surely as the leaves were burned after being swept into piles after the autumn gales had stripped them from the trees.

"My God, just look at Dave; you'd think it was Good Friday, not Christmas Day," commented Peter to Mark and Ken. "I just don't understand that miserable bugger." He snorted contemptuously. "Why can't he let go and enjoy himself for once? He'll make himself ill if he goes on like this."

"There's something seriously wrong" agreed Ken. "I wonder that the Novice Master doesn't do something to sort him out. I don't know about you, but I've tried to argue him out of his attitudes on occasion. The trouble is, his arguments are unassailable, if you take seriously the formation they're giving us here. We're taught to despise the world, so despise it he does. To bring the body into subjection by mortification, so he pastes the bejasus out of himself, as our Irish brethren would say. I suppose the authorities feel that most of us are kept on the straight and narrow by these methods; our natural inclinations to a life of ease and pleasure are tamed into moderation by a touch of severity, but they rely on our natural common sense to make sure we don't go too far. But if you follow literally the instructions we're given, especially in some of the spiritual books, then you end up like David."

He shrugged expressively. "After all, some of the saints whose lives you read must have been a real pain in the neck to live with, just like him."

Mark broke in, "But maybe in those lives, the authors just put in the bits that sound edifying, and leave out the things that made the saints ordinary human beings like the rest of us."

"That's it", agreed Ken. "But try and convince poor old Dave of that."

Peter kicked an offending piece of wood off the road.

"A priest once said to me that the mark of a good religious is a healthy mediocrity."

The others fell about laughing, and Ken pushed him.

"That's you all over, Pete; you're certainly a good religious, very healthily mediocre."

They were now nearing the monastery gates, and the little group trooped back into their cloistered world, and prepared for the delights of the Christmas dinner, which was shortly due to start.

The meal lived up to expectations; it was far more lavish than anything ever enjoyed by Mark or Peter before. Christmas dinner at home had meant roast chicken or more recently turkey with roast potatoes and Brussels sprouts, followed by Christmas pudding. But this was a meal that would have gladdened the heart of a mediaeval monarch.

It started with prawn cocktails, followed by soup, then the roast turkey with all the trimmings. Afterwards, the Christmas pudding was succeeded by Stilton cheese, crystallised ginger and various other delicacies in little dishes. A glass of sherry was followed by red or white wine, and liqueurs rounded off the meal for the community, though this final indulgence was denied to the novices.

The meal ended; though feeling scarcely able to move, the brethren set to with a will on the mountain of washing up with much noisy hilarity and the occasional broken plate. Later, lounging at ease in the armchairs of the community common room to which they had been invited as a special treat, the young men sighed contentedly as the more senior brethren sipped spirits and smoked cigars.

"The religious life isn't so bad after all" remarked Peter, and was immediately made the butt of a lot of friendly teasing by the others. The noise and smoke and general excitement created the sort of atmosphere he loved, but the general hubbub, together with the unaccustomed alcohol combined to give Mark a headache.

Finally, excusing himself to the others, he left the common room and made his way to the chapel for a moment's prayer before retiring to bed. Opening the door, all was in darkness save for the tiny flicker of light emitted by the sanctuary lamp. Kneeling at the back of the chapel just inside the door, he turned his thoughts to the day's events, thanking God for the gifts of body and soul they had enjoyed that day.

Suddenly with a start, he realised that he was not alone in the darkened room. Through the gloom he could just make out the dim form of a kneeling figure several benches further forward. The realisation struck him; he had not seen David since the meal, during which David had sat silently, toying with the food on the plates before him.

"God, help him" Mark murmured, the words a prayer rather than an exclamation, and he resolved to himself to try and be kinder in his attitude to him.

During the next few days, he tried to put this into practice, deliberately choosing David as a partner on the walks, but found every approach he made resisted with a polite but firm rejection. It was as though David had built a wall of bronze around himself, a wall no-one could ever breach. Peter noticed the efforts Mark was making, and slapped him on the back.

"It's typical of you to try, but you're wasting your time. It's a psychiatrist he needs, or he will soon if something isn't done."

Ken went so far as to bring the matter up with the Novice Master, who agreed that David's attitude was a little extreme, but he defended him.

"Brother Hetherington does perhaps take things a little too far at times, but you should all feel shamed by the example of his fervour.

After all, he doesn't do anything that the Saints didn't do; his attitudes and practices should encourage all of you to try harder. Greater experience of the religious life will lead to a moderating of his attitudes, but I would hesitate to discourage him."

Peter was disgusted when he heard of the results of Ken's well-intentioned intervention.

"Novitiate fervour my arse" he snorted. "David's a bloody loony; why can't they recognise that and do something about it?"

But the novices were obliged to leave it at that, and so David's isolation grew throughout the remaining months of the Novitiate.

FIFTEEN

It was during the Spring of that year that Mark was given a new outlet and opportunity; though that was not how it began. The community organist was suddenly transferred to another monastery, and so the brethren were reduced to the hit and miss attempts of the leading singers among them to start the hymns at Mass and Benediction.

"Do any of you know anything about music?" the Novice Master enquired after a couple of days of cacophony and near disaster in the liturgical celebrations. Hesitantly Mark raised his hand.

"Brother Kennedy - you claim to be an expert do you?"

"Oh, no father, not in the least" Mark stammered hurriedly. "But I did learn the piano for a while as a boy."

"Right, then. You are the community organist from now on."

Mark was aghast. "But father, I can't play..."

His protest went unheeded.

"In the religious life, brother Kennedy, what we think we can or cannot do is of no importance. To follow the directions of our superiors is what matters. You will be given ample opportunity to practice; just get on with it. You will be expected to play for Benediction on Saturday."

That gave him three days to master the intricacies of a strange instrument, and to dredge from the depths of his childhood the neglected remnants of his musical knowledge.

"If only I'd practised and worked at this years ago" he groaned.

Peter laughed. "You and your big mouth. That'll teach you not to put your foot in it."

For the next few days, at all sorts of strange times, the church rang with weird and wonderful noises as Mark struggled to learn an 'O Salutaris' and 'Tantum Ergo' in time for Saturday's deadline. Looking round from the organ loft, he could see any of the brethren who had ventured into the church to pray burying their heads in their hands to shut out the dreadful noise. Choosing the quietest stops he could find, he soldiered on.

Saturday night finally arrived; it was time for Benediction. Mark trembled during the introductory prayers, sheer terror gripping him. He knew that he could not play the two hymns through without a mistake. The priest rose, walked up the altar steps and inserted the key in the tabernacle door. This was the signal for Mark to begin. Hands poised over the keys, he said stoically to himself "This is it." The hands descended, the opening chord sounded. He played the introduction slowly, and then, without a change of stops, started the first verse.

The lusty singing of the community carried him along, and with reckless abandon, he pulled out louder stops for the second verse. It was a triumph. He caused the final notes of the 'Amen' to ring through the Church for several seconds before taking his fingers of the keys. His euphoria was short lived, however, as the 'Tantum Ergo' loomed menacingly nearer. This time, his worst fears were realised, and loosing his place after a panic-stricken pandemonium of wrong notes, he stopped playing, allowing the singers to carry on unaccompanied. He managed to join in with a tremulous 'Amen', but it was a considerably chastened Mark who returned to his place, not unaware of the nudges, winks and titters of the uncharitable brethren which had greeted his fiasco. Later, he had to endure the caustic remarks of the Novice Master, who used his downfall as an excellent occasion for humiliation.

Mark was crushed. "Let me give it up, father" he pleaded.

"No brother, this will be a valuable lesson in humility, obedience and perseverance. Not to mention a good penance for the rest of us," he added dryly.

So Mark was condemned to further embarrassment as public performances were demanded of him, regardless of the current state of his ability. But he began to enjoy the practice times as his musicianship grew, and he could soon manage several of the easier hymns without mistakes. His feet began to venture onto the pedals, and he thrilled at the booming, echoing sound made by the sixteen foot Bourdons and double Diapasons. Leafing through the hymn book, he found the Lenten and Passiontide hymns which used the chorales of Johann Sebastian Bach as melodies, and a new love of the stately Baroque counterpoint was born in him, a love which would grow and flourish throughout his life. So moved was he by the haunting beauty of some of these tunes and harmonies that he wondered whether his emotion was sinful, though happily his confessor was able to reassure him on that point.

SIXTEEN

The Spring had been late in arriving that year. But with the blossoming of the fruit trees, the Novices realised that it had indeed arrived, and hard on its heels would come the Summer, which meant profession.

By now, their numbers had been somewhat thinned; two of the St Saviour's boys had left within a short time of each other, in February.

"February is the top month for suicides" remarked Peter somewhat inconsequentially on learning of the second departure.

"I suppose you could call it spiritual suicide in a way, leaving the Nov." replied Mark. "If you throw away your vocation, that's like throwing away your life."

"Don't be daft, Mark" retorted Peter. "You give people a hard choice. Throw away eternal life if you leave, or go bonkers and maybe even really commit suicide if you stay. It's enough to drive you to suicide sometimes, this dump. It has been known, you know."

"I sometimes feel there's a tremendous pressure on people to persevere" added Ken. "It takes real guts to leave in the face of all the psychological pressure put on you to stay. I think they must be so desperate for vocations that they'll push anybody through, and be damned as to whether they're suited or not." He grinned. "You'll be OK, Pete; they'll put you through, no problem."

"Cheeky bugger" laughed Peter. "Just because I'm not a goody goody like the rest of you doesn't mean I don't love God, or want to be a priest, and a good priest. I'm going to invent my own type of sanctity." He grinned broadly. "The St Peter Clark school of Spirituality."

This naturally provoked much mirth and mockery from the others, who teased Peter for some days after this, asking how his new ascetical school was getting on.

More and more of the novices' time was now taken up with particular preparation for the taking of the vows, or first profession as it was called. This would be for three years, or until the candidate reached the age of twenty-one.

Detailed instruction in the vows and virtues of poverty, chastity and obedience was given, with the need for generous self-sacrificial offering.

"Poverty, my dear brothers" expounded the Novice Master, "is the giving up of all independent use of material goods. Everything you need is provided for you by the community; though of course everything that you have remains community property. We use the phrase 'ad usum' to indicate that what you have is simply for your use."

The Novice Master was getting into his stride.

"Technically, as ours is the simple vow of poverty, you can retain ownership of your patrimony, but its fruits must be used only in one of three ways."

The canonical jargon was duly explained. Passing on to the virtue of poverty, he explained that the good religious was not prepared simply to follow the letter of the law, enjoying every comfort as long as permission had been granted; no, the virtue of poverty demanded a frugal lifestyle and a union with Christ who though the foxes have holes and birds of the air have nests, had nowhere to lay his head.

Mark found the instructions uplifting, and was happy with the simple lifestyle to which the Novices had grown quite accustomed. Material wealth seemed to him to be so tawdry, cheap and unworthy of human endeavour in its pursuit. Peter was more cynical.

"Poverty; they don't know the meaning of the word" he scoffed.

"I've known times when my Mum had to hide when she saw the rent man coming, and here's us, with never a worry as to where our next meal is coming from."

"It's the spirit of poverty that counts" insisted Mark. "There's no virtue in starving to death in a gutter. The whole point of poverty is to release us from the cares that money and the need to earn it cause, so that we can be content to serve God like the birds of the air, or lilies of the field."

"That's fair enough" retorted Peter, "but somehow I feel that living a comfortable existence while other people are scratching around for a living without two pennies to rub together is not quite what Our Lord had in mind."

The young men were learning; all was simple and uncomplicated in theory; but in practice, questions were arising that would exercise their minds and those of the Church's deepest thinkers for years to come.

Chastity and obedience were more straightforward. Less time was spent on their explanation, as they involved, in Peter's splendid simplification, "no sex, and doing what you're told." Mark found the explanations of the role of chastity less uplifting than those on poverty. Everything seemed so negative; and the prohibitions regarding sexual matters added little to what the Church demanded of any unmarried man.

Also, there was something faintly disturbing in the idea of giving up the possibility of the love of woman so as to concentrate fully on the love of God. Were people who married thereby choosing sexual love in preference to the love of God? Did they lack the necessary generosity to choose the better, nobler path? Despite all insistence to the contrary in the explanations given, the impression remained that the married Christian was somehow second class; the religious were striving for a state of perfection; were married people therefore to be regarded as essentially imperfect? Again, to choose the love of Christ in preference to the love of a woman struck Mark as being somehow faintly distasteful, even having a hint of homosexuality about it. Female religious were known as the brides of Christ; "Though to look at some of them, they became brides of Christ because they couldn't become the brides of anybody else" Peter coarsely and uncharitably remarked after one of the talks on this subject. But what of male religious?

"The love of Christ isn't a sexual love" insisted the Novice Master when Mark privately voiced these feelings to him.

"We give up that kind of love completely so that we can dedicate our lives to a purer, nobler love. After all, the friendship of man for man isn't homosexual, yet we accept that as perfectly normal."

These remarks satisfied Mark for the moment, though they struck him as somewhat ironic in view of the lecture he and Peter had been read some months earlier on the dangers of particular friendships. Setting the love of Christ in the context of friendship or brotherhood made it seem fully healthy and acceptable again, but the problem remained to some extent.

His heart craved for a love that could be fully emotional, and somehow he could not fit the love of Christ into this category. There was part of him that was unfulfilled, bereft; the sort of emptiness known by the rejected lover whose beloved promises to be like a sister to him, though for the moment he did not see it in quite these terms. He was content to try and satisfy his need for love in seeking to deepen his relationship with God. His disappointment, he told himself, obviously reflected the weakness of his faith and charity. Others might be able to wallow in the sugary sentimentality of some of the hymns and the pink-cheeked effeminate pictures and statues of Christ, but Mark could find no such outlet for his emotional needs. They were to be offered up as part of the crucifixion demanded by the dedication he was undertaking.

Obedience caused no problem for Mark; all his life he had been accustomed to having his life directed for him, by his parents as a small child, and by the Order since joining St Saviour's. In fact, he enjoyed the freedom from responsibility that this system allowed.

"The gift of free will is one of God's greatest gifts to man" announced the Novice Master during one of the conferences on this last of the vows.

"And yet how misunderstood in our modern world is this gift of freedom. Liberty is confused with licence. Freedom does not mean that we can do as we like; it means that we are free to choose God, and therefore perform a meritorious act in our service of him. We are not free to reject him; not free, that is, in the true sense of the word. We may abuse our freedom and reject him, but this is not a true exercise of freedom; rather an abdication of it. You are now on the verge of making one of the truly great free decisions of your lives; the decision to commit yourselves to the service of God. At the threshold of life, the way of the religious life lies before you, or the way of the world. Which are you going to choose?"

He paused dramatically, then continued: "It must be stressed that to choose the married state in the Church is a good and valid choice for the majority of Christians, and that is a choice that lies before you if you have no vocation to the priesthood or the religious life."

"My God, it's some freedom" groaned Peter afterwards. "I always thought being free meant you could choose alternative 'A' or 'B' without recriminations; like choosing chicken or steak in a restaurant. Here, you're free to take it or leave it; but God help you if you refuse to take it."

Ken shook his head and kept his thoughts to himself; but he felt that the novices, especially the younger ones, could hardly be said to be making free decisions as the pressure to conform and bow to the system was immense.

He had chosen freely to embrace this life after some years in the adult world; but any tendency on their part to seek a wider experience would be seen by the young men themselves as disloyalty, a flying in the face of God's grace.

Mark recalled his earlier agonising over the question of vocation, and felt himself no nearer a clear understanding of what exactly was entailed by a vocation. It was explained, in the context of the vow of obedience, as God's call, to which one submitted oneself by a free acceptance. Yet how could one refuse such a call? It seemed that either God called you, or he did not. If he called, then there was no honourable way in which his call could be refused. Presumably, with the call he gave the desire and the strength to follow it. If he did not call one to the priesthood, then it must be supposed that there would be no inner urgings or promptings of conscience to embrace this way of life. And yet what generous-hearted young man could fail to be aware of the moral pressure? The Church needed priests urgently; vast numbers of the faithful were served by a handful of priests; what was going wrong? How could any conscientious young man who realised the need draw back? Even personal desires and preferences were to be denied if the experience of Jeremias, the unwilling prophet, was to be believed.

It was all very confusing, sighed Mark to himself, and as usual, he fell back on the in-built never questioned conviction that he had that his life was mapped out before him, with the priesthood lying ahead of him as inevitably as birth, marriage, parenthood and death lay before the average human being. It saved a great deal of heart-searching and agonising, and it could be comfortingly dignified by joining oneself to Christ in the garden of Gethsemane, saying with him "let this chalice pass me by; yet thy will, not mine be done." Christ did not want to be crucified, yet he accepted it; who am I to jib at the sacrifices entailed by the path God has decreed for me?

And so Mark moved confidently forward towards profession day, and the gift of his life to the service of God.

SEVENTEEN

The year's Novitiate rolled relentlessly on, with the arrival of the new postulants and the pre-profession retreat announcing the imminence of the profession day. Plans had to be made; families booked into nearby accommodation; with a mounting sense of excitement, the novices forged ahead with their preparations.

Walking in the grounds the evening before the big day, Mark enjoyed the peace of the fragrant summer's evening, the last of the sunshine casting a golden glow on the dappled green of the shrubberies and leafy avenues.

"Lord Jesus" he prayed silently, "let me be a good religious as I commit myself to you in tomorrow's ceremony; let me never lose the love and closeness I feel for you now; let that sense of being united to you be my strength in the years to come. Thank you for making me a member of the great family of our Order; keep the brothers who will be professed with me close to me and to you".

He walked slowly on, every detail he observed seemed drawn with a special sharpness, as though his senses had been tuned to a pitch of acuteness; he savoured the earthy smell of the woodland; the delicate shape of an individual leaf, the soft grey furriness of a squirrel, basking in the fading golden rays.

In another part of the garden, Peter thoughtfully sucked on a long stalk of grass pulled from a nearby clump.

"Am I mad to go ahead with this caper?" he thought to himself. Many of his family clearly thought so. "It's a crazy set-up in many ways, but then I suppose I'm as big a loony as the rest" he smiled to himself. "Mind you, God does choose the foolish to confound the wise; it will all make sense one day, in the light of eternity, maybe."

But Peter was not one for self-questioning and analysis as was Mark; his goal of the priesthood lay before him, and he would go through hell or high water to get there, or even put up with the ups and downs of the religious life. He was still the stubborn Peter who had dodged the flak with reasonable skill throughout his years at St Saviour's; the snub-nosed freckled kid from one of the tougher areas of Manchester was still just below the surface. His objective clear before him, he was content to take it one day at a time, making sure he creamed off whatever perks he could wangle on the way.

Ken was in his room; he had finished his packing, and the room looked bare. Only the things he would need the following day were still laid out; his army training sometimes came in useful. He thumbed through one of the books on his desk, humming quietly to himself, a slight impatience gripping him as he waited for the final hours to tick away.

His road ahead was clear; his decisions had all been made some three or four years earlier, before he had abandoned the promising career in accountancy that he had embarked upon to enter the "late vocations" college to prepare for the priesthood. Tomorrow was just another milestone on the way.

The Novitiate had been plain sailing for him; the crises, great and small, that had affected Mark and David had left him untouched. He had many gifts and positive qualities, among which intelligence, common sense and a calm serenity and maturity were prominent. He was not uncritical of the ways of the Order he was joining, but viewed them with an appreciative tolerance, often agreeing with the hot-headed Peter that certain aspects were worthy of criticism, but Ken saw the positive elements in things that Peter merely regarded as 'bonkers'.

The last rays of the sun slanted through his window, just managing to bathe the reveal in their golden light, and Ken too turned his mind and heart to prayer. He was not one for striking up mental conversations with God; instead, he slowly repeated the time-honoured phrases of the great prayers of the Church, the 'Our Father' and 'Hail Mary', letting the phrases sink in as he slowly turned them over in his mind. He offered the prayers for himself and his family, and his young companions, his thoughts turning especially to David, whose problems sometimes moved him to a sort of helpless anger with the system that could produce an effect such as that which afflicted the unhappy young man.

David, meanwhile, was inevitably on his knees in the Novitiate oratory. He cast his mind back over the year that was drawing to a close, and begged God's forgiveness for the missed opportunities.

"We are called to perfection" he prayed, "and I am far from perfect, Lord. There are so many ways I could have done more, suffered more, prayed more."

He recognised in himself the human weaknesses and desires that he could not root out, and begged God to help him subdue them.

Earlier that evening, he had visited the Novitiate confessor, trying to purge himself of the all-contaminating feelings of guilt that clung to him.

"Father", he had said, "I don't know whether I tried really hard enough to get those thoughts out of my mind; I tried, but perhaps I could have done more, maybe my consent to them was at least partial."

As on so many past occasions, the priest tried to console and encourage the troubled soul before him.

"You must learn to obey your confessor" he insisted. "Pride in your own judgement is a greater sin than any you have confessed."

David recognised the need to trust and obey, but felt unable to put himself totally in the hands of another.

"What if he doesn't understand properly what I've been trying to explain?"

He longed for the freedom from worry that complete trust in his confessor would bring, but could not rid himself of the nagging uncertainty. Now in the oratory he pondered on the events of the morrow, and continued in his prayer. The evening sun that Mark and Peter were enjoying in the garden cast its light into the oratory through the back window, and David studied the long, black shadow cast by his body as it stretched over the benches before him. Somehow, it seemed a fitting image of his inner state.

"I don't want to vow myself to you, Lord, in a state of sin; what a terrible hypocrisy that would be."

He tried desperately to cling to the assurances the priest had given him, knowing he could not nerve himself to return for further reassurance. A feeling of sick terror began to overcome him, and his heartbeat increased as the panic gripped him. Silently, he began to weep, and with the tears came a strange sort of comfort, and soon he felt that he recognised a presence of the consoling Spirit of God within him, and for the moment his fears were calmed; for how could the comfort of God be felt by anyone in a state of sin?

It was a calm that stayed with him through the rest of the evening, and so eventually, the candidates for profession along with the rest of the community slept the sleep of the just, awaiting the events of the following day.

EIGHTEEN

As in the previous year, the day itself was too busy and rushed for very much of the solemnity of the occasion to make a deep impression. From the usual early rise, the activity and preparation were non-stop. Mercifully, the fine weather of the evening before had proved to be constant, and so things augured well for a good set of photographs for the various family albums.

The bulk of the material preparations fell on the postulants, who worked with a will, cleaning, tidying, making sandwiches for the buffet meal which would follow the ceremony, and generally making sure that the proceedings went like clockwork. The profession ceremony itself was billed for ten o'clock, and at half past nine, anxious eyes began to look out for the arrival of the various families.

Mark and his companions had to contain their curiosity and excitement, however, as the minutes passed and it was eventually time to assemble in the sacristy. Habits newly washed and pressed, hair cut once again to the bone, the young men looked pink and eager as they paced restlessly up and down in the sacristy. The father Provincial had come to receive the vows; it was only occasionally that the Novices had the honour of the presence of such an August dignitary as the head of the Order in Britain. He now vested in the community's best set of white vestments, covered in exotic flowers embroidered in multicoloured silks and gold thread.

"Done up like an old tart" whispered Peter, unable to resist the temptation of shocking Mark, who blushed and put his finger to his lips in an attempt to stem the flow.

The bell tinkled, and the assembled religious processed solemnly out onto the sanctuary. Mark surreptitiously cast a rapid glance over the congregation as he turned after genuflecting, and was relieved to pick out the familiar face of his mother two or three rows back with Brenda beside her. But who was the tall young man with them? Not Brenda's boyfriend for sure, unless she had taken a new one in tow since he had seen her last, though surely she would have mentioned this in one of the letters from home? Anyway, he would soon know.

Dragging his mind back to the sacred events in which he was sharing, he joined in the responses automatically and after the readings for epistle and gospel, sat with the others to listen to the Provincial's address.

The solemnity of the occasion and the importance of what was taking place were reflected in the words he used, but later Mark could not remember more than a few disjointed phrases: 'love of God', 'sacrificing their lives', and 'dedicating all their energies', but perhaps the gesture of the young men publicly offering their lives to God was more eloquent than any words could have been.

The neophytes rose in turn and knelt before the father Provincial, who was seated in front of the altar for the reception of the vows. Mark read the words from the book that the Master of Ceremonies held at his right, but though his brain told him that this was one of the great moments of his life, the words themselves seemed curiously empty and hollow as they fell from his lips.

As he returned to his place, he felt a sense of anticlimax and disappointment; he would have liked the moment to have been one of the emotional peaks of his life. Later, after explaining this to Peter, his friend laughed.

"You would have liked to proclaim your vows in ringing tones with the massed heavenly choirs rising to a crescendo as you spoke the sacred words; just like a Hollywood film".

But at that moment there was no time to brood on his disappointment as the ceremony moved on and continued with the Mass. Peter and Ken did not share Mark's sense of flatness as they approached the solemn moment in a more matter-of-fact way. Neither was a particularly emotional type, though Peter knew a moment of madness as he was tempted to shock the assembly by saying something vulgar; it was the sort of impulse that comes over otherwise sane people who find themselves tempted to fall off the edge when peering over the brink of a deep chasm. Fortunately his normal sanity prevailed and the moment passed. They pronounced their vows in calm, clear voices, then returned to their places, conscious of a deliberation and definitiveness in the step they had just taken.

For David, the pronouncing of the vows had the solemnity of a sentence of death. Mercifully, he was spared the anguish of his doubts and scruples; the calm he had achieved the previous evening lasted through the night and the hours before the ceremony. But the moment held no joy for him; rather, he felt the weight of an immense burden settling on his shoulders as he pledged his life and freedom to his God of fear and justice.

Communion came and went; the rest of the proceedings ended with a slight sense of anticlimax, though the community with the newly professed at their head processed from the sanctuary with almost a martial air as the organ thundered forth a glorious voluntary; a visiting organist had fortunately been available, and Mark listened enviously to the stirring chords and dissonances as he made his way with the others through the sacristy door.

The young men were quickly swept up into a round of congratulations from their confreres, and then followed the family reunions. Mark eagerly ran up to his family as they left the main doors of the church.

"Mum, Brenda" he cried as he rushed up to them. After saluting the ladies briefly with chaste kisses, he shook hands with the tall young man beside them.

"Tony; I didn't recognise you" he gasped.

Tony had been a boy when he had left home the previous year. Now he was a man, and Mark felt a sense of shyness and loss as he realised that he had missed those vital months in his brother's development. He felt that the close and easy comradeship they had known as children could never be recaptured. It was the end of an era, and he could only hope that the future would mean the growth of a new, if different, relationship.

"The Order has stolen something precious from me" he thought, with a touch of bitterness. But the joy of reunion soon banished those thoughts from his mind for the time being at least, as he tumbled out a hundred questions to catch up on the family news.

The family too saw before them a new Mark, lean and gaunt, with the bones protruding, clear evidence of the rigours of the past year. But Mark's obvious happiness reassured them concerning his general welfare, and so they all settled down to enjoy the buffet meal and the rest of the day together.

Peter meanwhile had greeted his family; or at least those who had come. His mother and the younger children were there, but his father had been 'too busy' and the older children had not even made the effort to find a respectable excuse for their absence. Peter felt the pain of this rejection, but shrugged it off, welcoming those who had come with a new realisation of love. He had always had a take it or leave it attitude to his family, and as a child had never been too sorry to leave them, thus escaping the bitterness and anger that could so often be felt in his home. But now he looked at his mother and younger brother, and the adorable little five year old who peeped up at him shyly through a riot of brown curls, with new eyes. He suddenly knew the pain and struggles his mother had endured in keeping her family together, and hugged her warmly.

"I'm sorry Charlie and Mick aren't here, Peter".

"Don't worry, Mum, I understand", and Peter closed his mind for the moment to his elder brothers, who had stopped going to Mass as soon as they were able to shrug off their mother's authority and influence, preferring to share their father's indifference. But today was a day for fun and joy, so he picked up his little sister, the baby of the family, and the little girl responded warmly and affectionately to the love of the big brother she hardly knew.

Ken on the other side of the room was trying his best to give equal attention to the twins, who though scarcely four years old, already loved their uncle Ken, and demanded loudly that he make a fuss over them. They had been almost three when he had last seen them, and had grown considerably in the meantime. Dandling one on each knee, Ken was able to hold an intermittent conversation with the older members of the family, while the little ones played with the various cords and other parts of his religious attire that were more easily accessible, and fascinating to young minds.

Nearby, David sat with his mother and father, an older couple who though used to their son's quiet and withdrawn ways, realised that he had changed quite profoundly. Unable to understand, they accepted that the religious life was David's life from now on; they had given their only son to God, and no longer theirs, there would obviously be some distance now between them.

David answered their questions with quiet monosyllables where possible, smiling gently but distantly at his parents' attempts at lightness. It would be a year before they saw him again, yet already David, uneasy in their company, was wishing that they would take their leave and allow him back to his lonely prayers. But aware of their need, he stayed and gave them his company in body at least.

The afternoon wore on, and slowly the evening started to slip by, too. Mark realised that within an hour or so he would have to say farewell to his family once again. It was hard to have to leave them when he had only just seen them again after a year's separation, knowing that it would be a full year before he saw them again. But the Order made it clear that these brief visits were a privilege, and so newly professed and family alike had to make the best of it.

"It's bloody criminal" snarled Peter later when the last tearful farewells had been made. "Our folks long and pine to see us for all these months; they spend a fortune in coming to our profession, then the Order graciously allows us the privilege of a few hours with them before telling them to get lost."

Mark was silent. He too felt the justice of Peter's remarks, and bitterly reflected on the inhumanity of the system. But the system it was, and he accepted it, already looking forward to the few days' visit that would be permitted the following summer at the house of studies. Accustomed now to a life of privation and sacrifice, small mercies had a way of appearing as high treats, and tomorrow would see the beginning of yet another major chapter in his life.

NINETEEN

The next morning was a mad scramble as last minute packing was completed, and taxis ferried the young religious from the monastery to the railway station in the town centre, ready for the long journey to the house of studies, which was situated in the Midlands, near Birmingham.

They looked an odd sight in their black suits, with scrawny necks sticking out of their newly acquired Roman collars and feeling very conspicuous, they boarded the train, finding an empty compartment into which they crowded, glad to escape the curious stares of their fellow passengers.

"Thank God we're on our way" gasped Peter, as he pulled out a battered cigarette, a relic of the previous day's revels, and lighting up, he grinned at the disapproving faces of his companions.

"The prisoners were transferred from the maximum security block at Pentonville to Parkhurst on the Isle of Wight; enjoy your little taste of freedom" he remarked as he settled into his seat for the journey.

In truth, the young men resembled convicts being transferred from one prison to another in more ways than one; the short haircuts, their being unaccustomed to the outside world, coming as they did from an isolated, all-male environment in which freedom was very strictly curtailed; the only difference was that the young religious were there by choice, and so there was no need of accompanying warders.

"Well, another new beginning" sighed Mark. "Looking forward to the house of studies, brother; er, Pete?" he hastily amended. It had been constantly enjoined on them as novices that they must address each other formally.

Peter thought about Mark's question for a moment. "I suppose so; it can't be worse than the Novitiate, at any rate."

"I'm going to miss the Nov." replied Mark. "It was a tough life, but once you were into the routine, it was fine."

Peter laughed. "They should have given you a security blanket, Mark, not a habit."

"It's true that the Nov. made us feel secure, but too much security can be a bad thing; we can't be like ostriches, heads in the sand" Ken broke in.

"Leaving bum exposed for all comers to kick" agreed Peter.

The train started with a jerk.

"Well, goodbye Novitiate" Mark sighed.

"Good riddance you mean" retorted Peter, drawing luxuriously on his half smoked cigarette.

The train gathered speed, and the little group settled down to enjoy the journey gazing at the world which was at once familiar and yet alien, to Mark and David at least, cocooned as they were by the thick layer of religious trappings into which they had been carefully woven during the previous year.

The journey was long and uneventful; broken only by the packed meal which they had brought, and so it seemed an age before the train finally pulled into New Street station, Birmingham, where they had to change to a slower local train for the final stages of the journey. By now they had grown a little more accustomed to the unfamiliar Roman collar, and as the connection was almost immediate, they had little time to reflect on whether they were conspicuous or not as they pushed through the dense rush-hour crowds.

The local train was old and dirty, dust flying up in clouds as Mark incautiously patted the stained plush prior to sitting down.

"Stop it, you idiot" gasped Peter, as his nose twitched with the urge to sneeze.

"Not far now he remarked, "provided we get there without catching the plague."

Three quarters of an hour later, the little band stood forlornly on the platform of the branch line station which was situated about four miles from the seminary, and patiently waited for the battered station wagon that served as the seminary transport. They had been told that they would be met, and so after a short time, they greeted a wheezing rattling sound with relief as the ancient vehicle turned into the station yard. The brakes groaned as it stopped, still swaying gently as the door opened and a middle-aged priest emerged, habit tucked about his waist as though he was prepared for the discipline or lavatory, as Peter commented in an aside to Mark. The car was big enough to engulf them all, including the luggage, so within a short time the young men and their cases were squeezed in higgledy-piggledy for the trip to the seminary.

With many groans and judders and in a cloud of dust, they left the station yard and pulled out onto the country road, a fist-shaking cyclist having to swerve to avoid them. But without further incident, they trundled through the seminary gates, and along the drive that led to the magnificent gothic pile that would serve as their home for the next few years.

Alighting outside the front door, Mark stared up at the grey stone columns and mullioned windows, the evening sun throwing long shadows against the lichen covered stonework.

"They rang the bell and after a long wait, a shuffling sound could be heard along the passage as an ancient servitor came and withdrew a multitude of bolts and chains. With a creaking sound, the door swung slowly open. A gaunt, skeletal face appeared which in dismal tones enquired their business". Ken made the others laugh with his mock-solemn intonation as the group examined the facade of their new home.

The seminary was a converted stately home, set in several acres of garden and woodland, beautiful, but impractical. However, it provided the isolation that was deemed a necessity for the successful formation of the young religious, and a more beautiful setting could not be imagined. The house was tucked into a fold in the gently undulating countryside; it faced south-west, and so the evening sun in which it was now bathed showed it to best advantage. It was a large, rambling building, with the students quartered mainly in the converted servants' wing, over the classrooms which had been fashioned from the old stables and outbuildings below. Completing a square with the main building, a church had been built towards the end of the last century, shortly after the acquisition of the property by the Order. It had been tastefully designed to blend in with the character of the existing buildings, and so the whole property formed a pleasing and harmonious prospect which invariably enchanted the visitor, but which left the inmates with the sense of belonging to another world, which some found attractive, but others yearned for the day which would see their return to the outside world.

Perhaps predictably, Mark fell into the former category, and Peter the latter. On that first evening, gazing at the building before them, Mark knew that he would be happy here.

The door opened suddenly, and onto the front steps poured a seemingly endless procession of young men, as the students, about fifty in number, came out to welcome the newcomers. Many were already known to the ex-St Saviour's pupils, as they had been further up the school in earlier days. Now they all bustled about, anxious to make their newly arrived brethren feel welcome.

"Brother Kennedy?" Mark looked round to see a tall, distinguished looking student addressing him.

"Ah, so you are brother Kennedy? Welcome to St Augustine's. I'm brother Winterton-Smith, with a hyphen, you know."

The refined tones made Mark blink for a moment, but with a smile he accepted the proffered hand, and replied:

"Brother Kennedy."

I've been appointed your guardian angel; rather a decent scheme for showing you new boys the ropes. Follow me, I'll show you to your billet."

"My God, what have we here?" Mark wondered to himself as he followed his guardian angel along the narrow corridors and up the back stairs to a dusty passage with several small rooms opening off to one side. The passage had windows at regular intervals which overlooked the quadrangle, with the church to the left and the main building to the right. The rooms, originally much larger, had been subdivided so that each student had a small room with a window facing north. Traces of the former arrangement abounded, with ornate cast iron fireplaces in some of the rooms, and generally, the rooms were in pairs with the doors at forty five degree angles to each other just inside the original doorway.

"This is it, my dear fellow" announced brother Winterton-Smith, as he opened one of the doors, showing Mark into a narrow, rather dingy little room. He had one of the ornate fireplaces, and adorning the walls were three or four black and white engraved pictures, familiar from the Novitiate, showing the Order's founder and early saints. Brother Winterton-Smith sniffed fastidiously.

"Bit niffy, what? I'd better open a window."

Suiting the action to the word, he struggled with the ancient sash, which finally gave and opened slightly with a creak.

"That's better, my dear chap" he smiled. "I'm Neville, by the way. Neville Winterton-Smith."

Mark warmed to his unassuming friendliness.

"I'm Mark; what year are you in?"

"Third, old boy; just starting last year of Philosophy."

"What's it like, Philosophy?"

"All very dry and boring, really; though it isn't too bad in parts; sort of curate's egg, as you might say. Anyway, you'll soon find out; class starts tomorrow."

"Well, I suppose there's nothing like going in at the deep end" laughed Mark, as he heaved his heavy case onto the bed.

"Do you want to unpack now, or would you care for a tour of inspection?" enquired Neville.

"I can unpack later" agreed Mark. "Lead on, McDuff."

The two re-emerged onto the narrow corridor and Mark followed his guide along to the end and down the rickety narrow stair.

"There are the classrooms, Mark; note the bloodstains and pools of sweat and tears."

Mark peered through the door. The room looked much like any other classroom he had seen, though the desks and general appointments seemed older and shabbier than most he had come across.

"This one's Theology, Dogma; Philosophy is further down the passage."

Mark dutifully followed his mentor and entered the room that was to witness his struggles with scholastic philosophy over the next three years.

"Where do we sit?" he asked.

"Anywhere; it's first come, first served, as one might say. You'll get used to the system. The lectures are in English, but the text books are in Latin. Hope yours is up to scratch?"

"It's OK," replied Mark; "I found I could sort of understand the Latin Office when we recited it in the Nov. The general drift, anyway."

"You'll cope admirably, I'm sure. The text books are in dog Latin, anyway; you know, "Sanctus Thomas dicit quod haec mensa est in hoc loco" and all that sort of thing. Besides, the more intellectually inclined brethren prepare notes that everyone else copies. I'm generally considered to be one of the brain boxes," he added modestly.

"I'll be knocking on your door pretty often then" laughed Mark.

The two students then left the classroom, and passed into the main block in which the principal rooms of the old mansion were situated. Mark gazed enraptured at the faded splendour of a former age; the ceilings were adorned with ornately carved and gilded plaster, and venerable oil paintings were displayed on the walls, surrounded by battered gesso frames and torn silk wall hangings.

"We just have the more respectable paintings now," Neville commented. "When the Order first arrived here, apparently there were all sorts of generously endowed ladies exhibiting their charms. The artists must have used a devil of a lot of pink paint in those days" he added reflectively.

"But shock, horror! We couldn't have such temptations against holy purity in our midst, and so all the offending paintings were removed. Some of those old boys were fearfully strict, you know; Philistines, if you think about it. I mean, who could be tempted by a cherub's little pink willy? Mind you, come to think of it, perhaps the little pink bottoms might be more of a temptation."

Mark blushed and grinned.

"David, that's brother Hetherington in my year, would have had a terrible job keeping custody of the eyes; in fact he probably still will have, as not all the naked cherubs have disappeared."

He then explained about David, and Neville nodded understandingly.

"He sounds like a bad case, but there are one or two others a little like that here already. Not British, old boy. You can understand these excitable foreigners getting somewhat worked up and carried away like that. But your true English gentleman would have no truck with such extremes..

"Peter Clark advocates a healthy mediocrity in his school of spirituality" Mark smiled. "It sounds as though you have the same idea."

"Well, not exactly; a chap can be holy; dashed good thing, in fact. But he must always be a gentleman, which means preserving the old sang froid, and not making an exhibition of yourself. But enough of that. Let us proceed on our philanthropic way. The church is next on the agenda."

There was a covered walkway or cloister between the main building and the church, and so they quickly reached the side door of the stately building. On entering, Mark was immediately struck by the atmosphere. It was dark, as the sun had by now set, even though it was still quite light outside. The tall narrow windows, filled with stained glass, tended to cut out any excessive light, though there was sufficient for Mark to be able to appreciate the fine proportions of the building. Stone columns soared gracefully skywards, and drew the eye up to the magnificent vaulted roof. The sanctuary was fairly simple, with nothing more than low altar rails separating it from the main body of the church. A large, but not unduly ornate altar of stone was situated against the north wall, with a large, almost clear window above. At the other end of the church was the choir loft and organ.

"Magnificent looking organ" whispered Mark. "What does it sound like?"

"I'll play it for you if you wish," murmured Neville. "Follow me."

Opening a small door, he climbed a narrow spiral staircase with Mark following, until they emerged into the choir loft. Taking his place at the keyboard with Mark at his shoulder, he switched on. A light came on over the console and a low whirring sound indicated that the electric pump was supplying the necessary air.

"It's a two decker" commented Neville. "Great organ on the lower deck, with swell above."

Mark wondered at the seemingly endless rows of stops, while Neville selected several. Opening a music book, he commenced a prelude and fugue by Bach which he played with considerable panache and several flourishes. Mark listened spellbound. The magnificent counterpoint followed by the stupendous chord sequences of the ending re-echoed round the church for several seconds after Neville had finished playing, and Mark was unstinting in his admiration.

"You're obviously musical" observed Neville. "Do you play?"

Mark hesitantly revealed his Novitiate experience, and Neville moved along the bench, motioning Mark to slide along beside him. He did so with a certain reluctance, not wishing his playing to prove an anticlimax to that which had just finished. However, his desire to try the magnificent instrument overcame his reserve, and opening the hymn book, he tentatively played through a couple of his favourite hymns.

"Very promising" Neville observed gravely when Mark had finished.

"We'll make an organist of you yet. But now dear boy, we had better adjourn to the refectory, as supper will be served in about five minutes."

They duly arrived and found the other students massing at the door. On the given signal, the group processed into the refectory in an orderly fashion, the newcomers moving automatically to the junior places in the order already long established in the years at St Saviour's.

"Hi there, Mark, where have you been?" whispered Peter.

"Tell you in a minute" his friend replied as the grace began.

"I'm starving" murmured Peter a few moments later as they sat down to the sound of much scraping and creaking as the assembled body took their places at the aged refectory tables.

"Bet it's boiled ham and a tomato" whispered Mark in reply.

The reading went on only for a sentence or two before the father superior with a flourish rang the bell the customary twice for the allowing of conversation.

"Welcome to the new students" he announced, and in the time-honoured fashion, the reader intoned the "tu autem, Domine."

"My guardian angel has been showing me round" Mark confided to Peter a moment later, and proceeded to regale his friend with his adventures over the past hour.

"Neville Winterton-Smith?" remarked Peter. "Sounds a bit of a berk to me."

"No, he's fine" insisted Mark. "You'll like him."

But Neville and Peter were not destined to become fast friends. Mark often found himself as the common link between incompatible individuals; though somewhat reserved, he was able to make friends with very different people, not sharing the antipathies which prevented the forming of a circle among them.

"Anyway, Pete, what did you do? Have you had a look round yet?"

"Yeah, I've had a quick tour" agreed his friend, "trying to spot the obvious gaps in the barbed wire, and noting the positions of the guards and searchlights."

Mark grinned at him.

"It's not that bad, Pete. I think I'm going to like it here."

"You would", snorted his friend. "It's a bit too far from civilisation for my liking. Typical" he groaned as the trays emerged with the inevitable boiled ham and tomato.

"It's enough to make you want to become a Jew. Still, I'll hang onto my foreskin for the moment."

Mark, by now used to Peter's sense of humour, failed to be shocked. The young men ate hungrily, the long day they had spent giving them a hearty appetite. Rapidly demolishing the despised ham and tomato, they passed onto the cheese, which Peter demanded with much nudging and hissing, until it was passed down to him. Large quantities of brown bread and butter, garnished with generous slabs of cheese quickly vanished, and soon, appetites sated, they sat back while the monastery cat prowled round between the tables, hoping for and receiving the occasional morsel.

"It might only have been ham and a tomato, but I enjoyed that" sighed Mark. "I suppose they must be right when they say hunger is the best sauce."

"Yeah, not bad" agreed Peter. "What wouldn't I give for a nice fag now!"

His wishes were soon to be granted, as later, seated in the common room watching the news on television, the students greeted the senior member of their body with acclaim when he entered the room bearing several packets of cigarettes. This was long before the dangers of smoking became generally known.

"Two each" he announced as the packets made the rounds.

Peter immediately entered into frenzied negotiations with the non-smokers to obtain their supplies, and managed to secure an extra bonus two or three, which he carefully tucked away in his habit for future consumption.

"This is the life, and it's even legal" sighed Peter as he puffed luxuriously. As both cigarettes had to be finished before the end of the recreation period, the common room was soon filled with smoke as forty or so smokers puffed away industriously, for all the world like laboratory rabbits. The pungent blue clouds quickly stung Mark's eyes, but he persevered, the treat too good to miss. The television too, was a novelty, as they had not seen it for over a year since entering the Novitiate.

After the news, an enthralling drama series started, but no sooner had their interest been gripped when the bell signalling the end of recreation sounded. With a groan, the assembly rose, the television was turned off, and the brethren retired to the church for night prayers. To the relief of most, the superior granted the occasional privilege of short night prayers, irreverently referred to by some as 'short nighties', and so it wasn't too long before Mark was stretched out on the thin mattress of the iron-framed bed in his newly acquired cell. However, sleep was slow in coming as the events of the full day caught up with him, and the clickety-click of railway wheels seemed to drum and throb in his head. Lights out had sounded, so he dare not switch on his light to read, and so he fingered his rosary beads and soon, with joyful mysteries inexplicably mingled with sorrowful and glorious, and 'Hail Mary's' lost count of in spite of the beads, he fell into a sleep that was restless and interspersed with vivid dreams. Eventually he slept more deeply, but it seemed as if he had hardly drifted into unconsciousness when the strident tones of the bell woke him.

TWENTY

Clutching his aching brow, the result of the previous day's exertion and excitement, not to mention the smoke-filled atmosphere of the common room, he staggered out of bed to begin his first full day as a student. Making his way to the church half an hour later, he discovered that Peter was not in his accustomed place beside him. Morning prayer and meditation started, and still there was no sign of Peter. Ten minutes later, obviously unshaven and newly awakened, the latecomer finally arrived.

"Slept in" he whispered to Mark somewhat unnecessarily as he took his place with clatters and bangs as he clumsily kicked the kneeler. Mark grinned at him and then resumed the perennial battle of trying to stave off distractions.

Mass followed meditation as usual, with the bulk of the students attending the public Mass at the high altar. Others served the many priests in the community who were saying Mass at the numerous side altars sprinkled round the church. The soft murmur of the Latin and the tinkling of the little bells as the various ceremonies progressed filled the church with gentle activity, and Mark found that although it was a little difficult to concentrate on the main Mass with all the pious hubbub around, the general liturgical bustle that filled the church helped him to keep his mind on what was happening in general.

The smoke from the many candles tickled his nose, and the church grew heavy with the smell of candle grease. Then with a clatter, the main body of the students moved up to the altar rails to receive Holy Communion, and for a few moments, Mark managed to concentrate deeply on the presence of Jesus Christ within him. He saw the years stretching ahead of him as if looking across a mighty plain as he stood on a high mountain, and he prayed, thanking God for his gifts and the comforting presence of Christ on the long journey he saw lying ahead. He knew that there would be hard times, but just then he felt a comfort and reassurance that all would go well for him.

The final blessing and last Gospel roused him from these contemplations, and rattling through the three 'Hail Mary's' and the 'Hail, Holy Queen' for the conversion of Russia, he realised that he was hungry and began to look forward to his breakfast. Thanksgiving was now a mere quarter of an hour, a bagatelle after the seemingly endless half hour of thanksgiving they had to endure in the Novitiate, so it seemed like no time at all before the students were milling round the huge steaming coffee urns, drawing off pint mugs of hot, grey coffee to wash down the thick slabs of brown bread and marmalade that made up the meal.

Talking was allowed on certain days, this being one, and so a general babble of conversation filled the refectory.

"What happened to you?" asked Mark of Peter, who still unshaven, sat with his hands wrapped round the pint mug of hot coffee, brooding.

"Just turned over for another five minutes, and before I knew it, it was twenty-five to. My God, I feel shattered" he moaned, rasping his stubbly chin on the back of his hand.

"And it's those damned studies this morning. God knows what I'll make of them if the horror stories are true".

Philosophy was a subject that rumour had painted in the darkest possible colours; abstract, deep, difficult to understand, and altogether an exercise calculated to stupefy with boredom even the most adventurous of intellects.

"It won't be too bad, Pete," encouraged Mark. "Neville Winterton-Smith has promised me his notes, so I'll share with you. We'll manage fine."

"What the hell all that junk has to do with being a priest I'll never know" sighed Peter. "Come on," he continued as he gulped down the last of his coffee and popped the remains of his bread and marmalade into his mouth, "let's take a walk."

Quickly finishing his own breakfast, Mark hurriedly joined his friend.

"We've got about an hour before class starts, so we can have a good potter round."

At nine o'clock the new students had been ordered to assemble in one of the classrooms for a general introductory session with the Prefect of students. But that was still an hour away as Mark and Peter left the buildings and headed for the gardens. It was a bright September morning, and the warmth of summer had not yet departed, and so conditions for the stroll were perfect. The gardens were large and ornate, though somewhat overgrown. The remnants of a glorious past could be seen everywhere, with cast iron classical urns in stately rows filled with brightly coloured geraniums; gothic follies and Arcadian grove alternating with slightly overgrown lawns, arbours and rather stagnant ornamental pools.

"What a place this must have been once" sighed Mark. "It's beautiful, even now."

Wood pigeons flapped and clattered from the trees as they approached, squirrels darted among the vast branches of trees that had been young in the days of the first Elizabeth.

"It is beautiful" Peter grudgingly admitted. "But even so, I'm sure you could go barmy here even among the beauty."

"Mind if I join you?"

A small, wiry student with dark, curly hair and a freckled face came up.

"Why not? You can show us the ropes" answered Peter. "Mark, this is Jim Hunter, my guardian angel."

"Watch out, you've a job on your hands with Pete Clark" laughed Mark. "Keeping him out of trouble is a full-time job."

The threesome walked slowly towards the kitchen garden, with its neat rows of vegetables and fruit trees which lined the walls. Along one side, a row of venerable ramshackle greenhouses stretched, with the occasional missing pane.

"Come on, I'll show you the greenhouses" said Jim, and suiting the action to the word, led the two first-year students into the nearest of the rickety glass structures.

"Apparently, the greenhouses used to be heated" he remarked, indicating the wide bore, rusty cast-iron piping.

"Just imagine, peaches, nectarines, probably even oranges or lemons. It must have been a glorious sight."

In the next house, several vines spread luxuriously, weighed down by an immense crop of black grapes. Peter was clearly impressed.

"I look after these" commented Jim, "gardening is one of my hobbies, and fortunately, we have plenty of time for such things here."

The tour continued, and gradually led the little group back to the house.

"I'd better go and have a shave" sighed Peter, "then it's nose to the grindstone time."

Taking his farewells, Mark went to his room and quickly made his bed, and then finished off his unpacking. A bell sounded, and all along the corridor doors opened and slammed shut again as the students hurried to their respective classrooms. Mark joined Peter, Ken, David and Terry in a classroom with the legend 'St Thomas' on the door.

After a short wait, the door opened and a tall, angular priest entered.

"Good morning, everybody, I'm father McDonald, your Prefect of students."

"Good morning, father" the assembled group dutifully murmured, sizing up the man who would be directing their lives for good or ill over the next few years.

"I hope you are settling into St Augustine's. We try our best to make this your home, and home should be a happy place."

He then started the proceedings formally with a prayer, and coughing to clear his throat, he began to outline the years that lay ahead.

"You will be students here for seven years."

The image of a judge pronouncing sentence immediately sprang to Peter's mind.

"Those seven years will be years of formation; intellectual, spiritual, moral. Let's take these in order. The course of studies here as in all seminaries has two major divisions; philosophy and theology. Philosophy will be occupying your first three years here. This year, you will be introduced to philosophy, and you will also be polishing up other aspects of your education. Perhaps some of you will do 'A' levels in one or two subjects.

"Philosophy is designed to teach you how to think; to establish the rational groundwork of the Faith, and to prepare you for theology. It is often called the handmaid of theology for this reason. But besides philosophy, you will also be studying other, lesser subjects;

Church history, Scripture, Canon law among others; these will of course take you through to theology, too.

"Theology will be the main preoccupation of your last four years here; dogmatic and Moral Theology. Very broadly, Dogmatic Theology is concerned with the exposition of the teaching of the Church, the doctrine of the Church concerning God himself, the nature of the Church, the Sacraments and so forth. Moral Theology is a study of God's law and man's response to that law, particularly the negative response of sin."

The little group looked silently up at father McDonald, who paced up and down before them as he outlined the general programme of studies.

"It's all Greek to me" thought Peter as his brain reeled from the bombardment of facts it had received. After a few more remarks on the nature of studies for the priesthood and the approach to them adopted by St Augustine's, father McDonald then spoke in general terms about other aspects of their life in the seminary.

"They don't seem to worry too much about spiritual formation" Mark pondered to himself, accustomed as he was to the intensive approach of the Novitiate in this area. The outline at St Augustine's was decidedly sketchy. Perhaps the authorities felt that they had received about all they needed in that department in the Novitiate, he concluded. Certainly, the place accorded to spiritual formation seemed decidedly jejune after the high-pressure treatment of the Novitiate. David's views were similar; though he regarded the seeming lack of attention in this area as a much more serious omission. Mark was content to adopt "the Order knows best" as his motto.

Peter on the other hand felt, as he remarked to the others later when discussing these points, that they had already had too much of all that stuff; what they'd had should last them a lifetime. The proposed formation in fact amounted to a monthly retreat day, with a conference from the Prefect, and one more conference on a Sunday morning, which more often than not turned out to be a jokey quarter of an hour, or a moan about current deficiencies in the students' behaviour, according to the prefect's prevailing mood.

It was with mixed feelings, then, that the first-year students pondered their future when Fr McDonald had finished his introduction.

"Give it a chance, boys" pleaded Ken, as the little group sat on the desk lids after the departure of father McDonald.

"It's only our first morning. It's simply too soon to form an opinion."

The younger minds had already tended to polarise the issues, but Ken's stabilising influence proved invaluable, as was so often the case. The group adjourned for coffee, and then reassembled for the first lecture in philosophy. In the first year, the course would cover logic and the history of philosophy, and the students awaited their initiation with some trepidation. They would join their more senior brethren for the other philosophy courses, which were run on a cyclical basis. That year, epistemology, or the study of the theory of knowledge, was on the agenda.

The philosophy lector was the epitome of the absent minded professor. Elderly, with white hair, he frequently lost all track of time, and sometimes even the day of the week or month eluded him. On one famous occasion he had been known to say 'I was remarking to someone the other day; that is, about forty years ago...' But he was kindness itself, and so his introduction to the new students was relatively painless.

The lesson was taken straight from the Latin text book, which the young men followed as he rattled off an impromptu translation. Some of his listeners scribbled busily, trying to get down the gist of what he was saying, others simply gaped blankly as the unfamiliar concepts danced before them, their minds vainly trying to assimilate them.

"What did you make of that load of old cobblers?" Peter asked Mark later.

"Not a lot" confessed his friend as they strolled in the garden after lunch.

"If that's philosophy, I can see we're in for a tough time."

"Never mind, I'll have a word with Neville, and see if he can throw any light on it for us."

That evening, having gained the Prefect's permission as talking during the study period was strictly forbidden, Mark knocked discreetly on Neville's door. On hearing the invitation 'enter' uttered in those distinctively cultured tones, Mark opened the door, and asked timidly:

"Could you help me with a bit of philosophy, Neville?"

"My dear chap, I'd be delighted" he cheerfully replied. "Take a pew and confess all, omitting no detail, however slight."

Mark presented the Latin text book. "I can translate it, more or less, but it doesn't mean very much."

"Lesson one. You'll discover, Mark my dear fellow, that an awful lot of what we study here doesn't mean very much. It is what is known as the wisdom of the ages, which has been handed down from St Thomas Aquinas in an almost unaltered form and learned by heart, often without much understanding, by generations of the clergy ever since. Of course there is a good deal of truth there, but winkling out the gems is the problem. Always remember this. What is important is to know a thing, not to understand it. If you understand it too, that's an added bonus. In theology, we call that faith; knowledge without understanding. I think that there must be an analogous gift where philosophy is concerned. Now let me see. If I can find them, I may have something that might just prove invaluable here."

Gentleman he might have been, and fastidious to a fault in his personal appearance, but his room had about it more than an element of disorder. He rummaged among dog-eared folders and piles of notes stapled together, and eventually emerged with a triumphant cry, exclaiming "Eureka! the venerable notes on logic."

Mark took the proffered bundle of notes, and discovered that there was a flourishing black market in notes for the various courses that were handed down to their successors by the newly ordained priests leaving the seminary. The courses were identical from year to year, and so notes that first saw the light of day twenty years earlier were still just as valuable today, allowing for the occasional error in transcription. The story about 'send three and four pence, I'm going to a dance' developing from the original 'send reinforcements I'm going to advance' had its many counterparts in the transmitted wisdom of the philosophy and theology courses.

"This is how I passed my history of philosophy exam" remarked Neville, handing Mark a slimmer sheaf of papers. Written on these was a long series of doggerel verses that did not rhyme, but which read with a beat and rhythm as they unfolded the potted summaries of the key thoughts of the world's great thinkers.

"Of course, I understood a modicum, but I simply took the matter to be learned, and cast it in this verse form for learning purposes, then in the examination simply re-rendered it into the best flowing prose I could devise, and bingo! Ninety-two percent" he added modestly.

There were obviously ways and means previously undreamed of that made academic success possible, and Mark wondered what surprises would be unveiled next.

"That's another thing" continued Neville. "Write with flair and style in examinations; it covers a multitude of ignorance."

Mark could believe it. He felt that Neville would pass simply by writing his name on the paper.

"So endeth your first full day as a student. What do you make of it so far?"

"I think I'm going to like it" Mark smiled, "and maybe the studies aren't going to be so impossible after all."

"That's the ticket" approved Neville. "Nil desperandum and all that. You'll find that Oggies isn't such a bad old dump despite the moans and gripes emitted by all and sundry. Of course, it's important to keep your interests many and varied. It all helps to avoid the onset of incipient lunacy. Now. We have established that music is one of your interests. Any others?"

Mark pondered for a moment.

"It's hard to say. I'm a bit of a dabbler, I suppose. Though I must admit there's one thing I'm not too keen on, and that's sport."

"Excellent" exclaimed Neville with an austere shudder. "Dreadful business. Muddied oafs booting inflated leather about the place. Mind you, many of the brethren find it strangely fascinating, so its power to grip cannot be denied. It does have its advantages, however. It provides an excellent excuse for rather tolerable binges when our fellows play other colleges. Also, a strange madness grips the place on various occasions such as cup final day, Wimbledon fortnight, the Olympic Games, and so forth. Provided that the authorities at the time are infected with that particular madness, the regular observance develops as many holes as a string vest, offering much needed relaxation and relief for poor wretches groaning beneath the weight of a surfeit of meditation and similar afflictions. But pray continue, dear boy."

Mark realised that Neville, once embarked upon a theme, was as difficult to stop as an express train, albeit an express train of the better sort, with finely appointed Pullman coaches and an exclusive clientele.

"Let me see. I enjoy walking, gardening, reading, art, messing about with bits of wood and tools. I think most things interest me; I find I enjoy doing all sorts. I'm not easily bored."

"Well, dear boy, Oggies sounds like the very place for you. A dilettante's paradise, as the opportunities are endless, and provided you keep abreast of the swots, the authorities usually give the green light to most interests and activities, provided they are not things you could get arrested for. As you might gather, I too am something of a polymath, at least in embryo and intention. The Renaissance ideal of the universal man, and all that sort of thing. Now reading. We have an excellent library here. I simply devour books, on all sorts of topics. What are your tastes in literature?"

Mark smiled. "A to Z just about covers it for me, too. I love some of the classics of English literature; Scott, Dickens, the sort of book you can get your teeth into. But I also enjoy lighter stuff, such as Agatha Christie, Sherlock Holmes, even the 'Just William' books."

"Don't say 'even the Just William books, Mark, my dear chap. They will definitely be one of the classics of the future. I confidently predict that among the classics of the next century you will find the 'Just William' books, as we have the 'Alice' books of Lewis Carrol today. Also, mark my words, the works of P.G. Wodehouse, Ian Fleming, and possibly even your Agatha Christie, though I personally prefer the works of Dorothy L. Sayers. The 'William' books, like the 'Alice' books, are of course children's books written for adults."

Warming to his theme, Neville continued: "the whole area of literature is a hobby horse of mine. The tragedy is, of course, that for most people, English literature and even reading in general becomes literally a closed book owing to the fact that English literature is taught in our schools. Schools are the great enemy of education. Show me a student of English literature in your average school, and I will show you someone who has been put off Shakespeare for life. The average school course prods and pokes into imagined motives and meanings, and misses the breathtaking beauty of the whole Shakespearean idea. Straining at gnats and swallowing camels, that's education in schools for you. Education essentially should teach you to love a subject, not impart facts about it. Take care of the interest, and the facts will take care of themselves."

"I take your point", murmured Mark, a little overwhelmed by the barrage. "My love of literature didn't come from the literature course at school; more likely it came from surreptitious reading when I should have been studying other things."

"QED" announced Neville. "And now, dear boy, perhaps you had better bugger off, as the authorities would not look too kindly on your staying too long. But we shall converse further on these matters, never fear."

Thanking him for the gift of the notes, Mark returned to his own room, and carefully studied the first pages of the logic notes. Glimmerings of understanding came to him, and so later he passed the notes on to Peter, who gratefully accepted the grains of knowledge that Mark had managed to glean.

During the next few days, the new students became more accustomed to the pattern of student life into which they had been plunged with so little ceremony. The style of their future response was also quickly established: Mark, Ken and David managing competently if not brilliantly, though predictably, Peter was finding the going rather more difficult. But academic studies were not the only area of concern, and in other fields the emerging pattern was to prove rather different.

TWENTY ONE

After breakfast at St Augustine's, the sylvan peace was usually shattered by various students singing loudly, or declaiming passages learned by heart from sermons handed down for practice purposes from year to year.

On enquiring what was going on, the students were introduced to voice production. Neville was something of a nonconformist in this regard.

"I have a theory, my dear boy" he announced when Mark discussed the matter with him.

"The purpose of voice production is to increase vocal capacity so that one day you may be capable of bellowing your way through a mission sermon. The trouble is, according to my theory, tried and tested as it is by many hours of acute observation I hasten to add, that the more the voice develops, the more the brain shrinks. I'm sure that there must be a perfectly reasonable scientific explanation for this phenomenon. It's probably something to do with the rising demand for hollow space in the head to increase resonance. So don't overdo it, old thing."

"Do you have any sermons that I could use, Neville?"

"One or two, my dear chap, though you may find mine a trifle unorthodox. Everybody else does, when I preach them in mission academy."

Answering Mark's request for enlightenment regarding mission academy, Neville explained that each week, the student body assembled after tea on the chosen day, and two of the brethren then preached a short sermon, which was followed by public comment from students selected at random by the father Prefect. The younger students were not allowed to write their own material for these practice sermons, but made use of extracts culled from a venerable tome of sermons known as the 'blue book', or other approved sources. Some of the more enterprising students persuaded their more senior colleagues on the mission circuit to allow them to use extracts from their material.

Mark was given two or three specimen sermons to choose from by one of the other students; a piece on sin, one on hell, and for good measure, one on Our Lady.

"The blood and thunder ones are the easiest" he was told. "Try one of those first."

So Mark learned the extract from the sermon on sin first, and soon found that once he had lost his inhibitions, he was thundering out the denunciations with great gusto to an audience of interested cows or trees, according to the particular location chosen for his practice that day, and thoroughly enjoying himself.

"Drunkard", he would roar, "what will your death be? You live a drunkard, you will die a drunkard, for as a man lives, so shall he die".

Peter too enjoyed the vigorous preaching exercises, and so the two friends would often listen to and criticise each other's efforts.

"Balls like a bull" he laughed after Mark had let his sermon rip at full blast. "This preaching lark is something I'm really going to enjoy."

The first year students were quickly falling into the routine of St Augustine's. Morning lectures in philosophy, Church history, liturgy and scripture were followed by afternoons of varied activities, among which manual labour, walks, football and some private study and spiritual reading alternated, according to the day.

Peter was a keen footballer, and so on every available occasion, he donned the necessary togs and joined the other aficionados. He was a skilful attacking forward, and so quickly caught the eye of the older students responsible for selecting the college team. Mark played occasionally, though he was a rather plodding full back and so his services were only called on if numbers were short. He preferred walking, and when occasion allowed, would go for long walks in the beautiful countryside of the English Midlands around the college, his usual companion being either Neville or Peter, or occasionally Ken, Jim, or one of the other students.

Under Neville's wing, his musical interests prospered, too. He managed to practise the organ two or three times a week, and would often creep quietly into the church when Neville was performing. He never tired of the works of Bach, though they were a little beyond his abilities just then.

One day, the head student or Capo as he was called, announced after lunch that the normal spiritual reading and manual work had been dispensed, and 'W.W.P.' had been granted, which meant that the students could choose any activity involving work, walk or play. The football pitch was a sea of mud with the constant use it received and the autumn rains, and so not enough students wanted to play to make a game possible.

"What are you going to do, Pete?" asked Mark. "It's 'W.W.P.'"

"I think I'll pee, then have a kip" grumbled Peter, slouching off to put this plan into practice.

"Come on, Mark, we'll listen to a few records" suggested Neville.

In view of the weather, the Prefect allowed this plan, and so the two music lovers adjourned to the common room, where Neville sorted through the mixed collection boasted of by the student body.

"Load of rubbish we've got, really" he murmured as he busily extracted the discs he wanted Mark to hear.

"When a chap receives a record token, as we do from time to time, especially at Christmas or on a fellow's birthday, his is the privilege of going into town to pick a record. Unfortunately, about ninety-five percent of the brethren have abysmal tastes, and so we are snowed under with offerings such as "Oklahoma" and "One hundred favourites for the piano" and other similar delights. Now. A little Mozart, perhaps, with a touch of Vivaldi, and perhaps a soupçon of the divine Henry Purcell."

So the pair were soon lounging at their ease in a couple of the ancient battered arm chairs which graced the students' common room, while the music of the above mentioned composers delighted their ears. Apart from an occasional comment, they listened in silence, the rain drumming outside providing a constant background.

"Thanks, Neville, that was terrific" sighed Mark as the afternoon wore on, and time for tea approached.

"What was that piece by Purcell again?"

"Dido and Aeneas" replied Neville. "Super little work. Henry didn't write a great deal; died young because his wife locked him out after a binge, you know. But what survives is pure gold. Strange thing is, you either love or loathe that sort of music, it would appear. Same with writers like P.G. Wodehouse. A few of the fellows here are dotty about him, others just can't get to grips with that kind of humour. Have you tried him?"

Mark confessed his ignorance, so on the way to tea, Neville slipped into the library, emerging moments later with "The Code of the Woosters."

"Dip into that, and see what you make of it."

Mark obediently took the proffered volume, and tucked it into the front of his habit. Curiously opening the book during study that evening, he was soon immersed and enthralled, the bell for meditation jerking him guiltily back to reality, with the realisation that he had done no study at all that evening.

"Never mind, my dear boy" laughed Neville when Mark confessed. "A very valuable step in your education has been undertaken. Your time was far from wasted."

Obviously, there was more to education than the cramming of philosophical facts into the head, Mark mused. Life at St Augustine's was clearly going to be full of the promise he had foreseen on his first evening there.

TWENTY TWO

September and October had passed, philosophy and the other courses had become a way of life. Mark and Peter had managed to acquire a part share in one of the antiquated typewriters that circulated among the students, and so both soon were busily engaged in teaching themselves the rudiments of typing. Mark typed up the notes from the philosophy class using Neville's copy, but adding bits where the lector had inserted additional explanations and material, and gave a copy to Peter, who returned the compliment in the area of Church history.

Fantastic misspellings peppered the notes, especially in the earlier weeks as they struggled with the mysteries of qwertyuiop, but their expertise gradually improved, and soon they were turning out very creditable results.

As November progressed, the students began to split up on several afternoons each week into small groups, to which the members were admitted by special invitation. The Christmas plays were under way. Mark and Peter both eagerly accepted an invitation to join Neville's production of "Murder in the Cathedral" by T.S. Elliot. Neville himself took the role of St Thomas, while Peter was one of the knights, and Mark one of the monks. Ken had been co-opted into another group preparing "Journey's End," another perennial favourite in the seminary owing to its all-male cast. Mixed casts were occasionally allowed, though at that time there was a ban on any female part under the age of sixty, as a year or two previously, the father Provincial had been gravely shocked at how attractive and feminine some of the students could look when suitably made up, with padding inserted in appropriate places.

The play in question, Shakespeare's "Romeo and Juliet" had come down in song and story, and newcomers to the college were still regaled with the shocking details, including the priceless tale of the performer whose blue tights had split in mid-production. A paint brush with blue paint had been generously applied to his rear quarters, and the show had gone on.

There was a great deal of preparation in the production of the plays, and taking part was a much valued part of a student's activities.

Meanwhile, the weekly preaching academies went on, and eventually it was the turn of the first year students. Mark and Peter being next to each other in seniority were due to appear the same week. For three days before, the activity in preparation was frenzied. They preached at each other until they were blue in the face, each hurling rhetorical abuse at the other as though they were addressing a congregation of the most hardened of sinners. On the day itself, nerves necessitated frequent visits to the lavatory.

"Talk about the need for brown trousers" groaned Peter. "I'm a nervous wreck."

Eventually with tea over, the two neophyte preachers joined the others in the classroom set aside for this purpose, which being the largest, could just about accommodate all the students at a pinch.

Mark was first.

"An extract from a sermon on sin from the bluebook" he announced, having given father Prefect his typed sheet. The student body looked up expectantly. He started a little nervously, looking at the ceiling as he struggled to recall the words he had taken such pains to learn. His delivery therefore sounded a little stilted, but as he progressed, his confidence grew, and he looked his audience in the eye as he slated them for indulgence in the grosser aspects of moral debauchery. Warming to his theme, he bellowed forth the denunciations, but then catastrophe struck as his mind went blank.

Father Prefect hurriedly consulted the typescript and gave him the necessary prompt, but having lost his stride, the rest of the sermon was trotted out in a commonplace way. He managed another tentative flourish at the end, and then stood waiting for the judgement of his peers.

Father Prefect called on one of the more senior students for his opinion.

"Brother Kennedy made a brave first attempt; he obviously isn't afraid to throw himself into a sermon; promising, but a long way to go yet."

The Prefect pondered a moment. He then called for a second opinion.

"I agree with the first comment, though I didn't like his gestures. Probably he'll be better when he is preaching his own stuff."

A low chuckle emerged from certain quarters of the room, as these were the stock phrases used when a student with nothing particular to say was called upon to comment. The Prefect frowned slightly.

"Yes, brother. You show signs of promise; but bear in mind that preaching a sermon is not the rattling off of something learned by heart. What you are saying to your congregation has to come from the heart. But you have a good strong voice and you aren't afraid to use it, so I'd say very passable for a first attempt. Thank you, brother. Now brother Clark?"

Mark retrieved his typed sheet, and with a little embarrassed smile, took the chair Peter had just vacated. Peter in turn gave his sermon to the Prefect and mounted the rostrum. He coughed slightly.

"An extract from a sermon on Death from the blue book."

He then made the sign of the cross and launched into the sermon. Very quickly, he had the interest and attention of the student body as the sermon got under way. Peter was a natural, it seemed; his fist clenched and his eyes flashed as he gave the sermon with all his might. One or two listeners even jumped slightly in their seats when he stressed a point with more than usual vigour. He got through his material without hesitation and finished on a triumphant climax.

The silence that followed witnessed that the hearers were impressed. The first student called on to comment was unstinting in his praise.

"He's obviously going to make a great preacher; all I can say is keep up the good work."

The second commentator was equally generous, but added a rider that brother Clark would have to be careful not to overplay his hand. The border between drama and histrionics was rather narrow at times.

The Prefect endorsed this view, and added that even though the encomiums accorded had been deserved, brother Clark must not think that he had no work to do; he must build on his natural talents to produce the results of which he was capable.

Afterwards, Mark too added his praise;

"I didn't think you had it in you to be as good as that, Pete; you were fantastic; much better than in our practices."

Peter smiled. "I don't know what happened; I just saw all those faces in front of me, and it somehow inspired me to give it everything. There's a few buggers there that I aimed at personally, so I was able to really mean what I said when I was blasting them to hell."

He grinned a little sheepishly. "Maybe not quite literally, but it does seem to help a lot to be able to speak directly to an individual. But preaching is something I find I really like doing; it makes much more sense than all the abstract study we do, like philosophy. It's a much more real preparation for the priesthood."

The feeling of exhilaration lasted for Peter throughout the rest of the evening, and so he was able to attack his philosophy study with something approaching enthusiasm. Perhaps it wasn't such a rotten life after all.

TWENTY THREE

As November progressed, the evenings grew perceptibly shorter, and the weather colder. The rains that had started in late September had lasted through October into November, and the students sometimes felt that it would never stop. Away in the distance to the west, a faint line of hills could be seen, and the local saying was 'when you can see the hills it is going to rain'. A caustic rider had been added to this by some unknown wag: 'and when you can't see them, it *is* raining.'

David too had settled into the routine of St Augustine's, though his was still a lonely life. With the best will in the world, the other students tended to leave him to his own devices, since it was such hard work trying to make conversation with him. He only came to the recreation periods out of obligation, and left as soon as permission allowed. More often than not, he would sit apart in the common room for the allotted span, reading a religious magazine. He would never read a secular newspaper, and television was regarded by him as the ultimate self indulgence.

The authorities at St Augustine's were more concerned about his state than the Novice Master had been, and recognised the unhealthy nature of his fervour. The father Prefect tried to encourage him to moderate his behaviour, even going to the extent of commanding him to watch the television, invoking his vow of obedience. David duly sat in front of the screen with the others on this occasion, but steadfastly refused to focus his eyes and follow the programme. In his mind, he realised his unpopularity, but in line with the ascetical training he had received, he put this down to the hostility that could be expected by anyone trying to live a devout life in a lax atmosphere. The lives of the saints were full of similar instances.

There were one or two other students similarly, though not so extremely inclined, and since they were the nearest he could find to kindred spirits, he tended to associate with them whenever the occasion demanded that he leave his isolated state.

Mark still occasionally tried to be friendly, regarding the effort as a part of his obligation to perform penitential good works, but could never strike a spark from the flinty crust surrounding the lonely soul within. He was sometimes ashamed and disgusted with himself, and everyone else at the way David was shunned and rejected, but was obliged to accept that not much more could be done about the situation, at least by him.

But the scruples known by Mark in his Novitiate days did not recur; he could now approach the problem areas of his intimate personal life with a little more maturity and understanding. He joined in the community penances in the ordinary way, but was still uneasy in his use of the practice of self-flagellation. He recognised that in spite of the fact that he did not regard it as something pleasurable in itself, there was a side of him that found the idea and the practice exciting in a sexual way. He recognised the feelings as sexual in nature, as similar desires, more overtly sexual in nature, came to him at times, on occasion triggered by the sight of one of the attractive young women who came to the monastery church for Sunday Mass, or sometimes by his vivid and ever fertile imagination. Such desires were always rigorously suppressed in line with the ascetical training he had received, and the very thought banished as soon as it surfaced in his mind, prayer for the assistance of God and the Mother of Christ coming spontaneously to his lips. But he realised that what he was coming to regard as his darker side was something on which he needed more advice. But the shame he knew in the Novitiate when trying to broach such topics made him hesitate.

The situation came to a head, however, when one night he suddenly awoke from sleep, his heart thumping wildly and a hard lump of desire filled his throat. His imagination racing, he slipped out of bed, reached into the cupboard nearby for his discipline, and quickly shook off his pyjama trousers. As the lash bit into his shivering flesh, sanity returned and discarding the scourge, he crept back into bed, where trembling, he drew the covers tightly round himself. What was to be done? He felt that he had sinned, given way to a strange, unnatural lust. He could only hope that he had not disturbed his neighbour, as he did not know how he could pass off the incident if he were questioned. He resolved to go and seek the help of the father Prefect next morning, and with the decision made, he prayed for forgiveness. The prayer calmed him, and he soon fell asleep once again.

Next morning, with a sick feeling, he approached the Prefect's door. After a couple of false starts, he summoned up all his courage and knocked on the door. On hearing the call to enter, he opened the door. The Prefect smiled.

"Sit down, brother. Now what can I do for you?"

Mark began hesitantly.

"I don't know how to tell you this, father."

The priest nodded encouragingly.

"Come on, now, it can't be as bad as all that."

"It is," whispered Mark, staring at his knees as the tears threatened to flow. With a little more encouragement, he started his tale, and once started, the words flowed forth in a torrent as he explained his Novitiate experience, and repeated the advice he had been given then. He then outlined the events of the previous night.

"I feel so unclean, so disgusting almost" he added, his voice quavering near breaking point as he wondered what the older man must be thinking of him.

"Now then, brother, don't distress yourself" he replied in a comforting way. "The advice you were given was sound enough, but perhaps the time has come for more drastic measures."

Mark's heart leaped with sudden alarm. Was this to be the end of his religious life?

"Do you think I should leave, father?" he faltered. "Maybe I should seek the proper outlet for these needs in marriage."

"We all have these needs" the Prefect replied. "Chastity is the keeping of our physical needs and desires in check, diverting the energy into God's service. Chastity is the same for you as for anybody else; every man is prone to sexual feelings and desires; it's just that you must avoid things which arouse sexual feelings in you, things that would not trouble others. But we all have particular problems like this. No-one is what is fondly called 'normal'. Everyone has little quirks and aberrations from the norm, to a greater or lesser extent. You don't practise masturbation, do you?"

Horrified, Mark hastened to reply: "No, father, never."

The idea of deliberately arousing himself sexually in this way had never occurred to him as a realistic possibility for himself; it would be too obviously mortally sinful.

"In moments of strong temptation, I've been sometimes close to just touching myself, but the thought of mortal sin is always uppermost in my mind, so I couldn't bring myself to actually do it."

"That's fine" approved the priest. "You obviously have things well in control. Now regarding your particular problem, I feel that you should discontinue the use of the discipline, at least for the time being. Just join in the prayers, and no-one will notice that you are not actually performing the penance. But you must stop worrying. You are doing very well here at St Augustine's, and we are all very pleased with your progress."

For the sake of Mark's peace of mind, he then gave him absolution and a small penance, just in case there had been sin in what had occurred, and then with a sigh of relief, Mark left the room and busily prepared for the morning's classes, the relief which the release of tension had brought adding vigour and enthusiasm to his efforts.

TWENTY FOUR

Christmas was now only four weeks away, and the season of Advent served to remind the students of its proximity. It was very much a time to be looked forward to, as it involved a break in the ordinary routine lasting ten days or so. The purple vestments used at the morning Masses were a daily reminder that, in the words of the liturgy, 'the time was short', and so preparations of all kinds for the feast forged ahead.

The choir, which consisted of the whole body of students except one or two whose singing was so terrible that sheer necessity kept them from the ranks, painstakingly practised the ageless Gregorian chants of the Nativity liturgy, and polished up the more ornate but less used Masses for special feasts in the 'liber usualis'. A few weeks earlier, Neville had begun to organise a new, special group of singers known as the 'part choir', not because it formed a part of the whole choir, but because it was to perform hymns and motets in harmonic parts. Mark was one of the students who eagerly enlisted, and the select group totalled about fifteen when the numbers were fully made up.

The immediate task in hand was to prepare some carols for the Christmas midnight Mass, and so the group willingly devoted some of its free time to learning some of the more beautiful traditional carols, specially arranged for male voices, such as 'In the bleak midwinter', 'The holly and the ivy' and Novello's 'Adeste'. Mark was a member of the first tenors, a group of those with more flexible voices, while Peter graced the second tenors, a group with more modest talents, which required much painstaking rehearsal and preparation.

"The second tenors consist of the blind, the halt and the lame" complained Neville somewhat uncharitably when patience was stretched to the limit during one of the rehearsals. Ken lent his deeper tones to the basses, who lived in a world of their own, but who could always be relied upon to support the airier structures above them. Neville was a hard task master, but he knew his musical craft thoroughly and had impeccable taste.

"I sometimes wonder whether he's a bloody homo" grumbled Peter on one occasion, "but there's a touch of steel in him somewhere."

The plays too made good progress with the rival groups keeping as much of the detail of their plans as secret as possible. Peter revelled in his part, and the general consensus was that his knight would be a character to remember.

In December, the weather turned colder and dryer, the autumn rains finally dwindling away entirely. The mornings now were sharp and frosty, and often the students would wake up to find that ice had formed in thick encrustations on the inside of the windows as the vapour from their breathing froze on hitting the cold glass. Every available paraffin stove was pressed into service, the acrid smell from the ill-maintained equipment causing the users to emerge from their rooms after three hours of study red-eyed and smutty faced.

The more fortunate students, Mark among them, who boasted fireplaces in their rooms, were able to light log fires. There was always an abundance of timber to be had in the woods, as many of the trees were past their best, and not a few were mere skeletons, choked with ivy, which waved the ancient bones of their once proud limbs to and fro, until rotten with age, they collapsed into the surrounding undergrowth to provide insects with their homes, and the students with their winter fuel.

Peter would on occasion come along to Mark's room during study on the pretext of exchanging and formulating notes, but often he would bring a couple of slices of bread filched from the refectory, with butter and a little cheese. Welsh rarebits were the work of a moment as they toasted the bread on improvised toasting forks, and then holding the bread at a perilous angle, managed to part-melt the cheese onto it.

"Wood ash improves the flavour" remarked Peter after rescuing one of the not infrequent disasters from the hissing logs, and eating it hungrily. They would sometimes gossip away about the old days at St Saviour's on these occasions, and discuss present progress and problems. Mark confided some of his worries to Peter, including his difficulties with the practice of penance, which for some reason Peter found wildly amusing.

"Don't be daft" he reproved when Mark expressed hurt at his attitude. "It's just all so bloody funny when you think about it. Grown men smacking their own bottoms with bits of waxed string."

Mark had to laugh when Peter put it like that, and so it helped to keep things in perspective.

"Maybe these problems arise because we're so repressed" he added. "The Church has such a down on sex that no wonder it sometimes finds strange expressions if the usual ones are clamped down on so vigorously."

Mark remembered the words used by brother Thomas years ago.

"I used to worry about you chasing the girls at St Saviour's, Pete. Brother Thomas told me not to; it was good and healthy for you to do that. He said if you train a tree lightly, then it will grow into a fine specimen, but if you prune it hard and viciously, then it will assume all sorts of fantastic shapes as it tries to develop. I suppose going to St Saviour's at eleven years old meant that from our earliest days our paths were laid out for us; we never had a realistic chance to consider any other way apart from celibacy. I'm sure the priesthood is the path for me," he added hastily, "but maybe we should have been allowed to reach that conclusion in a healthier way."

Peter grunted his assent. "Purity isn't a big problem for me" he asserted, "though I do get a bit hot under the collar sometimes. Or should I say hot under the trousers?" he grinned. "I've masturbated on the odd occasion when things have got a little out of hand. Now that's a funny expression to use; it's when they're in hand that you're in trouble! Seriously though, it's happened sometimes, but not regularly. Somehow I don't feel too guilty about it. I know it's mortal sin and all that, but I just go to Confession if it happens, and that's that."

Mark wondered at Peter's matter-of-fact attitude. Mortal sin was an unthinkable disaster in his view of life, yet Peter seemed very offhand about it. When he thought about it later, he realised that he had always unconsciously regarded Peter as being rather lax, as he never worried too much about bending the rules where necessary.

"I'm a pompous bugger" he thought to himself. "What right have I to judge Pete, or anybody else? In many ways he's a damn sight better than me. He certainly seems to have a balanced, healthy attitude to life. Maybe I can't say as much for myself."

Mark was learning a little true humility, and so was himself slowly growing towards a new maturity.

Christmas was now only days away, and the many faceted preparations kept everybody occupied. Christmas cards were given out, rationed to ten per student, so peripheral members of the family had to be left out, with the hope that they would understand, or somehow hear on the grape vine that they had only been neglected by force majeure.

Under Neville's keen and demanding guidance, the choir was reaching a pitch of near perfection with the carols for the midnight celebrations being repeatedly practised until they could be performed faultlessly, even the second tenors manufacturing fewer testicles than normal, as Neville commented after one of the practices. The weather remained cold and frosty, but some of the younger students were still boyish enough to be hoping for a white Christmas. Some of the Irish students in the middle years were keen amateur wine-makers, and so the assorted smells of the brewing processes competed for attention against the perennial smells of cooked fish and polish which tended to pervade the atmosphere. A strange and wonderful collection of concoctions finally emerged; plum wine, damson, rhubarb, wheat and potato; in fact anything fermentable was pressed into service to provide the student body with alcoholic refreshment for the many celebration evenings, or 'gaudiosa' that were liberally sprinkled through the Christmas season.

In the last few days before the feast, the Post Office had to lay on special vans to bring the mountains of Christmas cards and parcels with which the college was inundated. Christmas cakes, sweets, totally unsuitable sweaters, even ties, much to the hilarity of the brethren generally. Mark received a large parcel from his family; a curious crowd gathered in his room to witness the unwrapping.

"Any cigs, Mark?" Peter wanted to know, but of course he was doomed to disappointment as most of the families had been indoctrinated with the idea that their offspring were denied such luxuries, and therefore it was useless to send them. When all the assorted delicacies were displayed on the bed, a critical audience surveyed them.

"A bloody great currant cake" commented one of the Irish home brewers disgustedly as he turned away. But Mark said nothing, a lump forming in his throat as he thought of the love and kindness represented by the displayed gifts. He took the plunder to the Prefect's room and was asked whether he needed socks, there being a couple of pairs among the gifts.

"I am a bit short, father" he confessed, and so he was allowed to use the socks himself, the rest of the presents being incorporated into the community.

Peter had managed to intimate his needs to the family in good time, and so discreet little parcels of cigarettes and hip sized spirit bottles arrived under plain brown wrapper with a few socks and handkerchiefs added to establish a guise of legitimacy, or as Neville put it, "to add verisimilitude to an otherwise bald and unconvincing narrative."

The crisp, cold but sunny weather coupled with the bustle of preparation somehow spurred Neville into attempting to tidy his room. One Thursday morning, Thursday being the general day off or recreation day, he set to with a will. Piles of rubbish quickly mounted up outside the door, clouds of dust and heaps of paper were scattered everywhere. A cynical bystander commented:

"The age of miracles is not yet passed: Winterton-Smith actually tidying his room."

"What do you mean, you cheeky bounder?" spluttered the outraged Neville. "I clean my room out once a week." Then he added a little sheepishly: "This just happens to be the first week."

About the only person in the community not infected with the general bustle of preparation was David, who was preparing in his own way, however, as he sedulously plodded his way through a venerable tome of Advent meditations and spent more time than ever in the church. Mark practised the Christmas hymns on the organ, and was assured by David, smiling his usual inscrutable smile, that the noise did not disturb him in the least.

TWENTY FIVE

Christmas Eve was spent, as in the Novitiate, in last minute preparations and in decorating the house and church. Crepe paper streamers were draped from lamp to lamp on the refectory ceiling, and the pulpit was so thickly encrusted with assorted greenery that the reader appeared to be performing his office from the middle of the jungle. The church was tastefully decorated with holly streamers, the leaves threaded painstakingly onto long strings, which were then wrapped round the pillars for all the world like Malvolio's cross garters. The effect was most striking; and was further enhanced by the placing of wreaths and candles on every window ledge.

The choir had a last rehearsal, almost like a dress rehearsal without the dress, and the performance could not be faulted. Supper came and went, and last minute bathings and scrubbings were completed. At about half past ten, Neville could be seen setting up the old fashioned spool to spool tape recorder with its green magic eye, ready to record the night's events for posterity.

Mark bustled about aimlessly, trying to keep busy as the minutes ticked by and zero hour approached. At about ten to eleven, the first of the lay people arrived; midnight Mass at the monastery was definitely the 'in thing' with the local Catholics, and soon, the area in front of the house was thronged with motor cars of the more expensive sort as the congregation trickled in.

Neville gave last minute instructions to the minion who would be operating the tape recorder, and Mark joined the rest of the part choir in the sacristy. Snowy white surplices were donned, freshly laundered for the occasion, and much last minute coughing and throat clearing took place. Peter carefully spat into his handkerchief, and commented to Mark:

"That was a good one. A real greasy green Gilbert."

Mark dug him in the ribs to express his loathing, and with a sharp clap of the hands, the assembled songsters were brought to order, and Neville, seeing the first winking candles appearing at the sacristy door, struck up the 'Once in Royal David's city' in best King's College approved style.

Lacking a boy soprano, the first tenors sang the opening verse, after which the carol was taken up by the whole choir, as the winding throng processed down the church and onto the sanctuary. The tape recorder minion was busily clicking and fiddling; Mark hoped devoutly that he was not making a mess of things, as he caught sight of the frenzied activity from the corner of his eye. The carol service went smoothly, as carol followed reading, and the biblical story of the Christmas Mystery unfolded. Peter proclaimed one of the passages in ringing tones, and the whole congregation listened intently as with inborn precision and drama, he made the words come to life.

On the stroke of midnight, the rest of the students processed onto the sanctuary and into the choir stalls, the Superior of the community taking up the rear as the celebrant of the midnight Mass. The austere Gregorian chant of the Introit now resounded round the church as the age-old liturgy began its majestic progress. After the Gospel, the Superior spoke a few words, wishing everybody a happy Christmas.

"Some of these buggers won't have been to Mass since this time last Christmas" whispered Peter uncharitably out of the corner of his mouth, and Mark thought to himself that a none too gentle reminder of the fact might have been in order, rather than the platitudes and good wishes that were being offered to the assembly. However, the Mass continued, and with the lights and incense, the music and an increasing tiredness, it slipped by fairly quickly, and before long, the whole community was processing out to the sacristy, to the rousing strains of 'Hark, the herald Angels sing', which Neville was playing with considerable éclat and style. After the last verse, he launched into a voluntary that had the walls vibrating as he called upon the services of just about every stop the organ possessed, and the church emptied in a fairly orderly manner.

Suddenly finishing on a crescendo, the last few worshippers were embarrassed to be discovered shouting to each other in the sudden silence.

"You always do that" smiled Mark to Neville in the refectory a few minutes later.

"I know; just can't resist catching out the types who dare to gossip in church; and what's more, dare to gossip instead of listening enthralled to the masterly performance."

"Big head" retorted Mark. "Happy Christmas, Neville."

The friends toasted each other in glasses of the rich dark altar wine that was often pressed into service when an occasional celebratory glass of wine was called for. Some of the students irreverently referred to it as 'pig's pee', a name which horrified Mark when he first heard it.

"After all," he protested, "this wine becomes the Blood of Christ in the Mass!" and in fact it was a very drinkable medium sweet sherry.

"And a most felicitous Noel to you too, young 'un" replied Neville, as he held out his glass for a refill to a passing student who was busily doing the honours.

"The music was first rate; the carols really did us credit, I thought. I do hope Bodger hasn't buggered up the tape."

Just then, brother Brookes, popularly known as Bodger, the seminary electronics wizard who generally looked after affairs of this nature, staggered into the refectory carrying the huge tape recorder, which he deposited on a handy table. Plugging in, he proceeded to regale the assembly with a replay of the evening's events.

"Capital, Bodger old chap" remarked Neville as a very passable rendering of the carols issued forth.

"Even the second tenors sound great" added Peter, who strolled up with his third glass of sherry at that moment.

"Happy Christmas, kid!" He nudged Mark, who smiled and offered Peter his own good wishes in reply. "How are you finding Oggies as a whole?" Mark asked, feeding Peter one of his favourite joke entry lines of the moment.

"As a hole it's not bad, but as a seminary, it's bloody awful" he duly obliged, laughing uproariously at his own wit, while the others grinned tolerantly.

"No, I must confess, we do have our moments. It's not such a bad old dump after all."

Mark had already grown deeply fond of St Augustine's, and Peter found it mostly bearable, never more so than on occasions such as the one they were currently enjoying. There was a warmth, a family closeness due in part to the Rule which bound them together as a community, but due more to a unique chemistry that seemed to pervade the place, at least to Mark's way of thinking. In later years, he always enjoyed going back; though for some reason wild horses would not have dragged some of the brethren back, a fact that he never ceased to find baffling.

The celebrations continued for an hour or so, and then gradually the group began to break up, as the weary revellers went to their respective rooms to grab what sleep they could before the 8.30 a.m. Mass; a modest sleep-in until that time had been granted, so many of the students were keen to make the most of it. A small group lingered on round the tape recorder, but eventually, Neville stretched wearily and observed somewhat obscurely:

"Dormiendum est omnibus, confratres. Aurora mox coelum rubescebit."

"What's he on about?" asked Peter.

"I think he means it's about time we hit the sack" laughed Mark.

"Come on, Bodger, switch off that machine, and let's scarper then" grunted Peter as the little group broke up. "See you in the morning, everybody."

"I would not care to accept any wagers on that eventuality" replied Neville, well aware of Peter's propensity for oversleeping on such occasions.

The last stragglers duly sought their rooms, with a certain amount of bumping and banging as they groped their way along the darkened corridors to the sound of querulous calls of "make less noise" and "stop that racket, some people are trying to sleep," but eventually, silence descended, and the community was able to pass the rest of the night peacefully.

Next day, the morning was taken up with the second Mass of Christmas at half past eight, which true to form, Peter missed. As the choir would be performing once again at the half past ten High Mass, Mark woke him at half past nine, having to shake him vigorously to rouse him from his slumbers.

"Wha, wha, oh, it's you, Mark. What time is it?" he asked, knuckling the sleep from his eyes. "My God, I've got a splitting headache. Must have been too much pig's pee last night."

"Come on, you lazy devil, you'll be late for the half past ten," urged Mark.

With a groan, the sleeper threw back the bedclothes and staggered to the wash basin. Bleary eyed, he considered the prospect in the mirror, and wondered whether he could restore himself to some semblance of respectability in the time remaining. Turning on the tap, he commenced operations.

Meanwhile, Mark joined the others for a quick stroll in the quadrangle, waiting for the moment for vesting to arrive. At about twenty five past, Peter staggered in, groaning "where's my liber?" to anyone who would listen. It was hastily found for him, and newly surpliced once again, he joined the procession which was ready to enter the church for the High Mass. Many of the items sung were the same as at the midnight Mass, so the choir sang with a certain careless abandon, thus making mistakes they had avoided the first time, so Neville conveyed his displeasure from the organ loft with frowns and grimaces.

On the whole, however, the performance was tolerable, though the effect was somewhat lessened too by the presence of many of the local children, who were busily engaged in trying out the newly acquired gifts that Father Christmas had left the night before.

Lunch consisted of cold ham and pork pie with egg in the middle, washed down with a bottle of beer. After partaking of this repast, some of the more energetic students went out for walks to prepare for the gargantuan gastronomic effort that would be demanded of them in the evening. Others took to their beds to catch up on a little of the sleep missed from the night before.

The short afternoon quickly merged into evening, the only sun visible that day had been a brief glimmer through the hazy grey clouds in the early afternoon. By four o'clock it was almost dark, and up and down the corridors the sleepers were awaking and washing, before hurrying down to the church for the renewal of vows, a short ceremony which took place each year at Christmas before the main meal. A bell sounded, and the community rapidly assembled in the church for the brief service. When everyone was present, the superior gave a short talk, and then everyone together recited the formula for the renewing of their commitment to the service of God in poverty, chastity and obedience. Duty done, the brethren then headed for the refectory, avoiding, but only just, any unseemly haste.

The meal lived up to its promise, as it usually did on these occasions, the brother cook and his assistants having excelled themselves. Crackers were pulled, paper hats donned, jokes and mottoes exchanged. Afterwards, Mark and Peter along with the others helped clear away the debris.

"I can hardly move" groaned Peter.

"I told you not to have second helpings of the Christmas pudding. Serves you right, greedy pig."

"It was worth it," he sighed, rubbing his distended stomach.

"It seems a pity that an otherwise all wise and provident Creator only saw fit to endow you with one anus, brother Clark. You're nothing but a bally walking alimentary canal." These strictures naturally aroused Peter's wrath, and Neville only narrowly avoided being caught on the side of the head by the extremely wet and smelly floor cloth hurled at him by the irate object of his abusive remarks.

The marathon washing up finally completed, the students retired to the common room, where the mediocre Christmas day offerings of the television provided a backdrop to the celebrations. It was only a backdrop, however, as a mere handful were actually watching. The rest of the students sat around in groups while the interesting concoctions of the home brewers were opened for sampling. The suspicious sniffing and sipping were soon followed by enthusiastic endorsement, and the assembly rapidly grew noisier and rowdier as the effects of the potent brew became apparent.

The dancing enthusiasts soon took over, and a space was cleared in the middle of the floor. The record player was switched on, and the Jimmy Shand records hauled out after a little rummaging. The music belted forth at full blast, despite the grumblings of the television addicts, huddled in a little group round the set. Soon, the floor was shaking as twenty or more strapping young men, liberally dosed with home brew, bounded up and down in a version of the eightsome reel that was distinguished more by its enthusiasm than by its elegance. Peter and Mark clumped around with the rest, while Neville sat on the sidelines, politely but firmly declining the repeated invitations to join in that were showered on him.

"It's my invariable rule" he explained to the red-faced and breathless Mark a few minutes later, "never to make an exhibition of myself in public. After all, a fellow has his image to maintain. People see you cavorting about, and they simply remark "There's

Kennedy making an ass of himself," and since you are an ass, there's no harm done. But if I were to indulge in such caperings, it would be an earth-shattering event, similar to the discovery of a cabinet minister in a brothel with his trousers down. It's what's known as lèse majesté, dear boy".

Mark laughed in spite of himself. "Neville Winterton-Smith, the arbiter elegantium. It doesn't do any harm to play the fool occasionally. You obviously don't suffer fools gladly?"

"Sit down, my dear boy, and charge your glass once more with some of this noxious, though potent brew."

So saying, he topped up Mark's glass with a yellow, cloudy beverage which came from a bottle labelled 'plum wine'.

"Your remark about not suffering fools gladly, Mark, my dear fellow. As a matter of fact, you have lighted on another hobby horse of mine."

Mark groaned and took a couple of generous swigs from his glass.

"Fire away, Neville; I know it would be easier to stop a charging elephant in its tracks than to silence Winterton-Smith when he's in full cry."

"Exactly, old comrade. Now. The only fools I don't suffer gladly are the fools who say they don't suffer fools gladly."

Mark shook his head, wondering whether the wine was more powerful than he had imagined. Neville, with the air of a professor expounding an abstruse philosophical argument, continued:

"I suffer fools with consummate joy for several reasons. Firstly, I flatter myself that I am a fool myself. A fool is one who can perceive and delight in folly in others; this was the role of the court fool or jester in mediaeval times. So-called sensible people on the other hand tend to be dead bores. How many grave, sensible chaps do you know who appreciate the works of P.G. Wodehouse, for instance? His works are inspired examples of sheer lunacy. This is their attraction.

"What a different world it would be if only some of our political leaders were able to realise what silly asses they make of themselves! The goose-stepping German soldier was a figure of fear. If he'd been ridiculed as a silly ass then perhaps world war two would never have happened. Political leaders are always fearfully easy to caricature. That's because the caricature is always nearer the truth than the reality itself. Imagine, for example, Hitler doing a Hitler impression. It would bring the house down. Instead, such men take themselves with utter seriousness, and the rest of the world takes the consequences."

He paused for a moment. "I seem to have undermined my own position. Perhaps I should make more of an ass of myself in public and join in your wretched dancing."

Mark laughed. "Don't worry, Neville. You're a big enough ass as it is without dancing. Maybe the mixture would then be too rich."

"Ah, yes, where was I? In the midst of my reflections on foolishness."

He took a sip of his wine and continued:

"Of course, the kingdom of God belongs to the foolish, too. So the Almighty suffers fools very gladly. In fact he doesn't suffer anybody else; in particular, he confounds the wise. So all in all, I'm on the side of the fools. The thing is, Mark, my dear chap, to be a fool is fine. But don't be a damn fool."

Mark was by now feeling more than a little foolish after all the home-made wine, and soon was roaring and laughing at the silliest things, as people do when slightly, or even more than slightly drunk. Neville retained his air of dignity, but his sang frôid became more than a little studied as the evening wore on, and his dignity became harder to maintain.

Peter, meanwhile, was one of a group trying to organise a game of 'bok-bok', a game in which two teams played a sort of hooligan version of leapfrog. The first team would form a line, rather like a Rugby scrum, but in a straight line, one behind the other. The second team would then charge across the room and leapfrog onto the line as far forward in one leap as possible. The object of the game was for one team to maintain its line unbroken while the other team had to get all its men perched on top. If the line broke, the leapers won, but if it held or the leapers fell off, then the line won.

The noise and commotion were indescribable, as bodies hurtled in all directions, and the crack of breaking furniture could occasionally be heard.

But eventually, all the wine bottles were empty and the cigarettes all smoked, and the television programmes had given way to the white dot. The last few groups of talkers started to drift away until Neville's group was the last remaining. The room reeked of stale tobacco smoke and the dregs and spilled pools of wine. Peter miraculously produced a few more cigarettes to hand round, and the half dozen or so students remaining gratefully accepted the illegal loot, and smoking, summed up the celebrations.

Mark was feeling parched and sore-throated from all the smoking, and dehydrated by all the wine he had drunk. He found a bottle of orange squash and a jug of water left by the more sober brethren, and thirstily drank a glass.

"Wait until tomorrow, Mark" commented Neville. "If I'm not mistaken, you'll find yourself suffering from a grade 'A' hangover."

The room was swaying gently, and as he lounged back, Mark looked at the ceiling which appeared to be revolving slowly.

"I don't care" he laughed, and at that moment, he didn't. It had been a memorable evening, a Christmas day he would never forget. He was content to listen as the others chatted on. Neville was giving forth on the history of father Christmas, explaining how the Christian St Nicholas and the pagan father Christmas, the disreputable old reveller of mediaeval England had become inextricably intertwined in the modern figure, but he was too drunk and too tired to follow the conversation clearly.

He began to realise that Neville was father Christmas, though a younger, beardless version of him. Peter, on the other hand, was visibly sprouting a beard, which was coming out of his face as he watched. He was really St Peter, and he began showing an interested father Christmas the net with which he had caught the miraculous draught of fishes. They were sailing on the sea of Galilee, the boat gently rocking to and fro, when suddenly, the storm hit them and the boat began to sink.

"Mark, we're sinking, wake up, wake up."

He awoke with a jerk to see Neville and Peter looking down at him, laughing.

"Come on, dopey, it's time to hit the sack."

Mark sleepily rubbed his eyes and stretched with a long drawn out sigh.

"OK, Pete, I'm coming."

The little group turned out the common room lights, and leaving the evidence of the night's revels behind, retired to their rooms. Mark was staggering slightly as he walked, chuckling inanely as he bumped into walls and doors on the darkened corridors, the others vainly trying to shush him. He reached his room without major mishap, however, stripped off his clothes and fell into bed, and was immediately out to the world.

Three or four hours later, he awoke with a raging thirst, a head which felt as though his brain had been replaced by a bag of squabbling cats, and an urgent need to relieve himself. He swayed along the corridor, found the lavatory and knew the bliss that the emptying of an over-full bladder can bring. He though he would never stop as the head of froth built up. After finishing, he turned to the wash basin and drank greedily. Feeling slightly better, he returned to bed and quickly sank back into his dream-filled sleep.

Crazy images of the previous day's events filled his dreams; the carol service was re-sung several times, but somehow the carols were all mixed up, and try as they would, the choir could not get them right. One minute Neville was playing the organ, the next he was in front of the choir, trying to put things right and explaining at the same time the origins and meanings of the carols. Eventually, the ecclesiastical side of the celebrations finished, and his image-filled brain recast the evening's events. This time, Mark was helping in the preparations. Vast quantities of turkeys had first to be caught and killed, the sprouts gathered, jellies made; everything imaginable went wrong until the meal was finally ready to serve. Then, as the trays were being carried into the refectory, he realised that there were no potatoes. He hared off to the kitchen garden with a spade and brought back a barrow load, washed and peeled them and finally got them on the boil.

The brethren meanwhile were noisily singing and drinking wine, just occasionally asking was the meal ready. Just as he finally had everything prepared, the bell went, signalling the end of the meal.

But the bell was really the bell for rising, and feeling shattered with a throbbing head and a mouth filled with sand, he sat on the edge of the bed and groaned. He was experiencing his first ever hangover. Somehow, he managed to go through the motions of washing and shaving, and bleary eyed but more or less respectable, he shambled into church with moments to spare.

"You look like something the cat brought in" whispered the more resilient Peter, who had somehow managed to be on time. Mark simply murmured back:

"I feel absolutely lousy, Peter. Hangover, I suppose."

He buried his head in his hands, and gave himself up to his thoughts. Images of death, doom and despair filled his mind. Life seemed such a brief flicker, a pain-filled episode of worry and care. The body was a fragile creature, threatened by countless dangers that could crush, tear and destroy it. Different ways of dying went through his head; not that he felt suicidal, but for some reason he could not banish the doleful thoughts and imaginings.

Somehow, he managed to survive the half-hour's meditation, but the Mass proved too much, and so half way through he staggered out as inconspicuously as possible and returned to his room.

After Mass, a solicitous Peter came up to find Mark slumped on the bed.

"How do you feel?" he asked sympathetically.

"Absolutely dreadful" he confessed. "I don't think I'll ever touch another drop of drink in my life."

Peter, an old hand in such matters, grinned consolingly.

"You'll get over it. Now take three aspirins and lots of water."

With that, he produced the tablets which Mark placed on his caked and swollen tongue. The water tasted like diluted battery acid, but he drank off the whole glass, which Peter immediately refilled.

"I couldn't, Pete" groaned the unhappy sufferer.

"Come on, it's the dehydration that's half the problem. You need plenty of water to swill out the system."

So Mark obediently drank two more glasses, almost retching at the effort, and then sank back onto the bed, his head reeling.

"Now sleep if you can" commanded his physician.

Sleep came with remarkable ease, and Mark awoke once more a couple of hours later feeling a little better. A visit to the lavatory followed by more drinking improved him still further, and he even felt he could manage a cup of coffee and some bread and marmalade. He made his way to the kitchen, where hot coffee was kept on the go all morning. A few minutes later, he was seated sipping the steaming brew, munching the brown bread and butter, thickly spread with marmalade.

"How's the wreck of the Hesperus, then?" asked Peter, a few minutes later.

"Much better, thanks" Mark managed to smile back at his friend.

"Fancy a drop of whisky in that coffee?" he asked, patting the front of his habit suggestively. Mark shuddered.

"I'm off the booze for a while after that lot," he sighed. "I don't want another hangover ever again if that's what it's like."

"That's nowt" replied Peter scornfully. "I once had a forty eight hour hangover."

"When?" asked Mark, mystified.

"Not here, idiot. Fat chance of a really decent hangover in this place."

"I don't know so much about that" groaned Mark.

"No, it was - let me see - it must have been the Christmas before last; our last Christmas spent at home."

Mark thought about his own childhood Christmases and smiled. Ginger beer was about the nearest he had got to alcohol before joining the Order.

"Yes, that would be it," Peter mused. "It was the New Year. There was plenty of booze about, and nobody seemed to mind, so I just piled in, mixing drinks without a care in the world. I got absolutely sloshed, pissed and pie-eyed, and didn't I know about it next morning! I went through hell for two days after that; those thoughts of death, doom and despair you mentioned were nothing to what I went through. It was forty eight hours of not wanting to go on living! Anyway, pull yourself together; make sure you eat a good dinner, because we're rehearsing the play this afternoon."

The main Christmas celebrations over, the frantic last minute rehearsals and preparations for the plays were put in hand. Props had to be made, or begged borrowed or stolen, and sets manufactured. That afternoon, one group put up the stage, which was three pre-made boards four feet wide by twelve long, the whole forming a twelve foot square, which rested on wooden butter boxes to give extra height. One end of the common room was reserved for the dramatic endeavours, so makeshift curtains divided the room into two, providing a stage and an audience.

Meanwhile, in the different classrooms, the several groups rehearsed. Mark was by now feeling more or less normal, and so he was able to play his part fairly creditably. Peter's knight was as impressive as everyone knew it would be, and Neville brought to the part of Thomas à Becket his most grave and dignified manner, and so all augured well for a successful performance.

TWENTY SIX

The first play to be performed was "Journey's End;" this was due to be staged the following evening, and so much hurried hammering and banging could be heard all that afternoon, evening, and the following day too as the set was prepared. Ken was to play the part of Lieutenant Trotter, an older steady unflappable type, and his usual air of calm stood him in good stead, as in this case fiction copied life.

After an early supper, the community gathered in the students' common room to enjoy the play. Bodger had rigged up a wonderful assortment of spotlights and footlights, made of old biscuit tins nailed to wooden frameworks from which assorted flex in varying stages of decay hung in festoons, which sparked and smouldered ominously on occasion. Bodger himself was seated in the wings at the control board, clicking his switches on and off, touching some rather gingerly as the insulation was far from perfect.

Everyone was seated, waiting patiently as the minutes ticked by. Suddenly, a head appeared between the curtains and a slight delay was announced, caused by 'technical hitches'. The audience laughed good naturedly, and finally, with gratings and creakings, the curtains parted and the play was under way.

Ironic cheers went up as the characters lit cigarettes, as the cigarettes allowed to the cast for dramatic purposes were always a much sought-after perk. The production went surprisingly smoothly as the story unfolded, and the makeshift theatre in fact helped to recreate the First World War dugout more effectively than a sophisticated professional production could have done. The audience laughed with Ken, and felt the anguish and pain of the main characters Raleigh and Stanhope as the drama headed towards its climax. Bodger excelled himself in the technical effects department, as in the final scene the dugout was demolished by a direct hit, and earth and planks cascaded down with alarming crashes from his carefully arranged ceiling-high booby traps.

"My God, Bodger, that was magnificent" remarked Ken afterwards, "though I was terrified all through the play that it would all come down by accident at any moment."

The audience enthusiastically applauded the players' efforts, and congratulated the actors, the producer and Bodger taking a special bow.

"Our turn next" remarked Peter to Mark as the audience dispersed

"I hope we do as well as they did tonight."

Two days later, after much frantic rehearsing and burning of the midnight oil as lines were learned and the stage area transformed, all was ready for "Murder in the Cathedral." Again, Bodger had the lighting and sound effects in hand as with nonchalant ease he kept his crackling and popping electric circuits in operation, somehow managing to avoid fusing the whole system.

Mark, Peter and the rest of the cast had been grease-painted and suitably robed, and precisely on time under Neville's orchestration, the production went ahead. Apart from a few frantic hissings from the prompter, all again went smoothly, Neville's Christmas sermon and Peter's dramatic and murderous attack being the highlights of the performance.

Once more the tolerant audience received the production kindly, and afterwards, with more of the home-made wine freely circulating, Neville thanked the cast and agreed that it had been a decent sort of show. Mark partook of the strong drinks rather more sparingly this time, and so avoided a repetition of the horrendous events of a few days earlier.

So the Christmas celebrations continued and finally came to an end with the celebration of twelfth night and the feast of the Epiphany. The decorations were removed, class started again, and life at St Augustine's returned to normal. As January progressed, the winter cold deepened, and one morning the community awoke to find everything blanketed by a heavy fall of snow. It took everyone by surprise, and the long drive which connected St Augustine's with the outside world was blocked by huge drifts, some several feet deep in parts.

Class was hurriedly suspended, and digging out parties arranged.

"My God, let's get on with it," exclaimed Peter as the diggers assembled. "This place gives me claustrophobia at the best of times. Even though I'm not going out into the outside world, I hate being cut off from it."

Mark stamped his feet, already numb with the cold as the party trudged along the drive, digging out the drifts, piling the snow in massive ridges on either side. He enjoyed the physical effort involved, however, as the easy living of the Christmas holiday had left his system feeling the need of some vigorous exercise.

"Pity we couldn't get Bodger to invent a snow plough" remarked Peter as they shovelled away.

"Don't encourage him, or God knows what sort of contraption he'll concoct," laughed Mark. Besides, I'm enjoying this."

So saying, he made a snowball and with an accurate flick of the wrist, caught one of the diggers twenty feet away on the side of the head. Retribution naturally followed, and soon war had broken out along a fifty yard front as snow flew in all directions, hostilities only coming to an end as the senior students present called for order so that the task in hand could be completed. Serious effort resumed and by late morning, the weary troupe trudged back, their task completed.

The brother cook had prepared a large steaming pot of soup, and so the workers were very quickly bringing warmth back to their stinging hands as they greedily gulped at the scalding liquid.

"I've never tasted soup so good in my life before" enthused Peter as he downed the steaming beverage, which he had liberally sprinkled with pepper.

"Old James has certainly got a magic touch."

"He does wield a rather nifty skillet on occasion" conceded Neville, who had lent his languid aid to the proceedings under a certain amount of mild protest.

Mark agreed enthusiastically as he dipped a chunk of bread into his soup.

"It looks so beautiful out there" he continued as he stared out at the grey sky, still heavy with snow, as scattered flakes continued to fall into the quadrangle. The church looked like a Christmas card, and beyond, the trees wore a silvery white delicate coat. Unlike Peter, he enjoyed the sensation of isolation that the snow introduced, and deeply appreciated the strange quietness that snow always seemed to bring.

Finishing his soup, he put his boots back on and went for a walk in the garden, revelling in the deep soft snow underfoot, thinking to himself that this is how Adam must have felt, the only man in the garden, as his footprints left their mark in the virgin snow. Nothing stirred or disturbed the ghostly quiet as he silently made his way deeper into the garden. A sense of loneliness suddenly struck him, and his thoughts turned to a realisation of how utterly alone he sometimes was in his life. The family was hundreds of miles away, and in any case the religious life had created a deep divide between him and them, living as they did in totally different worlds. The Order was now his family, and though he had found a sort of closeness to Peter and Neville, somehow they did not reach his inner self. He was conscious of a deep void there, which he knew should be filled by God, or so he presumed. Sometimes he felt this inner presence, or was he just trying to convince himself of it? As he ploughed on, the snow squeaking underfoot as he strode, he resolved to try and deepen his prayer life, so that this aching void could be filled.

The snow began to fall more heavily once again, and so with a sigh that shuddered through his frame, he cut across the snowy wilderness to form a circle which would lead him back to civilisation. The thick flakes obscured the grey of the trees, and Mark felt thankful that he had not far to go to reach safety.

Before long, he was back at the house, shaking the snow off his boots before climbing the stairs to his room. On the corridor he met Peter, who laughingly asked:

"Where have you been, you loony?"

"Enjoying the snow" smiled Mark a little wistfully.

"It's all right to look at, but you wouldn't get me out there without necessity" grunted his friend. "Anyway, get ready, it's almost time for particular examen."

Mark hurriedly shook the snow from his hair, dried it and brushed it before rejoining Peter on his way to the church.

That afternoon, some of the students, Mark among them, gave themselves up to winter sports. Makeshift sledges were soon careering down any available slope, and one enterprising student even managed to fashion a pair of home-made skis, the fronts turned up with a weird arrangement of struts and wires.

"Like Biggles in his biplane" spluttered Peter, who roared with laughter at the sight.

But that evening, reality returned to St Augustine's as the exams were not too far away, and the first term was rapidly nearing its close.

"My God, Mark," groaned Peter to his friend at the beginning of the study period. "How am I going to learn all this shit in time?"

He waved a thick wad of notes disconsolately in front of Mark.

"Now don't panic, Pete" insisted Mark. "We'll get through."

"You will, you mean," he grumbled.

"No, we will, Pete. I'll give you a hand. We'll do this together. I'll organise a programme of study, and we'll work through it together."

He set to with a will, divided the material into manageable chunks, and showed Peter the amount they had to get through each day. For the next few days, they studied and then tested each other on the various sections, and Peter eventually began to think that he might have a chance. Unfortunately, the emphasis had to be mainly on the principal subject, philosophy, so he was not able to give the same attention to the other subjects.

Mark took them in his stride, achieving a level of competence in them without too much difficulty, though it involved long hours of study. He was an occasional visitor to Neville's room too during these few days, whenever he hit a snag needing additional information or explanation. But he remembered Neville's words from a few months before; that it was more important to know things than to understand them, so a good deal of leaning by heart took place.

Whenever Mark went to Neville's room, he never seemed to find him hard at work; Neville was one of those extremely fortunate people endowed with an excellent memory and intelligence too. The studies in general were a walkover for him, and so he had plenty of time to indulge his favourite activities; extra study and reading round the subjects of the philosophy course did not figure largely in these. Something of a dilettante, he delved deeply into the byways, and was fascinated by the odder characters of history.

"You're a fund of useless information" laughed Mark after Neville had regaled him with incidents from the life of yet another mediaeval eccentric. But he was usually able to enlighten Mark too on the points of information he was seeking, and so progress towards the examinations was steady.

As the examinations drew nearer, Peter's nerves became more and more pronounced, until the evening before, he was in a flat panic.

"This is it, Mark," he groaned. "I'll be off to get measured for the blue suit as soon as this lot is over."

In common parlance, a student was said to be "going for his blue suit" when he was leaving, either at his own or the superiors' behest.

"Nonsense, Pete" encouraged Mark. "You'll do fine. You've coped with exams right through St Saviour's without catastrophe striking; or at least you've always survived. Why should this time be different?"

"School studies are a different kettle of fish" replied Peter gloomily. "You can always fudge through with them. But as a priest, you've got to know all this tripe."

"Balderdash, Peter," said Neville briskly, walking up at that moment. "Some of the most ignorant, stupid people I know are priests. We are blessed with some prize boneheads; far thicker than you."

Peter mused for a moment, uncertain whether to accept these remarks as insults or as consolation.

"If you fit the bill in other regards, the swots will never let you down. You've made your mark as a preacher; you'll get through. Mind you, I did warn you about overmuch voice production shrinking the brain."

With these observations, he passed on to his own room, leaving Mark and Peter to continue their conversation.

"Maybe it won't be so bad" said Peter bracingly, a little of his customary self-confidence returning.

"That's better, Pete" smiled Mark. "You've worked hard; surely it must produce some results."

Next day, the philosophy class assembled at nine o'clock sharp, nervously awaiting the arrival of their absent minded professor. About ten minutes late, he finally shuffled in, beaming benignly through his spectacles, and clutching a clutter of notes and papers.

After a prayer, the students took their places and two of their number were delegated to pass round writing paper and the duplicated sets of questions. There were four questions, any three to be attempted. Mark breathed a silent prayer of thanksgiving; two of the questions were topics he and Peter had exhaustively covered, and so he felt confident that they would both succeed.

He wrote busily, occasionally glancing over to Peter, who wrote sporadically and stared ceilingwards the rest of the time. Finally, their white-haired mentor looked up from the book he was reading and announced "Ten more minutes," which caused a sudden surge of frantic scribbling. Mark finished his three questions feeling fairly satisfied with his efforts, and hoped that Peter had done enough. Afterwards he went up to his friend and asked how it had gone.

"Bloody awful" he replied disconsolately.

"But two of the questions were a walkover" protested Mark. "We knew them backwards."

"That's the trouble" moaned Peter. "I knew the stuff backwards; I just couldn't express myself properly in putting it down forwards. And now I've got to think about the Scripture and Church history exams; I've done hardly any work for them. It's been nothing but blasted philosophy for the past couple of weeks."

Mark was silent. He felt a little helpless; Peter's study prospects still seemed hopeless in spite of all his efforts and encouragement. What else could be done? He could only hope that Neville was right, and that success in the studies was not the only thing taken into account when the superiors were deciding a man's future. Sighing sympathetically, he slapped Peter lightly on the shoulder.

"Come on, Pete, let's go for a walk; we could do with the fresh air."

The garden seemed marvellously fresh and clear after the hours spent in the stuffy examination room, and even though it was cold, with snow still in the areas not reached by the sun during the day, their spirits lifted with the sense of freedom it gave.

"They're not going to get the better of me with this bloody philosophy" stated Peter. "It's not going to stop me being a priest, I can tell you that. Just let them try to kick me out."

"They won't do that, Pete" consoled Mark. "Look at the Curé of Ars; there was never anybody worse at the studies than him, and he made it."

"He was a Saint, though" commented Peter. "I'm not exactly a saint, and they know that. I think one or two of those bastards would be glad to see the back of me. But they'll not find me a pushover."

"You've got a lot of the qualities they're looking for, Pete," added Mark. "They're not daft. They know that the studies we do now have little bearing on the work we'll be doing later. Surely they must judge us on what they think we'll be like working as priests in ten years' time? I bet if you set half the priests in the country that exam that we did today, most of them would do a lot worse than you."

"You're right" agreed Peter. "What the hell philosophy has to do with being a priest I'll never know."

Mark frowned in concentration, kicking aside a stone which lay in his path.

"I often wonder how much real use the preparation is that we get here."

"I thought your motto was 'The Order knows best'" observed Peter ironically.

"This is something wider than the Order" replied Mark. "It's the same, I suppose, in all seminaries. We do these studies that haven't really altered much over the past three and a half centuries or more, at the very least. Some of the stuff we study dates back to the Middle Ages. What would a time and motion expert make of our course here, I wonder? I bet you could cram the useful stuff into a two year course, and here's us spending seven years of our lives here. Maybe it's the time element that's important; perhaps it takes seven years to produce a mature priest."

"You make it sound like a cheese factory" laughed Peter. "Maybe it's a good simile with some of the mouldy old cheddar they serve up to us in the studies."

"No, seriously, Pete" insisted Mark, "an outsider might say: 'Right. What is a priest?' We define that, and then the question is, what is the best way to train him? A priest is a pastor; he needs to know the faith thoroughly, to be able to preach and defend it. He needs to know how to deal with people. He needs to have a good business sense if he's running things like parishes. So what have we got? Ideally, a course of study should contain these elements; theology, but tuned to preaching and apologetics, a bit of philosophy, but just enough to teach us how to think clearly; social studies such as sociology and psychology, and then basic business studies and lessons in practical administration."

"That sounds like a sensible approach," commented Peter. "You'd certainly be cutting out all the shit."

"Occam's razor" grinned Mark, who had recently come across the famous dictum of the mediaeval theologian in his studies. "Entia non multiplicanda sunt sine necessitate," or in other words, "cut the cackle and get down to the horses; strip away any unnecessary clutter".

Mark was to find this a most useful principle in future years. The Second Vatican Council was just round the corner, but it had not yet happened; his theology of the priesthood was still in its infancy, but already he had begun to be dissatisfied with the system, the received wisdom.

"I suppose we are too cut off from the outside world here" he sighed. "You're right in that, Pete."

"This place getting on your nerves too, at last?"

"No, I love it here; nothing's changed from that point of view as far as I'm concerned. But I do realise that as future priests in today's world, we need contact with that world; Oggies is something of an ivory tower. Even though I'm keen on ivory towers, I realise you've got to get your feet on the ground from time to time."

He breathed in deeply, sniffing the cold, clear air appreciatively.

"Mind you, there's lots of people who would give their souls to be living in a place like this. What have we got here, Pete? Beautiful surroundings, fresh air, no worries, apart from the occasional exam" he smiled at Peter. "Good grub, plenty of rest and relaxation, what more could you ask for?"

"Don't tempt me" replied Peter ironically. "You might not find not having a good time too much of a sacrifice, but some of us do. Young people of our age outside; what are they doing?"

"You can keep all that" laughed Mark. "What does it profit a man, etcetera?"

"You still haven't got over the Nov." replied Peter. "I know it's all worldly vanity and all that, but I find giving it up a real wrench."

The two friends walked on, enjoying a brief respite from the examination pressures, but lunch time brought them back to the house, and afterwards, the mood for talking had gone. Mark pressed on with his Church history and Scripture revision; Peter, still suffering from the stresses of the morning, decided to sleep it off and see if he could summon up fresh energies for the evening.

TWENTY SEVEN

The next few days saw the minor examinations out of the way; the pattern was repeated with Mark managing fairly easily and Peter struggling. The last exam was on a Saturday, and the new term was officially scheduled to begin on the Monday, so the students reacted with anger and dismay when the father Prefect announced that the intervening Sunday would be a retreat day.

"Bloody hell" complained Mark, the exceptionally strong language (for him) testifying to the depth of his feelings. "You'd have thought that they'd have given us a day or two off to relax and recover. This is crazy."

"They don't give a toss about us and our feelings" grumbled Peter. "Bloody farts, the lot of them, all those superiors."

The retreat day passed quietly enough, but few of the students derived much profit from it. Mark rebelliously spent the day reading novels, and strange to say felt no guilt about it.

Next day, the new term started, and the philosophy course forged relentlessly on.

"You're lucky" remarked one of the theology students to Mark when he complained about the automatic routine of it all. "Our Prof. in theology is even worse. At least you finished one section of philosophy and started another. Our man is so mechanical that if the bell went half way through a sentence on the last day of term, he'd start half way through that same sentence when he began the new term, even though the whole summer holiday had intervened."

But the grumbling soon died down, and as the term got under way, spring did not seem too far off. Peter's examination results were predictably poor, but passed without comment from his superiors.

One morning, a large parcel arrived for brother Hunter, Peter's guardian angel from the first few days at St Augustine's.

"What is it, Jim?" asked Peter, ever nosy.

"Not cigs, Pete, anyway. It's seeds; I sent off for the new season's seeds a couple of weeks ago. It's about time I got cracking with the garden. Would you like to give me a hand?"

Intrigued, Peter agreed. Jim unpacked the parcel, laying out on his bed the many brightly coloured seed packets that promised a beautiful summer in the garden. He answered all Peter's eager questions, describing the different flowers that they would be growing, and that afternoon, Peter accompanied him to the greenhouse and was soon helping to fill the seed trays with compost, and was allowed to sow some of the easier varieties. He worked with a will, soaking up the information with which Jim was bombarding him.

He soon recognised the difference between hardy annuals, half-hardies and the perennials. After sowing the seeds, they watered them thoroughly and then Jim lit an evil smelling paraffin stove. Coughing as the fumes caught his throat, Peter asked:

"What are you lighting that thing for, Jim?"

"There's always the danger of frost, and besides, the plants all come on a lot better with a bit of heat."

Wiping the smuts off their faces, they emerged into the cold damp February air, and as there was time before darkness fell, Jim took Peter on a tour of the gardens, pointing out the various varieties of trees and shrubs while he described his diverse horticultural experiments, including the grafting of fruit trees and crossbreeding flower varieties.

Peter was hooked. Here was a new interest that would blossom and flourish like the plants they grew. The greenhouse now became one of his favourite haunts, and his heart swelled with pride as the tiny new plants began to emerge. He would often smoke a cigarette as he pottered among his carefully nurtured charges, explaining to an amused and cynical Mark that tobacco is an excellent fumigant which destroys greenhouse and plant pests. Mark commended him for his altruism and devotion to duty, suggesting that he should be entitled to a cigarette ration from the father Prefect for horticultural purposes.

"In fact, Pete, I think I'll suggest it to him."

"Sarky devil" laughed Peter as he chased Mark back to the house where the demands of the philosophy course insistently awaited them.

A few weeks later, Mark's one and only decent pair of shoes finally gave up the ghost, the sole parting company with the welt. As the only other pair he had were on their last legs too, he approached the Prefect and obtained permission to cycle into the nearby town to buy new ones. The monastery had an account with one of the shoe shops, and so no money was necessary. Selecting one of the bicycles from the motley collection reserved for the students' use, he set out on the nine mile journey.

Squally showers ensured a brief drenching, but he revelled in the brisk exercise and the taste of freedom. A plastic Mac kept off the worst of the rain, and so it was a reasonably dry but somewhat overheated young man who arrived in town, where he made for the shoe shop without delay. He carefully propped his bicycle against the window of a ladies' clothing shop next door, as a pavement display prevented his leaving it against the front of the shoe shop.

As he propped it against the shop front, his eye was inevitably drawn to the display inside which consisted of lifelike window dummies exhibiting the charms of skimpy, frothy creations in pinks, whites and blacks. Bras, silky knickers, suspender belts; he couldn't take his eyes off the display. Fearing that he might be noticed if he stared longer, he dragged himself away and entered the shoe shop, his heart beating a little more quickly than the exercise entailed in cycling to town could explain.

To add fuel to his already heated imagination, he was served by Deborah, the owner's pretty daughter, a rosy cheeked seventeen year-old whose swelling breasts gave ample testimony to her blossoming young womanhood. In a voice which stammered with bashfulness, Mark made known his needs and the girl brought a selection of shoes for him to try. In crouching to help him fit the shoes, she somehow managed to afford him a tantalising view of shapely, silk-clad thigh, and even a momentary glimpse of stocking top, suspender and smooth pink flesh and the delights that lay beyond. Everything seemed to be conspiring to fuel his racing thoughts, and he realised to his horror that a pulsating warmth and hardness were becoming evident in his loins. Hoping that the suspicious bulge in his trousers was not too evident, he chose the first pair of shoes that seemed remotely suitable, signed the bill and beat a hasty retreat. The girl smiled and thanked him. She always enjoyed serving the bashful young men from the seminary who were always so polite, many of them handsome too, if somewhat reserved.

"What a waste" she sighed to herself as she turned to serve her next customer, a middle-aged lady.

Mark meanwhile grabbed his bicycle, trying not too successfully to avoid looking at the eye-catching display in the window. Gritting his teeth, he pedalled away furiously, his new shoes dangling from the handlebars as he tried to banish the seductively attractive images that filled his mind. Only then did he think about praying, so belatedly he mumbled an 'Our Father' and a 'Hail Mary'. As the journey progressed, the desire and excitement gradually faded as the exercise of pedalling along at a rapid rate tired him, and in its place, his conscience began to assert itself.

Had he stared deliberately at the window display? Even worse, had he looked up the girl's dress on purpose? He hadn't tried to look up it, he decided, but he certainly hadn't closed his eyes when the engaging view had been afforded him. My God, and what a view it had been! Maybe Pete was right about their having to give up a hell of a lot. His imagination clung stubbornly to the vision he had seen, and try as he would, he could not banish the thoughts. He realised that he was putting up a fight now, a fight that would absolve him from any guilt of acquiescence in the present moment of temptation, but he would have to confess the earlier episode.

"I'd better ride carefully" he thought to himself. "If I'm run over and killed just now, I wouldn't like to face God with that not sorted out in the confessional."

Happily, however, the thundering lorries all gave him a wide berth, and half an hour later he was safely on the drive, and before much longer was back in his room, the bicycle safely bestowed once more in its customary place.

Feeling hot, sweaty and thoroughly uncomfortable, he quickly washed in cold water, and then hurried down for tea before the evening study period.

"Hi there, Mark," whispered Peter, talking at tea that day not being allowed, "How did you get on? What are the shoes like?"

"OK, Pete, I think. I didn't look at them too closely. They fit, and that's the main thing. Trouble is, I had other things on my mind."

"Like dishy Deborah, you mean?"

"No, of course not" lied Mark. But Peter's knowing glance at Mark's blushes betrayed the fact that he had guessed right.

Afterwards, Peter continued to press his friend for details, and so Mark told him the tale, but merely the part involving Deborah.

"Lucky devil" commented Peter. "By gum, I wouldn't kick Deborah out of bed if I had half a chance."

But Mark's half-smile showed that his conscience still smote him, and so leaving Peter as soon as he could without appearing rude, he went to his room and prepared for confession. He sat at his desk, his head in his hands. Mortal sin was a terrible burden on one's shoulders; a sense of guilt and forebodings of doom seemed to oppress him; he felt cut off from good, decent people, the brethren surrounding him, a moral leper. The Church was the community of the faithful, those who had kept faith with Christ and lived pure, unstained lives. He was no longer fit to belong to this family, dirty sordid wretch that he was, reduced to goggling at ladies' underwear and stealing glances up girls' dresses.

But then his spiritual formation came to his rescue; after all, the forgiveness of sin was what the coming of Christ into the world was all about. "Not the just, but sinners to repentance."

"I'm a real sinner" he prayed. "Lord, you came to love and save the likes of me. Be merciful to me."

The sense of humility he knew comforted him, and so having prayed a little longer, he stood up, stretched briefly, the tension having stiffened his muscles, and then with heart beating a little faster, made his way to the room of one of the priests of the community.

He told the tale in a low voice, kneeling beside the priest's table, and in a slightly bored way, the priest gave him three 'Hail Mary's' for his penance and absolved him. Such was his release from the threat of eternal damnation.

Feeling a profound sense of relief, yet also a disappointing feeling of anticlimax, he returned to his room and faced once again the unrelenting demands of the philosophy course.

TWENTY EIGHT

The routine of the term made the time pass quickly, and very soon, the cold wet days of February and March gave way to the brighter fresh spring weather of April. Peter and Jim toiled in garden and greenhouse, while in the woods the new growth was everywhere evident. First snowdrops, then the momentum building, daffodils and primroses quickly followed. Lent meant an increase in the penitential aspects of their lives.

"More bloody fish" grumbled Peter morosely. "All this beetroot, too. I ask you: fried fish with boiled spuds and beetroot. The other day my pee turned pink, and I thought 'My God, it's my kidneys gone for a Burton', then I realised it's all this damned beetroot we're eating."

As Lent neared its end, the retreat loomed larger. This lasted all Holy Week, and was preached by one of the priests from another community. Preaching the students' retreat was not a keenly sought task, as the young men tended to be a rather critical audience. This year it was to be preached by one of the fathers not noted for his eloquence, and a general groan went up when the name was announced.

"I do hope it won't be just his Mission sermons rehashed" sighed Neville, "or some hastily adapted conferences from nuns' retreats. A couple of years ago we had an old buffer of a retreat master who insisted on addressing us as 'his dear sisters' every now and then."

"Maybe he wasn't too far from the truth" growled Peter, who still had his reservations concerning Neville's masculinity.

The talks proved to be predictably boring, though Mark conscientiously jotted down notes after the first two or three, in accordance with the Novitiate practice in which he had been trained, but even he gave up the effort after that. But he charitably tried to defend the hapless preacher against Peter's continual murmurings, hissing:

"The things he's saying might not thrill us to the core, but there's a message in there if you look for it, so shut up and try to keep the silence."

"Bugger off, goody goody" sneered his piqued friend, softening the remark however, with a playful dig in the ribs.

The topics covered included the perennial favourites of sin, confession, prayer and so forth, but the liturgical season was acknowledged with talks on the Eucharist on Holy Thursday and the Passion of Christ on Good Friday. Traditionally the last talk of the retreat was always on Our Lady, and so on the Saturday a couple of the more devout brethren built a special shrine on the sanctuary, decorated with the spring flowers which were plentifully available. In the talk, the preacher waxed eloquent about the virtues of Mary, and her many perfections. For some time, Mark had felt uncomfortable when devotion to Mary was overblown as it often was in the Church at that time. One or two of the students were devotees of the Montfortian system of the 'Slaves of Mary', a devotion which aroused much fierce controversy among the student body, and Mark often felt a certain sympathy with the Protestant view, which saw such excesses as 'Mariolatry'.

As the retreat master spoke, Mark felt the familiar sense of distaste and unease as the fulsome encomiums flooded forth.

"Mary is the mediatrix of all graces" enthused the preacher. "Every grace that comes to us from God, comes through her. We can only approach Christ through her. He only deigns to listen to us poor sinners because she intercedes for us, begging him to temper the wrath of his justice towards us."

"What a travesty of the merciful loving Christ he presents" thought Mark. "Christ is pictured as a petulant Eastern tyrant who is turned from an orgy of destruction among his enemies, which seems to mean all of us, by the intercession of his mother. Besides, why can't we as Christians have a direct, uncomplicated relationship with Christ? That retreat Master would have Our Lady butting in all the time. Christ certainly came to us through Mary, and maybe comes to us still through her, but surely" he thought, "it's too much to picture Christ as not deigning to deal with us personally, but only reaching us at second hand. The doctrine of his real presence with us in Holy Communion too, makes nonsense of this 'everything through her' business. As I see it, it's another job for good old Occam's razor!"

He shuffled uncomfortably through the rest of the talk, breathing a profound sigh of relief when it finally ended. Afterwards, he discussed his feelings with Peter.

"I hate all this sugary, sloppy stuff about Our Lady. It does nothing for our dignity as children of God. How can all this twaddle be reconciled with the idea of the dignity of the Christian as a son of God?"

"Keep your shirt on" laughed Peter. "What's got into you all of a sudden? It seems OK to me. I don't mind being a little child in matters of faith".

"It's not that, Pete" insisted Mark, his frustration growing as he tried to express himself.

"It's just that... oh, it just doesn't seem to be reconcilable with ordinary Christianity as we know it from the New Testament."

Later, he mentioned this at the obligatory colloquium that every student had with the retreat master, trying to describe his feelings as tactfully as he could.

"You aren't a convert from Protestantism, brother, are you?" he replied.

Mark laughed ruefully and gave up the effort to explain. But the sugary, devotional side to Christianity which was still such a feature of Catholic life had palled. He was looking for more solid meat on which to nourish his faith for the future.

Spring wore on and the daffodils became overblown, beginning to give way to May blossom and bluebells. The morning walks in the woods for voice production were a sheer joy as the gentle breezes played on the face, and the sunlight created moments of dazzling brilliance as it broke through the dancing young leaves, making the spiders' webs glisten as though strung with diamonds as the glancing shafts struck the droplets of morning dew. The flower beds were by now neatly laid out, with the bedding plants already full of the promise of an exotic display.

Peter and Jim had been busy, and were earnestly hoping that a late frost would not nip all their efforts in the bud. Taking Mark on a tour, Peter knowledgeably explained the difference between tagetes and French marigolds, salvias and antirrhinums, lobelia and alyssum. He kept a jealous eye on his tender charges, and woe betide any slug that dared to make an appearance within fifty yards of the flower beds. He would quickly pounce on the offending invertebrate and with a deft flick of his thumb, reduce the slimy creature to a pulpy mess. He laughed at Mark's shudders of horror.

"Jim says that it's a sign of being a true gardener to be able to do that."

"It's all 'Jim says' these days" laughed Mark.

"Well, he certainly knows his stuff about gardening. Anyway, you're as bad with your 'Neville this' and 'Neville that' when it comes to music."

The two friends ambled on, bickering amicably. Life was good at St Augustine's just then.

At about this time, Peter became involved in another new interest. Jim Hunter had fingers in many pies, all of them practical and creative, among which printing was not the least prominent. One day, he mentioned to Peter that a vacancy had arisen in the printing shop, due to the acquisition of a blue suit by one of the more junior inmates, and the position was his if he cared to accept. Intrigued, Peter investigated the matter further, and was soon enthralled by the wonders of letterpress with its lead type in many and varied faces, quoins, furniture and chases. He quickly became a devotee, and was soon spending some of his afternoon setting type and operating the small printing press which turned out a surprising range of products from ordination cards for the newly ordained priests to a vocations magazine which was distributed round the members of the vocations club, a loosely organised group of young men who had expressed an interest in the possibility of joining the Order at some later date.

Mark's interests were developing along more academic lines, and so he was drawn, under Neville's aegis, into the Literary Society, whose members met twice a month to hear a paper on some learned and literary topic prepared by the various members in turn.

These activities, coupled with the already busy programme of St Augustine's, ensured the rapid passage of time. The Summer holidays were now within sight, and preparations for family visits had to be made. The bed and breakfast establishments within easy reach of the seminary were quickly booked up; the season for visitors was very short, as it only involved the month of July, and if a family still had children at school, then the season was reduced to barely more than a week or ten days.

Mark drew up a list of the best places from suggestions made by the more experienced brethren and then pestered his family to let him know the dates they could come. They were only allowed three full days, and the two travelling days. Fortunately, family commitments posed no problems, and so armed with the dates suggested, Mark sallied forth one afternoon on his bicycle to make the arrangements.

The best dates were already taken at the first three places he tried, much to his dismay. But travelling further afield, he finally managed to find a not-too-pretentious situation for them. He wrote that evening to let them know, then sighed with relief: fixing up the accommodation for the brief summer visit was always a nerve-wracking experience.

May gave way to June, and once again the examinations were hovering like a black cloud on the horizon. Repeating the pattern of the previous February, Mark and Peter worked diligently away. June that year was blazing hot; so the afternoons were spent lying in the long grass on the edge of the hayfields armed with bundles of notes which quickly became dog-eared and sweat-stained as they anxiously pored through them. The first part of the afternoon was spent in solo study, then they would agree to meet at a prearranged time to go through the material together.

Inevitably, Peter's confidence began to ebb as the days slipped by, and his knowledge seemed pitifully thin.

"If only we didn't have to waste so much time in blasted class," he complained. "I just can't keep awake while they drone on with all that crap, and I could be using the time more profitably for revision."

Peter's sleeping in class was a standing joke with the others. On more than one occasion, he had been gravely embarrassed by the general commotion caused when his elbow, propping his sleep-filled head, had slipped off the desk causing a sudden collapse of his somnolent body. On other occasions, books had clattered to the floor, to be hastily retrieved by their scarlet faced owner. Trying to strike the right note, he had gone one evening to the philosophy professor's room to apologise, and being invited to sit down, had promptly fallen asleep once again while the kindly old man regaled him with his memoirs.

"Oh God, I don't know what it is," he groaned afterwards. "I get plenty of sleep at night, but try as I will, I just can't stay awake. If they'd make it more interesting, maybe I'd have more of a chance."

Mark tutted sympathetically, and pressed on relentlessly with the revision. Neville meanwhile spent his afternoons fishing in the ornamental lake that graced the old estate, languidly flicking through the text book in the evening, assimilating the details of the courses without apparent effort.

"My God," grumbled Peter to Mark one evening, "if that bastard put his mind to it, he could be a bloody genius."

"He certainly could do with a real intellectual challenge" replied Mark. "The studies here don't stretch him at all; he'd do much better at University. I suppose our standards are pretty basic, really."

"They're quite high enough for me, thank you very much", retorted Peter. "Don't go suggesting any fancy ideas to make life any harder than it already is."

Mark laughed, clapping his friend on the back.

"Come on, Aristotle, let's get this stuff crammed into our bulging, aching brains."

The examinations passed off much as before; Mark managing with reasonable competence, in spite of some anxious moments; Peter cursing and struggling like a drowning man. When the ordeal was finally over, a delirious sense of freedom ran through the college, the coming of the holidays meaning a relaxing of many of the less important parts of the structure of regular observance, though the ordination year students went into retreat to prepare for their great day, which would be in a fortnight.

The others went out for cycling excursions into the surrounding countryside, or lounged about the grounds when the weather permitted, since following an age-old law, once term had ended the fine weather broke, July coming in rather changeable. But there were some fine days, and Mark enjoyed one excursion with Peter to the ruins of a pre-reformation abbey, where they sat amid the grey broken arches, munching their sandwiches and thinking their thoughts of their ancient predecessors whose lives must have been in many ways similar to their own.

"It's fascinating to think that monks just like us walked along here, sang and said the office, and it was all part of the ordinary life of the country. Nowadays, people must think of us as weird anachronisms."

Peter grunted his assent, adding "And they don't know the half of it."

Lunch finished, they lay back looking at the grey and white clouds sailing serenely across the vast semicircular vault of the sky. Mark drifted off into a reverie; the air seemed to be filled with the smooth rhythms of the old plain chant, and the ghosts of his brethren of five hundred years earlier seemed to surround him. He felt a sense of peace and contentment, a belonging, or continuity with the past that was as real as the stones around them; the smaller fragments such as a slip decorated tile or a hinge embedded in lead making the past vividly present to him.

"I wonder, Pete" he murmured, "if we really are present with those monks who lived here. Time is the only barrier separating us from them. Eternity is the true reality; time is just a way of looking at things which is suited to our present limited state. But God sees all things as present, so He sees us here, and He sees those pre-Reformation religious here, in an eternal present."

He paused for a moment, then continued enthusiastically:

"Perhaps that's how you can explain the apparitions of ghosts. They aren't spirits surviving from the past, so much as glimpses of the past, the curtain of time slightly parting for a second. We see things for a moment in the light of eternity, and so because they are just as really here from that point of view as we are, we can see them. Maybe they can see us in the same instant; ghosts of the future to them."

Warming to his theme, he continued:

"Perhaps that explains prophecy; your Nostradamus and Mother Shiptons glimpse the future, already eternally existing in God's sight, through a crack in the curtain of time, in exactly the same way as a person sees a ghost of the past. It's quite weird to think that a person seeing a ghost is perhaps a ghost himself to the person on the other side of the curtain, so gives the ghost just as big a fright!"

"Shut up, you blooming gobshite" grunted Peter. "You don't half talk a load of rubbish sometimes."

Mark grinned at him, but felt slightly deflated as he stood up, dusting the twigs and leaves that were sticking to him off his jersey.

"Let's see if we can find a pub and get a pint" suggested Peter. "I've a couple of bob with me" he added mysteriously.

Wondering where he could have got the money, Mark shrugged and was content to cycle off with his friend to the nearby village and the sleepy pub at the heart of it.

Another day he went brass rubbing with Neville. Armed with rolls of lining paper and sticks of black cobbler's wax, they sought out a quiet country church mentioned in the brass rubbing books as having some notable examples. It was some twenty miles distant from St Augustine's, so an hour and a half cycle ride was needed to reach their destination.

"Let's hope the weather holds" commented Mark as they bowled along, the vigour of youth giving impetus to their pedalling.

Neville treated Mark to a learned disquisition on the brasses they were to rub, and soon Mark's head was filled with facts and figures relating to thirteenth century crusading knights, palimpsest and shroud brasses, and the techniques they would be employing in taking the rubbings. That topic exhausted, Neville passed on to a running commentary on the countryside through which they were travelling, regaling Mark with a hundred and one facts relating to it, from the sites of civil war skirmishes, to the canal-building feats of the eighteenth century engineers.

"Where do you learn all these things?" he marvelled.

"Oh, I don't learn them, dear boy" drawled Neville. "I suppose my memory is rather like a trawler's net that just scoops everything up. Once I've heard or read about something, it just seems to stay. My mind in consequence is an absolute rag-bag of bits and pieces, useful and otherwise; a walking old curiosity shop, as you might say."

With this pronouncement, the mobile emporium cycled on in his usual dignified fashion, continuing to pepper his protégé with a constant barrage of the choicest morsels of information.

The church finally reached, they first of all hungrily devoured their lunch seated on a convenient tombstone, and appetites sated, opened the creaking door to peer into the gloomy interior, where their nostrils were assailed by the odour peculiar to the Established Church; a mixture of mildew, dust and old hassocks with just a touch of incense and polished leather.

They quickly found the tombs they sought, and discovered a notice asking would-be brass rubbers to enquire at the vicarage. This they found to be next to the church, and so within the space of a couple of minutes, they were pressing the doorbell.

An elderly bespectacled mild mannered clergyman opened the door.

"Good afternoon, sir" began Neville politely. "We are Catholic students for the priesthood. We would very much like to make some rubbings of the brasses in your church."

"Ah, Romans, eh?" mused the reverend gentleman. "Why, certainly, of course. Normally we charge a fee of five shillings for the permission to rub, but I suspect a paucity of funds in your case, eh?"

"That's extremely kind of you, sir" replied Neville. "We really are most obliged."

"Don't mention it, my dear chap. It isn't of the slightest consequence."

Mark's gaze switched from one to the other like that of a spectator at the centre court in Wimbledon as these polite exchanges continued.

"Now then. You know where the church is? Of course, of course. Allow me to lead the way".

So saying, the amiable old gentleman pottered down the path and turned into the churchyard. Mark and Neville followed at a respectful distance, Mark struggling hard to contain his mirth. As they entered the venerable building, the vicar enthusiastically began to describe its beauties. Following his pointing finger, they duly admired the Norman arches, fan tracery and the mullioned windows, the rood screen and choir stalls with carved misereres. Eventually he led them to the tombs and continued:

"Well, gentlemen, I shall leave you to your labours. But do honour me by taking a cup of tea afterwards."

"We would be delighted, sir" replied Neville gravely.

After his departure, they set to work with a will, taping the long sheets of paper in place, and then, under Neville's direction, the rubbing commenced. Gradually, the picture emerged, first the ornate Gothic arch, then the solemn faced figure within, its fine proportions and majestic dignity apparent.

After about half an hour, the figure was basically complete, and Mark whistled softly.

"Magnificent, Neville" he breathed, and continued: "It reminds me of the Shroud of Turin."

"The image there was produced by a rather similar process" remarked Neville, "though the sheet was over the body of Christ rather than a flat, carved image. But in both cases, the results are rather startling."

A little further work to complete the finer details brought their operations to a conclusion, and removing the tapes, they carefully rolled up the completed work.

"Let's do another of this tomb" pleaded Mark, "I'd like one to hang in my room".

"Of course, dear boy" murmured Neville, and they quickly recommenced operations, this time producing the final result a little more rapidly, practice and familiarity rendering the task simpler. Similar attention was then given to a couple of the lesser brasses, and their operations complete, they returned to the vicarage to enjoy the promised cup of tea.

Afterwards, cycling homeward, Mark thanked Neville for what had been a fascinating day.

"Though that vicar would insist on referring to us as Romans," he grumbled. "It sounds almost as bad as 'papists'."

"Hardly that, old boy" replied Neville. "Besides, it does make a certain sense when you think of it. We call them Anglicans after all, so 'Romans' is a parallel usage."

"I wish people would just call us Catholics" Mark retorted. "After all, that sums up what we are; the universal Church. We aren't a local splinter like the Anglicans. Besides," he continued with the assumption of the monopoly of truth and legitimacy that was taken for granted among Catholics in those days, "all those churches and cathedrals should really be ours. They were stolen from us at the Reformation."

Neville laughed. "I think if it came to the push and we offered them a straight swap, their plant for ours, they'd snap our hands off. Those venerable piles, steeped in history as they are, must be positive millstone about their necks."

They cycled on for a few moments in silence, and then Neville continued;

"Don't be too quick to blacken all non-Catholics, my dear boy. After all, they are Christians with us; they share the same fundamental gift of faith and baptism. That means a great deal. We may have the fullness of truth, but they do have the truth too, and they deserve our brotherly respect."

This was a new approach to Mark, even though it could only be described as a moderately ecumenical outlook. In Mark's experience, dealings with the other churches had always been on a level of total suspicion and rejection. In his childhood, the thought of entering a non-Catholic church was anathema, especially if any sort of service was involved, even a marriage or funeral. Neville's words gave him pause for thought, and he came to realise that to think of the Christian Church in terms of the faithful and heretics was too simple a view, even though at the time it was still the common view.

Neville's outlook was a most unusual one for his time, and Mark's mind, which was already learning to question accepted positions rather than adopt the traditional views in an unquestioning way, soaked in the novel approach, and the beginnings of a newer wisdom took root.

TWENTY NINE

The family visit was now drawing closer, and Mark's heart ached with longing to see his loved ones once again. He had kept up the weekly letter to the family reasonably faithfully, though the week had occasionally stretched to ten days or so. The letters he received from home were full of the main events in the family's life, and yet somehow he felt remote from their everyday experiences. Brenda had decided to become engaged, while Tony was beginning to give his mother some heartache as he found his feet and began to sow a few wild oats. But Mark felt that he hardly knew them any more, and a bitterness towards the Order in consequence began to take root in his heart, even though at that time it was still a mere seedling.

But now that the brief visit was so close, he began to count the days, and indulge in exercises of the 'this time next week we'll be doing so and so' variety. By the same token, he thought that this time in ten days they will have departed again for another year, and so he began to suffer a sense of their loss even before their arrival.

Added to this, he worried about their safety on the journey, imagining all sorts of catastrophic accidents that could befall them, a precious little group in a fragile metal box on four wheels.

The weather improved, and a few scorchingly hot days immediately preceded the visit. He restlessly paced the gardens, kicking clouds of dust into the burning air, letting the anxieties of the situation gnaw at his soul.

"For goodness sake stop worrying" cried the exasperated Peter, as Mark confided his feelings. "They'll be OK. Just forget about their going away again and enjoy their presence. You think about things too much. You've got to learn to close your mind to things on occasion, or you'll go barmy."

Mark gratefully accepted the offer of an illegal cigarette, and the smoke calmed him for a time. His dreams in the hot, sultry nights were frustration dreams; he would dream about the visit, and every imaginable thing would go wrong. Idiotic things would delay their departure, the car would continually break down on the way, garages would unaccountably have no petrol, and he himself would be despatched on pointless errands that prevented his getting back to St Augustine's in time for their arrival. He would wake up, naked and drenched with sweat, gasping his relief at the realisation that he was only dreaming.

But eventually the big day came, and after a morning spent keeping himself occupied in every imaginable way, the moment he had been longing for finally arrived. He had been walking to a vantage point from which he could see most of the drive on and off for the past hour or so, but whenever he looked, he could see no sign of them. Momentary hopes were dashed by the discovery that the vehicle approaching was a bread van or the car of some other visitor.

Just when he had begun to worry that they must have had an accident, he was called to the front door by one of the other students with the words:

"Hurry up, Mark, they're already here."

The joy of the reunion was indescribable. He hugged Brenda and his mother, and playfully punched Tony, who just as enthusiastically greeted his elder brother. He quickly arranged some lunch for the hungry travellers, and caught up on all the news while they ate. He then changed into his Roman collar and black suit and accompanied them to their digs, sitting in the front of the car in the place of honour with his mother, while Brenda and Tony were squeezed in the back with the luggage.

The next three days were a mixture of heaven and hell, days of great joy as the family did the sort of things done by any family on holiday: visiting the local beauty spots and historic monuments, shopping in the nearby towns, and wandering round the spacious and beautiful grounds of St Augustine's, which Mark described with great pride as he gave them a conducted tour. Yet behind the joy lurked the ever-present spectre of their imminent departure, and try as he would, Mark could not put this out of his mind. The pain became so bad that by the evening of the third day, the eve of their departure, Mark found himself almost wishing them gone so that the wrench of separation would be past and the healing process could begin.

The family felt the same joy and pain, and when the time for departure finally came after a lunch eaten but not tasted, Brenda and his mother were in tears, while Mark and Tony bravely tried to keep up the appearances. The travellers took their places in the car, farewell hugs and kisses having been exchanged, and fervent promises of more frequent correspondence made, and then a cloud of dust swallowed up the departing vehicle, whose hazy impression Mark followed until it was lost in the shimmering distance.

"Come on, Mark" coaxed Peter softly, sympathetic to his friend's grief, and a walk round the ground with an outpouring of the soul went some way to healing the pain that filled his heart.

THIRTY

He could not nurse his grief for long though, as the seminary holiday was now heading towards its climax; the annual three weeks by the sea. Every year, the first three weeks of August were spent in a convent boarding school, vacated by its regular inmates for the summer. Much lobbying took place in the allocation of places in the various dormitories, large and small, and each group had its own special nickname. There was the English room, of which, needless to say, Neville was a denizen; the Irish room, populated by the home brewers and republican fanatics of various shades; the odds and sods, who were a cheerful miscellany of various types; David and the more pious brethren took a dormitory together which was promptly named 'Carmel' by the others, while the laziest dropout types clubbed together to inhabit a dormitory which rejoiced in the name of 'Punks' Paradise'. The squalor and smell were taken for granted, and it was rumoured that the inmates had even been known on occasion to urinate out of the windows. Cigarettes circulated freely, and the more respectable brethren only ventured within its sin-stained walls when prompted by strict necessity.

"Mark, my dear boy, would you care to accept a place with us in the English room?" murmured Neville one morning after breakfast. "I rather believe I can swing it with the others."

"Thanks, Neville" smiled Mark. "I'd like that very much. I don't know what Pete's doing, though."

"I'm not sure that my influence would stretch far enough to secure a place for Clark too," remarked Neville, thoughtfully fingering his chin. "He is English, I know, but there are certain standards. After all, the chaps wouldn't put up with farting in public, which as you well know, is a habit to which Clark is on occasion prone."

"I wouldn't want to be in the bloody English room" growled Peter when Mark mentioned this to him later. "You can go in with that bunch of potato-mouthed what-whaters if you like."

"Be fair, Pete" urged Mark. "They're all reasonable types, really. You can't blame them for being a bit patriotic; after all, the Irish do tend to put peoples' backs up with the way they carry on about the English oppression and all that sort of thing."

Peter grunted. "Anyway, I've been asked into Punks, so I think I'll just go in with them."

Mark threw up his hands in mock horror and let the matter drop.

"Anyway, we can still cycle there together if you like."

"Yeah, that'd be smashing" agreed Peter enthusiastically, and the two forthwith began to make provisional plans for the journey, which would take place in a few days' time.

The idea of cycling to the holiday house was an attractive proposition for many of the students; there were about sixteen bicycles in the common pool of varying degrees of antiquity and in varying states of repair. All were road worthy, but some had borne the burden of the heat of the day, and were calculated to raise an anticipatory gleam in the eye of any passing scrap metal merchant whose attention they happened to catch.

The students wishing to cycle entered their names into a draw in pairs, and as each couple were announced, their steeds were also drawn from an adjoining hat. The bicycles were easily identified from the desirable green racer, down to the lowly sit up and beg policemen one and two. Bodger and a couple of the more mechanically minded brethren worked earnestly to ensure that all of the bicycles were in the pink of condition, and a couple of days before the departure, the draw was made.

Cries of delight alternated with groans of despair as the names of the couples were called out, followed by those of the allotted machines. After the first few had been drawn, Mark began to feel that he and Peter and no chance; they would have to go on the bus with the non-cyclists and the also-rans.

"Winterton-Smith and Parkinson" called the teller.

"Tandem" rejoined his companion.

A roar of laughter went up from the assembly, as the tandem, while having its advantages, was not everyone's cup of tea. However, Neville and Parkinson, a rather superior theology student, accepted the decision with equanimity.

"Clark and Kennedy."

Mark jumped. "Black Raleigh and Hercules with aluminium mudguards."

"Not bad" commented Peter. "But you know what they say; go to Scotland on a Hercules and you'll come back with a B.S.A."

"What are you on about?" queried the mystified Mark.

"Haven't you heard that one?" asked Peter. "Come back with a B.S.A. Bloody sore arse."

Mark grinned. "Bags I the Raleigh, then."

The rest of the draw finished, and the cyclists all eagerly discussed their respective machines and the planned routes; the thwarted gloomily resigning themselves to the bus journey. Maps were produced and pored over, notable pubs and stopover places discussed and selected.

The day of departure finally arrived, an ideal day for the cycle ride, clear with a few fluffy white clouds and a gentle breeze.

"Great" enthused the athletes. "The record for the trip will be broken this year, I dare say."

The first departures were just after breakfast, athletic types intent on fast times.

"Bugger record breaking" commented Peter. "Let's just enjoy the trip."

The non-cyclists were busily engaged in heaping all the suitcases into a pile, some went back and forth to the kitchen stacking provisions, awaiting the arrival of the bus.

"Right, Mark" announced Peter when their suitcases had been added to the pile in the courtyard. "Let's get cracking."

Duly fortified with the ten shillings allowed for the journey, they took their allotted machines, and made final checks on tyre pressures and emergency puncture repair kit, complete with old spoons, and to the cheers of the others, set out.

Parkinson and Neville started a few minutes later, and a mile down the road, swept past majestically, Neville behind waving his hand as though he were visiting Royalty.

"Hope they fall off or have a puncture commented Peter, as the tandem, still gathering speed, disappeared round a bend a hundred yards further on.

"Right, let's get ourselves sorted" commanded Peter firmly, as side by side, they bowled along the quiet country road that was leading them west towards the distant Welsh hills.

"First of all, let's get rid of these bloody collars."

Suiting actions to the words, they halted briefly, removing the Roman collars which they stuffed into their saddle bags.

"That's better" gasped Mark. "I felt a right nit cycling along with that on."

"The damned things half choke you" agreed Peter. "Now let's see. I reckon we can get our first pints in Newtown; it'll be opening time by the time we get there. We've enough money for about three pints each and ten fags, with a bit of luck."

He winked at Mark. "Of course, there's always my contingency fund too, but I don't want to break into that if I don't have to."

He patted his jacket pocket. "A little holiday spending money."

Mark shook his head. "You're terrible, Pete. Incorrigible, I should say."

"I know, but you'll let me buy you a pint from these wages of sin, won't you?" replied Peter shrewdly, and Mark's shamefaced grin made him a partner in crime.

Remounting the bicycles, they pedalled steadily on, a rhythm developing which ate away the miles. As they rode, they chatted happily, admiring the rolling countryside through which they were travelling. Ludlow was soon reached, but with time pressing, they had little opportunity to admire the castle. Turning north, they followed the main road, finding the going fairly easy. But bearing left at Craven Arms, the haul over the edge of the Long Mynd began, and soon the pair were puffing and gasping as they followed the winding, hilly road, their goal on the Welsh coast seeming a million miles away.

"It'll be opening time a long way before we reach Newtown" gasped Peter. "Let's have a pint as soon as they open."

Mark, panting, agreed, and so they made a slight detour into the village of Bishop's Castle, where they thirstily demolished a pint apiece of the local brew. Sitting back contentedly smoking Woodbines and relishing the malty taste of the beer, they reviewed their progress.

"Not bad" announced Mark. "I reckon we've done nearly forty miles in about three and a half hours. I'd call that pretty respectable."

"How far still to go?" enquired Peter.

"Just over fifty, I make it" replied Mark. "We should get there easily for about six this evening, even allowing for stops on the way. But we'd better not dawdle, especially on these earlier stages of the journey."

So saying, they drained their glasses, stubbed out their cigarettes and bidding the landlord a cheerful goodbye, remounted their machines and recommenced their progress. They pushed steadily on until about half past one, and finding a pleasant wayside pub, stopped for lunch. Digging their sandwiches from their saddle bags, the friends munched greedily, washing down the slabs of bread and cheese with copious draughts of beer.

"Fancy another?" asked Peter when the glasses were empty.

"Better not" replied Mark. "Two pints would maybe knock the stuffing out of us."

"I'm having one, anyway", Peter pronounced. He marched up to the bar, paid his one and ten pence, and was very quickly half way down the glass.

The more of this stuff you have, the better it tastes" he remarked. "It's amazing how easily it slips down."

But he was soon paying the price of his overindulgence as the hilly Welsh roads took their toll.

"Bloody hell" he gasped, "it's like trying to ride up the side of a house trying to get up some of these hills."

"It's all that beer holding you back" laughed Mark, as moderating his pace, he waited for his struggling companion. A little further on, they spotted a couple of familiar bicycles outside another wayside inn.

"We must be well known on this route" commented Mark as they passed. "I bet the locals watch out for the annual migration of the mad monks to the sea."

"Leaving a trail of fag-ends and empty beer glasses all the way" agreed Peter, his second wind now helping him to make better progress.

The dusty August hedgerows, already rich with the promise of autumn's harvest of wild berries, slipped past as the pair pedalled on. The hills seemed to be growing steeper and longer as the journey progressed. The agonising, lung-searing, muscle-straining slog of the climbs had them both wheezing and clenching their teeth as they forced their machines, tyres rasping grittily in the loose gravel at the side of the road, up the steep inclines. Then it was with gusty sighs of relief that they sped down the other side, the wind fanning their faces and rushing through their hair. The quaint, drab little villages of Wales, cottages with gardens full of vegetables and lines of washing flapping in the summer breeze all came and went as the long afternoon wore on, and the miles slowly ticked by, until towards evening, their shadows starting to lengthen and their limbs aching with a desperate weariness, they neared their goal.

"Only about ten more miles" groaned Peter. "My backside feels like a piece of raw steak."

"I hope you won't feed it one" laughed Mark. "The very thought is enough to make you turn vegetarian."

He eased his position on the saddle, his own bottom feeling similarly afflicted.

On the outskirts of the town which was their destination, they stopped at another pub, quickly reckoned up their remaining change, and downed a final pint.

"Maybe this is what heaven is like" sighed Mark as he lounged back, his legs stretched out before him.

"Bloody hell, maybe not" he gasped as a sudden cramp gripped his thigh, making him stand in agony. A little brisk rubbing eased the pain, and he knew a blessed relief as the cramp relaxed its deadly grip.

"It was worth the pain, though. It's been a long hard grind, but it's been a day I've enjoyed."

He sucked at his cigarette, blowing out the smoke in a long sigh of bliss.

"Come on, then, kid, we'd better see if we can find this school, then."

Outside the pub, the temporary laymen became clerics once again as they donned the obligatory dog collars, carefully glancing round to make sure that they were unobserved. The soberly clad young men then resumed their steeds, mentally recalling the directions given them on how to find the school on entering the town. Happily, the directions being clear, the school being quite prominent and the town small, they were soon pedalling wearily through the gates, receiving a nonchalant welcome from the bus travellers who were already old hands, well settled in.

"Everybody arrived?" enquired Peter, wiping the sweat from his brow and rubbing his stinging eyes, irritated by the salty moisture that had escaped his handkerchief.

"No, only about half" came the reply.

"We haven't done so badly, then" exclaimed Mark, surprised, as he thought that they must have been the last to reach their destination.

The athletes had all cycled in, bursting with freshness and brim full of vigour, about two hours earlier, and now the less ambitious were straggling in, two or three more pairs arriving shortly after Mark and Peter. The inevitable phone calls started to come from the breakdowns some time later, the priest who had been appointed as holiday house superior ferrying home the remains of riders and machines from a twenty five mile radius in the battered seminary shooting brake.

Supper was at eight that evening, and by then, the whole community had been assembled and were noisily exchanging stories of the day's events.

"What's your room like?" Peter asked Mark while they hungrily demolished the meal of cold ham and a tomato, which as already noted seemed to have been ordained by some law of the Medes and Persians as the obligatory meal in all such circumstances.

"Seems fine" he replied. "It's a bit crowded, though. How about yours?"

"We've already got Punks off to a good start; it stinks of the sweaty clothes blokes have changed out of after today's journey. Did you hear about Carmel, though? What a laugh. Over the beds in there are notices which read 'please ring if you require a mistress during the night.'"

"What a waste" laughed Mark. "I suppose that room must be the sickbay or something. This seems to be quite a place, with playing fields, tennis courts, all mod.cons. We should have a great holiday here."

And so it proved. The next few days were burning hot, and most of the students spent nearly all day on the beach, basking in the heat and swimming in the sea. Most were sensible, careful not to let themselves get burned, though inevitably one or two spent their evenings gasping and groaning, dabbing calamine lotion on inflamed backs and limbs. The framework of the Religious Life was reduced to the bare essentials: morning Mass and a short period of prayer in the evenings, though all the students were expected to supplement this with a little private prayer, if only a rapidly mumbled rosary at some convenient moment during the day.

But some rules still obtruded; a provincial edict ordained that while it was permissible to disport oneself on the beach in normal beach attire, journeys to and from the beach, a matter of a quarter of a mile, should be made in clerical dress. This was largely ignored by tacit agreement, though on one occasion the previous year, to stress the silliness of the rule, one bright spark had taken to making the journey clad only in his bathing trunks with the Roman collar round his neck.

"People must think we're a right crowd of nutters" grinned Mark as he and Neville lounged in the morning sun on the beach towards the end of their first week. "Just look at Bodger."

Turning his head, Neville was treated to the sight of the slightly corpulent handyman, sporting a pair of tattered knee-length football shorts, with his spindly legs ending in feet encased in stained white tennis pumps, at least two sizes too large. Neville closed his eyes, shuddering delicately.

"What a positively unspeakable sight" he complained. "Bodger is a public menace and should be suppressed. We aren't with him, dear boy. If he comes over, pretend you don't know him."

As fate would have it, Bodger strolled across. "Lovely day, lads" he beamed.

"Smashing, Bodger" agreed Mark, winking and indicating Neville, who had raised his eyes to heaven as if making some silent supplication that the ground would open up and swallow either Bodger or himself.

"Neville was just admiring your sartorial elegance."

"Yes, rather nifty, eh?" replied the dandy, sand shoes flapping as he kicked at a pile of seaweed nearby. "These shorts allow the fresh air to circulate freely around the nether regions. Go to avoid athlete's dick, you know."

Bodger was referring to a minor epidemic of a rash that affected sensitive areas that had afflicted the seminary some weeks earlier.

"Frequent bathing and the use of talc would be more efficacious" pronounced Neville, giving up the struggle to remain aloof. "Really, Bodger, you are the limit. You certainly lower the tone. What must people be thinking, looking at you?"

And in truth, Bodger had attracted the curious stares of more than a few of the holiday makers with whom they were sharing the beach.

"Still, I'm no danger to the virtue of any of the susceptible young maidens around" he modestly averred, and proceeded to paddle in and out of the many pools left by the receding tide, striking up instant friendships with the children who were busily making dams and sailing toy boats.

Mark lay back, allowing the warmth of the sun to soak into his body. Bodger might pose no threat to the virtue of the susceptible young girls on the beach, but they posed a threat to Mark's virtue. His gaze kept returning to the smooth young bodies with their pert little breasts, bottoms wobbling slightly as they ran into the sea amid shrieks and laughter. He knew a moment of loneliness and separation from all that was meant by normal warm humanity, and thought somewhat bitterly that at least Bodger had warm human contact with the children. His mind turned momentarily to the crucified Christ in prayer, as was his wont when the burden of the sacrifice entailed by his way of life lay heavy on his shoulders, and he prayed briefly that he might feel something of the closeness to Him that he saw as the ultimate and only safeguard of his happiness and peace of mind.

"Penny for 'em, dear boy" interrupted Neville after a while. "You seem somewhat pensive this morning."

Mark laughed a little ruefully.

"It's nothing, Neville, really. I just couldn't help noticing the lovely young girls dashing into the sea, and regretting the insurmountable barrier that cuts us off from them. Holy celibacy! There are times when it fills you with a terrible sense of frustration!"

"Beauty is but a snare, as the wise man said" murmured Neville. "I feel personally that celibacy is an attitude of mind as much as anything. Perhaps in a sense this is what the ascetical writers were trying to imply in their notions about subjugating the flesh. Mind over matter, I suppose we'd say in our day. If you think celibate, you won't have too much difficulty in being celibate."

"My imagination must be too unruly" sighed Mark. "It definitely has a will of its own. I don't think I really and truly want celibacy in my life, maybe that's the problem. I want to want it, if you see what I mean, but that's not quite the same thing."

Neville nodded understandingly. "The classical spiritual masters generally maintain that the sincere desire is what is required in moral decisions; feelings do not enter into it. If you desire the celibate mentality, then essentially, you have the celibate mentality. Once it takes firmer root, then you will achieve greater mastery over your feelings and desires."

"Thank you, John of the Cross" laughed Mark. "Come on, let's have a swim. Until I attain the celibate mentality in its fullness, cold sea water is the best cure I know for the desires of the flesh."

"I know just what you mean, dear boy" replied Neville as they walked down to the water's edge and dipped in a tentative toe. "Origen would have found his self-inflicted operation totally unnecessary if he had taken to daily sea bathing."

The pleasant shock of the cold water had the desired effect, and the sparkle of the morning sunlight on the translucent green water, so clear that the pebbles on the white sandy bottom were clearly visible from the surface, soon chased away the more depressing serious thoughts that filled his mind.

The holiday passed with ever increasing speed as the three weeks drew nearer to their close. The weather remained generally fine and warm, though a few rainy days were interspersed. The time was spent mainly on the beach, though bicycle excursions were also popular, especially in the earlier days of the holiday before the money allotted to this end ran out. Several students joined the local library for the duration, and Mark greedily devoured mounds of light fiction, thrillers, detective novels and historical fiction being his staple diet. He tried his hand at tennis, though without a great deal of success, though he found the exercise stimulating after too much lounging around. But holidays, by their very nature merely intervals in the serious business of daily living, must inevitably come to their end, and so the break drew to its close. The cycle ride back to St. Augustine's, however, provided a fillip which avoided too great a sense of anticlimax at the end of the three weeks.

It was two bronzed but tired travellers who sat drinking cider in a pub about seven miles from home, at about six o'clock in the evening.

"Well, Pete, it's back to the grindstone. That's the holidays over for this year."

Mark took a long pull at his pint glass. "Not bad, this stuff, if you can't afford beer."

"It gets you just as drunk" agreed Peter, "and drunk is what I need to be to face another year in that dump. It's the bloody retreat in a couple of days, too. They're determined to weed out any sin that might have taken root while we were away."

Mark thought of the many pretty girls he had been sneakily ogling on the beach, and the hours frittered away reading rubbishy fiction. A desire for a cleansing touch of austerity came to him.

"I don't know, Pete. We probably need a retreat: I know I do, anyway."

"Masochist" retorted his friend, pulling out his battered cigarette packet. "Have a last fag and then we'd better get back to that hellhole."

They lit up and smoked in silence for a while.

"A year over and gone; it's a chunk out of our time at Oggies" Mark observed, breathing out a plume of smoke.

"It's passed pretty quickly, all things considered. It makes you realise that ordination will be here before we know it. It's true that as you get older, the time passes more quickly. Now we've done one year, the next will only seem half as long. All the more senior students say that."

"The quicker it passes the better as far as I'm concerned" replied Peter. "I can't wait to get out and get on with some real living. This endless preparation really drives me up the wall."

But Mark felt secure as he was, and thrust thoughts of the future and the demands it would make, out of his mind.

"Sufficient for the day, and all that" he commented, voicing and canonising his feelings. "Let's not wish our youth away; one step enough for me."

They smoked the cigarettes down to the filter, drained the cider glasses, and then cycled the last few miles back to St Augustine's, with frequent stops necessitated by the diuretic qualities of the beverage of which they had been partaking.

"It adds ammonia to the hedgerows" commented Peter knowledgeably as they added yet more nitrogen to ensure a verdant spring to the particular hedge behind which they were urinating. Mark laughed, and quoted a popular childhood saying: 'If a bean's a bean...'

"Home again" sighed Mark, as they put their bicycles away. "I think I'll have a hot bath, and then it'll be time for supper."

"Don't tell me" laughed Peter. "It'll be..." and the two chimed in together, "cold ham and a tomato."

THIRTY ONE

Term started, and as September gave way to October, the nights quickly started to draw in. The new students arrived, and Mark and Peter realised that they were well established as mature residents of the seminary as they showed the newcomers round, no longer the junior year.

The second year was passing in much the same way as the first, with the daily grind of Philosophy class, the panic (for Peter at least) of the examinations, and the monotonous routine of prayer, class, study, recreation and bed as the daily programme. Feast days intermittently added a certain spice to life, with the treats of cigarettes and a drink added to a more splendid meal than that usually served. Mark enjoyed the cosiness of the routine, the regular observance giving stability if not happiness to his life, though he would have described himself as generally content with his lot.

The spiritual awareness that the Novitiate had brought almost to fever pitch had relaxed somewhat, though his realisation of the presence of Christ within him was real enough, if not particularly inspiring. His daily reception of Holy Communion nourished this, though even here the danger of routine meant that the experience lasted seconds rather than minutes or hours. The weekly visit to the Confessional gave a slightly more urgent prod to his spiritual sensibilities, and by and large, Mark was the student his superiors saw him to be; reasonably hard working, well-intentioned and making the sort of progress that would ensure a slightly above average rather than spectacular passage through the seminary.

Peter's position was more precarious. Barely scraping through his studies, he was regarded as not very promising material. The rules and regulations, especially the lesser ones, he simply ignored or used to suit his own purposes. His spiritual life appeared to the outside view at any rate to be sketchy in the extreme. True, there was the saving grace of his preaching ability, a not inconsiderable factor in an Order dedicated in a special way to preaching the Word of God, but the general view was that unless things changed drastically for the better, Peter would probably not make the grade.

What saved him as he progressed by the skin of his teeth was the reluctance of the superiors to actually expel anyone. Vocations were getting harder to come by year by year, and unless a man showed himself to be an absolutely hopeless case, he was usually allowed to continue. Peter managed to leave sufficient doubt in the mind that he was always given a stay of execution in the hope that he would improve, or at least that the situation would clarify to make a negative decision more firmly possible.

David remained an enigma to his superiors. They recognised that his spirituality was unhealthy, closed in and shut off from the rest of the world as he was. Yet what was to be done? A man could hardly be asked to leave because he was too holy, or because he did not take sufficient relaxation. The general view was that he would probably grow out of it as ordination neared, and responsibilities in the outside world increased. In the meantime, he was left largely to himself, occasional sniping attacks aimed at curbing the more obvious excesses being the only form of treatment that occurred to the authorities.

In his own mind, David was right with the conviction that only the true fanatic enjoys. He was as certain that his was the right path as any Jehovah's Witness, and the cruel logic of his position compelled an unswerving obedience to his ideal. He deplored what he considered as the mass laxity all about him in students and superiors alike, but was saved from the need to condemn in an outright fashion by adhering to the biblical maxim "Judge not, and you shall not be judged." His studies merely tended to reinforce his position, as the emphasis in all areas was the same; Catholicism was presented as the all-perfect all-sufficient system of belief and living, with its laws and ideals clearly stated, so that all that was demanded of the individual was obedient assent, a submission that would bring perfection through a stretching and nailing of the individual to a cross comprised of these principles. Sin was the failure to match up to these demands, which God forgave through his mercy, though the obligation on the Christian was to hold these ideals before himself, and constantly measure his behaviour against them.

David accepted this view implicitly, while everybody else accepted it with a subconscious pinch of salt. David's was the more logical position, logical with the logical folly of the cross, though it was a view of Christianity which if accepted logically could only produce saints or lunatics. Opinion was divided as to which category David belonged, though the latter was the view which commanded more general acceptance.

Ken was proving to be as dependable as the Novitiate experience had foreshown. He was generally known as 'Rocky' since someone had felicitously remarked that he was as solid as the rock of Gibraltar. Neville tended to poke a little gentle fun at him, though he conceded that the name 'Peter' given to Simon Bar Jonah by Christ himself was really a biblical form of the same nickname. Nothing perturbed him; the studies he found manageable, though he was far from brilliant, and he could be counted on in any crisis. He tended to make his friends further up the seminary being a late vocation, though his relationships with Mark and Peter were friendly enough, if not particularly close. His early concern with David had tended to blend in with the general view that he was a hopeless case, and so apart from occasionally exerting himself to join the ascetic at recreation, he let matters take their course.

However, his worldly experience and background in the Forces during his National Service had tended to bring out in him a rather vulgar streak of humour, buried in his Novitiate days, which occasionally had the more liberal brethren in stitches, and the rest would raise their eyebrows in various stages of shock, depending on the depth of their piety. He kept a small black book of choice limericks, examples of which he would recite to Peter, who would double up with laughter in the most gratifying manner. Ken would dig out the best and most scandalous as Peter's reaction was so comical.

"Go on, Ken, tell us another" he would plead, so Ken would oblige:

> "Then up spoke the king of Siam,
>
> for women, I don't give a damn.
>
> You may think if odd of me,
>
> but I prefer sodomy,
>
> You'll say I'm a bugger; I am."

Another choice one went:

> "There was a young man of Pool,
>
> who had a red ring round his tool.

He went to the clinic,

but the doctor, a cynic,

said 'Rub it off, it's lipstick, you fool."

Neville contributed the rather more learned:

"There once was a student called Rex,

who had a small organ of sex.

When charged with exposure

he replied with composure

'De minimis non curat lex'

One of the Irish brethren offered:

"There was a young man of Coothill,

who swallowed a hydrogen pill.

His genital organ was found in Glamorgan

and his balls on a bush in Brazil."

Neville held forth with one of his disquisitions after a typical session of limericks and jokes, referred to by Ken as "Cock and ball stories."

"The clergy, I believe, along with the legal and medical professions, have the coarsest sense of humour of all groups. Navvies and stevedores can be pretty vulgar, but they lack the nice touches that put the professional classes in a unique position. Perhaps it has something to do with our educational system. It is well known that a public school education can produce all sorts of peculiar sexual manifestations in later life, possibly due to the severity of sexual repression inculcated at a tender age. Working class children, growing up in an environment in which sex is part of everyday living, accept it much more naturally. After all, how many homosexual dustmen does one meet?"

The others looked at one another blankly, wondering where Neville obtained the information to bolster up his unique pronouncements. But they had to admit that the notion of a homosexual dustman did seem a trifle improbable, and the probability of their encountering one seemed even more remote. Neville, meanwhile, was continuing his peroration:

"Sexual maladjustment, of which an excessive interest in lewd humour is a symptom, is perhaps a more or less exclusive preserve of the middle and upper classes."

"I'm not from the middle or upper classes" remarked Ken, "and I hope that my interest in lewd humour isn't excessive. Maybe I should draw the line a little more strictly, but you've got to admit that jokes about sexual topics can be very funny."

"My dear Ken, I trust you weren't taking my remarks personally" expostulated a slightly embarrassed Neville. "Of course these matters can be a rich source of humour. It could be said that we joke about matters for which we have the most regard. Sex, politics and religion are all topics of fundamental importance, cornerstones of human civilisation. Humour about them can be a safety valve enabling us to preserve their true worth. Jokes about them would not be amusing unless we held them in high regard."

"If one is to draw lines in these matters, I would reject stuff that degrades or ridicules sex, or is simply salacious. I don't think my limericks fall into that category."

"Absolutely, Kenneth. I feel that we are in total agreement here."

The discussion drew to an amicable close, though a not inconsiderable body of opinion in the seminary would have drawn the line rather more strictly than either Ken or Neville.

THIRTY TWO

Mark, Peter, David and Ken, second year students grappling with the intricacies of the Philosophy course, were fighting broadly the same battles, living more or less the same lifestyle, with a few concessions to the twentieth century, that their predecessors had fought and lived two hundred years earlier. But the cosy world of St Augustine's was about to be disrupted by events which had been simmering gently in parts of Europe for the past twenty years, and would shortly be breaking out into the wider context of the Church Universal.

The second year blended into the third, and with the autumn rains beating down as heavily as ever, one evening Neville poked his head round Mark's door.

"Have you heard, my dear Mark? The Pope has died."

"That's the end of an era" replied Mark, more prophetic than he knew. "He's certainly had a good innings, has Pius XII. It's funny to think that he was pope well before the time we were born. I wonder who'll be the next Pope; Pius XIII sounds a bit funny, somehow."

"It mightn't be Pius" replied Neville, although somehow any other name seemed preposterous. "It could be Leo, or Benedict, or anything, come to that."

A buzz of excitement went round the seminary, and everyone crammed into the common room at news time after supper each evening to follow events on the television. Even David allowed himself the occasional glimpse, religiously turning away once the newscaster returned to secular matters.

The cardinals assembled for the conclave, and along with the rest of the world, the students looked for the plume of white smoke from the Vatican that would announce 'habemus Papam'.

"It's some old geezer" exclaimed Peter in disgust when the news finally filtered through.

"Must have been chosen as a night watchman because they couldn't agree on a more positive candidate" murmured Neville.

Groups of students were assembled on corners, eagerly discussing the news.

"His Holiness John XXIII; what a funny name" mused Mark. "It doesn't sound very Pope-ly. Why couldn't he have stuck to Pius or Benedict?"

The new Pope's coronation was duly celebrated on November 4th with a recreation day, complete with plenty of wine, and so the new pontificate was inaugurated in rousing style in at least one of the world's Catholic centres. Life returned to normal, but not for long. The new Pope quickly made his presence felt in the Church; no night watchman he, but a whirlwind of change. Nervous Vatican officials desperately tried to back-pedal and apply the brakes as the word 'Ecumenism' began to gain currency in ecclesiastical circles, and more wonderful still, a Council was announced.

"What's all this about a Council?" grumbled Mark. "We have the Church's infallible teaching all established. What the devil we want with Councils, I don't know."

He would have received many a pat on the back in the corridors of the Vatican.

"Something about opening the windows and letting in a breath of fresh air" replied Peter. "I think maybe he has a point there. A dose of salts to get rid of all the crap might be a better metaphor, though."

"Well, it can't make much difference" Mark commented. "After all, there's nothing to define, and the Council of Trent gave us a pretty good summary of what the faith is all about and how it should be presented. It'll probably be about boring stuff like religious broadcasting, or preaching the Gospel in Bongo-Bongoland. Sounds like a right waste of time and money to me."

Certainly, it made no difference in St Augustine's for the time being. Such news about it as percolated through to the students tended to reinforce Mark's view that it was just an excuse for a glorified get-together.

But as the months passed, the first hints that perhaps it would lead to more fundamental changes began to emerge. Neville was delighted with the new ecumenical attitude that was becoming apparent.

"That's just because you've always had a soft spot for the Established Church" laughed Mark.

"Yeah, you'd make a right good Anglican with your plummy voice and your nose stuck in the air" jibed Peter, joining in the conversation.

"We should be humble enough to admit that we can learn from them" observed Neville to his somewhat scandalised hearers. "They have a great deal to offer us."

"But they're really just playing at it" protested Mark, who still largely unaffected by the Ecumenical movement, was voicing a view very common in the Church at that time. "Their orders are invalid; they lost the Apostolic succession in the time of Elizabeth the First. That's what it all comes down to as far as I can see."

"I think that view is open to question, saving his Holiness Leo XIII's position" replied Neville. "I certainly don't think that the validity of Anglican orders is a closed question. And besides, we have never questioned the genuine nature of their baptism. They are all Christians with us."

But to a generation reared on the slogan 'It is the Mass that matters', this seemed cold comfort.

"I can see that we should start being charitable and polite to them" admitted Mark. "But you can't change the facts. We are the one true Church, and any unity in the Church will mean eventually that the Proddies will have to come back to Rome."

But Mark had already started out on his road to Damascus, little though he realised it. Liturgical changes were the next results from the Council to affect St Augustine's. Modestly enough at first, they only meant that the Epistle and Gospel were read aloud in English instead of having to be repeated after the Latin rendition. This was generally acceptable, although already rumblings were being heard about a more fundamental reform. The sacred liturgical edifice, erected at the Council of Trent and meant to last until the Second Coming of Christ, or so it seemed, was beginning to crumble.

Furious arguments began to develop, the Latinists desperately trying to stem the swelling tide of reform.

"The Mass can be understood immediately wherever you go in the world; Latin is the hallmark of the universal Church" it was announced.

Mark, at first somewhat bemused by all the furore, began to take sides with the proponents of the vernacular liturgy, as participation by the people seemed of paramount importance to him. Peter, perhaps surprisingly, tended to be something of a die-hard, supporting the arguments for continuing with the Latin Tridentine liturgy.

"It's all just a fad" he stormed, "stirred up by bloody Continental trouble makers."

"Nonsense, Pete" retorted Mark warmly. "I'd have thought you'd be all for it. You can't understand Latin at the best of times."

"But it's this whole thing about change" protested his friend. "That's what we had over the Protestants. They change their churches as the whim takes them. We're supposed to be the unchangeable, timeless Church. Besides, anywhere you go in the world, the Church is exactly the same. That's what Catholic means. Doing away with the Latin will end all that."

"That's the argument from tourism" retorted Mark scornfully. "Do you expect the French to put up with the Mass in Latin so that the occasional Englishman who wanders in will be able to follow it, even if not understand it? Besides, it's not the essentials we're talking about changing, only the accidentals. After all, the Last Supper wasn't in Latin. Besides, I thought you were all for getting rid of the crap in the Church; that's what you said when the Pope spoke about opening the windows."

"That's different" grumbled Peter. "I only meant the mumbo-jumbo they keep churning out from Rome every ten minutes, giving us mountains of encyclicals and other pronouncements to try and learn for the exams."

Mark slapped him on the shoulder and laughed. "Maybe this Council isn't such a bad idea after all; there's no harm in looking at things even if you decide to keep them the same in the end."

Mark was beginning to appreciate that change need not be a bad thing, that infallibility did not mean the absolute immutability of a monolithic structure. But his attitudes were still fairly conservative, especially where he felt the Church's doctrine was at stake. But the impetus for change, once unleashed in the Church as it had been by John XXIII, rapidly snowballed and became at least for the time being, unstoppable.

Copies of the first books about the Council, by Robert Kaiser and Xavier Rynne began to circulate among the students.

"Read this, it's dynamite, my dear fellow" enthused Neville, thrusting into Mark's hands "Inside the Council" by the first mentioned of these writers. It was written like a thriller, with conservatives and liberals portrayed as graphically as the Chicago mobsters of the nineteen thirties. Mark was enthralled. The Council took on an entirely new meaning and aspect for him; he began to see it as a crusade, in which the proponents of an exciting new vision of the Church were embattled with the vested interests of those in power, who would sometimes stop at nothing to thwart the renewal and keep the Church from moving forward into the twentieth century.

The Curia in Rome took on all the worst aspects of the Inquisition; in fact, the Holy Office *was* the Inquisition, its methods admittedly not as bloody, but just as deadly as they had ever been. Peter declined to read the book, even though Mark tried to persuade him, and the gap between the two friends' appreciation and understanding of the Church grew rapidly wider.

"You've gone flippin' bonkers over this Council business; I don't know what's come over you" Peter grumbled. "These cardinals you keep slating too; they're good and probably holy men who've served the Church very well over the years. Why suddenly start seeing them like some sort of gang of ecclesiastical Stalins?"

"Maybe their intentions are good, but I'd even question that sometimes" retorted Mark. "But openness and truth is what we're looking for; surely there can't be any harm in that? Anyway, the Pope is certainly wanting change and renewal in the Church, so if you lot are so keen on the hierarchy and obedience to it, why not obey the bloke at the top and get on with it?"

So the arguments seesawed to and fro, not only between Mark and Peter, but among the students generally, and between liberal and conservative in the Church at large.

These were suddenly heady, exciting days in which to be living; not only as regards the Church, but in the world generally. Mark's namesake, John Fitzgerald Kennedy, was President in the United States, and echoes of the Cuban missile crisis struck the very heart even of St Augustine's, for all its isolation. For a day or two, the seeming near inevitability of a nuclear war had a noticeable effect on the attitudes of most of the students; a quieter, almost sombre attitude prevailed, and Mark personally stared death in the face for the first time in his life. The chilling reality of the danger would stay with him for many years, though mercifully buried in his subconscious.

In a lighter vein, the excitement of the 'swinging sixties' made itself felt even among the celibate young seminarians. Laggard though he was in the revolution in attitudes in the Church, Peter was in the forefront here. New trends in contemporary life did not escape his watchful eye for long; cut off from the outside world as he was in St Augustine's, he had his sources. For some time he had surreptitiously listened to the hit parade on 'Radio Luxembourg', and more recently, had managed to acquire an old but serviceable reel to reel tape recorder. Nobody knew how Peter, as efficient as any wartime black market spiv, managed to come by these illicit treasures, and Mark forbore to ask, taking the view that what he did not know would not hurt him.

By dint of much wheedling and cajoling, Peter had persuaded Bodger to assist him in organising a direct link with the radio, and so he was now able to tape the hit parade each week. His favourite haunt became the subterranean printing shop, deep in the bowels of the earth in the old cellars beneath the original mansion that comprised the main block of St Augustine's. His activities in this refuge suddenly took on a new assiduity, as with volume suitably muted, he diligently set type and ran off the various printing jobs, soaking in the stirring new sounds emanating from the Liverpool based groups.

One afternoon, Mark wandered down to have a chat, and as he poked his head round the door, Peter jumped guiltily.

"Bloody hell, don't do things like that" he gasped, "I almost shat myself!"

The tape recorder was churning out the latest hits, and Mark listened, fascinated.

"Great, isn't it?" enthused Peter, joining in the chorus of one of the songs: 'You're no good, you're no good, you're no good, ba-yay-be, you're no good' he crooned. "Wait for the next one; it's the Beatles."

Thus Mark heard for the first time the sounds that were sweeping the world, and was bowled over. The split which had been threatening to develop over their widening differences of view in matters ecclesiastical and theological was healed by a common love of the music that had gripped the imagination of their generation, although they had come to it rather later than their secular contemporaries.

"Twenty-one year old adolescents" remarked Neville at his most patronising.

"One can appreciate Bach and the Beatles" protested Mark, a view that was shared by more than one eminent music critic.

Thereafter, Mark would often slip down to the printing shop, and listening to the music, he was gradually drawn in and became a member of the printing fraternity, Peter showing him the ropes so that he was soon setting type and undertaking ambitious projects with the best. Peter was quite an arresting sight as he operated the press, habit tucked up to reveal fashionable skin tight drain pipe jeans, with his feet encased in winkle pickers or Cuban heeled boots. Wherever else he obtained his footgear, it was not from the hands of dishy Deborah in the duly approved emporium.

THIRTY THREE

Another term that began to be bandied about at this time was the 'New Theology'. Scholastic theology, with its set patterns of the thesis followed by demonstrations from Scripture, the Magisterium of the Church and the Fathers, had been the norm in the seminary since the time of Thomas Aquinas and earlier, and was still faithfully taught in St Augustine's, Mark and Peter by now starting that particular part of their education. Its concerns seemed curiously remote from everyday realities, even though it did not often go to the extreme of calculating how many angels could fit onto the head of a pin.

The New Theology, at least within the walls of St Augustine's, consisted of the exciting new works of the continental theologians which began to appear about this time in translation, courtesy of Messrs Sheed and Ward among others. The stylised line drawing of the stag was appearing on paperbacks by the score, and it was not long before the ideas expressed there began to make their mark on St Augustine's, which started to undergo the most profound changes in its attitudes, at least as far as the students were concerned.

One of the seminal works was "The Resurrection" by F.X. Durrwell, a French Redemptorist. Neville, by now in his second last year at St Augustine's, had continued his policy of introducing Mark to much of the stimulating literature available, and so one evening, Mark found himself opening a book that was to change his life more radically than any other single influence he had ever encountered.

Theology had always placed the crucifixion and death of Christ at the centre of the Catholic Faith, in a system of belief which saw Christ as the Redeemer, or the one who paid of the price necessary to atone for man's sin and gain him eternal salvation. God's justice demanded payment, and God's mercy gave us Christ to make that payment on our behalf.

But now a whole new vision of the Christian Faith was presented to Mark as he devoured the book, reading and rereading it as he soaked in the vast riches it contained.

Christianity, he realised, was essentially a very simple religion. Man is cut off from God by sin. The plan of God is this: to send his

Son to become man; not just a man, but *the* man, the head of the race. This is Incarnation. The Man Christ then journeys back to the Father by dying to sin on the cross and rising again. The Resurrection is a new birth, man's birth again as the son of God. All men are then called to share in this journey through death and Resurrection by being one with Christ, or by being his body, in this dying and rising. We die with Christ on the cross and rise again, sharing his new, glorious life. We do this through baptism and the other Sacraments which make us the Church, the living, risen body of Christ, the community sharing his death and resurrection.

This is the framework into which every Christian doctrine fits; everything else is simply an amplification or extension of this fundamental notion.

The sheer beauty and simplicity staggered him as it slowly dawned on him, and a growing impatience with the mounds of obfuscation with which the Message had been surrounded soon made itself felt. He tried to explain his new vision and enthusiasm to Peter, but somehow could not manage to communicate the magic of the vision as he saw it.

The Mass was not just a ceremony remembering the events of two thousand years earlier, or an offering to God of the merits of those events; it *was* those events in this time and place. The Christian was not just a believer in Christ and a follower; he *was* Christ incarnated here and now, offering himself to the Father in the timeless sacrifice of death and Resurrection, and offering himself to the world as Saviour and Redeemer.

In his efforts to share this notion with Peter, he found himself too easily slipping into the clichés so often mocked by the die-hards.

"Paschal bloody mystery" scorned Peter. "This new theology is just a heap of jargon. Transcending this, and encapsulating that in a sacramental cosmic weltanshauung."

"You seem to know all the expressions, anyway" laughed Mark.

"I hear various bods wittering on about them so often that I can't help it" retorted his friend. "My God, why tart things up with all this tripe? Just say your prayers and behave yourself; that's what it's all about."

So Mark's vision went unappreciated, though it brought new dimensions to his prayer and spirituality, and the sheer excitement stayed with him as he hungrily sought out and eagerly devoured all the works currently appearing, the names of Hans Küng, Piet Schoonenberg, Edward Schillebeeckx and Jean Danielou soon joining his pantheon of new theological worthies.

As his appreciation grew, so did his impatience with the dogmatic theology course he was following at St Augustine's, which jogged along as though nothing had happened.

"All this rubbish about the physical virginity of Our Lady" he exclaimed one day to Neville, who was in the middle of washing a hand basin full of rather smelly socks.

"Theologians talk about a miraculous birth of Christ, so that the physical virginity of Mary would not be affected. I thought virginity was all about lack of sexual intercourse. What the doctrine is really saying is that Christ was born of Mary, but of no earthly father, and that Mary never had sexual relations and so other children either. All this stuff about intact hymens. It's supposed to be theology, not biology!"

Neville, wearing a pair of socks on his hands like gloves, soaped assiduously. "Excessive interest in irrelevant physical details has long been a mark of scholastic theology. Take for instance the discussion about the meal of fish eaten by Christ after his Resurrection. He passed through closed doors, his body being glorified. But what of the fish? That was not glorified, so how could it pass through the closed doors? We were discussing that in class a couple of years ago, and Bodger, ever practical, came up with the brilliant suggestion that perhaps it went through the letter box!"

When he had finished mopping his streaming eyes, Mark gasped: "That deserves immortality. Bodger should go down in song and story for that one!"

"But don't simply write off scholastic theology for all that" continued Neville, by now rinsing the pile of socks in clear water before draping them over his radiator. "It is a positive mine of useful information and material for theological speculation, and my own view is that the dross should be stripped away, leaving the pure gold to be further enriched with the new biblical insights. The methodology is valid, I feel, and its discipline could well be adopted by the so-called 'new theologians', who if they have a weakness, suffer from a certain lack of methodology on occasion, hence the tendency to relapse into the jargon and verbiage that friend Clark berates so vehemently."

The arguments continued, and the student body had another group within it. As each student normally fell into several overlapping categories, there was no discernible split caused by the rise of the 'new theology'. So Mark and Peter, divided in their theological and spiritual viewpoints, still had many other areas of common interest to cement their friendship. It was tacitly agreed between them that potentially contentious issues would not be raised, and so they continued to enjoy one another's company as before.

THIRTY FOUR

The end of Mark's first year in Dogmatic theology saw Neville's ordination, and Mark helped him choose suitable cards, or small holy pictures, to commemorate the event. Each ordinand was allowed a free hand here, within certain spending limits, and the pictures were printed on the reverse with any text and details requested by the candidate.

Yesterday's choice had been the rather sugary, Italianate Sacred Hearts and Madonnas; now, with the liturgy well to the fore, the choice was stylised grapes and chalices, or assorted liturgical symbols. Mark and Neville, however, agreed on some rather austere engravings by Albrecht Dürer, which Mark then printed on the reverse with the text in Latin: 'Tu es sacerdos in aeternum, secundum ordinem Melchisedech'. The details and name were tastefully printed in various sizes of Bembo type, so called after the noted Renaissance Cardinal of that name.

"His Aunty Ethel will appreciate that" growled Peter as he operated the press, with Neville's cards being laid out to dry in neat ranks by his faithful assistant. Peter's tastes tended to favour the colourful effeminate Christs now despised by the cognoscenti.

The day itself was a sharp reminder to Mark that his own ordination was now only two years away, and he was still no clearer in his mind regarding his future life and work within the Order. He tended not to think of it too much; particularly as more recently the excitement of the new theological insights had diverted his attention from the hard facts concerning the everyday life of the priest in the contemporary Church. If pressed, he would have replied that he would like to go for higher studies and then teach; or failing that, simply to play his part in bringing the ordinary people to a new and deeper appreciation of their faith, to share the Vision.

Neville of course being otherwise engaged, Mark played the organ during the ordination and from his vantage point in the organ loft, looked down and followed the service in all its awesome detail, with a firm sense of the irrevocable nature of what was happening. "You are a priest for ever, according to the order of Melchisedech". He felt a pang of envy for the apparent courage and serenity of Neville and his contemporaries, answering clearly and firmly as the bishop put the ritual questions to them concerning their dedication.

His own final profession would be coming up within two or three months, he recalled with a sudden shiver. This was just as irrevocable a step in its own way as ordination; he would be dedicating himself to the Order for life.

A sudden rush of warmth and affection for his brethren filled his heart, and his resolution grew firmer. This was his family; he belonged, he would happily take the step which would confirm his lifelong dedication. The apostolate would take care of itself; in the immortal words of countless theatrical producers, it would be 'all right on the night'. But doubts about that still lingered as he thought about the world they lived in, a world so different from the anachronistic society of St Augustine's and the Order. Things they almost took for granted would cause shock, astonishment, mockery, or even occasionally respect if revealed to others; things like the corporal penances for instance. But the Church herself as she existed in the everyday world, seemed a million miles from reality sometimes. Mark would on occasion agonise for hours; what was he to say to people that would mean something to them?

He recognised the priceless treasure he possessed, particularly since his initiation into the mysteries of the 'new theology', but even this seemed worlds away from the swinging sixties with their everyday problems of working in factory or shipyard, the music of the Beatles, the nuclear threat, even the ordinary bread and butter facts of life like eating meals and going to bed. He cringed when he read of trendy vicars trying to make religion 'with it' for the ton-up kids, yet how could you bring a vision of Christ to twentieth century man? The apostolate ahead of him seemed woefully ill-equipped to meet the challenge. He sighed, looking down at the ceremony unfolding below, and coming to himself, hurriedly prepared for the next piece of music he would have to play.

"Congratulations, Neville - I mean Father."

Mark smiled as he knelt to receive his friend's blessing.

"Music very passable, dear boy - thanks" murmured the newly ordained priest. For once, Neville seemed a little subdued, overawed by the solemnity of the occasion. But next day at his first Mass, he brought style and panache to the liturgy, which he performed faultlessly with great dignity. It proved a temporary balm to Mark's doubt-troubled mind, as Neville's performance of the timeless rites made them seem much more living and real, though for the moment he overlooked the fact that what seemed living and real to him would not necessarily appear in the same light to the assembly line worker or shop assistant.

But Mark, by nature an optimist, soon left behind his gloomy doubts and it was in a positive state of mind that he duly pronounced his final vows two months later. His family was present for the occasion, and looked proudly on as in a clear voice he committed his future to the service of God.

"What a wonderful day" his mother commented afterwards; her son's future seeming so bright and assured in the service of God and the Church. Brenda confided in him that she hoped to marry within a matter of months now, her boyfriend, who was still the same one from three or four years earlier, having finally popped the question.

"We thought they'd be courting for the rest of their lives" remarked his brother.

"Stop it, Tony!" protested the blushing bride-to-be. "I'm only twenty three after all!"

Tony, more worldly-wise than the ladies, nudged Mark and said:

"You've gone and done it now, kid! But if ever you feel like ducking out and bolting, never be afraid: I'll back you up every time!"

Mark hastily disclaimed any such possibility, while his mother and Brenda gave the young cynic a severe scolding.

Peter's final profession had been postponed; the authorities putting off a final decision yet again, and so he simply renewed his vows for a further year.

"Bastards!" he had snarled to Mark when breaking the news to him some days earlier. Mark had comforted his friend as best he could, while privately wondering whether in fact it could be for the best if Peter did seek his vocation elsewhere, though he never intimated as much to him. He had succumbed, partially at least, to the view that Peter's academic abilities, but more especially his attitude to life, were more than a little at variance with the received wisdom on the model priest and religious.

But he couldn't help admiring Peter's determination and unswerving loyalty to his purpose. Mark sometimes doubted and questioned, if only in his heart. But Peter's inner attitude seemed serenity itself, and it was this limpet-like persistence more than anything that had ensured his survival. If he had once expressed a doubt to his confessor or superiors as Mark had on occasion, he would have been encouraged to leave.

David and Ken had been with Mark on the altar, the superiors having long given up any idea of altering David's attitudes. The general view among the students was that it was folly to allow him to continue; they saw more of him than the more remote authorities, but their views were never consulted. Many in the congregation that morning felt that the Order was storing up trouble for itself in allowing him to continue, but no one in authority had the courage to grasp the nettle and attempt to get to the heart of David's inner world, and so he too had dedicated the rest of his life to God, the Church and the Order.

THIRTY FIVE

"Erection, penetration, ejaculation; what a way to sum up the mysteries of the sexual relationship."

Mark, Peter, David and Ken has started Moral Theology, their last two years at St Augustine's. Neville had left at the end of the previous term, and as expected, had been sent to Rome to pursue higher studies.

The Moral Theology course was taught by a priest who sometimes gave the impression of being rather a worldly cynic, whatever the depth of his piety when once removed from the scholastic sphere. The academic world of St Augustine's still lay largely untouched by the Vatican Council, at least as regards the official curriculum, though this term, a newly qualified young professor fresh from the Roman Universities had arrived to take charge of the newly established liturgy course, which was at least a nod in the direction of renewal. He was also allowed to teach a little theology, under the guise of catechetics, to the younger students, but the mainstream of the intellectual life of the seminary progressed, or failed to progress, as before.

"It's bloody diabolical" grumbled Mark as he strolled to the greenhouses with Peter after breakfast.

September was nearing its close, and the grape harvest, watched over carefully by Peter, a zealous guardian, was ripening nicely. The Irish home brewers, like wolves round a Russian sledge, kept pestering him to allow them to make wine from the bumper harvest, but he was having none of it.

"Moral Theology should be describing the new life of Christ within us, how it should be expressed in our ways of living. I bet old Carver has never even read Häring".

Mark was referring to the book 'The Law of Christ' by Bernard Häring, which was in the process of revolutionising Moral Theology just as dogmatic theology in its turn had been turned upside down by the continental theologians. Moral Theology, classically, had been the scholastically based ethical treatise on the rules and regulations governing human living, covering the ten Commandments, the Sacraments, or at least the moral implications rising from their administration, and canon law. The Moral Theology professor was popularly known as 'Carver' because of his predilection for food, having gained the name one Christmas as he carved large slices off the breakfast ham. As his treatment of his subject had a certain ruthlessness about it, too, the name seemed doubly appropriate.

Peter stretched lazily in the morning sun, which still had a certain strength left in it.

"Oh, Carver's not too bad. At least we get a good laugh in his classes. I liked his crack the other day about the deaf wife with ten kids: 'Do you want to go to sleep or what tonight? What?' Mind you," he continued, "you've got to admit that at least Carver's stuff is practical. When someone in the confessional gives you a real knotty problem, you can't just waffle on about the new life of Christ and all that."

"I know all that's true" admitted Mark, kicking moodily at a clump of weeds beside the path.

"But you're supposed to inspire people to the right way of living in the Confessional, not just point out their sins in a technically correct fashion."

"Anyway, I'd rather have Aertnys-Damen as a text book than Häring; it's much easier learning principles than trying to soak up that more general, inspirational stuff."

The discussion was threatening to polarise along the all too familiar lines of old ways versus new, so Mark hastily changed the subject.

"Thank God your final profession has gone through, anyway, Pete."

Peter had just been given the good news a day or two before; the ceremony would be quietly performed at the end of the month.

"Yeah, they knew I'd stay whatever they said, so they just accepted the inevitable and made it official" grinned the unrepentant reprobate. "By the way, have you heard? We're going to start catechising in a couple of weeks."

Thus casually Peter broke the news that transformed the morning for Mark. A cold hand seemed to clutch at his heart, and a feeling of sick panic formed in his stomach. For the last few months, the superiors had been debating the possibility of allowing the senior students some pastoral experience in the shape of giving religious instruction to the local children, who could not attend Catholic schools as could their more fortunate city-dwelling contemporaries.

"It'll be great" continued Peter enthusiastically. "Getting out twice a week of an evening."

Mark stared thoughtfully at the trees surrounding the kitchen garden beautifully dappled with sunlight as the early morning breeze caught them. He turned to Peter and smiled.

"Yes, it'll be good."

"You don't sound too keen about it."

"It's a good idea" admitted Mark. "It just scares the shit out of me, actually trying to put the Faith over to somebody else."

"You've no bloody faith" laughed Peter. "It's all in here with you," he continued, forefinger tapping the side of his head. Mark shrugged his shoulders a little ruefully.

"You're probably right" he admitted. "Though I think I do have a spark or two. My faith makes me want to love and serve God; it just doesn't give me any confidence when it comes to putting it across to others. Especially kids. I can see it now; a group of them sitting in front of you, shuffling their feet and resenting it because they've got to come and listen to you instead of playing out with their pals. Grownups wouldn't be so bad. At least they have the politeness normally to keep their boredom to themselves."

"Talk about pessimism" retorted Peter. "Don't be such a pissmire. You're enthusiastic about the Faith; just be yourself and let it all hang out, as the bishop said to the actress."

With that, Mark had to be satisfied for the time being. Within a few days, the details had been hammered out, and the four found themselves detailed to cycle twice a week to one of the nearby villages, where the children from six to sixteen were to be assembled in four convenient groups according to age in the houses of two of the Catholic families. Peter was given the little ones, while David took the juniors. Mark was allotted the younger group of seniors, and Ken was to tackle the tough fourteen to sixteen's, a sullen group of gum-chewing lip-curling cynics, who by and large only came to Mass each week under protest.

"It's all right for you" grumbled Mark morosely to Peter when the details were announced. "You can get the little kids drawing and painting pictures, and tell them nice, simple stories. I could have managed that."

"I think it's a good choice" replied Peter, somewhat smugly. "You're the brainy one after all. You'll be able to answer all the awkward questions about the existence of God and all that sort of thing for the little buggers."

There was no use in crying over spilt milk. Like his disastrous first attempts at organ playing all those years before, this was something he would have to get on with, for better or worse. He duly ensconced himself in his room with any of the more modern catechetical works he could lay his hands on, and tried to map out a course.

His first attempt was disastrous; it looked like the table of contents of one of the more learned tomes of dogmatic theology.

"Where are you, Neville?" he groaned, missing the sage advice of his mentor. "What the hell am I going to do?"

He scrapped his first attempt, which started with various proofs for the existence of God, and decided to tackle things from a liturgical point of view, basing a course on the seven Sacraments. He always came back to the same point, however. How does one make religion interesting to thirteen year olds, and bolshy thirteen year olds at that? Eventually, he had a tentative plan of campaign mapped out. He would start with the death and Resurrection idea. Christianity was simple, so such an idea should be understandable and appealing to the pubescent youngsters committed to his care.

The day of the first lesson drew nearer, and Mark's panic knew no diminishing. He envied Peter his infants, but fatalistically accepted that he would just have to try his best. The afternoon of the day itself he spent in putting his final touches to the campaign, as often as not breaking off to visit the lavatory yet again.

At last it was time, and with a dry mouth and heavy heart, he joined the others in the courtyard, and with trouser legs securely tucked into socks, mounted his machine and pedalled off. The village was about five miles away, and was soon reached. He waved farewell to Peter and David as they made their way to the house that would be the scene of their endeavours, and he and Ken cycled on until they came to their own destination. Leaning the cycles against the side of the house, they approached the front door, which Ken rapped smartly with his knuckles.

"Chin up, Mark" he said briskly. "Just fix the little blighters with a firm hand and beady eye, and lay down the law."

It was all right for him, Mark thought gloomily. He had an air of authority about him, and could be sure that the teenagers would try no nonsense with him.

The lady of the house opened the door and welcomed them in.

"You're a little early, brothers" she said brightly. "The children have not yet all arrived."

Mark hoped that most of his would have been stricken with some not too serious disease, just enough to keep them at home. Inside, several youngsters sat quietly on settees and chairs, looking expectantly at the two flushed and perspiring young men who had just entered the room. Mark fingered his collar nervously, the sweat having started to bring out a shaving rash on his neck.

"Have a cup of tea while you're waiting" invited their hostess, and feeling like a condemned man granted a short reprive, Mark accepted gratefully.

The other children arrived in dribs and drabs, their parents having been informed of the arrangements by the priest who said an occasional Sunday Mass for them. Some of the children had scarcely ever been to Mass in their lives, and none had received very much in the way of religious education. Mark's heart sank further towards his boots when one of them addressed him as 'vicar.'

But further opportunity for depression and panic was not to be given him; downing his tea, Ken said suddenly, "Right, let's get on with it then."

So saying, he organised the fourteens to sixteens and led them into the kitchen. Mark was left with his group, the lady of the house tactfully making herself scarce upstairs.

"Let's get to know one another. I'm brother Mark Kennedy from St Augustine's. You all know St Augustine's?"

Several of the children nodded, but one or two looked blank. Mark explained about the seminary and the training for the priesthood, and then went round the group one by one, asking names and ordinary family details.

The lesson was going famously; no problem here, he thought enthusiastically. But then he recalled that he was simply engaged in the 'pourparlers', and was not yet down to the nitty-gritty. The lesson was scheduled to last about forty five minutes, and nearly twenty had gone by, so at least it was almost half over. Eventually the introductions had been completed, and there was nothing for it but to take the bull by the horns. Taking a deep breath, he plunged in.

On a sudden inspiration, he went round the group asking each in turn what the word 'religion' meant to them. He received various answers; 'going to church', 'being good', 'being kind to other people', 'saying prayers'.

"Do any of you enjoy religion?" he asked.

One girl whose mother was a regular fervent worshipper at St Augustine's dutifully replied "yes, brother", though the others muttered and looked a little sullen.

"Religion isn't really much fun, is it? Do you know something? I don't enjoy it very much, either."

He paused, and looked round. The girl was looking a little shocked, but some of the others looked slightly interested. This was something new, at any rate. He then described the boring aspects of religion, putting himself in their place, and painted a rather depressing picture, a not too difficult task.

Then he eagerly embarked on a brief description of the Vision.

"Religion is many things" he announced, "but first and foremost it is a new life."

He explained about dying with Christ and sharing his Resurrection, which was a new birth and so we are now alive with his life, a part of his body. The group looked at him solemnly. It was impossible to tell from their expressions what effect if any his words were having. He soldiered on, but as he spoke, the words he was using began to sound less heartfelt and more redolent by the minute of the currently fashionable theological new speak. Glancing at his watch, he realised to his profound relief that it was almost time to end the lesson. He thought he would ask a couple of questions to see what effect, if any, his words had produced.

"Right, boys and girls" he said briskly. "We've talked quite a lot about religion over the last half hour or so. Let me ask you again the question I asked at the beginning. What does the word religion mean to you?"

He received several replies again, some depressingly similar to the initial responses. But one or two spoke of 'sharing God's life', or 'loving God', and the child who had called him 'vicar' came up with 'it's Jesus living inside you', so all in all, he felt as though his first attempt had been not entirely fruitless. The end of the lesson, however, was the signal for a general stampede in the direction of the door, and so he was under no illusions as to the popularity of the class.

The relief, however, of having survived the first lesson induced a sense of euphoria, and it was a very different Mark who chattered away to the others on his way back to St Augustine's.

Thereafter, twice a week the same journey was made, though half terms and school holidays provided a welcome break. He kept plugging away at his central theme, illustrating it from the Mass and the Sacraments, and eventually felt that at least a little headway was being made. But it was not all plain sailing. Once the youngsters were used to him, keeping order became a regular part of the task, shuffling and pinching, sly slaps and digs with elbows being considered part of the give and take of the situation. Some days, all he seemed to do was to remonstrate continually with one or other of the habitual trouble makers, while the better behaved children hissed their disapproval at the mischief-makers, fondly believing that they were thereby helping Brother to restore order.

None the less, he often wondered how much real progress he was making, as he still felt that religion was more or less completely outside the ordinary experience of most of the children. They were able to talk a little more about 'sharing Christ's life', but did it really mean anything to them? Maybe he would have been better, he sometimes thought gloomily, sticking to the catechism, as some of the more traditional critics of the pastoral experiment maintained. He thought back to his own childhood, and one memorable occasion on which the nun taking the catechism class had belaboured one dim child with cuffs to the head as she repeated 'God made us to know him' (slap) love him (slap) and serve him (slap) in this world, (slap) and to be happy with him (slap) for ever in the next (slap)'. At least the need to love God wasn't being hammered into them, but they were to a large extent a captive, unwilling audience all the same.

But this was perhaps true of the Church at large. How many Sunday Catholics, he wondered, would keep coming to Mass if the obligation were to be abolished? Maybe the biblical imperative 'compel them to come in' had a perennial relevance. His thoughts turned to his own religious practice. Could he claim to be any better? How much did he do that he didn't have to? It always seemed to come back to the basic question: how relevant is religion to the 'common' man? The relationship with God should be as humanly satisfying as a man's relationship to his wife, he felt. True, the experience of Divine Sonship was on a different plane, only knowable by faith, so perhaps it all came down to the clarity of the Vision? One could not give faith to people; one could simply do one's best to present the message, and trust God to give the gift of faith to the hearers - he felt the weakness of his own faith, and prayed that he might see God more clearly, or know him more vividly in his life.

All in all, he found the experience of teaching the children a mixed blessing. He had a little success, a lot of frustration, and was not sorry when lessons had to be cancelled for any reason, but he enjoyed the contact with ordinary lay people it gave him, his first real contact as an adult apart from the brief, yearly family visits, and that was different. He enjoyed chatting to ordinary people about ordinary things, away from the ivory tower of seminary life. Before or after lessons, he would play games, especially with the little ones, and draw pictures for the babies. He soon became popular with the village Catholics and found that the constraints imposed by his situation fairly minimal.

On one occasion, visiting the family where Peter taught to collect his friend, the man of the house used a fairly mild vulgar expression in a moment of exasperation while doing a repair job, and immediately apologised, his wife murmuring something about 'using such language in front of the brothers.' Mark laughed with Peter afterwards.

"If they could hear the language in the printing shop when things are going wrong, they wouldn't know what hit 'em," Peter grinned.

Mark had the feeling that the lay section of the church in general would not know what hit it if half of what went on in clerical circles was generally known; but for all that, thought the gap between the two worlds most unhealthy. Perhaps some sort of void between the sacred and profane was inevitable, but need it be a separation aggravated by the Church's own attitude? Sometimes she seemed hell-bent on increasing the distance, while the whole meaning of the Incarnation, unless he much misunderstood the matter, was that such a dichotomy should no longer exist; in the words of St Paul, Christ was to be 'all in all'. These were matters that would assume an ever greater importance in his life, but already Mark felt the contradiction keenly, and sought ways to resolve the situation as best he could in his own outlook.

THIRTY SIX

"There's a letter for you, Mark," Peter announced one day after breakfast. It was a cold, autumn morning, and so Mark walked with Peter towards the greenhouses to refill the paraffin stoves, reading the letter as they went.

"Our Brenda is taking the plunge at long last with Bill" he commented. "The wedding is fixed for just after Christmas. It's a damned shame I'll not be able to go."

The pair walked on in silence, Mark gloomily trudging along with his hands in his pockets, having tucked the letter into his habit. The rule about students not being allowed home was still most strict; a very serious illness or death of a parent or brother or sister was the only reason for which an exception was permitted. One or two students had asked for permission to attend weddings, but this had always been refused.

"Go on, ask, you may as well," Peter urged. "You've nothing to lose, and there has to be a first time for everything."

"There's no point" Mark replied morosely. "They'll only say no. It's so unfair; families are expected to put themselves out and visit us for the measly three days a year, and then come to our professions and ordinations, and then we can't put ourselves out for them in the least. We've got to be grateful they allow them to come and see us at all. It's all take, take, by the Order, and no give."

Peter agreed. "There's our little Lucy, she's ten now. I've missed all her childhood being in this dump. She really hardly knows me, nor me her. Still," he continued, "by the time she comes to get married I'll be a priest, and I'll be able to do the wedding myself."

"Maybe she'll become a nun" Mark grinned.

"Not bloody likely" retorted Peter. "No sister of mine is going to be a nun if I can help it. The Church isn't going to get her claws into her."

"I know what you mean" Mark replied sympathetically. "It's O.K. for boys to become priests, but it seems so hard, a girl becoming a nun. Giving up marriage and children, it's a hell of a sacrifice, more so for a girl than a boy. People say 'what a waste' when a girl enters a convent. They should be saying 'how marvellous, giving her life to Christ', but it's difficult even for us to see it that way."

"Well, it's not surprising, some of the hell-holes that exist, with poor, frustrated down-trodden nuns trying to get a bit of human consolation where they can. If I was a girl, you wouldn't get me into one of them places."

Mark had a sudden vision of Peter with veil and wimple, his truculent face glaring forth from the stiff, white linen tunnel. He laughed and teased:

"You'd make a lovely nun, Pete" and then ran ahead to avoid his friend's avenging boot.

But at Peter's prompting, he duly put in his request to attend the wedding, but was met with the expected refusal. He was allowed to send a telegram, however, so at least he was able to acknowledge his sister's big day.

At about this same time, however, he was able to be present at more unhappy occasion; the funeral of his old friend, brother Thomas. During his years at St Augustine's, he had kept in touch sporadically with the brother, meeting him on one or two occasions and writing to him at Christmas. Somehow, brother Thomas seemed to go on for ever, and so his death, after a short illness, came as a severe shock to Mark . It was Peter who broke the news to him.

"Have you heard?" Old Thomas has kicked it at last. I wonder how old he was? He must have been knocking on a bit. A brother's life is not much fun, though, to say the least, so maybe it was a happy release" he added, with unconscious brutality.

His words, none the less, bore seeds of truth within them. During his later years at St Saviour's, Mark had come to realise that the brothers were on a different social plane to the priests in the Order: definitely second class citizens. Though he sometimes felt anger and shame at the situation, he had come to accept it, more or less unconsciously. The brothers were expected to keep to themselves and not socialise with the fathers: they always treated the priests with due deference and knew their place. Mark sometimes felt that they were used, 'unpaid skivvies' was a fairly apt, if somewhat uncharitable description of their role. Of course, in official terms, their vocation was dignified with the usual spiritual trappings, and many of the priests treated the brothers with courtesy and respect. But inevitably the caste system meant that their position in the social order was inferior, and most of the clerics treated them accordingly, though without malice or conscious intent.

Now that he was dead, Mark realised that he too had slipped to a similar position in his relationship with brother Thomas, and the Order's brothers generally. He bitterly reproached himself for this, blaming the system, though not absolving himself from guilt.

"The funeral's up in Liverpool" Peter continued, "and apparently they want to make a bit of a show of it, so they've asked if the part choir can go up to sing. My God, all those hours put in under Winterton-Smith are paying dividends at last."

Mark and Peter both still lent their services to the choir, which since Neville's departure for Rome had been run by a musically gifted young student two or three years their junior. Towards the end of Neville's reign, the services of the part choir had begun to be sought occasionally outside the confines of the seminary when solemn liturgical occasions demanded something special. Inevitably, the perks attendant on such occasions were a great attraction, so such excursions were welcomed with more than a little enthusiasm.

As the journey was the best part of a hundred miles, the coach hired to transport the singers arrived at St Augustine's at the crack of dawn a couple of days later. The shivering group climbed gratefully aboard, the acrid smell of diesel being more than counterbalanced by the warmth and comfort offered by the modern vehicle. Mark opted for a window seat, Peter naturally taking his place beside him.

"This is the life" remarked Peter breezily, failing to recognise his friend's pensive state. Mark would have preferred to be left to his thoughts, but good naturedly he smiled and took his part in the banter that the earliness of the hour in no way abated.

With a lurch, the coach roared away and was soon rattling down the drive and onto the main road. After a couple of miles, the conversation grew more desultory, and Mark was soon able to indulge his pensive mood. Staring out of the window at the grey, damp landscape, his thoughts turned to the ceremony that lay ahead.

Thomas was dead. It was the first time in his life that the fact of death had struck him so forcefully, though the death of his father had been an ever-present reality to him. Now the fragility of man's grip on life came home to him with a new intensity. Sickness seemed a hair's breadth away from health, and the strongest, most vigorous frame could quickly be reduced to a pale, feeble shadow. Life seemed so short, like the grasses of the field, he thought, in Biblical terms. Eventually, Peter broke in on these dismal meditations.

"Cheer up, you miserable devil. It may never happen." Mark turned and smiled at his friend.

"You're right, Pete. But it just makes you think. Old Thomas was a friend of mine; a good friend when I needed help and advice."

"Well, he's gone to his reward" replied Peter comfortably, "and we're in for a good binge, so cheer up and enjoy yourself."

But the mood stayed with Mark, and during the requiem Mass, the bare coffin stood starkly between the rows of choir stalls in which Mark and his companions were situated. It was a grim reminder of the harsh reality which had brought them together that day, and as Mark gazed at it he felt a deep sense of loss, and regret that he had taken the brother's friendship so much for granted, and had not valued it as it deserved. How little of a life remained; a pathetic bundle of already disintegrating flesh and bones. He had looked into brother Thomas' room before the ceremony, and a few shabby clothes and tattered books were the only tangible evidence of a lifetime of love and service. He shivered in spite of himself. His faith told him that an eternal crown of glory awaited them at the end of their years of self-sacrifice, but how unreal it all seemed when confronted with the grubby, mundane experience of today. Who gave a damn whether you lived or died in the Order? Before the Mass, the assembled brethren had gossiped and chattered, catching up on all the latest news. Get-togethers were rare enough, and the opportunity was too good to miss. But sadness or a sense of loss at Thomas' death were the last things in evidence, to Mark's mind at any rate. Any guilt that this might arouse was quickly assuaged by the reminder that the deceased had achieved eternal glory, and so the mourners were entitled to rejoice.

He stood by the grave afterwards, looking down at the coffin before the earth was heaped on top of it. He prayed silently, not for the brother whom he knew to be in glory, but *to* him, asking for his help and support in his lonely pilgrimage. He had his friends, especially Peter and Neville, but this realisation brought little comfort. He had no-one to love and treasure him; no-one to whom he was as the breath of life. The sacrifice of celibacy had a cruel harshness about it which came home to him with peculiar force at that moment. He longed for the comfort of arms about him, and knew that such comfort was for ever denied to him. With a sigh, he turned away and followed the others back through the garden to the monastery, where the pale substitutes of food and drink, laughter and the comradeship of the Order awaited him.

The experience served, however, to deepen the longing he felt for the human love and warmth he knew with his family. He communicated with them with a new assiduity, writing weekly and waiting for their letters with impatient anxiety. Then an event occurred which he could never have foreseen, even in his wildest and most improbable dreams.

That spring, a momentous decision was made at the highest level to renovate and extend the Seminary. The father Superior announced it at lunch one day, and informed the community that the father Provincial would be visiting in a few days to explain the proposals more fully. The high power delegation arrived as expected; the father Provincial and his assistant, the provincial bursar and an American gentleman in a very smart suit.

The Provincial explained to the assembled community that for years the students had had to make do with cramped quarters in dilapidated buildings, but now was the time to build for the future. Vocations, he claimed, were at an all-time high, and so the way ahead seemed most promising. The old students' wing would be demolished, and a smart, modern block would replace it, architecturally in tune with the old country mansion to which it was being joined. Of course expense would be a grievous burden, but a fund-raising campaign would be launched to meet this. The American gentleman, apparently, had been drafted in for this purpose. He was the representative of a high-powered American company which specialised in organising fund-raising for Charities.

Without more ado, he was introduced and before long he held the brethren spellbound with his eloquence. There was to be a massive campaign in each of the parishes run by the Order, with families being asked to commit themselves to fixed sum pledges, with the promise of a permanent memorial in the new building. Carefully chosen students would support the effort, their youthful yet manly appeal being used to back up the honeyed words of the American chrysologos. They would be on hand to encourage the faithful to sign their pledges. Also, it was proposed that the students be allowed home to spread the fund-raising among their own families.

"Bloody hell" whispered Peter to Mark, "it's an expensive ticket for a holiday, but I'm going if I can."

"Me too" whispered back his companion, and so it was that a few weeks later, most of the students in turn visited their families for a few days, any consideration of the ascetical need to eschew the world and its pomps set aside for the greater good.

Mark and his family were overwhelmed with excitement; a holiday at home after all these years. It was like Moses gaining his first glimpse of the Promised Land.

The train journey was an experience in itself. When he had last travelled on a train, the day he first came to St Augustine's, the journey had been made by steam train. Technical revolutions of immense significance had occurred in the meantime in the outside world, and now the all-pervading smell of diesel oil filled the stations, and the trains were pulled by throbbing, drumming monsters that with sleek and menacing grace crept slowly along the platforms, the yammer yammer of their immense engines telling of power that could quickly increase the speed of the hurtling trains to well over a hundred miles an hour.

Mark took his place in the main line express, the fabric of the seat feeling hard and scratchy compared with the softer plush of yesterday. The carriage was open plan, too; four seats to a table instead of the old, familiar compartments. He preferred this, as paradoxically he felt it gave him more privacy. He was much less likely to be buttonholed by some fanatic, attracted by his Roman collar, than he would have been in a compartment. He none the less felt vulnerable, as though the eyes of the world were on him, mocking his faith and all that he and his isolated world stood for. He had brought a book with him, and felt safer with his nose stuck in it, ignoring any curious glances his clerical state might attract. But the interest of the journey ensured that his morbid shyness did not last too long; also, the growing excitement of the anticipated reunion with his family meant that his mind soon threw off any last traces of gloom.

The time soon passed, the train rapidly crossing off the cities and towns on its way; Birmingham New Street, Burton, Derby,

Sheffield, York. The local train was soon whisking him efficiently on the last leg of his journey, the main line express having dropped him on time. Then with a raucous hoot like a braying donkey (or a big butch Avon lady, as Peter would have put it) the two carriage push and pull shuffled busily into the station of his home town.

With beating heart, he eagerly leant out of the window, his nose sniffing appreciatively at his native air, his eyes searching frantically along the platform. He suddenly spotted his mother and Tony, and waved excitedly.

The train juddered to a halt, and throwing open the door, he lugged his suitcase onto the platform.

"Oh, Mark," his mother hugged him.

"Hi, Mum" he greeted her shyly.

Tony picked up his case, and with a lopsided grin, said "Welcome back to the old home town, big brother."

Mark felt as though positions were reversed, and Tony was the big brother; he seemed so mature and confident, while he was opening his eyes to a new, strange world, very different from the world he had left behind six years previously.

They passed through the barrier, and soon reached the family car, a Morris Minor shooting brake that was showing signs of age, but was still sturdy and reliable. His mother climbed into the back seat, while Tony took his place in the driving seat, Mark beside him.

"Passed my test a couple of months ago" he announced proudly, and soon had the car weaving in and out of the busy town traffic as though he had been driving all his life. Mark marvelled at it all, and sat back, drinking it all in. Once home, his mother soon had a meal ready, and the family hungrily set to.

"So they've let you out when money's at stake" commented Tony, to be chided by his mother, who told him that Mark was home, and that was all that mattered.

The next couple of days passed with a dreamlike quality that almost blended into unreality. Tony was on holiday from college, and he and Mark wandered round their childhood haunts together reliving the past. The local shops had changed; the counter service grocers were now little supermarkets, though the hardware shop where they had bought wood and nails to make cages for rabbits and white mice years ago seemed much the same. Tony took Mark to the pub in the evening, his clerical collar forsaken for a convenient polo neck sweater, borrowed for the occasion. Mark bought a provisional driving licence and had his first tentative lessons in driving from his younger brother.

They managed a quick visit to Brenda, a wife of only three months in her new home, a small, modern terrace house on one of the town's new estates. That little house was her pride and joy; though the furnishings were all second hand, she was making a very creditable effort at setting up a home for herself and Bill, already well and truly under the thumb, as Brenda was a capable and determined young woman. Having been an elder sister to two younger brothers, keeping a man in his place was second nature to her, and Tony only dared laugh when safely alone again with Mark.

But the idyllic days were soon over, and Mark returned to St Augustine's with a sorrowful heart, and a pledge for two hundred pounds tucked safely in his pocket.

Peter's trip home was less successful, at least from the financial point of view. On his return, Mark was regaled with the story of his visit, which consisted mainly of nights of drinking and days of sleeping it off. However, he had departed with travelling expenses of ten pounds, and he returned with seventeen pounds eight and tuppence, so the visit was reckoned to be not quite a total disaster.

THIRTY SEVEN

The weeks and months were slipping by with increasing rapidity, and Ordination began to loom on the horizon. First a year away, as the class immediately senior to them received Orders and departed, then it was only a matter of a few months. Peter nervously wondered if there would be any hold-up, but the superiors appeared to have overcome any final reservations, and the path ahead seemed clear.

"We'll have to be choosing Ordination cards soon, Mark" he observed one day as they laboured away in the printing shop on a vocations newsletter that they printed and distributed round the group of boys and young men who hoped to enter the Order one day.

"What have you got in mind?" asked Mark.

"Oh, I think I'll stick to the Sacred Heart and Our Lady of Lourdes" answered Peter. "I suppose you'll be going all airy-fairy with those things Winterton-Smith used a couple of years ago; or maybe you'll choose St Patrick's bra strap?"

This was the irreverent name given to the old Irish prayer, known as St Patrick's breastplate, by Peter when trying to be facetious about tastes other than his own. Mark laughed.

"Yes, I've been thinking about a good text like that, or maybe St Francis' prayer about seeking to love rather than be loved."

"Why not Lacordaire on the priesthood?" replied Peter.

This was another perennial favourite, and spoke of a heart of bronze for chastity, and a heart of flesh for charity. It ended: "My God, what a life - and it is yours, O priest of Jesus Christ." It was a quotation more abused than used, especially when the students were feeling a little depressed about their future prospects. Mark dug his friend in the ribs.

"That would suit you down to the ground; I dare you to use it as your text."

The banter to and fro continued, but Mark realised how near Ordination now was. Six months was a matter of twenty six weeks; it seemed much nearer when it was expressed that way. A sense of awe and excitement began to dawn on the Ordination year. They began to celebrate 'dry' Masses, which involved taking over an altar in a remote side chapel, and using all the necessary equipment, chalice, paten, corporal and so on, the student would run through the liturgy, practising the gestures until the whole performance could be gone through without awkwardness or hesitation. Occasionally a helpful critic would point out areas of improvement, and the Prefect of students finally gave the performance his seal of approval, pronouncing the candidate ready to say Mass when the time came.

As the time grew shorter, preparations of all kinds intensified. There were the ordinary details of accommodation for family and friends to be arranged, invitations to be sent out, Ordination cards to be printed, celebrations to be organised.

Mentally and emotionally, a sense of calm came over Mark. In the early stages he had panicked slightly, as he looked ahead and saw the years stretching before him, years of grinding servitude in an apostolate that he found no more appealing in spite of the pastoral experience he was gaining in his catechetical efforts. He harshly chided himself for what he saw as his own cowardice; he appreciated the need of the Church for priests, and like the reluctant prophet Jeremiah, he was prepared to offer himself. If Christian living was not about laying down ones life with Christ on the cross so as to rise again to newness of life with him, then he had misunderstood the whole gist of the Message.

It never occurred to him to question or doubt his vocation; In his heart he knew that this was his calling; he did not 'want' to be a priest in a sense; he often wondered what 'want' meant in the context of a priestly vocation. How could you 'want' to be a priest in a similar way to that in which a person might want the fulfilment of any other goal in life? Perhaps some people did want to be priests in the same way as others wanted to be bus drivers, but this was not how he saw his choice of the priesthood. The biblical 'You have not chosen me, but I have chosen you' summed up his feelings on the question of vocation. He found little that was naturally attractive about the life. When a man was answering a call, what he wanted or did not want seemed hardly relevant. Thus it was that as the day of Ordination drew nearer, Mark was calm and accepted the destiny that lay before him.

Peter was looking forward eagerly to the day as it approached. His journey had been stormy, with many risks of shipwreck on the way. Even now he had his enemies who would baulk him of his goal, but as he had progressed so far, and there seemed to be no good reason to dismiss him, solid grounds for delay or rejection were wanting. It was not so much that the superiors wished to advance him; more a question of their not being able to conscientiously reject him. Mark's doubts about Peter's suitability had more or less evaporated, as Peter was just about coping adequately with the studies, and his pastoral experience was at least as successful as Mark's, if not more so. Peter did not introspectively scrutinise his own motives as did Mark; 'staring at your own belly button' was how he described this activity. His aims were simple, his needs obvious and direct; he wanted to be a priest, and never questioned the why's and wherefore's of this desire. He enjoyed the good things of life as and when they were available, and made sure he got his fair share of them, poverty and obedience notwithstanding. He accepted the ideal of perfect chastity, but lost no sleep over the occasional lapse, or 'wank', as he would crudely put it. Sin and grace were black and white; if he masturbated he sinned, and so went off to confession without worrying unduly about it. Mark had never masturbated, but in his attempts to remain pure, had agonised occasionally over thoughts, glances and desires, and his degree of culpability in them. He also still struggled against what he saw as his darker desires, which while normally quiescent, would occasionally rise to the surface like bubbles of poisonous gas in an otherwise serene lake.

Peter, unlike Mark, quite enjoyed the prospect of pastoral work. His preaching ability was first-rate, and though his material might be very much of the old school, he had a basic and direct approach which would probably appeal to the ordinary people when once he commenced his preaching career. However, their pastoral abilities would soon now be put to the test more fully than the catechesis of the local children demanded.

David had spent his career in St Augustine's in almost complete isolation from the ordinary life of the seminary and the other students; he unburdened his soul to no-one, except in part to his confessor. His ideals of perfection still demanded of him that he reject anything that gave him pleasure of any kind, and he still scrupulously confessed any lapses against his draconian code. In vain did his confessor attempt to change his attitudes, but in these last few months before Ordination a doubt began to arise in David's mind about his vocation. His conscience clung stubbornly to the conviction that the path he had chosen was the one way to holiness, but he felt the burden of sin on his shoulders, reinforced by the inevitable slight lapses from his terrible ideal. He felt unclean, unfit to be a priest. Perhaps he ought to pass the rest of his life in humble obscurity, devoted to prayer and penance in an attempt to expiate his guilt.

"No, brother" his confessor had insisted. "You have a vocation to the priesthood; God and the Church are calling you to a life of service. Of course it is a great dignity, but think of St Peter who was called to be Pope, even after denying his Master. No-one is worthy of the priesthood; we just thank God that he chooses us in spite of our sinfulness and unworthiness. But your way of life is too extreme; it produces obsessions about the danger of sin. You see sin or the danger of it in anything and everything. It isn't healthy."

But David could not accept the reassurance, and still his torment continued. He felt utterly unworthy of the approaching priesthood, and would have drawn back with a terrified 'Domine, non sum dignus.' He lashed himself until the blood flowed, trying vainly to purge the all-pervading sense of sin that he felt, and it was only his confessor's patience and encouragement that helped him to face the day as it drew inexorably closer.

Ken, like Peter, had no doubts or hesitations. His path through St Augustine's had been relatively smooth, with no major hurdles or stumbling blocks. The way of life suited him, with its routine which permitted steady work and a regular, if not too demanding, regime of prayer and spiritual exercises. Of course, Ken had his temptations as did the next man, but they were simply a part of a regular, mature outlook on life. He had absorbed certain aspects of the newer approach in theology and liturgy, but somehow the excitement of it all left him largely unaffected. As he saw it, the Church had progressed serenely on for two thousand years and would continue on for another two thousand, or until the Second Coming of Christ, whichever came first. His pastoral experience had been marked by a similarly calm approach; his presentation of the Faith to the normally turbulent teenagers had been competent without being exciting; though he had few behavioural problems with them, the young people responding automatically to the air of authority which emanated from him. His fellow students had summed it up with the nickname 'Rocky' and his superiors tended to agree; they foresaw a career that would be spent in the mainstream of the Order, hardly hitting the headlines, but providing the bread and butter type of loyal and dependable service that made the Order a stable force in the Church.

So the last few weeks passed, and the four young men faced the approaching day, each in his own way making his final preparations. A large number of guests would be coming; friends and relations they had not seen since entering the Novitiate several years earlier. Numbers were limited by the size of the church, but each was allowed thirty or so. The proud families easily made up these numbers, uncles and aunts, cousins, old school friends and neighbours all eager to come and share the big day.

Peter and Mark, ably assisted by one of the younger students to whom they had been passing on the mysteries of printing, just as they had been initiated in their earlier days, had completed the Ordination cards and the invitations, which had been duly dispatched.

A week before the date, the four went into retreat, a time of reflection and prayer, and the final material preparations were then left to others. For Mark, they were days of relaxation and calmness, the freedom from the ordinary routine of St Augustine's imparting a strange sense of isolation. Their meals were served apart from the others, and they ate in silence, while the main body of the community carried on as normal, their conversation a babble of noise which merely seemed to emphasise the silence surrounding the ordinands.

Mark spent such of his time going for long, solitary walks, and found that he was growing to like this hitherto not much used form of activity, enjoyable as it was to body, mind and spirit alike. It tended to give him gentle exercise, while allowing the mind to roam freely, an occupation congenial enough to his introspective nature. At Peter's prompting, he allowed himself an occasional stroll with his friend in secluded areas at the far end of the garden. The two of them walked among the tangled undergrowth of overgrown rhododendrons and ornamental yews, which had long since outstripped the cramped confines inflicted on them in the last century by the estate gardeners. Wood pigeons cooed in the tall, dark evergreen trees, and rabbits and squirrels fled silently at their approach.

"Almost journey's end, or journey's beginning, depending on your point of view." Peter inhaled deeply, drawing the smoke from a newly lighted cigarette into his lungs.

"It's been a long haul," mused Mark, his mind going back nearly fourteen years to the call of the missioner who had invited the small boy to follow his vocation. "I sometimes wonder what would have happened if that priest had been late for his supper, and so had missed our house out that day."

He explained the origins of his vocation to Peter, who laughed.

"You might have been an up and coming young doctor or solicitor, with a beautiful wife and two children, or then again, perhaps a navvy with a nagging shrew, who drove you out to the pub every night."

Mark sighed. "It's daft to think of might have beens; God has called and directed us in this way, and so tomorrow we will become his priests."

"My God, what a life" quoted Peter. "But life is what you make it," he added. "I know God gives us vocations and all that, but there's a hell of a lot of the individual concerned, too. It reminds me of the old story of the elderly man with the beautiful garden. The vicar, passing one day, said 'that's a beautiful piece of work you and the Lord have produced between you', to which the old man replied: 'You should have seen it when the Lord had it to himself'. I sometimes wonder if I'm here at the door of the priesthood because of God or in spite of him. It's been a bloody hard fight, with them buggers in charge fighting a rearguard action all the way." He paused. "But I've shown 'em" he added modestly, and Mark gave him a friendly nudge.

"I'm glad you did, Pete. I'd have given up the struggle in your place, I think."

"No stamina, that's you" laughed Peter. "Still, we'll give them a run for their money between us. Come on, kid, let's get back to the house, we'll miss supper."

The two walked slowly back towards the college buildings, which were silhouetted against the evening sky, the setting sun making them appear as a menacing dark mass against the rich variety of shades of yellow, gold, crimson and purple, an evening sky which at least as far as the weather was concerned, boded well for the morrow.

Book Two

THIRTY EIGHT

The Ordination was over. The rest of the day passed in a whirl. Trying to remember it all later, Mark had confused memories of imparting his first blessing to the Bishop, community, family and friends, and everyone else's' family and friends, then posing for photographs, hugging his family, and enjoying the celebration with them.

The young priests had started to recite the Divine office as deacons; this was the obligatory prayer of the Church, consisting of Matins and Lauds, the little hours, Vespers and Compline. Somehow this went by the board in all the confusion and the ordinands were packed off to bed at a reasonably early hour so as to be ready for their first Masses the next day.

Peter's was arranged for eight o'clock, with Mark's following at about nine. He was up in good time for Peter's Mass, and knelt as the new priest proudly enacted the age-old rites of the Church for the first time. Peter looked absurdly young in the ornamental white and gold vestments, but his Mass, a votive Mass in honour of Our Lady, went without a hitch. Mark remembered Peter's irreverent comments about the father Provincial on the occasion of their profession years ago, and smiled wryly to himself.

"Your turn next, kid," Peter murmured to Mark as he unvested in the sacristy later.

Mark chose green vestments, the ferial colour, as he wanted to see his Mass as the Church's worship rather than his own private devotion, a move which caused the raising of a few eyebrows as most newly ordained priests chose one or other of the votive Masses which could be freely chosen when the liturgy did not stipulate some special feast.

The family were kneeling in the front row, eyes alight with pride as Mark processed onto the altar for the first time. The liturgy was in a transitional state, some parts in Latin, some in English, and Mark too started his celebration faultlessly. The linen on the altar was of purest white, the polished silver and gold of the sacred vessels glinted richly yet austerely, the ruby colour of the wine in the gold of the chalice, the smell of the beeswax candles as they burned, all served to embellish what was for the young priest a deeply satisfying experience, both spiritually and emotionally. As the ceremony progressed, Mark found that his hours of practice stood him in good stead, and he did not have to think too hard about the mechanical details. His mind was free to concentrate on the meaning of the mysteries in which he was involved.

Closing his eyes for a moment, he was in the room of the Last Supper, then the garden of Gethsemane, and as he extended his arms in prayer, the words of consecration pronounced over the bread and wine for the first time, he was one with his crucified Lord in the once for all sacrifice that reconciled man with God. Raising the gifts of Christ's Body and Blood, the Son of God incarnate lifted up in death and resurrection, he prayed 'through him, with him and in him, in the unity of the Holy Spirit, all honour and glory are yours, heavenly Father, for ever and ever'.

In this celebration, he thought, the Son of God incarnate, the head of the human race, goes back to his Father through death and Resurrection, and we, mankind in every age, are part of that gift to the Father through the Mass in which we share. This is the meaning of the great Christian mysteries, Incarnation, Death and Resurrection, and this is how man shares in them. At that moment, he realised that in faith, he and his fellow worshippers stood in Heaven before the throne of God, engaged in the worship that summed up the whole meaning of existence. He resolved to try and dedicate his life and work to the ideal of sharing this vision, the practical details of how it was to be done far from his mind at that moment.

This resolve was strengthened through his union with his Lord in Holy Communion, an experience shared with his family as one by one, they received the body of Christ from his hands. Pausing afterwards before completing the ceremony, he pondered on all these things and asked God to bless his future ministry. A little restive shuffling among the congregation finally brought him back to an awareness of his surroundings, and he rose and finished the Mass.

"I thought you'd fallen asleep" remarked Peter afterwards, but Mark merely smiled, still immersed in his spiritual world. But he soon came down to earth; breakfast had to be organised for his guests, and then it was off for a week's holiday with his family.

After the brief meal, he waved goodbye to Peter and his family who were travelling north to Manchester by train, and then he climbed into the car with Brenda, Tony and his mother to begin his own journey home.

THIRTY NINE

"Hey, Mark, come on; the appointments are out".

Peter's knock on the door had Mark hastily scrambling to join his friend as they hurried to the notice board to discover their fate. The father Provincial was in residence at St Augustine's, having come for the final examinations which had taken place the day before. Mark, Peter, David and Ken had all faced the orals board in turn, being questioned by the examiners on their knowledge of Moral Theology and its application in the confessional. They had been priests for two months or more, but had still to receive the final accolade, the permission to hear confessions. All had come through successfully; Peter had caused the raising of the odd eyebrow, but his knowledge had been deemed sufficient, and so his academic career had somehow managed to reach a successful conclusion.

Now they would be discovering what lay in store for them in the larger, though still clerical world outside St. Augustine's. Mark's heart was pounding through nervousness as they hurried along the corridors. He knew that an appointment to Rome for further studies was a possibility, but no more than that. Breathless, and with sweating palms, the two joined the little group gathered round the notice board. Peter stared intently, then gave a delighted shout.

"Orf to Landon, innoi? he exclaimed in a mock cockney accent. "You're off to Rome, brain box. Serves you right!"

Mark sighed his relief to himself. At least he wouldn't be thrown in at the deep end, straight into pastoral work. Peter was still prancing about in his excitement.

"It's the best possible appointment" he enthused. "London; that'll be fabulous." The currently popular expression of enthusiasm fell naturally from his lips. Mark smiled at his friend's excitement.

"You'll be able to see Carnaby Street and all the dolly birds in their miniskirts."

Peter's appointment was to a busy London parish, situated north of the river, though not too distant from the Provincial house, which lay across the city to the south. Perhaps it was felt that he should make his pastoral debut well and truly under the eyes of the authorities. It was a challenging appointment and would give the young priest plenty of experience in all areas of pastoral work.

David was to join a different community in the midlands, where his time would be shared between parish work and preaching missions.

Ken was for the north, again to a community with a mixed apostolate. So the four would soon be widely scattered, each to a different community.

Meanwhile, the last few days of their time at St Augustine's slowly passed, and on the eve of their departure, there was to be held one of the traditional celebrations, or 'gaudiosa'. The home brewing tradition still flourished, though more recently, the celebrations had also been fuelled by crates of bottled beer. After supper, willing hands helped carry up the necessary bottles and glasses, and the party was soon under way as the corks popped and the bottle openers were busily plied, releasing golden streams of the frothing beverage into the eagerly held out glasses of the revellers.

During their final year at St Augustine's, Ken had served as head student, a post he held with discretion and moderation, as he transmitted the authorities' ukases to the student body and in turn, presented their views and desires. Now he handed over the reins of authority to his successor in the year below, and the new Capo, as he was called, asked for silence and proceeded to toast the departing foursome. He wished them good luck and God speed in their appointments, and as he raised his glass, cries of "speech, speech" filled the room.

Traditionally, each departing new priest spoke a few words, so Ken obligingly rose to his feet, and a silence quickly fell over the assembly, some of the noisier brethren being hastily shushed by their companions.

"St Augustine's is a great place" he commenced, to be greeted by groans and laughs. "No, seriously, it has been home for the last six years; a home is where a family lives, and I have appreciated the family who have made life here what it is. There have been ups and downs of course, but in all families, it is the mutual support that counts, and that is what I have always experienced here. Cherish that spirit; it's your most valuable asset here."

He then thanked them all, and sat down to cheers and claps. David was prised out of his shell next, and rose reluctantly to add a few quiet, conventional words which were politely applauded.

It was Mark's turn now, and rising to his feet. he took a quick sip of his drink. Already, the smoke from thirty or so cigarettes was swirling around in the atmosphere, and the student body gazed at him expectantly.

"I know none of you will believe me" he started, "but my years here at St Augustine's have been among the happiest of my life." Ironic cheers broke out, and a few shouts of 'it's all right for you, you're getting out.' "Seriously, like Ken, I have known a real family here, with a spirit that's second to none. This is an asset which is priceless. We received it from our predecessors, and we pass it on to you, more or less intact, I hope. Of course life here is sometimes difficult, even boring (more cheers) but I'm proud to be a member of this family. I won't walk out of here and forget you, and I'm sure the others feel the same. We're going out now to begin our apostolates or to study further, but I'm sure that anything we learn or achieve later on will be learned or achieved only on the foundations we've established here. Thank you, St Augustine's, and thank you, our family."

He raised his glass in salute, drank briefly and sat down, while the noisy listeners, already well plied with strong drink, cheered and called for Peter to add his word or two. Nothing loth, he rose to his feet and immediately contradicted Mark's effort.

"I'll be frank" he started. "I'll be bloody glad to get out of here. Oh, I agree with Mark about the family feeling, but Oggies is a necessary evil as far as I'm concerned. We put up with evil so that good may follow. The end justifies the means, and all that," he continued, slightly confusing his moral principles. "But my advice to you all is this."

Mark wondered what was going to come next.

"Grit your teeth, keep your head down, and stick it out until the date for your release is set. There'll be no time off for good behaviour, but the day will come. It has for us," he smiled smugly. "For the rest," he continued, "if you come face to face with a situation that seems impossible, remember that Clark survived worse. And he did it by giving it one with his knee in the right place, before it could get its hands round his throat. That's the secret of a happy and successful life, as far as I'm concerned."

So saying, he raised his glass, shouted "up the system," a Delphic toast which could mean anything to any hearer, and downed the contents. The students always appreciated Peter's asides, so his speech was applauded long and loud.

Lighting another cigarette, he turned to Mark. "That's that, then, duty done."

"They seemed to like your speech, Pete".

"It's what they want to hear. There's probably more of them with my way of looking at Oggies than yours. It's not a bad place in some ways; we've known some good times here, I'll admit that, but we are grown men when all's said and done, or at least people of our age in the outside world are grown men. You've got to admit they treat us a bit like kids in a boarding school sometimes."

Mark thought about it for a few moments, and ruefully admitted,

"I suppose you're right in some ways. I've must confess I feel far from ready to meet the challenges ahead of us. I've some growing up to do, I know that. But don't overlook the good points; a monastery is supposed to be a haven of peace in a troubled world, a place where you can have a chance to establish a relationship with God. Our Order is supposed to be contemplative as well as active; that side is reasonably well catered for. And the studies here are starting to get a bit more up to date. They're moving in the right direction there, sending me to Rome" he added with mock modesty.

Peter laughed. "Well, you can keep it as far as I'm concerned. You won't see me back here in a hurry. There are bods in the Province at large who haven't been back here since they left, twenty or thirty years ago. Someone once told me that one or two make a point of it."

The atmosphere was getting thicker as the evening progressed, the billowing clouds from the hurriedly smoked cigarettes made the eyes smart and burned the tongue.

"Come on, Pete, let's get a breath of fresh air" suggested Mark. Peter good naturedly gave way, and the two left the common room and were soon walking in the warm, evening air.

"That's better. I can't stand those fuggy atmospheres."

"I like 'em" Peter replied. "Good, healthy smoke. I'm sure it must kill off a lot of germs. Nicotine is used horticulturally to get rid of nasty pests."

"Maybe you should avoid it, then."

"Cheeky bugger. Smoking's done me no harm, so I can't be that bad." The banter continued for a few moments, then Mark sighed.

"It's the end of an era, Pete. We've been sitting next to one another in the Order's refectories for the past thirteen years or so now. It's a long time, and you get to know someone pretty well in that time. I'm going to miss you, my old friend."

They walked in silence for a few moments, then Peter said a little gruffly:

"Yeah, they've been good times. Thanks, Mark, I owe you a lot. Especially the last few years here in St Augustine's. I'd never have got through those studies without your help. People often think I'm a thick skinned bastard, but I'm as soft as shit, really."

Mark laughed at Peter's graphic expressions.

"Well, you've certainly lived up to your name and been a rock as far as I'm concerned. It's good to have a friend with that streak of toughness that can be relied on. I'm the one who's a coward at heart and needs encouragement and support. You've always given me that, Pete."

The discussion was threatening to turn a little maudlin, and a touch of banter lightened it again. It was nearly dark now, and in the deep blue of the sky overhead, the stars were emerging in the clear air. Mosquitoes and flies of the small, biting kind flew round them in clouds as they walked among the bushes and grassy paths. Peter hastily lit a cigarette in self-defence.

"I wonder what Rome will be like" Mark mused as they strolled on. In the distance the plaintive lowing of a cow calling for its calf could be heard, and Peter chuckled.

"You won't be hearing the sounds of the country, that's one thing for sure. Our lives are going to change with a bloody big bang. London, getting stuck into the apostolate, a lot more independence; you'll find the same, I'm sure. The blokes in Rome seem to have a marvellous time from all I've heard."

Mark thought for a moment.

"What do you feel about the prospect of pastoral work, Pete. Does it scare you at all?"

"Course not" Peter snorted. "What's there to be scared about? The job is pretty well cut and dried; there are things to be done, and lots of other bods about who can give you advice on how to do them, so there's no need to get into a flap about it."

Mark slapped at the clouds of buzzing insects.

"It'd have me crapping myself. Pete. What you say is true, I'm sure; I'm just so diffident about myself; maybe even unconvinced about the value of what we're supposed to be doing. Not of the priesthood itself, of course, but the way we live and work. What effect will what we do have on people? Will it make any difference to their lives?"

"You're like a dog with a bone; you keep worrying and chewing over these problems, Mark. Give it a chance! The Church has done O.K. for two thousand years so far; we're the strongest and biggest of the organised churches, and we can't be doing it *all* wrong. Priests do their job and run the parishes and a lot of people seem to get a hell of a lot of help from it all, so why be so negative about everything?"

Mark sighed. "You've got a point, I've got to admit. I know I'm a bit of a Jeremiah."

"More like a pissmire" Peter interjected, laughing.

"I don't know what it is" Mark continued, ignoring the interruption. "I know in theory what I'd like to do, to achieve; but making it a concrete reality sometimes seems impossible."

"Maybe it's a pity you're going to Rome, in a way" commented Peter. "Perhaps a good dose of the priesthood in action in the parishes and in missions would be the best thing in the world for you."

"You're probably right" Mark agreed ruefully, "But I can't say I'm sorry about being sent to Rome."

"Aye, well, it'll all come out in the wash" muttered Peter philosophically, and then added:

"Come on, let's get back and have another drink if there's any left".

So they retraced their steps through the darkening evening, the night scents of the garden sharp in their nostrils. Back in the common room, the party was still in full swing, so the two quickly obtained fresh supplies of bottled beer, lit fresh cigarettes, and proceeded to see out their last night together at St Augustine's in rousing style.

FORTY

The British European Airways Trident stood at the end of runway number one at Heathrow Airport waiting for permission to take off. With a dull whine, gradually rising to a high pitched roar, the three Rolls-Royce engines responded to the pilot's easing forward of the throttles, and then, like a greyhound unleashed, the jet leaped forward and began its rapidly accelerating takeoff run.

Mark peered through the small window, saw the red and silver wing vibrating slightly and the patched concrete and tarmac flashing past, then he felt the nose lift, and with a stomach churning leap, the plane was airborne. It climbed steeply, banked, and he saw the glint of sun on car windscreens far below. After a few minutes the warning lights forbidding smoking were switched off, and so lifting his plastic carrier with the duty-free cigarettes and whisky off the floor, he rummaged inside for a packet of cigarettes, lit one, and relaxed in the warmth and comfort, allowing himself to unwind, remembering the hectic few weeks he had spent since leaving St Augustine's.

He had spent some of the time at home, a week here and a fortnight there, but he had also been sent to a busy parish in the midlands to help out, allowing the regular staff to take some holidays. It had all been rather strange; the basic structures of the community life were similar, but he found it hard to settle into the routine. Somehow, he felt alien, very much an outsider in the group to which he had been temporarily attached.

But he had heard his first confessions, and found little problem there. He felt humble and privileged as he sat in the darkened cubicle, listening to the stories of human greed, weakness, stupidity and sheer goodness as they emerged from the hesitant penitents before him.

"Bless me, father, for I have sinned." That first Saturday evening he had arrived in the busy parish run by the Order in Birmingham, he had been thrust straight into the hurly-burly of parish life.

"Ah, father -"

"Kennedy" Mark had supplied.

"Yes, of course. Welcome to St Aelred's. You'll be hearing confessions tonight, starting in about three quarters of an hour."

No time for more than a quick wash and brush-up, a hasty cup of tea, and he was being shown into the church and the small, dark cubby-hole smelling rather strongly of sweat, and then no time for nerves, the first penitent was coming in.

"My God" he thought, aghast. "What am I going to do if I get some terrible problem straight off?"

But his first penitent was a middle-aged lady with nothing more serious to confess than gossiping about her neighbours. Mark gave her a little lecture on the need to appreciate people's good points, and asked her to pray for those she had gossiped about. Then a couple of children whose fingers had been in the biscuit tin without parental permission; the first hour passed remarkably quickly without too much in the way of major crime.

He heard sounds of activity in the church as the steady trickle came and went, and then the organ struck up; evening devotions had begun. The penitents petered out, and Mark peered through the curtain. The church was about half full, and the devotions were in full swing. He opened his breviary and hastily muttered his way through Matins and Lauds. He really must be more careful about the Office; he was getting into the habit of cramming it in at odd moments.

The main burden of the evening's confessions would come after devotions. The 'O Salutaris' and 'Tantum Ergo' came and went; the soft boom of the gong announced the blessing, accompanied by the 'ching-ching' of the thurible. The Divine Praises were followed by the 'Adoremus', and Mark knew the penitents would start coming again. The door on the penitents' side creaked, and Mark saw a glimmer of light and a hazy figure entering and kneeling.

"Father, can you help me?"

Mark's heart leaped as he realised this was something out of the ordinary. "Yes, that's fine" he whispered in what he hoped was an encouraging tone. "Just tell me in your own words what the problem is. How long is it since you've been to confession?"

"It must be five or six years, father, I'm not sure."

"Don't worry" Mark replied. "Now, what seems to be the problem?"

"I'm a married man, father" came back the reply. "Things are in a bad way at home between my wife and myself. It's this birth control thing. We've got five children, and we're at our wits' end. We just daren't have any more, but what are we to do? I'm frightened to touch my wife in case she gets pregnant again, and she's terrified of sex now. It's breaking me up. I've not been to confession because we've been using contraception. But I can't go on; either having sex and being in mortal sin, or being pure and abstinent."

Mark's mind wandered to the balloon-like objects one sometimes saw in the streets, especially in secluded spots where cars had parked the night before. The sight of them had occasionally fuelled his overactive imagination, and now he hastily banished such thoughts to concentrate on the problem unfolding before him. The penitent continued:

"What can we do? sometimes I've masturbated just to get relief; but how can we live and love normally? You've got to help us, father."

Mark took a deep breath and plunged in.

"What you must realise first and foremost is that God isn't a tyrant, scrutinising your every act, waiting to catch you out. He is a father, and he knows the problems we face, he wants you to love your wife and have a good, close, physical relationship with her. That's priority number one. Now children are important in a marriage; you've shown your appreciation of that; you've got five, after all. The Church is not against reasonable regulation of births; responsible parenthood, if you like. What she is against is the glorifying of sex for its own sake, out of the context of love, family, children. Keep your sex life in that context and you won't go far wrong."

It's getting to the nitty-gritty now, he thought. That's the general encouraging remarks over and done with.

"In practical terms" he continued, "make sure your relationship with your wife is basically sound; you can't live out your life in a state of sexual frustration. You have the right to a happy, contented life there. If using some sort of contraception is the only way you can achieve this, go ahead. Almighty God doesn't expect miracles of us; he simply sets ideals before us, and wants us to do our best to achieve them. The loving sexual relationship is the ideal here, not a sort of mechanical abstinence from using contraceptives. Certainly they aren't good things in themselves but they can be a necessary evil in a relationship, if you like."

He paused.

"You mean it's all right to use these things, father?"

Mark sighed. How could he put it?

"It isn't exactly 'all right', if you see what I mean. But if you try and look at your situation as objectively as you can, and then judge before God that it's the only way, go ahead, don't worry, you aren't sinning. Is that something you can accept?"

The penitent hesitated. Poor bugger, Mark thought. Up to now, the laity have looked to the clergy to tell them what to do, and then, like the six hundred riding into the valley of death, they have tried to do it. Getting them to adapt to a whole new way of sorting out their moral attitudes was going to be a hell of a job. But to Mark's relief, the penitent finally answered:

"I think I see what you mean, father. I'll try and look at things the way you've described them. Thanks for all your help."

Mark breathed deeply. Bloody hell, he'd be in bother if the Powers heard him giving this sort of advice.

"As a penance, buy your wife a little present to show you love her. Pray for yourselves, and me too."

He then gave absolution, and mopped his brow as the grateful penitent left the box.

The rest of the session passed without any other undue difficulty, and a tired Mark trudged along to the refectory to sup alone on the inevitable cold ham and tomato. However, there was a bottle of beer to wash it down, and so he managed to quite enjoy his supper. He joined the community ensconced in the common room for the Saturday evening football afterwards, but beyond the occasional nod or curious stare, his presence went largely unacknowledged. Not being a keen sports fan, he soon decided to retire to his room; there was tomorrow's sermon to brush up; his first 'for real'. He had worked briefly on it at home the previous evening, but much still needed to be done. The Epistle and Gospel readings suggested the topic of Christian witness, so he was soon deeply immersed in the why's and wherefore's of the best ways to approach what seemed to be for most people a big problem in their Christian living.

Eventually, he had the sermon worked out to his satisfaction, more or less. So he wearily climbed into bed, only then remembering that he had not finished his Office. He thought about getting out of bed and digging his breviary out of his suitcase to plough through it, but then reasoned that if the fulfilling of the obligation and that alone was his motive, it would probably do him more harm than good; he would be falling into the same trap from which he was trying to liberate his penitents. Besides, the obligation to Sunday Mass was dispensed for travellers; he had travelled from home that day, so he felt safe enough in considering himself to be in an analogous situation, and therefore free to snatch some precious sleep. It would be an early start in the morning; he had been appointed to the eight o'clock Mass, and would be expected to preach at a couple of the other Masses, too.

The bed was comfortable, and he soon drifted off, though his sleep was disturbed by nightmares in which he found himself on the verge of processing out for Mass completely naked, and then when finally vested after many frustrations, discovered he had completely forgotten his sermon.

Morning eventually came however, after a period of deep, dreamless sleep, and half past seven found the young priest busily engaged in his morning meditation in the community oratory, after a hurried recitation of Lauds for the day. The minutes ticked by, and at five to eight he made his way to the church, the elderly brother sacristan smiling a welcome as he approached the chest of drawers on which the vestments were laid out.

Mark produced the notes of his carefully prepared sermon, secure in the knowledge that he could always fall back on them if disaster struck; he then twirled the amice round his shoulders, tying it about his waist and tucking it in at the neck. Next, he donned the crisp white alb, and knotted the cincture round his waist. Stole and chasuble completed the vesting, and the altar boys meanwhile carried out the cruets of water and wine, and lit the candles. A brief moment of reflection, and then he picked up the chalice with its green cover matching his vestments, bowed to the crucifix, and the altar boys taking the cue, the little procession wound its way onto the high altar for the first Mass of the day.

The church was about three quarters full, the worshippers seeming only half awake. Mark began with a brisk sign of the cross, and Mass was under way. The introductory prayers, Kyrie, Gloria, collect; he was soon at the readings which he delivered in a clear if somewhat stilted voice; the tension was hard to bear, and tended to constrict his throat.

"This is the Gospel of the Lord." The congregation responded; the moment had arrived. He looked down from the pulpit over the scattered crowd before him; the mother with the fidgeting children in the front row; the old lady already nodding gently, though she had only just sat down. A man noisily clearing his throat so as not to have to cough during the sermon. A moment later, silence descended, and he tentatively began.

"Is 'Jesus Christ' anything more than a swear word for most of our fellow citizens? How real is he for us, come to that? Our faith teaches us that he is the centre of our lives, the most important factor in them, and yet how important, or how real is he to us? Wives, is he as important to you as your husbands; children, is he as important to you as your parents? We must be ruthlessly honest with ourselves here. Our faith tells us that he is, but when we say it, do we really mean it?"

"This brings us to the heart of the problem of faith. God reveals or gives himself to the world. He does this in his son, Jesus Christ. He gives Christ to us in many ways; Historically, he became man two thousand years ago. But is he any more real to us than any other man from about the same era, Julius Caesar, for example? He comes to us immediately and intimately in the sacraments, especially Holy Communion. But do we really find him there, vividly present under the appearances of bread and wine? Do we treat Holy Communion as very much more than the eating of a little bread, the drinking of a sip of wine?"

Mark was getting into his stride now, and continued with enthusiasm, fist clenched dramatically and eyes alight with enthusiasm for his theme.

"The answer to the problem lies in the words we heard in the Gospel: "As long as you did it to the least of my brethren, you did it to me." Christ comes to us in our fellow-men; so he comes to our fellow-men through us; so we must be the living presence of Christ in this twentieth century world in which we live."

He then went on to develop this theme, showing how the Christian must first receive Christ through faith, in Sacrament, Scripture, prayer and the witness of his brethren, and then full of the Spirit of

Christ, he could make the reality of Christ a reality for every other person he met. He had to realise that the way in which Christ had chosen to be present in this day and age was through him, the Christian.

"You are the living, breathing, loving presence of Christ in the world at this moment, in this place; but to what extent and how effectively Christ is present is up to you."

The minutes were ticking by, but Mark went on, finally realising that one or two of the congregation were becoming a little restless. He glanced at his watch, realised that he had been speaking for nearly twenty minutes, so he hurriedly wound up his remarks, and finished with the sign of the cross.

Well, that hadn't gone too badly, he felt, as the congregation took up the Creed, and then the responses to the bidding prayers. The preaching experience had been very different to the practice Mission sermons preached at St Augustine's. He felt it had been a reasonable first attempt, all in all. The brother sacristan confirmed this when he was unvesting afterwards, "though a little on the long side, father; normally the people are used to ten minutes on a Sunday."

The rest of his stay in Birmingham had been fairly uneventful. He felt like a stranger, even though he knew one or two of the community, including David, who had recently taken up his appointment there. After the warm and friendly atmosphere of St Augustine's, this was a little disconcerting. However, it was no skin off his nose, he felt, and was not sorry to take his departure when the time came.

"Drink Sir?"

Mark came to himself with a start as the stewardess smilingly repeated her question.

"Yes, please; whisky and soda" he replied, feeling very much the man of the world. A few minutes later, sipping the drink which in the pressurised cabin seemed to make him light headed, his thoughts returned once again to the recent past.

It was only yesterday that he had arrived in London, lugging his two big suitcases with him on the underground, then staggering from the station to the nearby parish community house where he had arranged to spend his last night in England. Sweating and feeling most uncomfortable, he fished in his pocket for his common key; most of the houses of the Order in Great Britain had front doors that opened to the same key; it was a very useful system, and Mark always felt it was a good symbol of the community life they shared. He opened the door, and carried the heavy cases into the porch. There on the wall was the notice board, giving a list of the members of the community. Last of all came 'Fr P. Clark', so obviously Peter was already in residence. Nobody was about, and so he mooched about the ground floor, in and out of the kitchen and refectory and common room until he came upon one of the brethren who found out for him which guest room had been allocated to him. He kindly gave Mark a hand with his luggage, and left the perspiring young man sitting on the edge of the bed, the counterpane crisp and clean beneath him, the wooden floor highly polished under his feet. Wearily he rose and washed, and feeling refreshed, checked the time. An hour before supper; he would go and see if he could find Peter. He paced the corridor, peering at the names on each door, but could find no sign of Peter's name. Climbing the stairs at the end of the corridor, he repeated the procedure on the upper floor, coming at length to the door bearing the legend 'Fr P. Clark.'

He knocked, and was relieved to hear the familiar tones calling out 'come in'. He opened the door and poked his head round. 'Hi there, pig face' he called.

"Bloody hell, Mark, come in, you old bugger. Nice to see you. What do you think of the old homestead?" he asked, proudly waving his hand, indicating the salient points which proclaimed the excellence of his abode. Mark strolled in, clapped his friend on the shoulder, and allowed himself to be impressed by the many features of which Peter was giving an enthusiastic description.

"Look at the view. You can see the garden, of course, and that's the centre of London in the distance."

"I suppose you can see the Houses of Parliament on a fine day" remarked his listener somewhat ironically. But he was pleased that Peter had apparently settled into his new community so well, and so he asked him how he was getting on.

"Fabulous, Mark; they're a funny old bunch of codgers, but by and large they're O.K. The nearest in age to me is about twenty years older than me. But they make me feel one of the team, so I've settled in pretty well. Of course, I miss having someone to talk to;

recreation is all reading the papers and watching the telly, but you're usually so tired that that's all you want to do anyway."

He then described his ordinary daily routine, which had Mark staring in amazement. He had the impression that the parish was a seething mass of people, living in the closely crowded streets making up the three or four square miles of which the parish consisted. Peter described the parish school in which he was involved, the hospitals to be visited, the hundred and one families with their many problems. The parish was in an area which had gone slightly to seed, and overcrowded, poor housing was very much a feature of the district. As Peter spoke, a new sense of respect began to dawn in Mark.

"My God, Pete, you've certainly been thrown in at the deep end; and you seem to be coping really well. I'd be absolutely lost, I know."

"Get away" scoffed Peter. "You'd be fine. There's nowt to it, really."

"Don't you ever feel that the sheer size of the task and the million problems that you face is just too much?" wondered Mark.

"No, you just say to yourself that there's so many hours in the day, and you give the required time to the job, and leave it at that. You're not a bloody miracle worker. I do my whack, and that's enough for me. And I'll tell you this, Mark; some of these old buggers here don't do that; the eat, drink and sleep brigade I call 'em. There's one or two who do damn all. They say Mass, hear confessions if they're on, and toddle out to take tea with their friends. And that's it. The school, hospital, youth club, etcetera etcetera get left to those willing to do the work. It's become an unwritten law that you just don't ask more than the minimum of some of them."

"Maybe the size of the job has just got them down" mused Mark. A slight depression came over him. "It must be a bloody discouraging job, trying to make some impact on a place like this."

"You won't change it, kid. It's just a question of keeping the system ticking over."

Mark had a mental picture of a large, fat, lazy animal that had to be fed by perspiring workers; contributing nothing, yet requiring the efforts of its enthralled slaves to keep it going. Was this the Church as she existed in the average parish?

"There's about five thousand plus Catholics in the parish, or that's as near a figure as anyone can give;" Peter continued, "there hasn't been a census of any sort since Adam was a lad. I've inherited visiting books that are years out of date. You go to a place and discover that the person you're looking for perhaps died seven or eight years ago. People whose grandad was a Catholic are still on the books; they maybe turn up for a wedding or a funeral and that's it."

He chuckled. "It wouldn't be a bad idea getting Occam's razor to work on these books" he added, remembering Mark's often quoted axiom from the distant days of philosophy.

Mark sighed. "I don't envy you, Pete. It'd drive me up the wall."

"Oh, I don't mind; as I say, I do my bit and that's it, take it or leave it. If you thought about it too much, you'd go bonkers, as you'd say. But there are consolations; you can sort out a problem for someone in the parlour or confessional, help someone to see the Church as something just a little bit more than an interfering busybody or bloody nuisance, and suddenly it all seems worth it. You've got to be thankful for small mercies."

"So you've settled in, and you're managing O.K." smiled Mark.

"Yeah, as I say, the community are fine, and I feel very much at home. The lazy sods who do nowt are O.K. to live with; it's just that they don't contribute very much."

It was nearly time for supper.

"That's meddy neatly dodged" Peter grinned. The rest of the community would be nearing the end of their evening meditation.

"Come on, let's get down, and we'll tag on to the others as they go into the ref. No-one will notice we weren't there. Afterwards we'll adjourn up here again; I think I can supply a bit of lubrication."

At this, they went downstairs and diplomatically slipped into the casual procession that wended its way into the refectory. Mark was formally welcomed by the superior, and talking was allowed. The meal, perhaps surprisingly, was not cold ham and a tomato, but macaroni cheese, and the generous portions were soon disposed of, bottled beer providing a welcome accompaniment to those who desired it. Afterwards, Peter told Mark to join the others in the common room, while he mysteriously disappeared. About twenty minutes later, he reappeared and gave Mark a summoning wink, and the two repaired once more to Peter's room.

"Whisky" he announced proudly, holding the bottle aloft.

"Don't tell me how you got it, I'd rather not know" grinned Mark. "Just pour me a drink."

Peter duly obliged, dispensing the whisky into two rather grubby tumblers, topping up the spirit with water from the cold tap in his hand basin. Moments later, they were sipping their drinks, and smoking a couple of cigarettes Mark had produced. Mark gave Peter an account of his own experiences since they had parted company on leaving St Augustine's, and his listener was soon enviously commenting on the amount of new-found freedom his friend seemed to enjoy.

"By gum, it's right what they say about you Roman geezers; two months and more doing bugger all, just enjoying yourselves farting about."

He was lying full length on his bed, head propped at a convenient angle for conversation and the consumption of whisky. Mark lounged in the battered armchair boasted of by Peter's abode, and laughingly protested that his summer hadn't all been dedicated to the pursuit of the pleasures of the flesh.

"I did that stint in Brum; not that it was anything like as tough as the routine you have here," he added conscientiously. Peter waved his empty glass in Mark's direction, and taking the hint, he recharged the tumblers with more of the whisky and water.

Settling down, they began to reminisce, recalling the days of long ago at St Saviour's, and their more recent shared experiences at St Augustine's. The night wore on; the bell for night prayers came and went, and the sounds of the brethren in the adjoining rooms retiring for the night prompted them to a considerate and diplomatic lowering of their voices.

Eventually, a sizeable dint having been made in the contents of the bottle, Mark stretched wearily and observed that he had better be getting a little sleep, or he would be shattered the following day.

"Right enough, kid" yawned Peter in sympathy. "I'd better show up for meditation tomorrow, or I'll be in the shit."

At the door, they whispered their final exchanges.

"If I don't see you in the morning, have a good journey. Keep in touch; you'd better, or I'll want to know the reason why."

"Course I will, Pete" whispered Mark. "Don't overdo it here; let me know how it's all going with you too."

"Go on, bugger off quick or we'll have the neighbours complaining." Mark smiled, and waving his hand in a gesture of farewell, tiptoed down the corridor, and after a slight hesitation, found his room.

Getting into bed was the work of an instant, and as he lay there, a sense of loneliness came over him. He would miss Pete, and the familiar things he had so long taken for granted. But the thrill and challenge of a new country and the sights and sounds of Rome in prospect soon reconciled him to the future; Neville too would be in Rome, so it wasn't as though he would know nobody out there. Feeling somewhat cheered, he soon fell asleep.

FORTY ONE

The pilot's voice over the intercom roused him once more, and he duly admired, thousands of feet below, the snow capped Alps and the wooded slopes and tiny villages. Lunch was served, and Mark enjoyed the plastic meal eaten from its plastic tray; he eagerly drank in all the new experiences as they presented themselves. But the flight was soon over; an hour and three quarters after takeoff, the descent to Fiumicino began, and as the aircraft dropped, the Italian countryside, baked brown by the summer heat, came into focus. He wondered what new experiences lay in store for him, but his reflections were cut short by the descent of the plane. The objects below rapidly grew in size as the aircraft lost height; the engine note changed and his heart missed a beat. Then with a sudden lurch and thud, they were on the ground once more, and the rapid deceleration as the pilot reversed thrust had Mark gripping the armrests of his seat. They taxied in and came to a halt. Mark joined in the general scramble as the passengers headed for the exit. Following the throng, he passed quickly through passport control, and then anxiously waited as the luggage appeared on the conveyor belts. He spotted his cases without difficulty, however, and soon found himself outside in the hot Italian sunshine.

Carefully avoiding the siren voices of the taxi drivers, he boarded one of the airport buses and relaxed, enjoying the journey along the dual carriageway that led to Rome. A sense of excitement grew as they neared the city, and he eagerly leaned forward, gazing out of the window, trying to spot any of the landmarks familiar from countless pictures and photographs. As they neared the centre, the noise grew gradually louder, the traffic more dense, until they seemed to be surrounded by a sea of snarling, hooting traffic, the grating of gears and the squealing of brakes competing with the fascination of the buildings and glimpses of the well known tourist attractions for his attention.

Eventually the bus came to rest, and within a couple of minutes, Mark stood on the pavement with his two cases and plastic carrier. A taxi driver offered his services, and Mark, remembering the advice he had received about using only 'official' taxis and even then being careful about the fare, smiled his tentative acceptance.

He gave the address of the Order's mother house, which would be his home for the next two or three years, and was immediately plunged back into the chaos of the Roman traffic. A ten minute journey brought them to the gates of a tall, grey Renaissance style building, graced here and there with statues of venerable saints and naked cherubs. It was tucked away down a small, winding street and Mark wondered how the driver could find such seemingly obscure places with such apparent ease.

He paid off his chauffeur who fortunately was honest, from his slim sheaf of Italian currency and hauled his heavy suitcases into the courtyard. Moments later, he was greeted by a well remembered voice:

"Mark, dear boy; a thousand welcomes."

Neville had emerged from a side door, and grasped his compatriot warmly by the hand.

"Good to see you, Neville; I didn't know when I'd be meeting up with you; they told me in London that as far as they knew, you were in Germany or somewhere."

"Just got in last night; couldn't have planned it better if I'd tried."

The courtyard was a large, airy place, even though it was surrounded on all sides by the gaunt grey walls of the building. All around the sides, citrus fruit trees grew in raised beds, with roses rioting over rustic trellis work. In the centre, a fountain played gently, its waters trickling softly into a deep pool, formed by huge curved stone slabs, ornately carved with now scarcely decipherable scenes. In the pool itself, water lilies graced the surface, and in its crystal clear depths, the vague shapes of huge golden and mottled fish could be discerned.

Leaving his suitcases where they stood, he gazed around in wonder; and then Neville took him on a brief conducted tour, pointing out the features of interest. Oranges, lemons, grapefruits, huge spiky aloes in ancient terra cotta pots, all in turn claimed Mark's fascinated attention.

"The fountain is exquisite" Neville commented; "it was presented to the monastery in the early sixteenth century by a lecherous nobleman making amends for his life of sin by pious donations. I believe the scenes round the pool represent various biblical incidents involving water, but I have never been able to decipher any of them."

The weather and the rough and tumble of the centuries had mellowed it to a miscellany of figures and shapes, obviously human, but more than that could not be discerned. The late afternoon sun slanted down, barely touching one corner of the courtyard, but the air was languorous and rich with many scents. Mark drank it all in greedily, feeling already at one with his surroundings. Neville eventually broke into his reveries with a smart dig in the ribs.

"Come on, Mark; you've all the time in the world to enjoy these delights. Let's ascend to the dizzy heights in search of your room, and then we might indulge in a cup of tea."

With these words, he led the way indoors, consulted a list in the porter's lodge, and then took Mark along to a rickety lift. The suitcases and their owner, together with his mentor made a full load, and pressing the button, Neville induced the creaky machinery to protestingly perform its office, raising them four stories to the floor on which Mark's room was situated. Feeling a sense of relief that they had arrived without mishap, Mark waited while Neville slid back the gates, and then emerged onto a wide, airy corridor. Moments later, they were at the door of the room which had been allotted to him.

On entering the austere looking chamber, Mark plonked his cases onto the bed, and then went to the window. He opened it wide, and then following Neville's instructions, wound a handle which raised a slatted wooden shutter. Immediately the muted rumble of the city was apparent, and he leaned out to survey the view. All he could see was the rooftops of the nearby buildings, a crazy jumble of sloping terra cotta pantiles and haphazardly added sheds and penthouses. Washing was festooned here and there, and the occasional potted plant, its leaves covered in dust, eked out a precarious existence at high altitude. In the street far below, he could see children playing, and a couple of mangy dogs sniffing at pieces of garbage. Every now and then, a car or small lorry would come smartly round the corner into view, hooting at dogs and children alike if they impeded its passage.

"My room overlooks the garden; it's on the floor below this. You must come down and we'll catch up on all the gossip. Meanwhile, permit me to leave you to your ablutions, dear boy."

Neville smiled and bowed slightly, and with brief instructions to Mark as to how to find his room, took his leave and told him to come down when he was ready.

Mark thanked him with a smile and cheery wave of the hand, and turned to his washbasin. He felt like a bath to remove the sticky grime that the journey seemed to have deposited on his person, but contented himself with stripping stark naked, and washing himself thoroughly in cold water, an experience which invigorated him. Quickly dressing in clean clothes, he left his room and found his way down to Neville's without undue difficulty. On knocking, he heard Neville call 'Venga', and correctly assumed that he was being invited to enter.

He opened the door to be greeted by the expected chaos that always seemed to surround Neville in his domestic arrangements, and carefully stepping round piles of books, free standing cupboards and the occasional discarded garment, joined his friend at the table by the window.

"Delighted to have you join our select company here in the eternal city" he murmured, indicating a rush seated chair onto which Mark perched himself. "Have a cigarette."

"No, have one of these." Mark hastily proffered his duty-free pack, and Neville exclaimed "Capital, dear boy", replacing his German cigarettes in a drawer against harder times.

"I rather think that you'll find Rome something of an Arcadia, if I may be permitted to coin a phrase."

Neville drew elegantly on his cigarette. "There is so much for the connoisseur to admire and appreciate. You must allow me to introduce you to the multifarious and manifold splendours of 'La bella città"

Mark smiled. Neville hadn't changed, at any rate.

"I'm dying to see so many of the places I've read about, especially the Forum and the Coliseum. St Peter's too, of course," he added hastily. "What are the studies like out here? I hope they won't be too difficult; it's all right for you, of course, with that high power intellect. We lesser mortals need to put in a lot of hard work on occasion."

Neville smiled modestly. "Even the most gifted of us need to cudgel the old cauliflower from time to time. But in general, you'll find the studies here in Rome what Marie Antoinette might have referred to as a morsel of gateau. The dear old Angelicum and Greg have been designed to cater for the dimmer sort of Latin who frequent them. The Anglo-Saxons generally patronise them too because the lesser demand they make in the academic sphere leaves one free to pursue the true education that Rome offers; her history and culture. Some keener types and the earnest Germans tend to flock to a newer upstart, the Anselmo, a Benedictine college for those with a hat size in excess of seven and three quarters. The lowest forms of life tend to emerge from beneath their stones to glean the meagre crumbs of learning that can be obtained from the Lateran university. And apart from specialist places like the Biblical institute and the Russicum, where the Eastern Uniate wallahs congregate, that just about sums up the educational scene here in Rome. Affiliated to the Lateran, by the way, but of considerably higher reputation, is the Alphonsian Academy, an establishment devoted to the study of Moral Theology. There, luminaries such as Häring dispense their wisdom."

Mark relaxed on the rickety chair and exhaled a cloud of smoke, aiming it at a particularly irritating fly that kept buzzing around.

"I've been told to sign on for the licentiate course in theology at the Angelicum."

"Capital, my dear chap. I did mine there; it's like falling off a log. I'm here for my final year, doing a doctoral thesis, so I don't attend any courses now."

"What's your thesis on?" asked Mark.

"Mediaeval English Spirituality; Julian of Norwich, the Cloud of Unknowing, Margery Kemp and all that sort of thing. Somewhat esoteric, I concede, but of considerable interest in the researching. What I am attempting to do is to establish and outline the spirituality of the times, though I have to be careful not to get bogged down in the mysticism aspects of it all. But my dear Mark, you must be parched. Let us adjourn downstairs for tea, and then perhaps we could potter along to one or two of the local places of interest."

They descended once more to the ground floor, and after a quick cup of tea made with those curious continental tea bags on the end of strings, emerged into the courtyard and then on through the gates into the street.

"Glorious place" said Neville, sniffing appreciatively. The multifarious smells of Italian cooking were beginning to percolate through the mild evening air. The sun had just set, and the light was beginning to fade. Neon lights flickered on in the little shops as they passed, Mark admiring the displays of smoked ham, various large and withered looking preserved sausages, and fascinating types of hitherto unknown fruits and vegetables.

"Carciofi; artichoke hearts; food of the gods" remarked Neville enthusiastically, indicating one of the items on display.

"Italian food is one of the loves of my life. You'll appreciate it, I know. Perhaps we'll treat ourselves to a pizza later, and give the monastery supper the go by."

They walked on for about a quarter of an hour, then suddenly emerged into a large square, the dominant feature of which was the Pantheon. Mark gazed in wide-eyed wonder as Neville described its history.

"Amazing to think that the Romans could build a mighty dome like that two thousand years ago" Mark commented in an awed tone as they strolled about inside, looking up at the huge vault overhead with its central aperture. The realisation that the enormous building had survived that time struck him forcibly, too. "It's amazing to think that it was there just after the time of Christ, much as it is today" he mused.

They strolled out once more into the Roman evening, Mark soaking in the atmosphere as they went. When it was almost dark, they reached the Trevi fountain, beautifully floodlit and bustling with people.

"A trifle vulgar, perhaps, but one of my favourite places in all Rome" Neville confessed.

The clear greenish tinted water seemed to refresh by its very sight, and Mark sat on the low wall beside it, his heart full and contented.

"Come on, let's get that pizza" smiled Neville.

They entered a nearby trattoria, and to Mark's astonishment, the proprietor greeted them with a cheerful 'Buona sera, professori', an obvious reference to their clerical status. They were not wearing clerical dress, and so Mark asked Neville how the proprietor knew that they were not ordinary tourists.

"Some sixth sense, dear boy. They can pick out a clerical student no matter what he's wearing; maybe we have all been marked with the sign of the Beast."

They were ushered to a table, and given menus. Neville explained the various items to Mark, adding descriptive comments to some of the items.

"Tortellini in brodo; small rings of pasta in soup. Some of the brethren refer to them as foreskins, but they are delicious. In the same vein, they refer to the thinly sliced dark smoked raw ham as 'scrotum'; descriptive titles, but they belie the quality of the food. Italian food is quite simply superb, as I think you will appreciate after some months here."

However, on this occasion they settled for a 'pizza capricciosa' and a carafe of the ice-cold dry white wine from the Frascati region. Mark ate hungrily, giving both food and drink his unstinting endorsement.

"Va bene, professori?" asked the proprietor, and Neville replied "Siamo molto contenti, grazie."

"Is Italian difficult to learn?" asked Mark.

"No, very straightforward; at least as regards basic conversational Italian. You'll soon pick it up. I'll give you a couple of books and any help you need; you'll be jabbering away like a native in no time."

"A native of the African jungle, maybe" laughed Mark.

The atmosphere was warm and friendly, and several Italian families were eating there. They nodded and smiled in the direction of the two students, though one man hissed 'questi preti' between his teeth.

"The Italians are a very friendly race, though there is more than a touch of anticlericalism in Rome especially. Strange to find it in the heart of the Church. Besides, less than ten percent of the Roman people go to Mass on Sundays; the men folk think that churchgoing is effeminate; something for the nonnas and the bambini."

It was a new insight for Mark, something which surprised him considerably.

"Familiarity breeds contempt, I suppose. They always used to say in St Augustine's that what the Church needs is a dose of persecution."

"Blood of the martyrs is the seed of Christians, and all that" said Neville. "Perhaps that's true, but I often feel that Christianity on a popular level at any rate is too woman centred; it appeals to women, that is, rather than men. Now Judaism and Islam are male-orientated religions. Perhaps much could be learned from them as regards the aspect of acceptability to men. How could we make Christianity a creed with which the ordinary man in the street could feel at home, and so to which he could commit himself?"

Mark murmured his agreement.

"Perhaps the answer lies in the 'new theology', he suggested. The Vision, he felt sure, if presented to people in preaching and discussion could inspire them to a new appreciation of Christianity. It had certainly revolutionised *his* life, in attitude if not in depth of religious practice.

"If only we could get across that Christianity is not just a creed, a list of beliefs, but a new way of life; a living experience of death and rebirth. People need something in the way of shock tactics to help them realise that baptism makes them Christ dying and rising again."

"There's a lot in what you say, dear boy" replied Neville thoughtfully, spearing the last of his pizza and inserting it into his mouth.

"I know it all depends on faith, a man's vision in the end" continued Mark, "but we've got to work out new ways of communicating it. The tired old methods of yesterday don't stir people."

"Yet one has to beware of simply instigating a facile enthusiasm; an emotional appeal based on the 'new theology' is not going to be radically more effective than the old emotional appeal of devotion to Our Lady or whatever."

"It's not just an emotional appeal" insisted Mark , "though an element of emotion must come in; Christianity is a rebirth of the whole man, not just his mind or soul. In fact the Scriptures keep on about a new heart and a new spirit. What's needed, I think, is a way of introducing people to a new way of life, inspired by the Vision, as I call it, or the view of faith which sees Christianity as a living experience of dying and rising again with Christ."

Neville drained his glass, and Mark, sensing that the meal was drawing to its close, followed suit. The wine was refreshing, yet curiously potent.

"You've certainly taken F.X. Durrwell to heart" smiled Neville, "and rightly so. Maybe I'm an intransigent cynic at heart, but I sometimes feel that getting the faith across to the ordinary man in the street is something of a losing battle. Maybe we'll always have to fall back on duty and obligation to ensure that people follow their faith."

Mark shuddered. "I hope not; and I'm sure that's not the lesson of history. Mediaeval man was deeply religions, and I'm told that the Italians today have a deeply religious cultural background. Perhaps what's needed is a way of making religion a part of the life of twentieth century man, as it was of that of the early Christians or people in the Middle Ages."

Neville sighed. "I agree with many of the points you are making, Mark, but remember that man in classical times, or mediaeval man, was not conspicuously superior to modern man in real goodness in the last analysis. Maybe that's the paradox of Christianity; though man is reborn into the Christian faith, he needs to continually undergo the same experience of rebirth throughout his life. No matter how good and holy his life, he is always man the sinner at the end of the day."

He signalled to the proprietor who was hovering nearby.

"Il conto, per favore."

Taking a couple of thousand lire notes from his wallet, he paid the bill, and then smiled at Mark.

"Come on, we'd best be heading for home. The gates are locked at half past nine, and we'll be in the cream of tomato if we find ourselves locked out for the night."

They left the trattoria and the evening air, still warm, felt fresh on Mark's face as they hurried through the streets back to the monastery which they reached a quarter of an hour before the gates were due to be locked.

Later in bed, he found it hard to sleep. It had been a full day, and his mind was racing. Rome promised to be an exhilarating experience; he was determined to make the most of it in every sense of the word. Several times he switched his light off and tried to sleep, only to switch it on again to read a couple more pages of a paperback he had brought with him from home to read on the plane. Eventually, a hundred pages and a few cigarettes later, he nodded off.

FORTY TWO

The sun was already high in the sky when he eventually awoke. Hurriedly rising and dressing, he went down to Neville's room.

"Slept in" he confessed with a grin on answering Neville's summons to enter.

"Don't worry. It's liberty hall here. No-one will check up if you miss meditation."

"I'll try and make it as a rule" Mark promised conscientiously, and then proceeded to ask Neville for directions to the Angelicum.

"I'll take you, dear boy. It's about time I visited the old Alma Mater to pay my respects. Just take a pew for a jiffy while I finish this letter."

Mark lit a cigarette and smoked while Neville busily finished his correspondence.

"I'm all yours" he smiled a few minutes later, and hastily stubbing his cigarette, Mark pronounced himself ready.

"We'll take in a couple of the local places of interest while we're out" announced Neville as they left the front gates. "But first, duty calls."

The city was full of bustling crowds, busily going about their business in the warm morning sunshine. Mark drank in the atmosphere as they went; the tall, slightly dilapidated buildings that could have been situated in any European city of any size; the bars with tables and plastic chairs outside; the posters advertising new and exotic products; the young men whistling at the pretty girls as they passed. It took them about twenty minutes to reach the Angelicum, and Mark entered the imposing complex of buildings with a slight feeling of trepidation. The sunshine brought out their rich, brown warmth, and so any nervousness was quickly dispelled by the pleasantness of the day, and the friendly reception given him by the Dominican in charge of enrolment.

The priest smiled, and with Neville acting as interpreter, quickly completed the necessary formalities. He then tapped the desk in an earnest manner, emphasising with the gesture a point that he was making verbally.

"Lectures begin tomorrow" Neville translated obligingly, "and he is telling you to make sure you attend faithfully and punctually. Some of the Latins have been known to sign on at the beginning of the course, and then turn up for the exams at the end. What they do in the meantime is anybody's guess."

As they left the university, Neville added: "The lectures are in Latin, of course, but that shouldn't present any problems. It is of the most basic kind; Cicero would be revolving in his grave like the armature of a dynamo if he could hear it. And so, my dear Mark, let us stroll in the direction of the Forum: a little classical culture would not go amiss on this splendidly sunny morning."

So the two strolled at a leisurely pace down to the Forum, and spent a happy hour pottering about among the noble remains, which Neville described to Mark in some detail.

"I think we shall have to forego the Coliseum today, or we shall miss lunch" he remarked after they had paused for an ice-cream at the gates of the Forum. "But 'morgen ist auch ein Tag', as our German brethren are wont to pronounce on occasions such as this."

The next few days were spent in sightseeing, and studying the rudiments of Italian, which Mark found he was picking up fairly quickly, as Neville had predicted.

One day, Neville took Mark to the bursar's office, where the Order's students were accustomed to draw money to meet the various expenses incurred during the course of their studies. They each drew ten thousand lire on the account of the English province.

"Books" murmured Neville as he filled in the necessary chit with details of the object for which the money was required.

"We shall be purchasing books, I have no doubt, by various authors, but of course Maldonatus will figure among them to some extent."

Maldonatus was a mediaeval writer, and certain portions of the money were always laid out in his name. None of the tomes purchased were in fact by him; the 'maldonatus' literally 'ill given' referred to the use of money for the very necessary element of recreation and relaxation for which they could scarcely draw official funds.

Later, they caught the bus over to St Peter's, and explored the vast basilica together. The sheer immensity of the place was overwhelming, and respect and admiration for the builders were feelings that accompanied the profound sense of being at the heart of the Church. They climbed to the top of the dome, and Mark's cheap plastic camera was soon clicking busily as he admired the panoramic view of the city, the Castel Sant' Angelo and the Tiber in the foreground, and various famous landmarks discernible in the distance, pointed out by Neville. Rome became a city of golden browns and terra cotta, the sky overhead turning from pale blue to white as the heat grew and midday approached.

Descending, they crossed the piazza and went to the Vatican post office, where Neville invested in the most recent collection of Vatican stamps, and Mark bought postcards and the stamps necessary to send them.

"We had better hurry or we'll miss the book shop" urged Neville, and so they hurried to the large shop at the top of the Via della Conciliazione. They browsed among the tomes printed in almost every conceivable language, Mark clicking his tongue and exclaiming at the prices as he translated the cover price of the 'Stag' books and realised that the price in Rome was considerably higher than he would have paid at home. He chose a couple of books, one in English, the other an Italian translation of a well-known continental work.

"I'll kill two birds with one stone" he explained to Neville. "I'll learn a bit of theology and a bit of Italian at the same time."

"Either that, or the one will prevent you learning the other" smiled Neville as they took their purchases to the counter. "Now for a cappuccino in the midday sun, supposedly only patronised by mad dogs and Englishmen."

Neville led the way to a nearby cafe situated at the terminus of the number sixty four bus, which they would be catching shortly to return to the monastery. They were soon sipping the fragrant brew and smoking while Mark scribbled a few hasty lines to friends and family at home.

"Dear Pete" he wrote, "Rome is fabulous - have just visited St Peter's. Promise will write soon."

"I think I could quite enjoy being a tourist" he sighed as he relaxed with his coffee. Neville laughed.

"You will enjoy Rome, my dear Mark. There are opportunities galore for seeing the sights, but your Roman career begins in earnest tomorrow."

The realisation brought him down to earth again, and he shivered slightly as he wondered what the morrow would bring.

He need not have worried. As Neville had predicted, the Latin of the lectures was simplicity itself. The material was the 'Summa Theologica' of St Thomas Aquinas; the course could scarcely have changed for several centuries. It was almost like travelling back in time, fascinating from one point of view, but Mark soon began to wonder whether it had any relevance to life in the twentieth century. However, much of it was new to him, and there were practical projects or 'tessinas' to be prepared, so he found that there was plenty to keep him occupied. He spent long hours in the library, searching through the dusty volumes of Migne's 'Patrologia Latina' as he conscientiously researched the views of the Church Fathers on the essay topics he had chosen. In his room, he pored over the pages of the 'Summa', his head nodding as the boredom of it rapidly induced a state of somnolence.

But as Neville had promised, there was plenty of opportunity for the would-be tourist. Lectures occupied the mornings only, and so some afternoons were spent wandering round the venerable streets of the city, though on others he succumbed to the traditional 'siesta', awaking with a throbbing head and dry mouth after two hours of deep, dream-filled sleep. Occasionally, he would go with other English speaking students to patronise a small cinema in a suburb of the city which showed English language films to a capacity audience of English-speaking clerical students (with perhaps the occasional lay person), an audience which was there in defiance of edicts from the Vatican forbidding visits to the cinema for clerics.

The evenings were spent in mind numbing sessions of study of the 'Summa', an activity he relinquished thankfully on occasion to visit a trattoria or ristorante with Neville or others of the English speaking fraternity with whom he had made friends. An easygoing soul, Mark made friends too with several of the other students; the monastery was the mother house of the Order, a world-wide institution, and so attracted students from every quarter of the globe. The Germans tended to mix with the English speakers, and so Mark became quite friendly with an earnest young man from the

Rhineland, who frequently upbraided him because of what he saw as his idleness. On one occasion, to Mark's astonishment, he had even remarked that if he did as little work as Mark, he would consider himself to be in mortal sin.

"And I thought I was working quite hard" he protested to an amused Neville, who replied that the Germans made a religion not of Christianity but of Theology, and the more abstruse it was the better.

"In fact, dear boy, one Australian student of my acquaintance did his doctoral thesis at the Anselmo a year or two ago, and though it was highly praised, he was told that it was too clear and simple; he should make it sound more learned."

FORTY THREE

The months slipped by, and almost before he knew it, he was staring the licentiate exams in the face. The brief Roman winter had come and gone, and with the spring, Easter soon indicated that the summer and the end of the first year were getting dangerously close. The temptation to sunbathe on the flat roof of the monastery or to take the train to the beach at Ostia could only be indulged in occasionally; much hard work needed to be done to revise the year's work. On many a warm, sultry night in late spring and early summer Mark sat at his desk, windows wide open but shutters closed, desperately trying to cram the Latin texts and notes he had taken.

"My God", he felt, "it's a near impossibility trying to assimilate this lot."

Neville's thesis was finally ready, and Mark took time off to go and listen to him presenting and defending it. He lived up to expectations, his presentation and defence a model of languid elegance, his manner as much as his material obviously impressing the examiners, who awarded him a 'summa cum laude'. The celebrations afterwards at one of their favourite ristorantes lasted until late at night. Besides Mark and Neville a couple of Americans and a New Zealander were present, and all during the meal indulged freely in various wines and several Zambuccas afterwards. The brother porter had been carefully bribed to admit them back into the monastery at the late hour at which they would be returning, and so it was five very merry young men who emerged onto the streets of Rome at about half past eleven. One of the Americans spent several minutes attempting to pick up paint spots from the road, convinced that they were lire pieces, but apart from a few stares from interest passers-by, the safety of the monastery was reached without mishap.

"Magnificent evening" sighed Mark afterwards in Neville's room, where he was sharing a last brandy with the newly qualified doctor of theology.

"Your turn next, dear boy; week's time, isn't it?" The cold panic returned to grip Mark's stomach.

"Yes," he groaned, burying his head in his hands. "Maybe Norbert was right when he called me idle. I haven't a cat in hell's chance of passing."

"Nonsense" retorted Neville firmly. "You'll do capitally. You've worked jolly hard, for an Englishman, that is."

But the week that followed was one of the hardest Mark had known. He studied at every available moment, desperately trying to cram the seemingly nonsensical facts into his head. He knew moments of hope, and others of black despair as his mood alternated between a slight optimism and a certainty of impending catastrophe.

"Don't worry" insisted Neville. You've got to be dashed thick or bone idle to fail at the Angelicum, and you're neither. So buck up, old boy, and bite the blinkin' bullet."

So upbraided, Mark managed a slight smile and pulled himself together once more. As Neville had predicted, the examination was something of an anticlimax, and though he had spent several heart stopping moments panicking outside the room, when once inside facing the examiners, a sense of calm came over him. The questions, he found, were fairly elementary; obviously the examiners were keen to pass as many of the candidates as they could, and Mark emerged feeling immensely relieved, and even rather foolish.

"Not too badly" he replied sheepishly to Neville's enquiry as to how he had performed, and sure enough, when the results came through, his name was comfortably among those who had succeeded.

The hustle and bustle of the journey back to England now took over. Neville was returning for the last time, his course complete. He had waited on in Rome to accompany Mark on a lazy, meandering return journey through Europe, and so the day following the publication of the results found the friends boarding the express for Florence at the Stazio Termini near St Mary Major's.

"A good first year?" enquired Neville.

"Mm, it's been absolutely terrific" sighed Mark, leaning out of the window waiting for the train to start. "I'm looking forward to getting back to England for the holidays, but I won't feel too bad about coming back in the autumn. The Alphonsian Academy sounds great, too."

Mark had written to his Provincial, suggesting he do a further year in Rome, specialising in Moral Theology. Leave to do this was granted, with the possibility of a further year if the situation and needs back in Britain allowed.

With a sudden lurch, the journey across Europe started, and Mark took his seat as the city began to slip by, finally giving way to the open countryside. He lounged back, chatting idly with Neville, and almost before he knew it, the train was drawing into Florence.

"It's been a quick three hours" he commented to Neville as they left the train to spend a day in that city.

"One fellow missed Florence on his way back from Rome; kept looking out for it, but remarked later that he'd only seen a place called Firenze. Absolutely true story, I assure you."

They found a modest pensione, and leaving their luggage safely looked in their room, set off to explore the city. It was early afternoon, and so they had plenty of time for their exploration. Neville was keen to show Mark the majolica work of the della Robbia's, a particular favourite of his, while Mark himself was anxious to see as much as he could of the works of Benvenuto Cellini, whose life had kept him spellbound for a magical week earlier in the year. There was so much to see, and as they had only allowed themselves a day, there was no time to be lost. Ignoring the growing problem of tired feet, they made their way round the city, visiting the Ponte Vecchio, the Duomo with its magnificent bronze doors, the museums and art galleries, Mark being duly impressed with the work of the della Robbia's, and finally finished their tour in the piazza della Signoria, where Mark stood gazing admiringly at Cellini's 'Perseus'. The vivid account of its creation came back to him, and he was storing away memories to last a lifetime.

"Right, my dear Mark, a spot of nourishment is indicated, I feel."

Neville broke into Mark's reveries, and added the comment that if he kept staring for much longer at those naked male bodies, people could begin to misconstrue the situation. With a laugh, Mark turned to Neville and said briskly:

"I've many problems, but that's not one of them, thank God! Right. Food it is. Let's look for a trattoria."

And so they were soon demolishing generous portions of spaghetti, and disposing of large amounts the excellent dry white vino da tavola. Afterwards, they wandered around the darkening city savouring the atmosphere until at length, finding themselves back at the pensione, they decided to call it a day.

Next morning, there was the hustle and bustle of departure once more, and by eleven they found themselves on the train bound for Venice, their next objective.

"Of all the cities of Italy, Venice is the most perfect" declared Neville as Mark sleepily yawned over his book as the train sped north.

"Very smelly, so I'm told," he replied.

"Nonsense, dear boy. That's the atmosphere people can smell."

"I always wondered what it was about your room wherever you live; now I realise it's the atmosphere."

The express rattled on, and at midday, many of the passengers began to unpack picnic lunches. The two young priests had brought rolls, cheese and a bottle of wine with them, and so they were able to join in the general dedication to the exercise of alleviating the pangs of hunger and thirst. An Italian couple with a young child politely offered some of their food, which the two Englishmen gratefully accepted, offering wine in return. Soon the conversation became quite animated as Neville explained in his fluent Italian that they were English clerical students on their way home for the summer. Mark could follow most of the conversation, and was able to chip in an occasional contribution, and so the journey soon passed. Eventually, the family left the train with many polite and cheerful good wishes and farewells, leaving the two young men alone as the train continued on the last leg of its journey to Venice.

The cooler temperatures of early evening were prevailing by the time the train was crossing the causeway and pulling into Venice station. With much stretching and groaning, Neville reached for the suitcases, and feeling somewhat weary, the two travellers opened the carriage door as the train finally came to rest. The early evening light seemed to add depth, brilliance and contrast to the scene that greeted them as they emerged onto the quay.

"Magnificent" breathed Mark, as he took in the surrounding grandeur.

The mood stayed with him as they caught the vaporetto, purring along past the moored gondolas and assorted small craft, the crumbling palaces forming a picturesque backdrop as they approached the Rialto bridge.

"How now, Bassanio; what news upon the Rialto?" quoted Neville as the boat moored and they alighted. "Nearly there," he added as they struggled along with their suitcases. After a few minutes, their cases making their arms ache as they made their way along the narrow winding streets, they suddenly came upon a small square, along one side of which ran one of the many small, secondary canals. On the far side stood the small, baroque church with attached monastery that was their goal.

The brother porter, consulting the guest list, opened the door and politely showed the two visitors into the parlour, then hurried away to confirm that their rooms were ready. Moments later, they were climbing the narrow staircase leading to the upper floors, and were quickly settled in the small guest rooms allotted to them. The brother who had shown them the way was about to leave them when Neville, thanking him for his help, intimated that they wished to say Mass. Obligingly, the brother led them back down stairs and along to the sacristy, where they quickly sorted out the necessary equipment. Mark had brought his small, English missal, and so after vesting, they made their way into the dark church, and started their devotions on an altar decorated with gilded cherubs and other florid baroque ornamentation, the light from a single overhead spotlight increasing the contrast with the surrounding gloom.

Later, they joined the community for supper, where the nature of the welcome they received gave Mark much room for thought as he recalled his experiences in visiting houses of his Order in Britain. Here, he felt the warmth of the family spirit and was deeply impressed with the cheerful kindly interest taken in them. It was good to belong, he felt, and mentioned as much to Neville.

"I don't know what it is, whether it's stiff-upper-lipped British reserve, or sheer indifference. Whatever it is, I agree that our Continental brethren can teach us a thing or two about a true community spirit."

The next three days were a sheer delight as they enjoyed the friendly hospitality of the confreres, and relaxed amid the beauty of Venice.

"Rather like sitting in the middle of a Canaletto painting" commented Neville as they sipped coffee in the open air in the Piazza San Marco.

"All we need now is a little Vivaldi playing in the background" added Mark as they lounged back, watching the pigeons clatter skywards as the children ran among them.

Later, they admired the bridge of sighs connecting the Doge's palace to the infamous prison known as the 'leads'. As they gazed, a young man dressed in the height of fashion approached them. In a heavy French accent, he asked if they were British.

"Yes, we are; how could you tell?" asked the wondering Mark.

"I have the eye for such things" replied the stranger. "You know who was the most famous prisoner to cross the bridge of sighs? It was Casanova. Like him, I too live only for the fucking".

Mark blinked and stammered a noncommittal comment in reply.

"And you, what do you do?"

"I, er, well..." Mark mumbled, feeling that he could scarcely reveal that they were priests.

"Business school graduates on vacation" announced Neville briskly, sensing the awkwardness. The young man invited them to join him for a drink, but making polite excuses, the two young Britons fled in a certain amount of disordered confusion.

"That's the 'world' as castigated by the ascetical writers if you like" remarked Neville. Mark agreed, feeling very green and sheltered. There was a lot to be said for the serenity of monastic life, even though it lacked some of the obvious excitement available in other walks of life.

Their all too short stay in Venice quickly came to an end, and it was time to resume their journey north. Looking back years later, Mark could recall the idyllic journey, made in the warmest summer he had ever known. The train took them through the Brenner Pass into the mountainous scenery of Austria, and so into Germany.

Here, they stayed for a couple of days near Cologne, Mark savouring the atmosphere of a different country once again. The sausages and sauerkraut, the sharp, fresh taste of the beer and the fiery schnapps, even the crusty bread and butter and sliced meats had a flavour all their own. They stayed with a German family that had befriended Neville a couple of years earlier while he was studying German at the Berlitz School in Cologne, and Mark was overwhelmed by the kindly hospitality. They seemed to do little else all day but eat and drink, then visit the local places of interest in the family's Volkswagen. Tea consisted of huge fruit tarts, served with mountains of whipped cream, but their healthy appetites coped admirably.

They celebrated Mass in the local parish church, starkly modern with a Germanic cleanliness and precision, the quality of the fittings being very apparent. In England, Mark thought ruefully, a similar church would have had all manner of flaws, with cheap and nasty accessories. As their hosts were present, they concelebrated Mass in German, Neville taking the lead, and Mark joined in as best he could, his knowledge of German being of the slightest.

The warm weather and the heavily flowering grass had his nose and eyes streaming with what he thought at first was a very bad cold. 'Heuschnupfen' diagnosed his friendly hosts, and Mark fell victim for the first time in his life to hay fever.

The last stage of the journey took them from Cologne to the Hook of Holland, and leaning on the rail of the ferry as it left port, Mark recalled the highlights of the journey.

"Well, at least we have managed to afford you a modest introduction to the delights of Continental travel. You'll be able to enjoy more over the next year or so. Time for me to settle down once again, I'm sorry to say."

Neville was to commence his teaching career in St Augustine's that autumn, and Mark commented:

"You'll fall on your feet, I'm sure. The professors' common room always was more like a gentleman's club than anything else; you'll add even more style to that establishment."

Neville smiled. "A modicum of civilisation will certainly do some of the inmates there more than a little good; why, some of the dashed bounders are known to break wind in public."

"One thing I'll say about St Augustine's" Mark observed thoughtfully. "At least it seems to have something of the community spirit we saw on the Continent. Some of our monasteries back home are diabolical from that point of view; they don't give a damn whether you're there or not. I see this

Community business as being crucial to our future. A man entering the Order has a right to expect a warm and loving family environment. That's something I felt was real, particularly in Venice. But in England, it's bloody awful. When we accept the vow of chastity, we renounce the right to a wife and children, the situation where most men find the love and closeness to others they need. We still need the love and closeness, so our community has to supply it."

The boat was now clear of the breakwater, and heading into the open sea. Neville stared thoughtfully at the rising and falling foam flecked waves, and replied with a slight frown:

"Don't expect too much from the community, Mark; celibacy entails a certain sacrifice, a loneliness that is part of the burden the Lord lays upon us. His burden is light and his yoke sweet, perhaps, but it is a cross to bear, none the less."

"I accept that, Neville, but at the risk of sounding banal, perhaps, one could comment that the Holy Family lived chaste lives, but they were a loving family all the same. We've only given up sex, not love."

"But don't let yourself become too dependent on emotional love, my dear fellow. I repeat that if you expect too much, then you'll be disappointed."

Mark was silent. His thoughts turned to the ever-recurring problems of sex and love in his life. 'My God, what a life' he groaned within himself as he leaned on the rail, watching the seagulls as they swooped on the flotsam and jetsam drifting by, carefully extracting any edible titbits from it. Chastity was very much a deep, personal struggle for the young priest, who though he did not indulge in practices such as masturbation, nevertheless found much in his personal life with which his conscience reproached him. His gaze would linger on the alluring figures of young women in their summer dresses, his imagination stripping them naked as a vivid realisation of their desirable soft, rounded bodies filled his thoughts. Struggle though he would against these images, he could not banish them. Almost any stimulus was sufficient to trigger his thoughts and emotions; the mere sight of a wispy bra in a shop window, slips and panties prettily displayed could bring tumult, quickly enslaving his part-willing feelings. The bold glances and calls of the Roman prostitutes had him wondering what a moment's madness might mean, and when the frustration became too much and even prayer would not serve to keep the teeming thoughts at bay, his darker thoughts and urges would occasionally arise, as if his desires, denied their natural outlets, would seek any remedy to relieve his yearnings.

But it was not simply physical desire that gripped him; he yearned too for the comfort of arms about him; he would see the obvious happiness of a young couple in love, and bitterly envy them their joy. He too longed to love and be loved, and felt crushed by the harsh cross of chastity that he had taken up. But it was his lot, the destiny to which God had called him, and the burden at times seemed far from light, sweet being the last word he would have chosen to describe Christ's yoke.

"Anything wrong, dear boy?" Neville's question interrupted the gloomy self-examination.

"Oh, nothing", smiled Mark a little lamely.

"Come on, let's see if the bar is open. A brandy or two would not go amiss."

The warm spirit tasted like distilled fire, burning Mark's throat as he sipped and swallowed. But it cheered him; the discussion and the meditation that followed had made him a little depressed.

"I'm not asking for the world, Neville" he continued, taking up the theme once more, "and I'm certainly not asking for a celibate version of happy families. Just a community life with something of the spirit we have seen on our travels."

Neville sensed Mark's need for consolation and encouragement, but respecting his friend's privacy, forbore to press the matter further. But he thought to himself that with his needs and expectations, perhaps Mark would find himself with more than his share of heartache and disappointment in the years to come. Being something of a cynic and emotionally independent did tend to mean an easier passage through the often turbulent waters of community living in the Order.

As Neville was to conduct Summer schools for most of the time before he took up his appointment at St Augustine's in the autumn, he was making his way home for a quick holiday before starting. So he and Mark parted company in London, Mark making for the London house in which Peter was stationed to spend a day or two, while Neville was heading for the midlands. Mark felt a sense of loss and regret as he waved goodbye, but soon cheered up as he recalled that he would be seeing Peter once more. Neville was a good friend, a close friend even, but somehow Peter was always the one with whom he could completely relax. He did not have to prove himself, or live up to any ideal, real or imaginary with Peter, whereas to enjoy Neville's company meant entering his world, congenial though it was, and to an extent, therefore, playing a part.

The reunion was as warm and friendly as he could have wished. Mark arrived just in time for supper, and Peter's face lit up as he came along the corridor with the community after evening meditation.

"Hi there, Mark" he whispered. "Come on. I'll see you get a place in the ref. next to me."

Leaving his baggage tucked in close to the wall near the notice board, Mark joined in the procession keeping a diplomatic silence so as not to offend the others. A couple of polite nods greeted him as the group milled about the open door, waiting for the signal to enter the refectory, but Mark was glad of Peter's presence; he felt very much the stranger. However, the superior formally welcomed him, giving permission for conversation, and so the two friends were soon catching up on all the news.

"My God" murmured Mark discreetly, "I don't know how you stick this place. It's like a morgue."

"Oh, it's not so bad" replied Peter. "You've got to get used to the blokes, make allowances for 'em. There's some miserable old buggers among them, but maybe you'd be a miserable old bugger if you'd led the sort of life that they've had."

"That's true, I suppose" Mark agreed, "but it makes you wonder what's the point of it all. If you can't be happy in the Order and the service of the Lord, then something is wrong."

"I thought you were the one who was always on about the need for self-sacrifice, dying with Christ on the cross, and all that rubbish."

Mark gave Peter a pained look, then grinned reluctantly.

"Hoist with my own petard. I suppose you're right, Pete. We shouldn't look for too much. But I sometimes wonder what should be our rights and expectations regarding basic happiness. That's the corny line people always used to crack: 'are you happy in the life, brother?' I'm finding that harder and harder to answer. Sometimes,

I don't think I'm happy in the life; content, maybe, but that's not the same thing. What about you, Pete? Are you happy here?"

Peter thought for a minute or two.

"Yeah, I suppose I'm happy enough. I don't really think about it too much. It's not a bad life; it's what you make it yourself. I see it as a job to be done, and so I just get on with it. It's bloody hard work, I know that, but I have good times, too."

Mark felt an affection for his friend as he spoke; and an admiration, too. Life certainly seemed more liveable if you simply got on with the job in hand, instead of philosophising and agonising over the why's and wherefore's of it all.

The conversation took a lighter turn as each regaled the other with incidents from the past year, Peter roaring with laughter as Mark told him the story of how the students of one Roman college had foiled the efforts of a prostitute neighbour who used to throw down her key to visiting clients; collecting up all the old keys they could find, they threw them down just as the lady threw hers to a prospective client, thus causing no little confusion and frustration. He appreciated too the story of the amorous Frenchman they had met in Venice, and in turn described the sort of pastoral activities that took up most of his time in the Parish. Mark once again felt a sense of inferiority steal over him. Peter seemed so self-assured and competent, going into the local school three times a week, facing those hardened, bored kids, and seemingly managing to keep them under control. He ran the Youth Club, and had more than his fair share of parish visiting to do, and he appeared to be thriving on it.

"Of course, it isn't nose to the grindstone all the time. I get my treats too; every now and then I nip off to the West End to see a film or a show, or have a meal. Sometimes I go alone, but it's nice to have company when you can; in fact, we'll do that tomorrow if you're staying. I've got Youth Club tonight; come along if you like."

Mark was hesitant, but Peter insisted cheerfully:

"You'll be fine, you daft bugger. You don't have to do anything else but chat to the kids about anything they want to talk about. Besides, you can catch up on the latest pop music."

Mark smiled as he recalled the halcyon days in the printing shop at St Augustine's.

"I've rather lost touch since the Beatles, but of course, they're still going strong, aren't they?"

After supper, they made their way to the adjoining Parish hall where all hell seemed to have been let loose. Table tennis, impromptu games of five aside football with rolled up balls of socks, dancing to the latest pop tunes as they blared forth from a battered looking stereo gram donated by a kindly parishioner; the scene hit him like a blow in the face. A group of the young people, mainly girls, quickly gathered round the two priests, and Peter made the necessary introductions.

"They like flirting with the handsome young priest" Peter explained modestly in a discreet aside to Mark, as the girls flocked around.

The visitor quickly relaxed, and was soon trying to answer the questions which bombarded him from all sides as he explained who he was, and described his life in Rome. In turn, he asked the youngsters about the latest fashions in music and trendy gear, while sipping the coke someone had thrust into his hand. He felt flattered as one or two of the girls flirted coquettishly with him, their youth and fresh prettiness was something he found most appealing.

"It's something you've got to watch carefully" explained Peter afterwards. "You know it's innocent fun, and usually they do too, but sometimes one or other of them can develop a real crush on you, and there could be a temptation to exploit that. Besides, there's always some flipping busybody somewhere who'll try to make a scandal out of anything they can."

The following day as promised, Peter took Mark on a tour of the London sights.

"We'll have a good potter about, then a pub lunch, followed by a film in the afternoon, how about it?"

Mark agreed enthusiastically, and ten o'clock saw them already on the tube, bound for the West End. They wandered about Piccadilly, its shops full of Union Jacks and other tacky tributes to the swinging capital of the world, then strolled round Trafalgar square, and so back up to Leicester square.

"Come on" suggested Peter. "Let's have a look at Soho."

Mark knew its sinful reputation, and agreed to the tour with a vague feeling of naughty excitement.

"It's a good job we're in mufti" he laughed.

"You'd probably find that Soho is crawling with priests and vicars if the truth were known" retorted Peter at his most blasé.

As they made their way through the narrow streets, Mark was amazed at the number of strip clubs with their pneumatic ladies displayed on the entrance door photographs in all their ample charms. Sleazy doorways boasted several bells, bearing improbable legends which stated that French lessons were available, or that model was willing to pose, for the benefit of any enterprising gentleman who cared to apply his finger to the bell push.

"This you must see" exclaimed Peter as he opened the door of one of the many sex shops, and the two curiously peered in. A couple of middle aged men were browsing among magazines which from their covers, portrayed the female body as something incredibly ugly, Mark thought as he gawped at the close-up shots of female genitalia looking like open wounds. On the shelves were hideously grotesque open mouthed blow-up rubber dolls, while hanging up were whips and all the paraphernalia of the bondage fanatic. He gasped at the huge knobbly phalluses which appeared to be afflicted with varicose veins and warts, and unmentionable implements the use of which he could only guess at. He nudged Peter.

"My God, I've never seen anything like it in my life! It wouldn't excite me; it would more likely terrify me. I've never seen anything so horrible in my life."

"But it does all have a certain ghastly fascination, don't you think?"

"I suppose so" Mark gulped "but let's get out of here before that man asks us if he can help us."

Feeling rather dirty and ashamed, he left the shop while Peter grinned tolerantly.

"You always were easily shocked" he remarked as they walked on down the street. "It's a part of the scamier side of life that it's good to know about; sex isn't all sweet romance and red roses, it's grunting, sweating bodies too. Besides, you meet cases in the confessional of people who have become involved in all sorts of way-out behaviour. They're sometimes drawn to these places and need your help and advice."

Mark felt a sense of relief that celibacy meant an escape from having to come to terms with the experience of sex; an experience which must take some getting used to if what he had just seen was anything to go by. Forgotten for the moment were the yearnings that sometimes tormented him; perhaps the reality would effectively extinguish any such longings. Purity suddenly seemed so simple and attractive.

"It's a bit hard to see sex as something beautiful and innocent when you see it in a situation like that" he commented to Peter as they made their way to a pub for their lunch. But as the sense of shock wore off, a curious fascination and desire to see more began to make itself felt, and he realised that the subject of sexual desire was a minefield of danger and confusion, and much prayer was needed to help him adjust happily and healthily to it. He shivered in spite of the warmth of the day, and it was not until they were in the pub downing a pint of beer that his pensive mood left him and he felt able to shrug off the dark and threatening thoughts and feelings, and enjoy his day in a relaxed way. The hitherto untasted delights of chicken in the basket served to complete the exorcism, and he ate hungrily, the beer and fried food combining admirably as a gastronomic experience. Soon, he was laughing and joking about what they had seen, and Peter felt a sense of relief. He had begun to think that taking Mark into Soho had been a mistake.

The film they went to see afterwards was the latest 'James Bond', which they both thoroughly enjoyed like a couple of overgrown schoolboys, and it was two happy young men who returned to the monastery in time for supper, after a full and varied day.

"Thanks, Pete, it was great" sighed Mark as they opened the door and entered the porch.

"Half an hour before supper; you can go to meditation if you like."

"Maybe it wouldn't be a bad idea; I feel like a bit of a pagan sometimes" confessed Mark. "In fact, before I go home, I'd better go to confession; it's about three months since I've been. What are the blokes like here? Anyone you'd recommend in particular?"

Peter thought for a minute. Then he mentioned a name that Mark found acceptable, and so Mark planned a visit to this confessor for the next morning. He duly made his way to the priest's room next day after breakfast, having prepared in the oratory beforehand.

"Bless me, father, for I have sinned."

This time it was Mark who was the penitent, and he hesitantly yet conscientiously displayed his life and inner thoughts as he knelt before the seated priest, an elderly, kindly man who was rather gaunt and tall.

"I'm careless about prayer, father, particularly the divine office. I often miss one or other part, sometimes several- in fact some days seem to go by without my saying any at all, It's not that I deliberately refuse to say it or anything; it's just that I haven't successfully organised my life round it."

"The obligation to recite the office is a grave one" commented the priest, "though I wouldn't regard it as a hanging matter to miss it occasionally. But by and large, the office, and the whole office, must be a part of your regular prayer life."

"I'll try my best to make it so, father" promised Mark, blushing at the gentle rebuke. He then mentioned his unruly imagination and the sexual thoughts and feelings that sometimes pestered him. Somewhat shamefaced he told the priest about the previous day's visit to the sex shop.

"I think it was simply unhealthy curiosity rather than a deliberate wish to seek sexual gratification, father."

"Chastity is a delicate flower; it can so easily be damaged or even crushed" replied the older man, "especially while you are younger, the urges and desires of the flesh are always lurking just below the surface. Let sleeping dogs lie is a good motto here. Avoid the occasions of sin, or you are asking for trouble."

Mark resolved to intensify his efforts to be a healthy, clean living young priest, avoiding the contamination that so easily came from careless glances and an undisciplined imagination. Receiving his penance, he made the act of contrition while the priest absolved him, and with a kindly 'go now and sin no more', he was sent on his way. Feeling cleaner and more wholesome, his heart full of the finest resolutions, Mark returned to his room and began to make preparations for his journey home. After lunch, he made his farewells to Peter, who made him promise to call in on his way out to Rome again, and then headed off to the tube with all his luggage.

FORTY FOUR

That summer long remained in Mark's memory as one of the happiest times of his life. Newly returned from Rome, he had three months of freedom before him; of course, there were occasional duties and responsibilities, but these were of the lightest, and they also provided him with the money needed for his travelling and day to day expenses.

For three weeks he supplied in his home parish while the parish priest took his holiday. The curate was in residence, and so Mark's duties were simply to be available for daily public Masses, and to hear confessions on the Saturday, and say two of the Sunday Masses, preaching at both. He lived at home, and apart from these commitments his time was his own.

Tony, by now at work and courting, was able to devote some time to Mark: often in the evenings he would take Mark out for driving lessons, and then they would go to the pub for a drink, along with Elizabeth, Tony's girlfriend. Elizabeth was a friendly, tolerant girl, and so she and Mark soon became good friends; though Mark was anxious not to be a constant third to their twosome. He insisted on Tony and Elizabeth being able to be alone, a move of which his mother approved.

There was always plenty to do in the family's large, somewhat ramshackle house, and so Mark's time was taken up with sorting out some of the many maintenance tasks, and in the evenings, when not out learning to drive with Tony, he would sink down in front of the television, still a luxury to him though very much part of everyday life for most people. He soon became a regular patron of the local hardware store, and after his morning Mass and leisurely breakfast read of the papers, he would set to with a will, finding much satisfaction in hammering, sawing and gluing as he put up shelves, repaired creaking doors and windows long since jammed shut, and dug the garden.

"You're a real treasure, Mark" his mother beamed, while Tony grinned sheepishly at the implied rebuke.

"When Tony and Elizabeth marry and set up home, he'll need to pull his socks up" Mark laughed.

On Tony's days off, they would all pile into the Morris Minor and head for the coast, or one of the nearby inland beauty spots with a picnic. Mark, for so long starved of the ordinary pleasures and experiences of family life, revelled in it all, and thoroughly enjoyed his summer. His priesthood became almost an unnoticed part of his life, restricted as it was to his daily Mass and a rapidly mumbled recitation of the office. He tried to follow his confessor's injunctions about regular dedication to his breviary, but with only limited success. But he consoled himself with the reflection that God, and the things of God, was often consciously in his mind and heart, and never far away at any time.

After a blissful month, he had to report to one of the houses of the Order for a short spell of supply work, and he chafed at the empty days and nights that were involved; the duties being almost as light as those in his home parish.

"I could be at home" he grumbled to himself. Always he felt the stranger, casually acknowledged, but rarely warmly welcomed. It was with some relief that he bade farewell to the brethren, returning home for another brief stay before departing for the Continent once more. As promised, he called into the London house to see Peter, and so in due course, found himself once again back in Rome.

FORTY FIVE

His second year was academically more exciting than his first; it was to be spent in the Alphonsian Academy. Many of the latest ideas in Moral Theology were being propounded and it was with real enthusiasm that he undertook the courses on conscience and law and their respective roles; courses that were in retrospect to shape the whole future of his life as they helped formulate his attitudes to ecclesiastical authority and the primacy of conscience in all major decision making.

His view of Christianity deepened and broadened during this year too as he assimilated the ideas being put forward, and fitted them into the Vision. A new appreciation of the role of the Sacraments grew as he began to see them as a living, daily sharing in time of the timeless events of Good Friday and Easter Sunday; a consecration of the many facets of human life, whereby they are made to share in the central mystery of redemption. He studied the law of Christ, learning that Christ himself was the law, and Christian living consisted of a man being Christ in this place, at this time. A study of the psychology of sin and temptation helped clarify his attitudes to sex and the question of sin; all in all, it was an immensely stimulating year that helped him emerge as a wiser, more mature priest, Christian, and human being.

In St Augustines, Moral Theology was still being taught from the traditional text books, and quite a ground swell of discontent was making itself felt among the students. The superiors gave way partially, the Provincial contacting Mark, asking him to break off his studies at the end of the year that he was spending in the Alphonsian academy, so that he could return to St Augustine's to add a little freshness to the course. The mainstream of the course would continue as before, but Mark's task would be to give supplementary lectures in some of the newer ideas.

"I've hardly begun to assimilate them myself" he pondered as he read the Provincial's letter. But the Roman experience, enriching though it was had left him with a feeling that now was the time for him to do more, become more involved in the life and future of the Order back home in Great Britain and so he was not altogether sorry to see the end, for the time being at least, of his Roman career.

"Maybe I'll be able to return to continue and do my doctorate after three or four years' teaching" he mused to himself as he packed, ready for the journey back home.

New challenges lay ahead. Mark felt that he had a great deal to offer the students; not that he felt in any way competent to offer it, but the Vision that nourished his own life had been intellectually established and cultivated in Rome, and he was burning with the desire of communicating it to his young confreres. The challenge made him shiver with nervous anticipation, but he knew that he had to do his best, and he was more than willing to try.

It was with these thoughts in mind that he hurried home in late June, the course examinations safely taken and passed, with no desire to repeat the idyllic journey of the previous summer. It was a more purposeful Mark that stepped from the plane at Heathrow, his thoughts already turned to the coming September. The Roman days were over.

There was time for a last, carefree holiday, however, before buckling down to his new responsibilities, and so he spent some time with Tony and Elizabeth, who had married during the course of the year. They had spoken of waiting until he came home to solemnise it for them, but Mark had insisted that they go ahead.

"If it had been a matter of a month or two, fair enough" Mark had answered when they approached him by letter in Rome, "but we are talking about six months. You go ahead; I'll be with you in spirit."

And so they had married in the early part of the winter, shortly after Christmas. Tony had found a job in a town about thirty or forty miles from home, and so Mark divided his time between the newlyweds and the family home, where his mother now lived alone. Brenda lived nearby, and so he was able to keep in touch with her, too; she was by now the proud mother of a bouncing baby boy. On one or two weekends during the summer, the whole family got together; Tony and Elizabeth coming over on the Friday night, and Brenda, Bill and the baby coming on Saturday.

"It's great to have a close and loving family" sighed Mark as they all sat eating round the table. "It's perhaps something you take for granted when you're at home all the time, but when you're cut off in a religious Order for the amount of time that I've been cut off, it means so much more."

He smiled at them all, and the answering smiles reassured and warmed him. The baby gurgled happily, and Mark felt surrounded by a cosy domesticity that seemed to welcome him back to the human race. The Order sometimes had the effect of making him feel so isolated from the ordinary warm, human details of living.

With Tony's help, he took and passed his driving test, and so was able to take out the faithful old Morris Minor on his own. Tony even let him borrow his Mini on occasion, so Mark came to know the glorious freedom of the road. That summer he managed to clock up many miles and a great deal of driving experience.

The summer days quickly sped by, however, and for Mark, finally petered out in the first days of September. It was time to report to St Augustine's to begin his teaching career. It was with mixed feelings that he anticipated the morrow as he sat with Tony in the pub on the eve of his departure.

"It's a challenge; you'll enjoy it" encouraged Tony as Mark stared thoughtfully through the clear amber liquid in his glass, held in his cupped hands, his elbows leaning on the table.

"I suppose so; it won't be too bad. But it's always hard starting a new phase of your life. I always worry in case I'm not going to be able to cope. Besides, I always feel so damned diffident, not only about my own abilities, but about the relevance of it all. What the hell am I doing, teaching theology? Does it really matter? You and Elizabeth know bugger all about theology, but you are happy and your lives have purpose. Can I say the same about my own?"

His deeply creased brow, indicative of the depth of his concentration, did not go unnoticed by Tony, who drank deep of his beer.

"Look, Mark; I once said if ever you felt like ducking out, I'd back you up all the way; that still goes, you know, priest or not. But meanwhile, don't sell yourself short. The priesthood is a fantastic life, an important life; maybe we lay people realise that more than you clergy. You sometimes feel useless and unwanted, but the message you carry gives meaning to all the things we do. And you as an individual have a lot to offer the priesthood and the Church. She needs priests like you who are always ready to prod and question, not lazy and self satisfied. So get in there and do a good job."

"Thanks, father" smiled Mark, encouraged by his brother's rousing little pep talk. "Maybe you'd have made the better priest."

"Maybe I would" answered Tony, "but somehow I don't think my willy would have agreed."

"Mucky devil" laughed Mark, and the atmosphere lightened once more. They enjoyed the simple pleasures of good beer and one another's company for the rest of the evening. After an hour or so, they adjourned to Tony's house, picking up a Chinese take away as they went, and passed noisily through the front door chuckling and giggling like children, to meet the tolerant sighs of Elizabeth and their mother, who had come over with Mark to spend the evening before speeding him on his journey the following day.

FORTY SIX

The rain was beating down monotonously the day after when the seminary car drew up outside the front door of St Augustine's. Mark's mind was drawn back irresistibly to the occasion so many years ago of his first arrival there. Then it had seemed a haven of religious peace; now it was vaguely threatening, though the earlier impression still made itself felt.

With a determined cheerfulness and optimism, he climbed out of the car, and with an untidy scramble, got himself and his belongings into the front porch. Neville was not there to greet him, but on enquiry, Mark discovered that he was due to arrive next day. One of the brothers showed him to his room, larger and more comfortable than the one he had known as a student, and he sat down at the table, surrounded by his damp luggage. His books were already there in a large wooden crate; they had arrived some weeks earlier direct from Rome.

"I've got a week before classes start" he thought to himself. "I've a hell of a lot to do; I'd better get on with it."

The next few days saw some frenzied activity. The crate was prised open, books and notes removed and heaped in piles round the floor. Mark had decided to call his course 'The theology of Christian living: an introduction to Moral Theology', and so Roman course notes, the 'Law of Christ' and similar works were pored over sedulously as the skeleton was gradually constructed. By the end of the week the plan was more or less complete; all that remained was for him to put flesh on the bones as the term progressed. Neville studied the schema Mark had produced, offered one or two comments, and generally commended it.

"Very suitable, dear boy. That should give the young blighters something to think about."

Neville taught Dogmatic Theology, also in a subsidiary position. The senior lecturer was the one who had taught the subject since the dawn of creation, or so it seemed. But progress was being made; newer ideas were getting through to the students who drank them in greedily as they were offered. The older tradition had demanded strict segregation between staff and students, a system that still held fast on Mark's return to St Augustine's. Neville adhered to it, being a believer in a hierarchically structured life in the Order. But

Mark, a democrat by nature, resolved to try and establish a greater air of familiarity with the students.

"After all" he confided to Neville, "it's only two years since I was one myself."

Besides, he thought to himself, sheer good sense and self-defence would seem to indicate the wisdom of such an outlook; Neville had the intelligence and the air of omni-competence that could establish a credible master-pupil situation; Mark felt that it would be sheer foolishness for him to try and put across such an image. Thus it was that on greeting the students at the start of his first lecture he announced:

"I too am a student; I have had the benefit of a couple of years' more study and experience than you, but the course I am going to give is to be an exploration, a learning together; you will be teaching me as well as me teaching you."

In this way he made plain from the start that his was to be a different approach; he would not be pontificating; he was there for the benefit of the students; he was their servant in their search for knowledge.

The response was warm and friendly; the lack of respect that Neville had predicted in dire terms did not materialise, and at the end of his first week's teaching, Mark was well pleased. The students seemed to admire his disarming frankness, and he soon began to be recognised as an ally in the perpetual struggle the students had to obtain recognition of their rights and grievances.

"Bloody anarchist" one or two more senior lecturers muttered, but by and large, the reaction among the rest of the staff was reasonably tolerant. "He will learn the hard way" was the general view.

But Mark soldiered on, and though he found the preparatory work for his lectures a nightmare at times as he struggled to complete his lectures on time, he realised that he was enjoying himself, and relating happily to the student body. Approached by one group, he agreed to take a part in one of the Christmas plays, hitherto an unheard of practice for a member of the teaching staff. A small group of the students began to seek his help as a counsellor and confessor, and humbled by the realisation of his own sins and problems, he was able to lend a sympathetic and understanding ear to the halting stories they told.

By and large then, at this time in his life, Mark would have described himself as happy had anyone asked him, in spite of his continuing personal problems. He found satisfaction in what he was doing; his mind was busily addressing itself to the challenges confronting the Order and the Church at large, and he was excited by the possible solutions that were beginning to be discernible. Spiritually, he felt a closeness to Christ, a oneness that his admittedly disordered prayer life fostered, and his imagination and emotions nourished. His Sunday sermons and homilies, both to the students and to the wider body of the faithful on the Sundays he found himself supplying outside St Augustine's were heartfelt and impassioned, delivered with an intensity which though curbed to acceptable levels, none the less seemed to favourably impress his hearers. He was wont to remark that in all his sermons he was preaching not just to his hearers, but to himself too, and thus the sermon became at times almost a public examination of his own conscience.

During this period too, he began to have more involvement with the apostolate generally. One of the main pastoral works of the Order was the preaching of parish missions, such as the one at which Mark's interest in the Order had first been aroused. They had changed very little since those days; the main outline of the exercise was the visit to the parish of the two man mission team, usually for a fortnight. The first week was spent in extensively visiting the families of the parish, practising and lapsed, encouraging them to attend the second week, which consisted of a nightly service, the heart of which was the mission sermon. These sermons were on the major points of belief and practice; salvation, forgiveness, the Eucharist, prayer, marriage and sexual morality and so on. The object of the mission was to bring back the lapsed to the practice of the faith, and the strengthening of the faith and practice of the regular church goers. Most missioners had a fund of stories about the marvellous conversions that resulted, but Mark had his doubts as to the effectiveness of the missions as they were then organised.

"I'm sure they give the faithful a boost, and that can be no bad thing" he admitted, "but to what extent they bring about a fundamental change in a parish generally, or even in the lives of most of the parishioners individually is another question."

These were very unorthodox views, and Mark was to learn to his cost that they were most unpopular. Any criticism of the missions was tantamount to a questioning of the whole purpose of the Order; an attack on the way of life of the brethren. To suggest that their lives and work were in some way irrelevant to the real needs of the Church and the world at large was heresy of the most heinous sort.

Mark's first mission was the result of a request by one of the seasoned missioners, whose regular partner had proved to be unavailable on this occasion. The staff of St Augustine's was occasionally called upon to help out in such situations, and thus it was that Mark was summoned to lend his assistance, an interruption of his course being deemed to be of relatively little moment.

He was given his orders by the senior partner in the team; he was to present himself in the busy south London parish on the Saturday night preceding the opening of the mission, and further directions would then be forthcoming. In the meantime, he was asked to prepare mission sermons on three of the topics; the Mass, prayer and Our Lady. The older missioner was reserving for himself the more important sermons dealing with sin and confession, and the eternal truths of death, heaven and hell, not to mention the perennial favourite, marriage. Mark resolved to do the best he could with the topics allotted, and so applied himself industriously to the task of writing the three sermons. He found the task easier than he might have thought; once he had commenced operations, the thoughts flowed freely. He took the finished efforts to Neville for his comments.

"Very creditable" he pronounced, looking at Mark over the top of his reading glasses as he sat leafing through the pages. "Perhaps a little too much of a theological lecture rather than a sermon, but then again, my view is that instruction of the faithful is absolutely necessary if any rebirth of their faith and Christian living is to be forthcoming."

Mark resolved to try and make the tone a little less academic, and a little more inspirational. He retyped the sermons with this end in view, and finally felt reasonably happy with the results. The Saturday of his departure dawned, and with Neville's farewell encouraging remarks still ringing in his ears, he caught the London train.

'My God, it looks quite a dump" he thought gloomily to himself a few hours later as he inspected the rather dirty looking Victorian building that was to be the scene of his labours. "Still, better make a start, I suppose."

So saying he pressed the door bell of the adjoining presbytery, and moments later, a kindly grey-haired old lady opened the door.

"Come in, father. You must be Father Kennedy. The other missioner is already here."

She ushered Mark into the sitting room where his co-worker was engaged in the demolition of a large piece of fruit cake, washed down by a cup of tea. An elderly priest, presumably the Parish priest, and a thin, earnest looking young man in spectacles sat at the table with him, and on Mark's entry, the older man jovially called on him to join them.

"Park your backside over there, father," indicating a chair. "All ready for the fray eh?" he continued, his large plump face beaming benignly. Mark grinned sheepishly, and taking his place, gratefully accepted the cup of tea and piece of cake proffered, and then briefly introduced himself.

"It's my first mission, so I hope it'll go well" he concluded.

"Of course it will, father" boomed the parish priest. "You Order men know how to blow the dust off the rafters in the church. What the people need is a lot of good, rousing stuff. A bit of strong, vigorous preaching will do them the world of good."

The thin young man, the curate, sniffed deprecatingly.

"Empty vessels make the most noise" he commented. "I hope you'll be giving us some good, meaty sermons with a dash of Vatican Two."

Mark smiled. "I'll certainly do my best."

"Vatican bloody tripe" bellowed the Parish priest. "Get 'em shaking in their shoes; there's nothing like it."

Mark's partner hastily intervened. "I think perhaps there's room for both; our tradition is a bit like that of the police; a hard man to scare them and break them down, then the nice, kind one to win their hearts. I've had the experience; I'll give them the hard time; father Kennedy here is a nice young man not long back from Rome. He'll be able to make the most of the soft sell."

Mark nodded a slightly uneasy agreement, and resolved to play the whole thing by ear. Later, having been shown to his room, he relaxed for a quiet half hour, anxiously running through his sermons. The local priests seemed not too bad on the whole; the parish priest appeared to be a bluff, kind-hearted man; he hoped the curate would not prove to be one of the slightly superior, condescending snobby types one met occasionally who despised missions. Mark could understand the feeling but he was convinced of the potential value of the parish mission, as an idea if not as it was generally implemented. He realised that it could be made into a potent vehicle for renewal in the Church. He resolved that he would stoutly defend the missions along these lines if challenged.

Next day, the mission started in earnest. The senior missioner preached at all the Masses, letting the people know in no uncertain terms that something Big was in the air. One minute he was bellowing denunciations at the hapless parishioners, castigating them for their indifference, and the next he was using a sort of coarse flattery to try and wheedle them into coming to the mission. Mark cringed as he listened, at times wishing that the ground would open up beneath him. Later in the day, the curate made some patronising remark, and it was enough to make Mark's hackles rise. He ended up not only defending the missions to the hilt, but his partner's experience and expertise, though he did concede that his own approach would be different.

"But there's nothing wrong with passion and commitment in preaching" he insisted, "In fact, all the biblical evidence points to Christ and the apostles eliciting an emotional, enthusiastic response from their listeners."

The curate responded somewhat testily, "That's all very well, but emotional responses are short-lived; it is the reason and will you must reach."

"I'm not saying that it is all emotion; that, admittedly, would he hollow and false, but the emotions must be allowed to play their part. I'm sure Paul on the road to Damascus, or any of the saints when they underwent sudden conversion, were not simply responding with intellect and will like scholastic automata, but with the whole man. I think that scholastic philosophy and theology have grossly underrated the importance of other factors in the human response; man is a very complex animal, and cold, intellectual aspects cannot be isolated in the real world; they are simply convenient abstractions."

The curate somewhat grudgingly admitted the point, and Mark felt a wholly unreasonable satisfaction at having squashed his opponent. Normally, debating was not one of his more obvious skills; he tended to become too emotionally involved to engage in the cut and thrust of debate with full competence; he allowed his often valid arguments to be defeated by well placed cynical sneers.

Monday saw the start of the visiting. Armed with a rather battered map showing the area in detail, and a well thumbed grubby visiting book given him by the parish priest, he set out, feeling more than a little reluctance and trepidation.

"I hate this bloody carry on" he groaned to himself as he prepared to knock on his first door. The response he received was to prove an all too familiar pattern.

"Who? No, that's not me. I think there used to be people here of that name about five years ago."

"Are you Catholics?" Mark asked hopefully.

"No, I don't really go in for that religion stuff."

Murmuring a polite word of thanks, he retreated down the path, looking at his visiting book to see which number came next. As luck would have it, his next call was at the home of one of the parish stalwarts, and so he was given a warm welcome, and a morale boosting cup of tea. Three quarters of an hour later he made his farewells, realising that this was not the way to complete the visiting, and ruefully resolved to try and get his skates on. His morning passed with rather mediocre results; daytime visiting, he came to realise, meant that one met the old, the mothers of young children, and precious few people besides. But he had encountered a few of the practising Catholics, and politely invited them to attend the mission.

We'll try and come on one or two nights" was the general response, and Mark felt a little diffident about pressing them to a more wholehearted commitment. He tried, but despised and disliked the hectoring, bullying tone his remarks seemed to adopt in spite of himself. He also met one or two of the lapsed, and there, his efforts were very difficult to assess. He met with several different responses, from the "I'm as good as those who go to Church" brigade, and the "I can pray at home just as well" fraternity, to the polite, slightly baffled "I think I was baptised a Catholic, but I've never ever been to church" type of response. One or two had horror stories to tell of sadistic nun teachers in primary school, or ogres in the confessional to account for their non practice, and Mark found himself constantly on the defensive, trying to get across the message of Cod's love and the sacramental relationship he was offering, but his words seemed to fall largely on deaf ears. He handed out his mission bills and posters, pleaded, argued and cajoled, but by lunch time, felt that little concrete had been achieved in the way of results.

Lunch was plentiful, as was the drink provided to prepare, accompany and follow it, so consequently, Mark felt totally disinclined to tackle the afternoon session. But he struggled on, finding that as the day wore on and evening began, more and more of the people were at home, and he had to scribble 'sorry to miss you' fewer and fewer times on the mission bills he left at the unanswered doors. One or two more positive responses came his way later in the evening, but again, time was his enemy and he could not afford to stay too long in any one house to discuss the faith in general and the mission in particular.

By half past seven, he felt he had done enough and he was feeling tired and hungry. With a sense of relief, he retraced his steps through the wet, darkened streets to the presbytery, where he swapped notes with his senior colleague and the parish priest as he downed a reviving whisky and soda.

"You'll have to be snappier about the individual visit, father" commented his superior. "A quick in and out, 'come to the mission, and God bless you' is about all you can afford."

No wonder these blokes get round a whole parish in a fortnight" Mark mused to himself. But what's the point? There has to be a better way of organising the whole thing than this.

But keeping his own counsel, he relaxed with the others while planning the labours of the morrow. The rest of the first week passed in similar style, though one or two of the mornings were spent more fruitfully in the parish school. Mark enjoyed talking to the children, their round, innocent faces gazing up at him as he told them stories, and explained about the new life of Jesus in ways suitable to their age.

"It's like this," he started, addressing one of the classes of juniors. "The life of Jesus is like a flame."

He produced a large candle and half a dozen small ones. Lighting the large candle, he held it aloft and said: "This big candle is like Our Lord, giving light to the whole world. But he needs us to help him bring more light to the world."

He called up six of the children, who eagerly volunteered in a mad scramble. Following his instructions, three lit their candles from the big candle, passing the light on to the other three.

"We get our life from Jesus, we share his life; it's the same life, just as the little candles get their flame from the big candle. And we give Christ's life to one another just as we can pass the flame on from one candle to the next. The flame gives us a good picture of what Cur Lord's life is like. A flame gives light and warmth; Our lord's life gives us the light of faith and the warmth of love. But it isn't just given to us for ourselves; we've got to share it."

He produced a small, metal container.

"What happens if we cover our flame and try to keep it to ourselves?"

Suiting the action to the words, he placed the container over one of the small candles. The children looked expectantly. "The flame goes out."

Uncovering the extinguished candle, he said:

"That's what happens to us when we let Our Lord's life die within us, and if we hide it away, then it will die sooner or later. But thank goodness we can be given the light again", as he re-lit the candle from the large candle. "That's what confession is for; re-lighting our candles."

Soon, all the children knew the missioners well, both from the classroom talks and playtime sessions, when the two priests would have hordes of children milling round, bombarding them with questions and inviting them to share their sweets and crisps. Mark revelled in their company, and quickly became a firm favourite. He organised mission poster painting competitions, and soon, all over the parish, the results of the children's' work could be seen in windows, where parents had to display them, willy-nilly, at the insistence of their offspring.

The second, preaching week thus started with most of the parish realising that something out of the ordinary was happening, and as day followed day, the attendance at morning Mass and evening mission service gradually increased. The two priests preached on alternate evenings, the ringing declamations of the older missioner producing a stunned silence in the congregation as he painted the awful picture of Man the sinner, lost forever. Mark's sermons were quieter, but in their own way just as forceful as he put his heart into every word, bringing home the message of God's love and new life to his attentive hearers.

Afterwards, there was at least half an hour to spend in the confessional, and Mark healed and comforted, encouraged and inspired the penitents as best he could, nine out of ten being run of the mill confessions of ordinary, practising Catholics. But even here he tried to lift and enthuse. The tenth was the lost sheep with a burden of guilt fit to reduce both confessor and penitent to tears as relief at the releasing of guilt fuelled firm resolutions of new beginnings.

Mark felt immensely privileged and humbled as he listened to some of the stories, lives spent enmeshed in torment of conscience over sexual problems too difficult to be borne or overcome. He confessed to one:

"I too sin in this way; I would despair if I didn't continually rely on God's understanding forgiveness. Forgive yourself; he forgives and heals; all you have to do is to accept the forgiveness."

Later, he thought to himself, "how many sexual cripples is the Church responsible for? The Pharisees were condemned by Christ for binding burdens on men's backs too heavy to be carried, not lifting a finger to help. For too long the Church has done the same."

He had heard the stories of men whose natures had been twisted by fear and self repression, the impulse to physical love cramped and distorted by their terror-stricken consciences until their sexuality seemed only able to find expression in compulsive imaginings and guilt-ridden touches. Even where these extremes were not reached, sex and sin had become virtually synonymous, the noble desire of man for woman almost totally eclipsed by the preoccupation with evil.

The mission drew to its close; the attendances had been fairly good, it was generally felt. A handful of the lapsed had been drawn back to the Church, and Mark thought that all in all, given the approach, the mission had to be called a modest success. "There is more rejoicing in heaven over one sinner who repents than over ninety nine that do not need repentance." Certainly, he had been able to help a few troubled souls in the confessional, and many of the practising Catholics had been to the Mission on several occasions.

"But is it just a temporary lift, or have we sowed the seeds of a new, vigorous plant?" he wondered. Surely there was room for the sort of exercise which would institute an ongoing, growing, living renewal in a parish.

"Our present missions seem to ignore to an extent the fundamental nature of the Church" he commented to Neville on his return home. "The Church is a living, growing body. The shepherd and sheep analogy, biblical as it is, is only one analogy. We can't just go into a parish and expect to bring about a total transformation, bringing back the lapsed and the sinners and converting the pagans like a tidal wave hitting the place. I think our job is to sow seeds, plant and establish new beginnings. The Church, the body of Christ in a particular place is like a vine, to use another biblical analogy, and it will grow and spread if it is healthy. If it doesn't grow, then there is something wrong with the Church in that place."

"Absolutely, dear boy" remarked Neville. "Our task is to help the laity to realise and live out their Christian vocations in a situation; if we enable them to do this, then the Church will grow. This is the method of growth and development established by Christ himself. He used the analogy of the leaven in the mass to express this. But beware, my dear Mark. Saying too much about the missions in a critical manner will not go down well with the brethren, I'm telling you here and now."

Neville had not given missions; he had not refused to do so, but it had become generally understood that it was not his scene, as the contemporary jargon was beginning to say. But being a lover of peace, he forbore from making provocative comments about change and renewal, preferring to go about things quietly in his own way. Mark felt a much stronger commitment to the sense of community, and so felt obliged to speak out on issues he felt important to the community, even though he courted resentment and unpopularity by so doing. He resolved to write an account of his views on the future of parish missions, for possible publication in the internal newsletter that circulated among the communities three or four times a year. If nothing else, it would at least start people discussing these issues which he saw as crucial to the future of the Order, and perhaps new approaches to the missions might even be encouraged.

FORTY SEVEN

The weeks and months were passing quickly, Mark being busily engaged in his principal work of teaching, but his services were called on for further excursions into the apostolic work of the Order from time to time. He gave one or two retreats to religious sisters, an exercise which he found helpful in formulating a coherent presentation of the Vision, as these retreats entailed the giving of about fifteen conferences or talks over the space of five days or so. He was able to develop his theme with enthusiasm and even passion as he spoke to his audience of willing listeners. In turn, this experience helped his teaching, which progressed painfully but reasonably satisfactorily, his views on the Church and Christian living in the Church growing and developing as he studied and pondered, before passing on the fruits of his labours to the students.

But the struggle for peace of mind and soul in sexual matters was growing more intense. His imagination was still as unruly as ever, the stimulus of a wisp of silk or a delicately curved hip being sufficient to trigger his thoughts and desires. Frustration sometimes threatened to boil over as he tried to quench the flames. The fruits of celibacy were hard, withered and bitter, he commented ironically to himself as he resentfully examined his life and the prospects for contentment and peace of mind which seemed so remote. Up until this time, he had managed to preserve intact his physical integrity, the lessons of purity inculcated from his childhood being stronger in their influence than the urgent desires of his body and mind. But their sway was waning; the moral imperatives which commanded that thou shalt not even think about it, let alone touch, were weakening.

At the public Masses in church, he found himself staring at the swelling breasts and curved hips of the women present, and one day, found that he could not drag his gaze away from the soft, round bottom of a buxom young woman of about twenty eight. He could plainly see the outline of her knickers on the tight, smooth material of her stretch pants, and a pounding, racing sense of urgent desire took over. Not stopping to think too closely about what he was doing, he hurriedly left the back of the church and went to his room, where he locked the door. He had never masturbated in his life, but now the urge to do so, and the rational justification seemed irresistible. Anything to obtain relief from the images and desires that tormented him.

In Rome, when discussing these problems, one fellow student had described the view of the eighteenth century moralist Caramuel, known as the prince of laxists who had described masturbation as being simply equivalent to pissing. Mark did not know whether he was sinning or not, such was his state of mind, and he was in no mood to agonise over the decision. He resolved to close his mind to the moral issues, wasting no more time in self argument.

Quickly lowering his trousers, he lay on the bed and grasped his semi-erect penis. Cold sweat beaded his brow; he closed his eyes and conjured up the image of the young woman he had seen. He mentally stripped her and pictured her soft nakedness, his heart thumping painfully as he slowly moved his hand up and down. His movements quickened as his penis hardened, and it was all over in a moment as the climax came, his body arching and convulsing as the seed flowed in exquisite relief. With a long gasping sigh he relaxed and lay back, physically and emotionally drained. He must have slept shortly afterwards, and he awoke some twenty minutes later, and shamefacedly set about the task of cleaning himself up. A dreadful sense of guilt and self-loathing came over him as he dried the sticky liquid from his stomach, and immediately the tortured self questioning of motive, awareness and deliberation took over.

He felt sinful, but could not say to what extent he had sinned. His sympathy and wisdom, so readily offered to his penitents, was of no use to him in his self examination. He prayed, asking God to forgive whatever sin there had been, and dressing himself, resolved to go to confession as soon as possible. He went to his usual confessor in the community, and in simple words confessed what had happened.

"Chastity is a lifelong struggle" the priest commented somewhat nonchalantly, seemingly making little of the story he had just heard.

"But I feel as if I have failed in a major way, father" confessed Mark. "My vow seems a sham, somehow."

"Don't take it to heart" advised his confessor. "You'd be surprised how many priests have a masturbation problem; you aren't the first one to meet these difficulties. You aren't alone by any means."

Later, Mark turned over the whole incident in his mind and the beginnings of anger and resentment at his celibate state began to stir once again.

"What the hell are we struggling for?" he thought to himself. Many reasons for priestly celibacy were advanced, from the simply practical ('a priest cannot dedicate his life and work to the Church and look after a wife and family at the same time') to the sacred ('a priest cannot fondle a woman's body one minute and handle the sacred body of Christ the next'). The only motives that Mark could recognise and admire were the spiritual motives of witness and love; the celibate was a reminder to the Church and the world that mankind is already redeemed, living a risen life, in which in its fullness, marriage and sex will be superfluous. 'We have not here a lasting city.' Man is a pilgrim, with staff in hand, he thought with grim irony. Sex and marriage are good, but of this present age, while all the time mankind is being reborn of water and the Holy Ghost into the future, the fullness of God's life. All Christians are called to love God; celibacy and marriage are two complementary ways of following this same vocation. The celibate reminds married people not to mistake the sign for the reality it signifies.

He began to see as contemptible the practical motives of availability and especially the argument from economy ('The Church can scarcely afford to keep the priest, let alone a wife and family too.') If that is the case, he thought savagely to himself, the Church doesn't bloody well deserve any priests. All in all, celibacy was a hell of a sacrifice, and only made sense as a voluntary self deprivation for the highest motives. But why should obligatory celibacy be linked to the priesthood? There seemed to be no valid argument for so doing, and celibacy, far from enhancing the priesthood, was possibly destroying some priests. Mark wondered whether it might possibly be destroying him.

He knew that the Order had its fair share of misfits; priests and brothers who to say the least were not able to make much of a contribution to the life and work of the community, and he realised that most other orders were probably in a similar position. Masturbation, according to his confessor, was by no means an uncommon problem, and he knew that other priests sometimes took to the bottle. He had heard occasional horror stories of the child molester or homosexual predator among the clergy; Neville had once told him of the case of an older priest who had tried to grope him in the not too distant past.

Obviously, the priest was a man under many pressures, and the Church had to pick her priests carefully, and then train and care for them with the utmost diligence, but why crucify them with celibacy too? Celibacy should be recognised in the Church as a special vocation, requiring particular gifts and strengths; it should not be tacked onto the priesthood willy-nilly.

But Mark recognised that as a religious, he was called to celibacy through his vow of chastity, and so in prayer, he tried to deepen his appreciation of the nature of this call. But the taboos surrounding masturbation which had kept him physically virginal until now had been fatally weakened. Having succumbed once, successive occasions saw his resolve weaken further and further until his efforts to be chaste relied solely on the spiritual motives for celibacy that he recognised, and on his self-respect which constantly struggled to assert itself. It seemed to him to be a shameful, degrading practice, but the need to give way became rapidly almost compulsive. He was fighting a losing battle, and before long, found himself giving way to the impulse two or three times a week; incidents which no longer tormented him with self accusations of grave sin, though he continued to mention them in the confessional, but which made him despise himself as he realised that any witness to celibate values that he gave was gravely flawed.

Each occasion was going to be the last, he kept telling himself as he constantly tried to make a new beginning, but eventually he came unconsciously to accept that for better or worse, it had become a part of his life.

FORTY EIGHT

In other respects, his life carried on much as before; his relationships with the students generally warm and friendly, and with most of the community at least polite. But changes and upheavals of other types were on the horizon. In line with his resolve following the mission, he wrote a paper outlining his views on the apostolate in which the Order was currently engaged.

Over the last two or three years, new interpretations of the Order's purpose in the Church had begun to be circularised, mainly stemming from the Continent. ('Bloody trouble makers' in Peter's succinct view). Parish missions as given in Britain were now growing less and less common in Europe, where the concern for evangelisation was interpreted in a more definite identification with the world about them; so in Europe the Order was engaging more and more in teaching, social work and similar activities.

One phrase in the constitutions became a key phrase for the future, especially in Mark's view. The Order, it was said, should concern itself with preaching the gospel to the poor and underprivileged, or the 'P and U's' as they came to be called in the jargon of the students. The parish mission could only be called evangelisation of this type by stretching the imagination almost to breaking point. Mark, in writing his article, began to realise that entirely new ways must be sought. It was a fallacy to say that the Order's work was the preaching of missions, simply because historically this had been the case, and then think that updating meant cobbling together a new approach that somehow embraced the notion of preaching to the poor and underprivileged, just because a tiny fraction of those reached through traditional means could in fact be described as socially and economically poor. The correct approach, he felt, was to start from the opposite point of view. The poor and underprivileged could be identified easily enough; (he could have no truck with the hypocritical notion that interpreted the poverty and lack of privilege as being spiritual poverty, so that even the middle classes and the wealthy could be so described).

They were those living in depressed areas, racially oppressed minorities, those generally considered to be the dregs, the rejects of society; how could one bring Christ to them? The example of Mother Teresa of Calcutta and the little brothers of Charles de Foucauld was there before him; surely the only way of bringing the saving love of Christ to people in these desperate situations was to live and work among them, sharing Christ's love by sharing their lives and sufferings, establishing communities among the poor in the multi-storey flats, the slums, or wherever they were to be found. He shrank from the thought of embracing these conditions himself but felt that the notions should at least be aired and debated, so that the Order's conscience would be prodded and the dangerous self complacency so often evident would be disturbed. If challenged to form such a community, he would offer himself, though God alone knew whether he would find the great strength necessary to succeed.

Having dealt with these ideas, he then turned to other questions. Obviously, the whole Order could not simply drop all other tasks and responsibilities and move en masse into the slums of Britain. He felt that the Order should recognise that the setting up of at least a pilot effort in this direction would show that it was serious about seeking new ways of preaching the Gospel to the poor and underprivileged, even if the main stream of the work carried on in the parish missions and similar apostolates such as retreats for various groups of the Faithful. As for the missions, he recognised the validity of the exercise, though he felt that the historical methods were wrongly regarded as sacrosanct.

Again, the object of the exercise should be examined, and the ways chosen, without prejudice, which would best achieve the object. What then should be the purpose of the parish mission? Not necessarily the conversion of sinners or the reconciliation of the lapsed, though these were by no means to be ignored. But in line with the idea of the Church as a living, growing organism, the mission should seek to help establish a healthy local church with this vital potential within it. Parishes were too often dead or dying structures, the lives and energies of the clergy sacrificed to maintain the crumbling edifice. So the practising Catholics should be brought together and given a new insight and inspiration regarding their faith and their missionary vocation to the neighbourhood in which they lived. The mission should consist in the team going into a parish to help establish family groups with house Masses, to give the people an experience of the faith as a real part of everyday living. A coherent series of services built round the basic Christian themes should be included, to draw the parish together as a whole, as an introduction to the real work of the mission; mission, in other words, was henceforth to be the apostolate of the parish community.

Neville shook his head sadly when Mark showed him the finished article.

"It's suicide, my dear boy" he remarked mournfully. "However true it may be, the brethren won't stand for it, you mark my words."

But true to his resolution, Mark sent in the paper, and it was duly published and circularised. As Neville had foretold, it aroused many bitter comments as the senior missioners with years of experience behind them, strongly resented the inexperienced newcomer who by implication condemned their life's work, or so they felt, and more than one muttered about the wisdom of having young firebrands stuffing the students' minds with such ideas.

"Put him into the field; give him some pastoral experience; that will soon knock the nonsense out of him."

The father Provincial agreed, and at the end of the academic year, Mark was informed of his impending change.

"Two or three years in a busy working-class parish will help you to gain the necessary experience of everyday living in the Church, father. I am appointing you to St Margaret's parish here in London."

"So that you can keep an eye on me" thought Mark, but at any rate he was glad that he would be joining Peter again after their three year separation, St Margaret's being the working-class parish community to which Peter belonged, across the city from the Provincial house, which was a bigger, better off community with a large and flourishing parish.

Mark was sorry to be leaving St Augustine's again, so soon after his return, but he shrugged and admitted that pastoral experience would do him no harm. When Peter heard, he was pleased and relieved. Phoning his friend, he gave vent to his feelings.

"Bloody hell, Mark, you don't half live dangerously. I knew it was a mistake sending you out to Rome. You'd have been much better off doing what I did."

"I don't know, Pete" replied Mark. "I agree that there is no substitute for pastoral experience, but I wouldn't have missed Rome for anything. It has helped me form what I consider to be very important ideas about the future of the Church and the Order.

It's no good just having experience if you learn nothing by it. Anyway, I'll be getting experience now whether I like it or not."

Early September saw the time for Mark's departure for the London parish. He realised somewhat ruefully that the freedom and long holidays he had enjoyed in the academic sphere were now over, but he had managed that summer to spend a certain amount of time at home, and with Tony and Elizabeth, who had recently become parents for the first time. Mark felt a warmth and tenderness glow within him as he held the squalling scrap of humanity in his arms, kissing the wrinkled little face. He duly performed the baptism, calling the baby Paul.

"Paul Kennedy: it has a good ring to it" he commented to Tony as he downed a pint of beer at the party afterwards.

"It's marvellous having you, Elizabeth and now baby Paul as my family; being a priest can be a hell of a lonely life sometimes."

Tony nodded sympathetically. "You must treat us just like that, Mark; we are your family, and we regard you as one of us; always a bed here for you, and you can come and stay whenever you like. What we have is yours."

A lump rose in Mark's throat at Tony's words; his brother's kindness and love were quite overwhelming.

"It's good to see the next generation, and feel that your family and name will carry on; celibacy involves a terrible sense of sacrificing the future. I know in faith it is an affirmation of the future in God's terms, but the bread and butter details of the way we live it tends to hide all that." He shivered. "It's not my favourite virtue just at the moment. I sometimes have a horror-filled vision of my future, in which I see myself as an embittered old man, living out my remaining days in a community which is simply an institution. We all need warmth, love, common humanity, whether we're married or celibate."

"You'll always have that warmth and love with us, Mark, you know that. So if ever you feel you can't stand it and need a break, just jump on a train and come."

Mark put his arm round his brother's shoulder and squeezed him gently. The tears were glistening in his eyes and he hastily turned away and pretended to be absorbed by his glass of beer, and the christening presents which he closely examined without seeing.

He saw Brenda on a few occasions when staying at home, and learned that she too was pregnant.

"I'd begun to worry about our Brenda" confided his mother. "I didn't like to say anything, but I know she's been wanting another baby, and nothing seemed to happen for long enough."

Later, Tony remarked that maybe it was because she didn't let Bill have his way with her often enough.

"I just can't imagine our Brenda as a passionate lover somehow, and Bill is under the thumb, so if he's not pestering her, maybe the poor bugger only gets it a couple of times a month."

Mark laughed. "That's a couple of times a month more often than me," he replied, his imagination telling him vividly what it was he was missing. Resolutely shutting such thoughts from his mind, he turned his attention to the impending move south, and at the end of August, returned to St Augustine's for a couple of days to pack and move.

"All the very best in every way, my dear boy" murmured Neville, as Mark called in to finally take his leave.

"I'll miss you, Neville." Mark smiled as he shook his friend's hand. "I'll miss Oggies, too. I'll be back, though. I'll come up for retreats and so on; they'll not get rid of me as easily as that."

Neville paused in silence for a moment.

"Let me give you a word of advice, Mark. I've mentioned this before, and now it seems more important than ever. If you are to lead a reasonably contented life in the Order, you must find more inner peace and self-sufficiency. Don't rely on the likes of me for the comforts of love and friendship that you may feel you need. You have my love and friendship; that goes without saying. But do not rely on them to such an extent that without them you cannot function. I value and cherish your friendship. But to be brutally frank about it, I can take it or leave it if the occasion demands. Try not to be emotionally dependant on others; you must learn to be your own man, able to live and work as a priest with or without the company and friendship of others."

Mark felt the implied rebuke keenly, as a sense of rejection flowed over him. He realised that in many ways Neville was right, and he was too vulnerable, too open to the suffering that the loneliness of a celibate life could cause. He had long realised that both Neville and

Peter were more emotionally independent than himself, and he recognised the practical value of an independent stance. But he felt that his own natural needs were amply catered for, in theory at least, by the new emphasis on community that was being propounded by the theologians; the closeness implied by the doctrine of the mystical Body seemed to him to be the ideal for which the religious community should be striving. Oneness with Christ, brought about through oneness with the brethren; the Vision showed him a Christianity which saw each other person as a living incarnation of Christ.

In a sermon, he had once put it like this: "When I see you, I should fall on my knees before you, kiss your feet as I would the feet of Christ himself if I met him in person, because in meeting you, I *am* meeting Christ; I would in fact be kissing the feet of Christ. This explains the seemingly extravagant gestures of some of the saints who kissed the sores of beggars and devoted their lives to the service of others. We don't love others because Christ commands it: we love others because they *are* Christ; and because we too are Christ, our mutual love brings the Christ-life to birth more fully in each other. This is the importance of the giving and receiving of love in our human relationships."

Mark sighed. "You are right, Neville, at least from a practical point of view. I leave myself wide open, I know."

"Your vision of Christianity is genuine and valid, Mark, but it is an ideal; all I'm saying is that like all other ideals in this world it isn't often that you will be able to realise it very fully, and so you could easily be hurt by the disappointments that you will inevitably meet."

He smiled. "Now cheer up, dear boy, and go on your dashed way rejoicing."

So saying, he slapped Mark on the shoulder and took him down to the courtyard where the car was waiting to take him and his bundles of assorted belongings to the station.

FORTY NINE

"Home sweet home" thought Mark a trifle ironically as he passed through the front door of the London parish house to which he had been appointed. Somehow it felt different; on every previous occasion he had merely been a visitor, and had felt glad that he was not a member of the community.

"Soulless, institutional places" he thought to himself as he considered most of the religious houses he had seen on his travels, though his mind harked back a little nostalgically to the one or two continental communities he had visited. Perhaps they were just as soulless when you stayed for more than couple of nights.

Leaving his luggage by the notice board, he climbed the stairs up to Peter's room, and knocked on the door. On hearing Peter's invitation he opened the door and peered into the room.

"Come in, you bloody heretic" called his friend enthusiastically, and Mark, smiling, entered the room, accepting the cigarette held out to him.

"Great to see you, Mark. Welcome to the metropolis. You're just what we need here; another youngish face to brighten the place. Most of the bods here are so ancient you've got to prod 'em every day to see if they're still alive."

"Yeah, it'll be good getting down to some hard work with ordinary people" agreed Mark. "I've been too long in the rarefied atmosphere of Oggies and Rome; it's all very well, but a bit stifling."

Peter glanced at him sharply.

"That sounds like the right approach; I thought you'd have been bewailing being dragged away from your beloved seclusion."

"I like seclusion too, but I sometimes feel I need to meet and mix with ordinary lay people. The clerical atmosphere can be rather suffocating."

"Well, you'll certainly get all you want of that here. We'll just finish these fags, and then I'll take you to the boss's room."

The boss was the superior and parish priest.

"He's O.K." commented Peter. "It's up to you how much work you do; all you have to do to keep him happy is to stay up to date with all the official stuff. Some of it, in fact nearly all of it, is a dead bore and waste of time, but it's got to be done. Stuff like deanery conferences with the secular clergy, committee meetings of various sorts. Apart from that, as long as you do your appointed stint in the confessional, preach when you're told to and turn up for a good proportion of the community acts, then you can do what you like. How much you visit or get involved in the parish organisations and so on is up to you. I get involved 'cos I'd go barmy if I didn't. There's some damn nice people about too! You'll be O.K., Mark."

Mark relaxed. Peter made it all seem so straightforward; he even began to look forward to his involvement with some enthusiasm. Shortly afterwards, they found themselves knocking at the Superior's door, and on entering, Peter cheerfully announced:

"It's father Kennedy just arrived to take up his appointment."

"Come in, father." The superior was a heavily built man with greying hair, in his early fifties, Mark judged.

"Father Kennedy. I think we've met before. You've stayed here on your journeys to and from Rome, I believe."

"Yes, father. You were superior here the last time I stayed."

"Humph." That noncommittal grunt could signify anything, Mark thought. But a moment later, the older priest smiled and said:

"I'm sure you'll be happy here, father, and an asset to the parish team."

"I'll do my best father" replied the rather relieved Mark.

"Father Clark will be able to show you the ropes. It's all fairly straightforward. It's a busy parish, so I'm sure you won't be bored or find yourself twiddling your thumbs. Regarding parish visiting, we all have areas. I have your predecessor's visiting book here somewhere."

He rummaged around on his desk for a minute then rose and crossed to a tall file, with miscellaneous papers heaped on top.

"Ah, here it is."

Mark took the proffered slim volume, and quickly flicked through it. It looked rather like the one he had used on his first mission.

"I wonder how out of date it is?" he thought a little gloomily to himself. As if reading his thoughts, the parish priest commented:

"You'll probably find it a little out of date in parts, but by and large it'll give you all the information you need."

"That's it, then, kid," remarked Peter laconically as they walked back down the corridor afterwards.

"Come on, I'll get the car, and we'll have a quick tour round your district."

As they chugged round in the battered parish Ford, Peter pointed out the places of interest. The streets seemed gloomy and dispirited, the houses drab and all jumbled together.

"Bedsitter land, this" observed Peter as they drove down a street comprised of tall, three storey houses each with about half a dozen bells on the front door.

"You'll probably find your visiting book hopelessly out of date for this area. They're all here today and gone tomorrow."

But the total area allocated to Mark did not seem too unmanageable. He thought he should be able to take it in his stride without undue difficulty. Later that evening, Peter produced one of his mysteriously obtained bottles of whisky, and the two chatted on into the small hours, catching up on all the news and gossip. Mark carefully skirted round the more contentious issues that had precipitated his departure from St Augustine's, knowing that he and Peter would never agree on them. But he was content to bask in the ties of their old friendship, welcoming the fact that he was with one of the few people with whom he could relax more or less completely, provided he steered clear of controversial issues.

Next day, he decided to take the plunge.

"No time like the present" he thought as he strode out into the busy streets shortly after ten o'clock. The beginnings of his area were within a ten minute walk of the church, and so before long he was hesitantly knocking on his first door. The experience was similar to that of his mission visiting; but on this occasion, he felt justified in spending more time in each house. His morning consisted of depressing arguments with the more self defensive of the lapsed, encouraging little pep talks to the partially lapsed or indifferent; pep talks which sounded irrelevant and hollow as his listeners stared blankly at him.

"Do you mean that white thing?" one asked when he was trying to discuss the importance of Holy Communion.

"I'd be as well speaking in Chinese" he thought to himself. "It would all mean just as much to them."

He began to realise what was meant by the phrase 'post-Christian era', and found himself unconsciously starting to act like one of the television caricatures of the priest that irritated him whenever he saw plays on television featuring the clergy. But then he would be cheered by meeting at the next house the warm, friendly welcome that nearly all practising Catholics give to their priests.

Within a few weeks he came to know quite a large number of the parishioners, especially those in his own area. On the Sunday following his arrival, Peter introduced him to many of the 'regulars'; old Bert who helped in the sacristy and was never out of the place; an ex-army man, Bert had been born in the area, and after seeing much of the world in the services, was now retired and living in the same haunts he had known as a child.

"Pleased ter meet yer, farver," he said gruffly.

"Bert keeps us all in order in the sacristy and on the altar; he's a terrific M.C, and I just don't know what we'd do without him" said Peter, giving Bert a familiar little nudge.

As Mark soon discovered, there were very few parish activities in which he was not involved. He kept the sacristy spotless, served at least one of the daily Masses, was a member of the S.V.P, or society of St Vincent he Paul, which looked after the poor and needy in the parish. He also helped to run the parish weekly bingo sessions, and was a stalwart in the social club, where a fair proportion of his army pension ended up in the till, in payment for the generous, and occasionally excessive amounts of beer and whisky he consumed. Nearly every parish has its Bert, and God help it if it doesn't. Mark warmed to him immediately, recognising a dependable ally.

"Hello, Bert" he smiled, extending his hand. It was taken in a grip like iron as the older man grasped it firmly. His respect was immediately apparent, and Mark found it humbling.

"Here am I" he thought, "a mere whippersnapper with no experience of life, and a man like this looks up to me."

The respect and regard of the faithful for their priests was something that never ceased to amaze him. "If only they knew," he thought ruefully to himself. It was a factor he occasionally found stifling too. He never objected to people calling him by his Christian name; Neville had sometimes warned him against this tolerance. But Mark had a deep-seated desire to be regarded as an ordinary person; the clericalisation which set the priest apart was not a factor which appealed to him, though on the other hand a brash over-familiarity was not welcomed either. Meanwhile Peter, anxious to introduce him to more of the parishioners, was digging him in the ribs.

"Snap out of it, dopey, come and meet Phyllis and Pat."

These two ladies were in their early thirties, with young families, and once again were obviously key figures in parish life. They were both vivacious and attractive ladies, and Mark felt a momentary pang of envy as he thought to himself what lucky men their husbands were. They quickly dispelled any tendency to shyness Mark might have had in his approach to them, and very soon he was swapping badinage with them as if he had known them all his life.

They were very deeply involved in parish life, he soon discovered, and came to weekday Mass two or three times, besides helping in the youth club and bingo sessions, where Phyllis had been known to scandalise staider parishioners on occasion by showing a flash of thigh when the caller announced 'legs eleven.' But they were good women with generous hearts, and Mark quickly came to regard them as firm friends. One or two older members of the community commented a little sourly that they should be spending more time with their husbands and children, but Peter, conscious mainly of their irreplaceable contribution, would not hear a word against them. In fact, their non-Catholic husbands regarded their involvement with an amused tolerance, and to the outside eye at least, all seemed to be reasonably serene on the domestic front.

Another regular helper was Maureen, an older woman from a poor background, whose husband was a hopeless drunk and gambler who was not above physically maltreating her on occasion. She was obviously seeking an escape through her involvement, and yet she seemed to bear life's burdens without complaint, and her devotion at Mass indicated real holiness. Her children always seemed to be in trouble with the police, and try as she would, she could not get them to Mass or to any of the other parish activities.

"That woman's a bloody saint" commented Peter. "Where she gets her strength I'll never know. She waits on that family of idle scroungers hand and foot, and all they ever do is push her into the shit."

He obviously had a warm affection for Maureen, and as Mark discovered, treated her a little like the mother whose love had been one of the few redeeming features of his difficult childhood days.

Going round his area, Mark soon became acquainted to a greater or lesser degree with most of the Catholics, though some he could never catch at home, and others he never seemed to get round to visiting. Like most priests, he got into the habit of treating certain houses almost as homes from home; houses where he could always drop in unannounced for a cup of tea and a chat when the burdens of his regular work got him down.

There was Mary, the Irish nurse whose timid Catholic husband obviously adored her; she had a couple of boisterous children who soon treated Mark almost like a favourite uncle. Mary obviously ruled the roost and quickly made her displeasure felt in no uncertain terms, using strong language and a loud voice, but she was always laughing and joking the next minute. She treated Mark like one of the family, shouting at him with the rest, but welcoming him just as warmly. He made sure he kept in her good books, though occasionally he became involved in good natured arguments.

There were several other families with whom he quickly became on warm, friendly terms, and he was soon recognised as a familiar figure around the district. He studiously kept up his visits to the lapsed, but found that he made little if any progress there, thus reinforcing his idea that the Church could not spread by exhortation; its development had to be an organic growth. He began to consider the possibility of organising house Masses in his area, but when he broached this idea with the parish priest it was discouraged, as one part of the parish could not be seen to be developing along lines other than those followed by the parish as a whole.

"We shall think about such a programme for Lent, father" encouraged the superior, not wishing to totally dampen Mark's initiative.

Mark quickly became involved in most of the other parish activities. Peter drafted him in to help with the youth club, and Mark decided to learn to play the guitar as part of his involvement. He broached the idea to Peter:

"There's a young social worker living in my area who's a fabulous guitarist, Pete: I think I'll see if he'll come along and help us in the youth club; he'd be great giving lessons to some of the kids, and I'd like to learn myself."

Thus it was that a couple of days later, Mark approached the young man, a Scot with a rollicking sense of humour and a magic talent for music.

"I've seen you at Mass, Alan, every Sunday. Have you ever thought about getting more involved in the parish? You could certainly give the sort of help that we could use."

Alan scratched his head.

"Aye, I suppose I could, father" he replied a little reluctantly.

Mark enthusiastically described the sort of contribution he felt Alan could make, and quickly began to foresee all sorts of areas in which he could be invaluable.

"We could even perhaps start a folk Mass occasionally; and you could be a terrific help at the social events."

Alan was overwhelmed by the flood of eloquence, and agreed to give things a try.

"There's my girlfriend, father; I don't know how she'll feel about my giving up some of my free time; she isn't too happy when my caseload takes up some of the evenings."

With the oblivious selfishness that on occasion can be a characteristic of the enthusiastic priest, Mark overruled these objections, saying that he could get her involved, too.

So it was that the twanging of guitars became a regular feature of youth club night in the parish, and Mark made rapid progress, quickly getting to the stage where he was able to help in the coaching of the younger beginners.

FIFTY

As the autumn drew on and winter approached, preparations for the two major social events of the Christmas season had to be undertaken. A committee of dedicated lay helpers was formed to organise the Christmas bazaar, and Bert began to arrange the collection of goods for sale, with the ladies circle and pensioners groups busily involved in making various articles of craft work. Rivalry, sometimes not too friendly, often developed in the efforts of the rival stall holders and it became a matter of pride in some quarters as to which group had the best laid out stall at the bazaar, and which made most money on the day.

Mark was thankful he did not have much to do with the organising; his role, along with Peter, was to encourage the efforts of others by every means possible. He enthused politely over the knitted tea cosies and table decorations; ooed and aahed at the mounting collection of tinned and packeted food, and congratulated Bert on the growing number of bottles he had collected for his bottle stall. In the announcements at Sunday Mass, he and Peter cajoled and browbeat the Faithful regarding the purchase of raffle tickets, and though everyone knew moments of blind panic, it was generally felt that all was proceeding in a most satisfactory manner.

The other major event was the parish pantomime. The two young priests had a much larger part in these preparations. Between them, Mark and Peter put together a script, based loosely on the story, with many topical references to the current political situation, and with many a dig at the parish priest and other parish worthies, all with the greatest good humour.

The cast was drawn from the youth club, with one or two of the ladies' circle and parish helpers drawn in. Phyllis and Pat were recruited, Phyllis making a splendidly leggy principal boy. A demure beauty from the youth club played Cinderella, while Alan took the part of Buttons. Mark and Peter were to be the ugly sisters, Mark finding that he was able to behave as outrageously as he liked, while Peter's natural acting ability enabled him to produce the show, besides making an invaluable contribution in his part. Rehearsals were held on a Sunday afternoon, and at first, it was hard to shake off the natural torpor induced by a busy morning of preaching and Masses followed by a traditional Sunday lunch. But the production came on apace with more and more skilled assistants being roped in, from scenery painters and designers to electricians, carpenters and humble tea ladies. The local dancing school was approached to provide a team of young dancers to grace the occasion, and before long the production was almost at the performance stage.

Meanwhile the pastoral work went on, with Mark becoming more and more involved in his district. One of his regular calls became the weekly visit to an old lady known to everyone as 'Gran', with Holy Communion. Her devotion was touching, and her asides hilarious. But on occasion, she gave Mark pause for thought. Commenting on one of the many tragedies that fill the screens of the television and the pages of the newspapers with a seeming inevitability, she murmured:

"Never mind, father, God looks after us all; at least He does his best."

Mark, used to the notion of the all-powerful God, was amused at first, but soon saw new depths in the saying. The helplessness of God was a notion that was needed to complement his omnipotence; the gift of a will that was truly free meant the notion of a God who had tied his own hands. When it came to trying to make some sense of the problem of an all-powerful God who permitted the vast amount of suffering in this world, it seemed to make more sense than the sterile old wranglings of the theologians trying to reconcile the notion of free will and predestination.

"You teach me a lot about God and about life, Gran" he commented.

"All I know, father, is that he's good to me, and so I love him and say my prayers to him," she replied, smiling her toothless smile and pulling her shawl more tightly round her skinny shoulders.

Later, he mused further on the problem of evil and suffering, and began to wonder what was really meant by the doctrine of hell. The mediaeval picture of flames and pitchforks, eternal, mind boggling agony, seemed to be totally at odds with the notion of a just and loving God. The general view of most theologians seemed to be that hell exists, but seems so impossibly frightful that perhaps nobody ever goes there. Mark wondered whether the phrase 'eternal death' might mean just that; those who had dedicated their lives to selfishness and had fundamentally refused to respond to the revelation of God's love or to basic goodness as they saw it might simply cease to be; 'homo naturaliter immortalis' was, after all, a supposition of philosophers taken from the Greeks rather than a datum of revelation. Eternal life as God's gift would then be seen to be truly a supernatural gift, a gift beyond the rights and expectation of mortal man. It certainly seemed to make more sense that the commonly received doctrine, which was often reduced to postulating universal salvation, as the alternative was unthinkable. Certainly, Scripture and tradition seemed to support a view which by no means implied that all would be saved; on the contrary, a depressingly large number would not be. A view depicting man as naturally mortal, in body and in soul, to whom the gift of eternal life is lovingly offered, seemed to accord better with this view than the more orthodox interpretation.

But Mark hastily banished any notion of speaking publicly about such views; he had already discovered that to speak one's mind was not always the wisest policy in the Church, as in any other walk of life.

His contact with families, ordinary people from old age pensioners to toddlers and babies, began to deepen his appreciation of ordinary humanity. His heart would bleed for some of those whom he met in the course of his pastoral duties; a tenderness towards them would sometimes threaten to overwhelm him. Vulnerability moved him deeply; he hated the insensitivity he often saw in himself during moments in which he appreciated the importance of every other person. The sight of a grubby child clutching its broken toy, or a woman deserted by her husband, bravely keeping the fragments of her life together as she counted out the pennies, working out what she could afford would wrench his heart, and tears would come into his eyes.

He found his contact with people rewarding, and enjoyed being part of their lives, if only for a few minutes at a time. But this very contact served to reinforce his sense of isolation and loneliness, and he sometimes longed for a sense of closeness and belonging; he grew to resent more and more the clericalism of the priesthood which seemed to be a major factor in shutting him out of people's ordinary lives, even though initially, it gave him admittance to their hearts and homes.

He felt a sense of revulsion growing from the attitudes and life styles inculcated by his long association with the Order and the Church. 'The world' was a place to be avoided despised, and guarded against; the truly privileged children of the Church were the priests and religious; the laity were a second class citizenry to be patronised, and those outside the Church were almost non-persons, unless regarded as conversion-fodder. He knew a growing desire to be one with this world and its people, to come down from his ivory tower. But for the moment, parish life was sufficiently demanding for him not to have much free time for such broodings, the demands of school, hospital and the many families with their myriad problems were sufficient to keep him more or less fully occupied.

There were moves afoot within the Order at this time to increase the importance of the sense of community among the brethren; moves enthusiastically welcomed by Mark, though Peter was more sceptical.

"What does it amount to?" he scoffed. "More bloody community meetings and the occasional concelebration. We've enough community meetings as it is."

Many of the older brethren tended to agree with him. One of them commented when he heard that a conference or study session on the subject was to be held at St Augustine's that in his experience, the things you learned at these events could have been put on the back of a postcard at vastly less expense; "or even on the back of the stamp, for that matter." Mark had to laugh at the comment, but was more hopeful, acknowledging nevertheless that a study session and a few community meetings were not going to produce miracles.

"What's needed, Pete, is a whole new attitude. We need to apply the theology of community to our lives; to learn the importance of a new love and respect for one another; to start treating one another as the body of Christ."

"Oh, bollocks, Mark" groaned the exasperated Peter. "I'm perfectly happy just doing my job and enjoying the perks as and when they arise."

And it was true, Mark acknowledged to himself. What was it that gave Peter his uncomplicated approach (at least it seemed so on the surface) while in his own case a maggot of dissatisfaction continually gnawed away at his heart? He recognised the fund of goodwill among his brethren; they were sincere, hardworking priests in the main, but he was looking for something more, something that perhaps he would never find, he admitted to himself, remembering his parting conversation with Neville.

But before he knew it, the Christmas season was upon them. At the bazaar, Mark was drafted in to play the part of Father Christmas, and he spent a frantic Saturday morning manufacturing a suitable grotto, assisted by Bert who helped with suggestions and the labour of his willing if not too skilful fingers. The ladies wrapped the presents for his sack, coding them suitably for boys or girls. At two o'clock the doors opened, and the hall and parish rooms were soon inundated with bustling throngs of people, many of whom Mark had never seen in his life before. After a preliminary potter about and last minute check of his grotto, where Bert was busily fending off over-inquisitive youngsters, he went to his room and donned his Santa suit. Then sneaking round to the main door to the hall, he rang his bell, and with a few loud 'ho ho ho's', soon had the children flocking round, the older ones trying to dislodge his beard to discover his identity. After declaring the bazaar open in his official capacity, he retired to his grotto to tackle the hordes of eager small customers. He was fascinated by the wide eyed wonder of the little ones, some of whom he knew from his visiting or chatting outside the church on Sundays after Mass, and thoroughly enjoyed a hectic hour and a half.

Eventually, the visitors to the grotto finally petered out, and he was able to beat a diplomatic retreat to his room to change back to father Mark. He then had time to tour the rest of the bazaar, trying for the bottle of whisky on Bert's stall, but only winning a child's bottle of fizzy pop. Alan was busily engaged in running a horse racing game, played with cards, in which the punters bet on the progress of a suit of cards up a green baize race course, as Alan turned over the pack one by one.

"Roll up, roll up, only ten pence a go" he roared in his strong Glaswegian accent, and the crowds pressed round, eagerly holding out their ten pence pieces. Winners doubled their stakes, and so with the odds firmly in his favour, he was steadily making money.

Peter was running a darts game, and on several occasions had narrowly escaped being impaled by the inexpertly thrown missiles of the excited juvenile participants. He hailed Mark's approach with relief.

"I feel like a bloody pin cushion" he groaned when granted a moment's respite, but almost immediately was compelled to minister to the needs of another eager player.

Mark rapidly toured the ladies' craft stalls, complimenting them on the sales they had made, astonished at the way in which the heaped tables of an hour or so earlier were now looking distinctly threadbare. Smiles of satisfaction wreathed the stall-holders' faces, and predictions were confidently made of a record breaking result. The noise and general pandemonium were incredible, and a warm fug generated by the milling human bodies filled the hall. Crying children were reunited with parents, and Mark mopped his brow with a sense of relief as the time came for the drawing of the raffles.

In his best sergeant major voice, Bert called for silence, and in a surprisingly short time, obtained it. Mark's family had loyally bought books of tickets, which he now consulted in case they had won anything. But no such luck. The winners all seemed to be non-parishioners he had never heard of, though one or two smaller prizes were won by the more familiar faces.

Shortly afterwards, the crowds began to depart, and once the exodus commenced, it quickly gathered momentum. After another half hour, priests and helpers were standing among the debris in the deserted hall, knocking back drinks from the illicitly opened bar of the social club, though many of the ladies made do with a cup of tea. As predicted, the results were distinctly gratifying, and the parish priest pronounced himself well pleased.

"Well done fathers Clark and Kennedy, and congratulations and thank you to all the helpers."

There was a satisfied glint in his eye as he bore off the financial spoils, and Peter grinned.

"That should cheer the old bugger up a bit" he commented to Mark in an undertone, and Mark laughed and stretched.

"As Alan would say, he sometimes has a face like the smell of gas, but that's certainly put him in a good mood, but it's a hot bath for me, and then it's my stint in the confessional."

Penitents never seemed to think about the clergy's other commitments, he thought wryly. Some years back, he recalled, people had even come for confession during the World Cup final between England and West Germany, or so he had been told by one or other of the brethren.

As he lay soaking in the bath minutes later, he mused to himself about the trivialisation of the sacrament of Penance. The Church earnestly recommended the frequent use of the sacrament, even on a fortnightly or monthly basis. But so often grown men and women came along to mechanically confess the same sins they had committed since childhood. Certainly there were the occasional souls in the throes of desperate guilt and sorrow; confession should be mainly for such occasions in life, he thought to himself. In the early Church, it had been a once or twice in a life time experience when a man who had wilfully rejected God and the Church could come home again; surely it should return to being something of the same sort of experience? Perhaps more frequent than once or twice in a life time, but it should be linked to more important moments in life, or a fundamental change of direction.

"We've trivialised the notion of the sacrament of Penance, because we've trivialised the idea of mortal sin" he concluded as he lay in the warm water, watching the steam rising from the surface. Mortal sin could only make sense as a definitive wilful rejection of God, either conscious or implied by the sheer wickedness of the action undertaken. In everyday Catholic thought, it was something that could be committed by seemingly trivial actions undertaken with full deliberation, such as a lustful thought or glance. Realistically, however, it seemed to him that masturbating teenagers (or priests, for that matter) were hardly monsters of wickedness; most people were basically well-intentioned, bumbling through life with a mixture of motives, good and not so good. One's basic commitment to good or evil did not seem to be much affected by the occasional moment of sexual desire, or petty dishonesty. He sighed.

"Better get a move on", he thought, rising from the water which cascaded off him as he struggled shivering to his feet. A brisk towelling down and some clean clothes rapidly donned left him ready for the onslaught of the Saturday night sinners once again.

FIFTY ONE

Christmas came and went, the pantomime was a great success, its demands wreaking havoc with other activities, but January saw things back to normal. For two or three weeks, visiting became very difficult as arctic gales and blizzards swept the country, London not being immune from such rigours. But gradually the weather moderated, and with the clocks being put forward in March, the evenings too became lighter.

But one day about this time, Peter came along to Mark's room with a bombshell.

"I'm being moved" he announced out of the blue. Mark blinked.

"Bloody hell, Pete; that's a bit sudden; where are you going?"

"North" he replied gruffly. "I'm to start giving Missions. I don't know who you'll be getting here. I only hope it's someone with a bit of go in him, or you'll be in the shit."

There wasn't much time for condolences or mental preparation when appointments were made; they took effect immediately. Two or three days saw Peter's affairs wound up, and he took his leave from Mark in typically brisk fashion.

"Keep in touch, let me know what's happening down here, and I'll see you around, kid."

Mark felt bereft once more. Peter had been his big ally in the parish. They had discussed their work and the common ventures; the parish priest, taken up with the official details, had been content to leave a lot of the social side of things to the younger men. In the Order, the harmonisation of the life and activity of parish and community had always been something of a problem, the Order not being dedicated by its constitution to parish work. The older brethren in particular tended to be inward looking, seeing any parochial duties and activities as peripheral to the main stream of their lives. Peter and Mark had felt the opposite in their commitment to the parish; they tended to stand apart from the rest of the little community, who by a tacit understanding, left them to get on with their major involvement. The parish priest allowed this, as being superior also of the community, he acted as a bridge between the two elements. He was involved with the parish on the more mechanical level, leaving the everyday details to his two juniors. There were several other older priests attached to the establishment, but of these, one was away a good deal preaching retreats and the occasional mission, and the others, like the parish priest, tended to keep their involvement to what was strictly necessary.

Mark prayed for someone young and dynamic to be sent to join them; but for a couple of months he had to soldier on more or less alone though the others did manage to help by relieving him of some of the pressure in the more formal areas of parish life. In the early days of May, however, Peter's replacement finally came through. He was a youngish man, three or four years senior to Mark and Peter, but he was known to have had his ups and downs in the priesthood and the religious life. Mark groaned inwardly.

"We need help badly" he thought to himself "and all they can do is to give us someone who very likely will turn out to be another passenger."

He immediately took himself to task for prejudging the issue, forcing himself to have more sympathy and understanding. He was beginning to have a better idea of the pressures that could cause a man to break down, or stop giving of his best.

"It's been a long time, Ollie."

Mark extended his hand and grasped that of the new corner. Father Oliver Brady smiled faintly.

"Nice to see you, Mark."

They had never been particularly close in the seminary, the seniority in those days making more of a difference than it did by the time Mark's year had reached the upper levels. Mark had come across father Brady on occasion since, but they had been like ships that pass in the night. Mark had heard rumours of drink problems and brief disappearances, but he resolutely thrust all such thoughts from his mind and resolved to take as optimistic a view as he could. He was pleasantly surprised by the way in which things turned out. Father Brady was a willing and imaginative worker, and he and Mark were quickly on friendly terms. He was something of a thinker too, and so Mark once again had someone with whom he could discuss his ideas on the future of the Church and Order.

Father Brady settled into the community, where the older members regarded him with suspicion and a cautions tolerance. Eagle eyes would fix on him whenever he had a glass in his hand, as though expecting him to descend to the worst depths of alcoholism.

"I'm not an alcoholic" he averred to Mark when discussing the subject on his own initiative on one occasion, "but I have hit the bottle pretty hard in one or two instances when things were going badly."

Mark gathered that it was an escape when the pressures became too great. He hoped St Margaret's would not prove too much for Oliver; other appointments had ended somewhat disastrously, and he was rapidly gaining the reputation of being an unwelcome addition to any community, but for the first few months of his stay at St Margaret's, Oliver seemed to be doing very well, and little by little, suspicions died down, and Mark was able to relax, as disaster did not seem to be imminent.

But imminent it was, and one evening out of the blue, Oliver disgraced himself by saying the evening Mass in a semi-drunk condition. It slowly dawned on Mark with mounting horror as the Mass continued. Hurriedly donning a surplice, he went discreetly onto the altar, kneeling at the side to be ready in case things became any worse. After Communion, he managed to get Oliver to sit down while he distributed Communion to the faithful on his behalf. It was a nightmare. He did not know what to expect next, and on one or two occasions Oliver started muttering, and Mark wondered desperately if he was going to become belligerent. Somehow they managed to get to the end of the service without major mishap, and with a deep sense of relief Mark ushered him off the sanctuary. In the sacristy, the flood gates were opened.

"You're a bloody fucking busybody" he spluttered in slurred tones, as Mark tried to help him unvest. The unflappable Bert was on hand and to Mark's relief, intervened.

"Come on, farver," he said gruffly. "What you need is a good lie down."

With Mark's help, he managed to get Oliver to his room, where they quickly put him to bed.

"He'll be orl right when he's slept it off, farver," Bert observed "It's a shame when the drink takes control. I've seen it often enough in me army days." A quick examination of the room disclosed two or three empty spirit bottles, and Mark tactfully disposed of these. Oliver must have been drinking for some time, he thought to himself. Why the hell hadn't he noticed? Alcoholics were expert at concealing their problem, he realised; well, he had certainly been fooled, for one. Next morning, Oliver was all apologies, and seemed no whit the worse for the experience.

"I'd have been nursing a king-size hangover" Mark mused, "but Ollie seems perfectly normal this morning."

The resilience of the alcoholic was also a factor new to him. In their relationship, Oliver carried on as if nothing had happened, but Mark was now wary. He felt that he could not trust him; he recognised the other man's good intentions, and appreciated his qualities, but felt that he could not rely on him in a crisis any longer.

The weeks and months seemed to speed by as Mark, taken up with the busy life of the parish, immersed himself in his work. The strains were beginning to tell on him, too; his prayer life, never particularly orderly, tended to suffer as the demands of his duties often left him too tired to give himself over to the routine exercises of the religious life. He was with people nearly all the time, and yet his sense of loneliness grew.

His sexual problems simmered away beneath the surface, masturbation bringing him a momentary habitual relief, though it tended to leave him feeling depressed and disgusted with himself. What added to this sense of self loathing was the occasional introduction of other elements into the practice which seemed even more squalid and obscene to him. He would occasionally buy magazines of doubtful reputation from the top shelf of a newsagent's diplomatically distant from his home territory, using the graphic illustrations to stimulate his desire; after a day, or even a couple of hours, he would destroy them with a sense of self-cleansing and purification, as he resolved to put these things behind him yet again, and try to be more worthy of his state. He still mentioned his problems when he went to confession, but the advice he received became as routine as the problem itself.

He began to look forward to any little break from the parish that he could arrange; a few days' retreat twice a year, usually up at St Augustine's, or at one of the other houses of the Order, situated in a northern seaside town. During his retreats, he would spend long hours walking by himself, sometimes quietly content with the sense of freedom and relaxation, sometimes trying to resist the thoughts and temptations that were threatening to become obsessions. On other occasions he would turn over in his mind the mounting problems in other areas that seemed to be filling his life, or daydreaming about a Utopian world or Church.

But frequently too the calm and peace would help him to pray, and he felt that although the Divine Office was to say the least merely an occasional part of his life, he had a relationship with God of a contemplative sort that meant that Christ was never far from his mind or heart. His celebrations of Mass became very much the heart of his day, and brought him a deep sense of peace, even when his thoughts were otherwise occupied with the many problems in his life, both personal and professional.

He split his three weeks' annual holiday into three equal parts, finding it more valuable to eke out the precious days in this way. Consequently, two or three times a year he would thankfully bid farewell to London, and take the bus north from Victoria coach station to spend a few days at home and with Tony and Elizabeth, whose family was growing with the addition of a new baby, Catherine. He loved to play with the babies, bath them, take them for walks for all the world as if he were their doting father, but close as he was to them, the loneliness in his inner core remained. He grew to accept this as an inevitable part of priestly celibacy, though sometimes he had to check a fierce surge of envy when his ministry brought him into contact with an obviously happy family, or a young couple in love preparing for marriage.

"What the hell am I giving up all this for?" he would sometimes ask himself, and the customary litany of the motives for celibacy tended to sound more platitudinous each time he rehearsed them to himself.

The Order was feeling the manpower crisis in the Church as keenly as the other religious establishments and secular clergy generally; consequently Mark's services were occasionally sought in other fields. He gave one or two missions, this time on a solo basis and so was more free to follow his own ideas in organising the exercise, within the constraints of the traditional fortnight.

One he gave in a small market town in the midlands, where the Catholic community formed an identifiable group organised in a single parish. He set to with a will, designing striking posters and handbills, visiting the parish for a weekend about two months before the mission so that he could preach at all the Masses and let the people know that something exceptional was in the offing. He drew up a programme of sermons outlining the Vision; the Gospel, or good news, enthusiastically proclaimed, would win a warm response, he was confident. Out were the threats of hell, meant to jerk the guilty backsliders out of their sinful slumber, as were the moralising denunciations of contraception and divorce of the sermon on marriage. What he could hope to attain in a fortnight, he realised, was a revitalisation of the faith and Christian commitment of a core of the Mass-going Catholics, brought back through his efforts to a new appreciation of the beauty and importance of the life of God they shared with perhaps a modest number of the lapsed returning to the fold through his efforts in visiting. If he could help the local Church to become a more healthy, living body, then the organic growth ultimately sought might be brought realistically closer.

He arrived in the parish with his plans fully worked out; his opening Sunday service was not a separate afternoon event, but the Sunday Mass itself with specially selected readings and a sermon based on the need of every Christian to listen and respond to the good news. His first week was the traditional visiting of school and homes, but with the addition of house Masses each evening in different areas of the parish. In these, he gathered as many of the faithful Catholics as could be persuaded to come, in the home of one of the families, and then tried to give them an example, an experience of the importance of being Christ's body as the Church.

"This is the Church at the grassroots, and therefore at the most important level" he said to the little group gathered round the dining room table. The importance of sharing the Mass in such intimate surroundings tended to help those present to a new, deeper awareness of their faith, and this was further helped by the informal discussions over the cup of tea that followed. It was hardly the Jerusalem experience of the apostles in the days following Pentecost, but it was a start.

The Parish priest he found co-operative and helpful, appreciative of what he was trying to achieve. He thought wryly of his first mission, and the old fashioned shepherd of the flock who treated his parishioners just like a load of sheep. The second week started well, with another appeal on the Sunday to the parish to come and hear the message of God. On each evening during the week, Mark then took one of the basic themes: conversion, sharing the life of Christ, the Church, the Sacraments, love of neighbour and witness, and developed it in the context of the Mass, with specially chosen readings and hymns. He gave shorter versions of the same themes at the morning Masses for those who could not come in the evening, and stressed the desirability of the people attending every day where possible, so as to be able to see the Vision as a whole.

He managed a very creditable turnout over the full week, and ended on the final Sunday, again at all the Masses, with a sermon on the theme 'Ite, missa est', or 'go, and share our faith with those around you'. But he could not resist a dig at the weekly Mass-goers who had resisted all appeals to come to the mission.

Discussing it with the parish priest after the final Mass, he was happy that he had achieved at least a limited success regarding his objectives; people would remember him and the mission; he hoped that they had managed to obtain even a glimpse of the Vision that inspired him.

Arriving back in St Margaret's, he was upset to hear rumours of snide comments that he was never in the place, comments made by one or two of the parishioners. Deeply hurt, he rang Peter to talk about it, but Peter just shrugged it off.

"Ignore the bastards" he replied. "If you're trying your best to do a good job, you can forget all the moans and groans; some people are never satisfied."

Mark tried to follow this advice, but the hurt lingered on. The injustice of it was wounding, because although he had to admit to being absent a little more often than a secular priest would have been in a similar situation, he was obviously busily employed in the duties and exercises of his calling, and there were always sufficient priests at home to ensure that nothing was neglected. But it all helped to build up Mark's sense of disenchantment and resentment; sometimes the priesthood seemed to hang about his neck like a millstone, the Church a cruel and relentless taskmistress.

"You've got me nailed in your cross; what more do you want?" he was tempted to cry.

But the Vision remained intact, although its relevance to the daily details of his life often seemed curiously remote. It inspired his sermons and instructions to converts, couples to be married and the older classes of schoolchildren, but his life when held against it seemed so tacky and unworthy.

The pattern of his life seemed to have been established; he sometimes wondered whether he would still be doing the same sort of things in forty years time. In general, it seemed to be an acceptable life, if crucifyingly difficult at times, but the thought of something radically different never crossed his mind. His sense of vocation was still strong, his obedience to God's will the paramount driving force behind it.

And so the months and years began to slip past, as spring, summer autumn and winter with their corresponding liturgical seasons came round with sometimes frightening rapidity. His life was a never ceasing round of visiting his parishioners, the school, the hospital, saying Mass, preaching, hearing confessions, enduring clergy meetings, and keeping up as best he could with all the routine paper work. The diet was varied by the occasional absence to give a mission or retreat. His own spiritual life seemed to flourish and stagnate by turn, his personal problems sometimes to the fore, and at other times simmering quietly in the background. He visited his family regularly, especially Tony and his still growing family, sometimes going on holiday with them for an idyllic week or few days.

Mark, then, was reaching his mid-thirties. His life was settling into a rut, even if a not particularly comfortable one. But then he met Madeleine.

FIFTY TWO

She came into his life almost by accident. It was a day in early spring; he had been at St Margaret's about six years, and was conscientiously carrying out the routine duties allotted to him; the daily round of parish visiting, the activities of youth club and other parish groups, the school and hospital; he seemed to be spending so much of his time enabling the creaking machinery to keep on turning. He would not have described himself as happy, but he had come to more or less accept his lot in life and though the pressures from various quarters, both personal and vocational weighed heavily on him at times, he was managing to keep his head above water.

On this particular day, he was intending to tidy up his visiting book. Against one entry for a house at the furthest edge of his area was the note, presumably made by his predecessor, 'Divorced; no point in calling.' He had never bothered to call before, but something made him decide to call; if the visit proved fruitless then he would cross the entry out once and for all. He went up the path and pressed the door bell. After a pause of a few seconds, the door was opened by a rather attractive lady, between forty and fifty years old, Mark judged to himself.

"I'm father Kennedy from St Margaret's, he announced with a smile.

"Come in, father. It's been a long time since a priest has called."

Mark went in, and admired the room into which he was shown. It was an interesting room; it was strange how often the general furnishings and appearance of a room spoke volumes about the person living there. The room was furnished with excellent taste, though the fittings were far from new, but everything was spotlessly clean.

"Mrs Gray isn't it?" Mark asked, and the lady smiled.

"Madeleine Gray. My ex-husband was the Catholic. I almost became a Catholic at the time of our marriage, but somehow, it never came to anything."

Perhaps with a little encouragement, the interest in the Church might revive again, Mark thought to himself. He instinctively liked Madeleine, recognising a generosity and good natured warmth about her. She made a cup of tea, and told Mark all about herself and her family.

"I have a son, now living away from home; I see him occasionally, but I live by myself now for most of the time."

She had been left by her husband several years earlier, while her son was still more or less a child, and the young man who was now about twenty had left home the previous year. Madeleine had a job in one of the factories on the North Circular road, which sometimes involved working night shifts.

Mark told her about himself and his work, his hopes for the future of the parish, his disappointments and the frustrations that accompanied the life and work of the priest. Somehow, she was easy to talk to, and an hour slipped by before he realised it. Glancing at his watch, he hurriedly made his excuses, and started to take his leave.

"You must come again, father" she smiled. "It's good to talk to a priest who doesn't preach to you, or talk down to you. I like the way you describe Catholicism, too; it sounds much more attractive than I'd imagined."

Promising to call again, Mark waved a friendly goodbye, and resumed his visiting. Somehow, the morning seemed brighter and more cheerful; definitely worth following up, he decided, making an amending note in his book.

In the days that followed, she was frequently in his mind, and he soon began to think to himself what an attractive woman she was. Slightly plump with a soft, peach-like complexion and curly brown hair; he wondered in an erotic moment what she would look like with no clothes on. The thought excited him, and he hastily pushed it out of his mind. But it was eminently reasonable to go and see her again, to see whether he could help draw out her interest in things religious.

On his next visit, about a fortnight later, the sense of attraction quickened; there was the scent of a soft womanliness about her; a beautiful physical quality that would have made her an ideal artists model. But true to his purpose he dragged his mind resolutely back to the matters in hand and found her genuinely interested in the

Vision, as he tried to expound his ideals. She asked him to call again so that they could discuss the Church more fully, and the many peripheral topics that had always fascinated Mark. Very soon, they were fast friends, and Mark began to call on a regular basis, working through an informal series of discussions on the faith, discussions that were often side-tracked down all sorts of fascinating byways. Their ideas often coincided, and Mark found her both a sympathetic listener and an imaginative thinker.

One day, they were deep in discussion, sitting side by side on the settee, her soft thigh somehow touching his. Mark suddenly realised that she was giving him signals of her interest in him, consciously or unconsciously. Almost without realising it, he was answering the gentle pressure and to his horror, had to stop himself from cupping her warm, round breasts in his hands. His body was not waiting for his will to agree, and devastated, he hurriedly made his excuses and left.

Later in the church, he prayed earnestly that he be given the strength to resist the almost overwhelming attraction that he felt, and for a few days, he manfully resisted the temptation to go and see her again. But finally, he could not resist his need any longer. Somewhere in his studies on the psychology of sin and temptation, he had read that the best way to face and overcome a temptation is to confront it; you cannot run away, he told himself. If a priest avoided every woman he found attractive then his work would rapidly become impossible.

Thus he found himself once more on her doorstep, ringing the bell. After a pause, through the frosted glass of the door, he could see her coming down stairs pulling a dressing gown hastily round her obvious nakedness. Her face was flushed from sleep, her hair all over the place, but she greeted Mark with obvious pleasure. Inviting him to come in, she explained that she was on the night shift that week, and had been asleep.

"But I'll be dressed in a minute. Go and make yourself at home in the living room."

So saying, she hurried back upstairs. Mark hesitated momentarily in the hall, and then quickly and quietly followed her upstairs.

Nothing seemed to matter any more; at all costs he had to see her naked body, and take her in his arms. His heart thumping madly, he approached her bedroom door, and quietly opened it. She gave a little gasp of surprise, and clutched wildly at the dressing gown she had been about to hang up. Blushing deeply, she paused, and then let it fall, and walked slowly across the room towards him, her full breasts swinging slightly, her beautifully rounded stomach and hips inexorably drawing his gaze to the softness of her pubic triangle. He groaned softly and held out his arms. Moments later, he was hugging her to himself, his hands gently kneading the warm, smooth flesh of her buttocks, his lips seeking hers in passionate entreaty. Quickly, she helped him undress, and together, they climbed into her still warm bed where they lay together silently in each others arms for several minutes.

"You're crying, Mark" she whispered as they lay there. "What's the matter, darling?"

A vast feeling of emptiness had come over him. He wept for the death of his desire, which had disappeared as they lay down together; he wept for his priesthood and the values he saw slipping beyond his grasp. He wept for the wife and children he did not have; he wept for Madeleine whose goodness and kindness touched him to the depths of his being.

She let him weep, softly stroking his hair as he poured out his heart to her, and he found a sort of cleansing and comfort in the confessions he made. Later, dressed, they shared a cup of tea downstairs and Mark continued to try and describe his feelings to her.

"I feel so shabby and selfish, trying to use you as an answer to my sexual problems." He gripped her hand as he shivered uncontrollably, the reaction setting in. He gulped at the hot tea, attempting to glean some comfort from its warmth.

"No, Mark, you are not using me. You need some tenderness and love, perhaps some sexual comfort too. You must feel able to come to me whenever you need to."

"But I'm a priest, Madeleine; my vocation is clear, and this whole area of life is and must remain closed to me."

He felt the conflict keenly, but she merely smiled gently. "Let's not look too much to the future; we must take life one day at a time. Perhaps you needed me today; perhaps you'll need me in the future, for whatever I am able to give you. Don't treat me as a sin, that's all I ask."

He smiled, cupping her face in his hands.

"My beautiful, innocent Madeleine" he whispered. "I would never think of you and sin as being in the slightest way connected. If there is, or has been any sin, it is my sin, not yours."

Promising to contact her again, he kissed her tenderly, almost as though she were a child, and took his leave. He had known a certain peace in sharing his fears, his guilt, his torment and loneliness with her, but as he neared the monastery, his heart was far from peaceful. The anguish of the conflict tore him apart; he was aware of an urgent need to find some solution to the sexual problems that beset him. What sometimes seemed to be the palliative of masturbation was not a cure in any sense for his frustrations, he realised; and yet he felt an urgent need to masturbate, to reassure himself after the disastrous death of his desire as he lay with her. On the other hand, he longed for the childlike innocence of chastity; he desired to be free from the compulsive needs that were threatening to reduce his life to utter ruin.

Back home, he tried to masturbate, finally managing to achieve orgasm after strenuous efforts of imagination and will. But the reassurance it brought was only temporary and partial. But for the present, it brought a curious sense of peace, and he later went down to the church to pray. He begged God to help him resolve these problems and to become a good priest and religious; he pleaded that he be freed from the compulsive need to see Madeleine that he admitted to himself that he felt.

A sudden inspiration came over him. He was due a few days of retreat; what better time than the present to take them? Hastily leaving the church, he hurried along to the superior's room, where he asked if he could be allowed to go away for a few days' retreat. Though somewhat surprised at the suddenness of the request, the superior agreed, and so Mark telephoned St Augustine's to make the necessary arrangements for his arrival there the following day.

Next morning, he set off without saying Mass; he felt unable to approach the altar until he had confessed the happenings of the previous day.

"Neville, I must talk to you."

On reaching St. Augustine's, he had hastily thanked the driver who had met him, and hurried straight up to Neville's room.

"Come in, dear boy. this is an unexpected, though none the less most welcome pleasure."

Mark sighed, and plunged himself heavily down in the chair indicated. Neville had not changed; the room was just as topsy turvy as it has always been, and it reassured him.

"I don't know how to begin" he stammered, and Neville smiled encouragingly.

"Just relax, and tell uncle Neville all about it" he murmured.

"Nothing is as bad as it seems" he added, sensing the burden under which Mark was labouring.

Hesitantly, Mark began, and once started, the whole story tumbled out. He scrupulously withheld names and places, feeling that to do otherwise would be to betray Madeleine, but he graphically described the compulsion he felt, and the frustrations that he saw with their roots in the distant past.

"1 know just how an alcoholic feels" he confided. "The dreadful need to do this thing; I don't want to make excuses, but my will and determination were like jelly; I was helpless. I even prayed as I walked up the stairs, but I could no more have prevented myself going than I could have stopped my heart beating."

"How do you feel about her?" asked Neville.

"I have a very great affection and regard for her" replied Mark, "but I don't think it's love in the sense of wanting to leave and marry her: I don't think she wants that, either, but I need her, or I need someone or something; I couldn't just say no, I will not see her again. I don't know what I need, that's the trouble," he added a little mournfully.

Neville stared pensively out of the window, his elbows on the table, his fingers pulling at his bottom lip as he pondered on the story he had just heard. The classic advice would have been to tell Mark that he must not see her again; he must seek strength of will through prayer and penance, and at all costs avoid the occasion of sin. But he knew that such advice would be pointless.

"You could ask for a move, dear boy" he mused, "but in all honesty I feel that such a course of action would not meet the case. "What do you feel?"

Mark answered without hesitation. "It's something I've got to face, Neville. This particular lady happened to give the right signal, and that's all that was needed. I probably haven't had this problem earlier because the opportunity never arose before, but I sometimes feel that I would meet the same problem wherever I went unless I shut myself away in an enclosed order, and went slowly mad."

"And enclosed orders aren't for refugees from the battle of life" added Neville. "No, my dear Mark, you must go back to London, and live your life there as the good Lord will ordain. A priori it must be supposed that you have a vocation to chastity, as you are a priest vowed to celibacy, but that must be proved in the crucible of life. Have your few quiet days of rest and reflection, and then we'll just have to see how things develop. But keep me informed; and at all costs, don't get hurt, or cause hurt more than you can help."

With that, Mark had to be content, and receiving absolution, he left Neville's room and made his way to the church where he prepared for Mass. One of the students offered to serve, and so he was soon engaged in a thoughtful celebration of the ageless mysteries. The softly murmured liturgy in the darkening church was powerfully soothing, and he felt a sense of comfort as he handled the bread and wine which he adored as the Body and Blood of Christ as he offered his tawdry, shabby life with the timeless sacrifice of that of his Master.

The comfort remained as he unvested, and sat alone in the church afterwards, watching the flickering sanctuary lamp as it cast its dancing shadows round the gloomy building. Chastity seemed an immense, insuperable problem, but he felt he could do no more than pray.

"My life lies open before you, Lord; you know me better than I know myself. If you want me as your priest, give me the help I need in this time of crisis."

The dim light cast its uneven glow over the tabernacle, at which Mark gazed earnestly, as though willing its silent Occupant to give him courage and confidence. Eventually with a sigh, he rose to his feet and slowly made his way to his room. He felt immensely weary, and foregoing supper, lay on his bed in the darkness. He soon fell asleep, and some hours later awoke, shivering; the noises of the community retiring for the night rousing him. He slipped out of his room, made his way to the kitchen, and finding bread and cheese, was soon munching hungrily while sipping a scalding cup of sweetened cocoa.

"There you are. I've been looking all over for you."

Neville smiled as he appeared in the doorway. "I missed you earlier, so I called at your room just now to see how you were."

"I'm fine, thanks, Neville" Mark murmured, smiling at his friend through the fragrant steam. "Just relaxing as you recommended."

"That's excellent" commented the relieved Neville. "You've a lot to offer, Mark; don't burn yourself out; and don't break yourself against the rock of Peter. Just let life give you what it will give; and remember the words of the Scripture, that no-one is tried beyond his strength. If you simply try to walk serenely in God's presence, you can take life as it comes, and nothing that happens need be regarded as a disaster. Here endeth the first lesson; that's your sermon for tonight. I'll leave you to your cocoa."

He slipped quietly out of the room, and Mark, quickly finishing his Spartan meal, returned to the welcome warmth of his bed.

The next few days brought a much needed sense of relaxation. Rising late, Mark celebrated a leisurely Mass and then spent what remained of the morning reading quietly, praying, and playing the organ. In more recent times, he had not given so much attention to music, but now he found a certain solace in the rich, mellow tones with which he filled the church. The afternoons he spent in walking, enjoying the crisp, seasonal weather. The trees were just beginning to show green, and the roadsides were speckled with primroses and the other flowers of early Spring.

But Madeleine was never far from his thoughts; sometimes he would think wistfully of her, and at other times, the hot, urgent desire would flood over him, setting his heart pounding, and a feverish shivering would seize him. The retreat drew inexorably to its close, and as the time for his return to London approached, the implication of what it meant in terms of nearness to Madeleine and the opportunity it accorded him in terms of sexual excitement would grip his throat like a fist of iron, leaving his mouth dry and his limbs trembling.

"Dear God, am I a sex maniac or what?" he wondered somewhat anxiously. At the same time, he realised that this burning desire was something with which he had to come to terms. It was not simply a question of could he or mustn't he indulge it; it was more a question of could he resist the craving that gripped him, a craving that he could only liken to that of the heroin addict for the needle. But his moral sense, surprisingly not too deeply outraged by his own attitude to the problem, was more concerned with Madeleine, and the possible harm he could do her. He still felt committed to the priesthood, and while along with the sexual desire for her that possessed him, he knew a fondness, even a tenderness for her, he did not know whether his feelings could be described as love. How could he use her in this way?

Time alone would tell how the situation would develop. He felt that in many ways he was a prisoner of the situation, though he could not wish himself out of it, even though part of him longed for release from the torment it brought.

"No wonder Origen cut his balls off" he remarked ruefully to Neville at their final chat before his return.

"Don't proceed to that extreme; he was said to have been much afflicted with headaches later" smiled Neville as he encouraged his friend, trying to help him keep his problems in perspective. Remember the old adage about the 'via media', Mark. The casualties of life are those who fall into one of the extremes. Man, confronted by the situation in which he finds himself, can react in three ways. He can sit back and bemoan his fate, doing nothing; or he can fight tooth and nail against the situation, trying to act as though he is not in that predicament, like a bird breaking its wings against the bars of its cage. Or he can take the via media; accept his situation, and then see how he can best live his life in the given circumstances. That is the task you must set yourself; you are the

Mark Kennedy that God created and placed in this time and place, among these circumstances, with this temperament and character. You are not abstract man, a body-soul composite faced with a particular temptation. In this given set of circumstances, God is calling on you to be Mark Kennedy, not Peter Clark; or even Neville Winterton-Smith," he added modestly.

Mark gave his friend a sad little smile, and sighed.

"It all sounds so comforting and sensible the way you put it, Neville. But living in the situation is bloody agony."

Neville nodded sombrely.

"I was simply trying to clarify the position, with the obvious danger of over simplification. Of course it is agonising; I know it must be. But keep a sense of proportion. To put it bluntly, you and I are very small cogs in a very large machine. True, we all have our unique irreplaceable importance" he added, bowing to the conventional wisdom "but at the end of the day we'll probably be asking ourselves what all the fuss was about. Look at it this way; who knows or cares what happened to a particular curate or parish priest in Birmingham in the year 1880? You see? It is all so small seen against the vast background of salvation history, the history of mankind, and eternity. Just be yourself as best you can here and now, and let the Almighty take care of the rest; that's the way to a life of peace and tranquillity."

Mark chewed his lip thoughtfully and let the wisdom he had heard sink in. It was true, there was no earthly use in getting himself into a state over his problems; far better let the good Lord guide him through. He only hoped he could keep a sense of balance, and come through it as a wiser, more mature person at the end of it all.

"If you want me as your priest, Lord" he prayed later as he mooched round the garden kicking at the piles or leaves still left from the previous autumn, "You'll have to help and guide me. The only hope I have rests in You."

He thought about praying for the gift of chastity, but somehow could not bring himself to ask for it. "I don't know whether I want it, Lord" he compromised, "but if you want me as your priest, show me what you want of me there."

He was relatively calm as the train took him back to London. He deliberately tried not to think of Madeleine, knowing that if he let himself, he could very easily find himself the victim of that heart-stopping desire that fascinated, yet frightened him; he sometimes felt ill with its intensity.

But shortly after arriving home it seized him, and without more ado he was hurrying through the semi-deserted streets, his thoughts whirling round tumultuously inside his head, his stomach churning with the not to be denied feelings. She opened the door to his fevered knock and hardly waiting to greet her, he took her in his arms, hungrily kissing her while his hands started to pull up her dress.

"Mark, people will see" she gasped, blushing hotly as she tried to restrain him, struggling to ensure that no-one could observe the goings on through parted curtains. Taking his hand, she quickly led him upstairs, where she let him pull her clothes off, helping him to remove his own a moment later. Within seconds, they were beneath the covers, kissing passionately as his roaming hands stroked her satin skin, his excitement mounting as he found the curly roughness of her pubic hair. But after some minutes, with a growing sense of desperation, he realised that his penis remained obstinately limp, and as the realisation gained ground, his caresses faltered. He felt distraught, emasculated. A sense of bitterness at what he considered the Church had done to him filled him, and Madeleine immediately realising the problem, instinctively embraced and comforted him.

"It doesn't matter, my darling Mark'" she whispered, cradling his head on her bosom. His body shaken by deep sighs, he allowed her to soothe him, and gradually he relaxed, his hand warm between the comforting softness of her thighs. They slept for a while, a sense of peace having gradually replaced the bitterness, and with the calm, his desire began gradually to return. He immediately began to kiss her, and gently, she allowed him to touch her and explore her body as he would.

"You have nothing to prove, my love," she told him quietly as she caressed him in return. "When your mind and body are ready, everything will turn out as it should, you'll see."

She took his penis and softly stroked it, constantly reminding him to relax and take his time.

"If we do not make love this time, there will be time again, my darling."

It was not to be on that occasion, and though his mind and will urgently desired the fulfilment of orgasm, he had to be satisfied with her almost maternal tenderness. He allowed her to soothe him gradually, and when a relative tranquillity reigned, they rose and dressed, Mark shivering as he quickly pulled on his discarded clothes. He followed her downstairs, and his heart filled with a mixture of tenderness, sorrow and frustration, he put his arms around her, nuzzling her neck and drinking in her perfume as she made a simple meal of warm toast and tea.

"Maybe it's the vow of chastity protecting me from myself" he pondered as they sat side by side before the fire. "My life is laid out for me; the priesthood is my destiny; why can't I accept that tranquilly and get on with it?"

He tried to explain this to her, but the words sounded hollow even as he uttered them. She merely smiled and replied:

"That may well be the case, Mark, that the priesthood is your destiny; but not as a sexually frustrated priest. My poor darling, I know you will never be able to settle until you shed this burden you are carrying; only then will you be able to decide what the future holds for you. Let me help you."

Once again he tried to protest that he felt that he was simply using her.

"Perhaps we are using each other" she replied, "but sometimes people need to use one another. As long as we bear each other's needs in mind, then no harm will be done."

He put his arms round her.

"How are you using me?" he whispered.

She smiled a little sadly. "I am a woman, with a woman's need for tenderness and love. I can live without sex as such, I think; it's a gap in my life I have learned to live with."

She looked at him. "Usually, women can accept the lack of physical sex more easily than men; but we need to be loved and caressed. You are a gentle, caring, tender man; that's what you give to me. So we can give each other what we need, even if it is only partially, and perhaps only here and now. But that's how it has to be. You can't make any decisions about your life in a state of bitterness and frustration. These are the immediate needs we must see to in each other."

He stared at her in wondering admiration. "You have a wisdom which is deeper and wider than all the text book stuff I've relied on, all these years" he murmured as he hugged her,

"And me a simple factory girl" she mocked gently. "When you are left on your own, penniless with a young child to bring up, you find that life is the best teacher. Not being a Catholic, I think that the rights and wrongs of a situation are simpler to understand; that's why I can see us as we are, while you, my poor Mark, have to try and fight your way through the years of Catholic upbringing and training to return to the simple, uncluttered appreciation of a human problem. Not that I don't value and appreciate your faith; I would very much like to have the faith and purpose in life that your religion gives to you. I do go to Mass sometimes, and perhaps one day, even one day soon, I could become a Catholic too."

Later, back at the monastery, Mark realised that he was caught in a situation that he could not resolve. One part of him saw the way ahead as a simple, if terrible, struggle to be chaste, true to the vows he had taken, his visits to Madeleine to be seen as almost unavoidable lapses to be repented. The priesthood and sexual experience were irreconcilable; an honest life demanded utter fidelity, or a serious attempt at it; or on the other hand, realistic capitulation. But Madeleine's words had prompted another train of thought which on reflection, could possibly be reconciled with the consensus he had reached a few days earlier in his discussions with Neville.

Who was Mark Kennedy? He had presumed that he had known the answer to that for all these years. But now he began to realise that he hardly knew himself at all. Whole new areas in his life were beginning to become apparent. He had always forced out of his mind any serious examination of such considerations. What about chastity? He was slowly coming to realise that he had to allow himself the consideration of the possibility that perhaps after all it was not a viable way of life for him.

Bloody hell! Viable? That was a laugh, he thought ironically to himself as he recalled the long, lonely struggle of the years since his early teens; what might have been as he remembered the passionate infatuations of his boyhood and adolescence; the tender love he might have found with his ideal woman. There was the constant battle with his imagination, and the sensual images that lurked round every corner; his occasional temptations to indulge the darker side of his sexuality. More recently there was his habitual masturbation, and the grubby, pathetic temptations presented by the sight of the soft porn sex magazines in the newsagents', or in the displays of the silkily seductive ladies' underwear in the chain stores. And latest of all his furtive visits to Madeleine. Where would his constantly restless sexuality lead him next?

All he needed, he sometimes felt, was a few more years added to his age and a tatty raincoat, and he would be a prime example of the archetypal dirty old man. He recalled reading of the case of a wretched priest arrested for boring holes in toilet cubicles; could that sort of thing be the next development for him, he wondered?

A sense of revulsion welled up inside him; he was disgusted with himself and the shoddy sort of life he was leading. The struggle for chastity was a losing battle; that had become glaringly obvious especially in more recent years. The only realistic thing he could do, he felt, was to call a truce with his conscience. He would visit Madeleine as and when he felt the need, and thrust aside the guilt feelings. Only time would tell what the situation would bring, and in the meantime he owed it to himself and to the priesthood itself to try and resolve the problems that were overwhelming him on a more or less permanent basis. Of course, all priests have their problems with chastity: but he was not all priests. Could he, Mark Kennedy, live with celibacy or not?

But his conscience was not going to accept the truce without a struggle. The image of the naked bodies of himself and Madeleine lying together brought beads of perspiration to his brow as the incongruity of the situation and his official status struck him. How could he do such things and still preach goodness and morality to the people? Considered in isolation, his actions did not seem by any means to be the ultimate in human wickedness, but when seen against the backdrop of everything his life had been and meant up till now, the contrast was painful in the extreme. His reason might tell him that the truce was the only temporary expedient open to him that made sense; but conscience has its roots in aspects of the mind and heart deeper than reason. He tried to pray about the situation, but his prayers seemed a hollow sham. Finally, he had to simply resort to the most basic of all moral imperatives, do good and avoid evil. He was trying, struggling in his own way to do good and avoid evil; his intentions were just, so he told himself, and so every other consideration had to be secondary to this.

FIFTY THREE

Meanwhile the pattern of his priestly life continued much as before in other respects. His sense of vocation remained as strong as ever; his commitment to preaching the Gospel was rooted firmly in the Vision that still survived as the basic motivation of his life.

One of his many duties was to give the occasional talk to the sisters in two or three of the convents in the vicinity. He would enthusiastically develop one of his favourite themes for them; prayer as communion with God in listening and responding to the Word as it is revealed in daily life or the Christian as Christ's revelation of himself here and now. Another favourite theme which he found fascinating was the idea of man as a microcosm of Salvation History.

He would paint for his hearers a picture of the panoramic sweep of God's dealings with man, from creation through the Old Testament to the coming of Christ. The founding and growth of the Church followed, with the final bringing of the whole of creation, with Christ as its heart and head, to the Father in one great act of self-giving love and worship; creation's complete response to the Creator. He would then point out that each of the phases of this great plan has its counterpart in the life of each one of us. We have our own personal creation in conception and birth; an Old Testament aspect in the sin and need of redemption experienced by every man. Christ is born in the Christian through baptism, just as he was born into the world two thousand years ago. Just as the Church grows through the preaching of the Word and the administration of the Sacraments, so does the individual grow through hearing and partaking, until he is fully integrated into the body of Christ, meanwhile playing his individual part in the task of revealing Christ to the world, which is the role of the Church in the present age.

Thus the vision still gave meaning and purpose to his life and work. But the daily reality of the Church in which he lived and worked seemed far removed from the Vision which inspired him. So often it came across as a cold and unfeeling bureaucracy, or as the meaningless irrelevance it had become to the majority of his countrymen in the world of the twentieth century.

When Peter visited the community, he would endlessly argue with him about the Church, the reticence on such subjects long since dead. Peter often came to London to make his retreat and see some old friends, taking in some of the good things a trip to London always meant for him. On one such occasion, they were going at it hammer and tongs:

"Of course the Church isn't irrelevant, Mark. Look at the numbers we get at Mass every Sunday. Agreed, the Proddies are largely a dead loss with their hymn singing and empty churches" he continued, apparently oblivious to the slight element of contradiction contained in his pronouncement, "but the Catholic Church always commands attention. When you get films and plays on the telly with a bit of religion in them, the bloke with the collar on is always a Catholic priest and never a vicar, you'll find. Whenever the Proddie clergy are featured they are just a figure of fun. But people take notice of us, I tell you."

Mark sighed impatiently. "I agree that the Church is relevant to you and me, and possibly to the churchgoing faithful at large" he admitted. "Though even there I often wonder. What do you think would happen if the Church suddenly abolished the obligation of Sunday Mass, and told people they were encouraged to come, but not strictly obliged to; attendances would drop like a stone. Within a year, our churches would be as empty as everybody else's. So that doesn't say much for the effect the Church has even on the daily living of our practising Catholics. The laws about contraception and sexual matters generally are largely ignored; people grumble if the sermon's a bit too long; sometimes you can even feel them a having a battle of wills with you after the gospel, remaining standing for as long as possible, wishing you'd start the Creed."

"I know the feeling" chuckled Peter, "but I just say to myself 'sit down, you bastards; you're going to get a sermon whether you like it or not."

"The people are good and conscientious" continued Mark. "That's a different thing. They make me feel ashamed of myself sometimes. But when the Church does touch their lives, it's so often in a negative way; witness the poor sods who can't keep away from the confessional because they're guilt-ridden over some sexual problem that our notion of morality has inflicted on them in the first place."

On another occasion they were discussing the structure of the Church and the priesthood. Peter was proud of his status as a priest, though he angrily denied this when Mark accused him of it.

"There's nothing wrong with liking the name 'father' he remonstrated. That's what you are; father to your people. They look up to you and respect you as such."

Mark tried to explain his vision of the Church.

"The Church is the body of Christ, a living reality. You can't confuse that with the bureaucratic organisation we've got with parishes and dioceses" he protested. "The bishop in our set-up is an administrator, cut off from the people. The Church in essence is the group of believers gathered round the Lord's table, which nourished by his Body and Blood, then brings him into the world round about."

The more he discussed it and thought about it, the more his ideas grew.

"Look Pete" he continued, "the organisation only exists to serve the essence, the essential notion that describes the Church as she is. We need to get behind the facade to see what's there. A cynic might say take away the facade and there's nothing there. Maybe we are afraid of proving him right, the way we cling to our structures."

He paused, frowning in concentration.

"What I'd like to see" he went on, "is a real return to basics, to the idea of Christianity as it's described in the New Testament. The Church is the body of believers gathered round and filled with the Spirit of their crucified and risen Lord. In ordinary terms, that means we should be small groups of closely linked, like-minded people, leaders emerging naturally as leaders will. These leaders are your priests. Ordain them sacramentally, of course, but they should be the leaders of the group fitted by grace and nature, and therefore called by God, to inspire, direct and unify the group; they would not be a special, separate professional caste."

Warming to his theme, he continued:

"That's what gets me about mission countries. We take a black man out of his mud hut, send him to Rome for seven years, completely taking him out of his ordinary world, and then expect him to come back and be the priest for these people. We think that this is an advance on the position of trying to build the Church round white, missionary priests put into their midst. In that situation, it's the catechist who should be the priest, the man who lives and works with the people, doing an ordinary job most of the time, but being the focal point and organiser of the bread and butter Church. You don't need seven years shut away in a seminary to be a priest; a basic catechetical course in the fundamental truths of the Faith with a bit of down to earth theology and scripture; that's enough. Then ordain the guy and let him get on with it. If I had my way, I'd ordain a chap like Bert in our parish tomorrow. He's a natural leader and organiser; he should be a priest."

"In practical terms, it shouldn't be impossible to implement such a vision of the Church. What it would mean is this: all the existing grades in the hierarchy would gain instant promotion of a degree. The priest would be the leader of a small local group; perhaps only comprising half a dozen to a dozen families. He would be an ordinary bloke like any other, with a job and a wife and family. He would organise his little group, in contact and co-operation with similar groups round him.

"The man we now call the parish priest would be the bishop, with his diocese about the size of the existing parish. This would be the local Church in reality, and every bishop would personally know all of his flock; it wouldn't just be a theory as it is at present. The local Church would gather once a week round its bishop for Sunday Mass, the priests concelebrating with him. Or perhaps it would be once a month, with weekly Mass in the small family groups."

"To take the idea further, the present bishop would become the archbishop, and so on up the line. The clergy as a cut-off professional class would cease to exist; promotion would be from within the ranks, so a man could be married at any stage, even as Pope. After all, the first Pope was a married man. There would be a place for celibates and theologians, both necessary vocations in the Church. But every priest wouldn't have to be a celibate theologian, that's the point."

He paused, deep in thought, while Peter remained silent, apparently having given up the idea of stemming the tide.

"The Church gets and will get the priests she deserves. We talk about a vocations crisis, with one priest to look after umpty thousand people in Latin America or here for that matter, and then we try to dragoon young men into the system with emotional and spiritual blackmail. We pray like men demented for God to send us priests, and then close the door in the faces of all the natural candidates with an attitude of celibacy and professionalism. And we haven't even mentioned the possibility of women priests. Why the hell we're so dead set on an entirely male priesthood beats me. Even that noted misogynist St Paul said that in Christ, there is no male and female. Just because the social attitudes of the past two thousand years made the idea a non-starter, we've canonised that into a theological ideal. Sometimes it all makes me bloody sick," he brooded.

Peter shook his head slowly.

"You and your crazy ideas; they'll be the death of you, Mark, I'm telling you. That's the way to discontent and disillusion. Work hard, pray hard, and play hard is my recipe for a successful life as a priest; you blokes with your fancy ideas; there's priests dropping like flies all round us, and that's the reason."

It was the mid Seventies, and the time when the greatest numbers of priests were seeking laicisation. Peter was clearly worried that such a fate would befall Mark.

"For God's sake, Mark, get a grip" he urged. "You're playing with fire. The priest who leaves is like a leper; he never fits in anywhere, and the Church as good as washes her hands of him. It could happen to you, the way you're talking and going on; you need to settle down and accept things as they are. Sure, we can change and adapt" he added generously, "but be patient."

Mark shook his head, and smiled sadly, gazing down at the floor. "I'm a priest and I accept what that means, Pete; but the sort of change the Church has in mind and the sort that's really needed are worlds apart."

Later, in the quiet of his room, he wandered to himself what Peter would think if he knew about Madeleine. Shaking his head and sighing, he thought to himself:

"I'm a lost cause. Time was when I was the observant, goody-goody or so I considered myself, and Pete was the reprobate. Roles seem to have been reversed."

The thought of Madeleine soon had his pulses racing, and with a feeling of self disgust mingling with the raw physical excitement that always gripped him, he hurried round to her house.

"Mark" she smiled as she greeted him. "It's late for you; you're normally an afternoon visitor."

"I had to see you" he said thickly, his throat feeling as though he was being strangled by the desire that had taken possession of him.

Within seconds, he was hungrily kissing her, his hands frantically caressing and rummaging with her clothing.

"Gently, Mark, my darling" she murmured, taking him upstairs. "You rush so desperately at things. As I keep on saying to you, relax, and let nature take its course. There is a natural way with these things; let your body react as nature intends; don't try to push it and force it."

He quickly undressed and climbed into bed, while Madeleine went to the bathroom and prepared for bed as though it was any other night of her life. In the semi-darkened room, Mark stared at the partly open door, awaiting her return. The thumping of his heart moderated, and his loins slowly stirred in anticipation. After almost ten minutes, she appeared in the doorway, her nakedness silhouetted against the flimsy material of her night dress. She quietly drew back the covers and slipped in beside him. Then slowly and calmly she allowed him to hold her in the crook of his left arm, while his right band gently caressed the soft curves of her body.

Thrusting his body towards her, he became aware of a satisfying hardness developing, encouraged by her fondling. He eagerly sought to mount her, but she murmured:

"Not yet, my love; I too need to be ready."

But moments later, submitting to his urgent entreaties, she lay on her back, bending and spreading her legs wide, and guided the novice lover as he thrust against her. Penetration eluded him, however, and so she quickly and discreetly employed a little petroleum jelly as a lubricant. Again they tried, and this time, his excitement rapidly increasing, Mark realised that at last his moment had arrived. The additional lubrication permitted penetration, and as he pressed close, he suddenly knew an indescribable sensation of velvety smoothness as he entered her. With a low cry, he shivered as his body wound itself up to orgasm, and gripping her tightly to himself, he gave himself up to the explosive spasms that shook him as his seed came.

An immense feeling of calm and peace flooded over him, and he murmured endearments as he clung to her, her own excitement now beginning to grow. Gasping, he withdrew, and following her murmured instructions, caressed her intimately until she too climaxed, arching her body against him. Content, they lay together, arms and legs entwined, drifting on the edge of sleep. Madeleine stirred sleepily and kissed him.

"My wonderful lover. You are such a romantic, my sweetheart."

"A real Rudolph Vaselintino" Mark murmured mischievously, and then grinned sheepishly.

She smiled and hugged him. "Now sleep, my darling."

Ignoring the first faint stirrings of his conscience, he settled down contentedly, snuggling close to her, and was soon asleep, his arm curved possessively round her.

The next thing Mark knew was the dawn chorus, and the first shafts of light from the rising sun. With the new day came a growing feeling of guilt, and a sense of uncleanness. Though he had logically thought out his position, more than logic was at stake. He felt dirty and besmirched, and quickly rising, he went to the bathroom where he washed himself in cold water, scrubbing himself vigorously with the towel. Returning to the bedroom, he hurriedly dressed. The activity wakened Madeleine, who realised immediately that Mark was in the throes of guilt and conflict. She rose, dressed and sat with him in the kitchen as he drank a hastily prepared cup of tea. She tried to comfort him, but he yearned for the comfort and reassurance of confession and absolution, though he was fair enough to blame himself entirely for what had happened.

"You are so good and kind, Madeleine; far better than I deserve. I'm just a selfish brute who uses you."

"I love you, Mark" she replied quietly, stroking his hair. "I don't want to trap you or lay any claim to you. Your life is your own; you must decide your own future. Just let me help you."

"You have helped me" he lied bravely, though at that moment he was far from realising the truth of his words. Madeleine smiled gently as he hurriedly took his leave, the tears only coming once he had departed. She did not feel any bitterness towards him; her love was too generous for that.

Mark hurried back to the monastery, his guilt mingling with fears of the shame of discovery. What if someone had seen him leaving her house? What if she were pregnant? He knew little of the mysteries of womankind, but knew that it had to be a theoretically possible result of what had happened. Suddenly, perversely, he almost wished she were; he would then leave the priesthood, marry her and help bring up their child. The decision would have been taken out of his hands.

The attraction of life outside the priesthood suddenly gripped him. He had never seriously considered the possibility of any life other than that of the priesthood. Could he dare allow himself the consideration that another life was possible? He shuddered, the enormity of what was before him terrifying yet attracting him. But the time for such deliberations had not yet come.

FIFTY FOUR

Mark slowly settled back into a kind of normality. Feeling too ashamed of the enormity of what he had done to confide in one of his fellow priests in the community, he crossed London to go to confession to a priest he had never met or even heard of before, and meekly accepted the verbal scourging he received. He had simply confessed to having sexual relations with a married woman as a priest and religious, and agreed that he would not see her again. His assent to the confessor's insistence on this point was automatic, even unthinking. He suddenly felt that perhaps this would be best for all concerned. He new a desire to return to the simple, uncomplicated life he had known before Madeleine; or before sexual desire had so insistently disrupted his peace of mind.

He threw himself into his priestly duties with an almost frantic urgency, welcoming the tiredness and utter weariness each evening brought. He tried to bring a little order into his prayer life, making a new effort to recite the divine office on a more regular basis, though with only partial success. He tended to grow more irritable and intolerant, finding it difficult on occasion to present the image of the nice, kind, cheerful father Kennedy that everyone knew and took for granted. The grumblings of the devout, middle aged women who were so prominent in many of the parish activities seemed to assume a new ability to penetrate beneath his skin; the excuses of the lapsed and the carelessness of the practising Catholics brought a new sarcasm to his lips in his conversations with his fellow priests.

On one occasion, he found himself regarding the simple happiness of an engaged couple he was instructing before marriage almost like a slap in the face for his barren celibacy. He was tempted more and more to regard the laity, particularly the married, as second class Christians, with scant commitment to the Gospel of the God of love on whose cross he was slowly being crucified.

At times, he took himself sharply to task for these thoughts, but he realised that without the greatest diligence, he could soon become just another bitter, disillusioned priest. He had met some in his time, men whose commitment had turned sour, who spent their time indulging their own selfishness, going through the motions of their duties. Some sought solace in the bottle, others more acceptably but just as ruinously in genteel pursuits such as music, learning for learning's sake, or even whacking golf balls in all directions.

The strain soon began to tell. One night, he suddenly awoke in the small hours, gripped by the blackest depression he had ever known. He lay there with the spectres of doom flooding into his mind and a great grief gripped him. Slowly, the tears began to trickle down his cheeks, splashing onto the pillow beside him. His life seemed hollow, barren, loveless. He felt utterly alone, bereft, destined to be deprived for ever of the simple joys and comforts that human life ought to bring to every member of the human race. He stared through the darkness at the well-known lineaments of his room suddenly hateful in their oppressive familiarity, like the features of a gaoler seen every day.

He tried to pray, but then God seemed to have become the gaoler, mocking him in his despair. Even the crucified Christ normally his comfort in distress, seemed remote, offering no consolation.

"You had a brief passion to undergo, Lord; three days and it was over. You ask me to undergo mine for a lifetime."

Mercifully, sleep soon returned, and next morning, the bright sunshine seemed to put things in a new light. The horrors of the hours of darkness were once more safely confined in the deeper recesses of his mind.

Once more he fought on, visiting, preaching, baptising, and suffering the frustrations of the endless clergy meetings, stultifyingly pointless though they seemed to be. He smiled to himself as he recalled one of Peter's comments when confronted with yet another commission meeting:

"They'll be establishing commissions to examine ways of wiping your arse next."

His resentment and sense of rebelliousness grew; sometimes the Church seemed to treat her priests like mindless drones who were expected to labour on patiently without question, like so many donkeys. He began to see obedience as the brutally efficient tool the Church had devised for keeping the machine running smoothly, thinly veneered with the trappings of virtue. It repressed questioning, and ensured the problem-free running of the organisation. Priests and religious were the cannon fodder needed to support the system, and Mark often felt used, his sense of vocation taken advantage of.

He tried valiantly to comply with the counsels of his confessor, resisting the urge to visit Madeleine, but the compulsive need proved too strong; and though he sometimes deliberately masturbated to forestall his need, he found himself inevitably drawn to her every three or four weeks. Recognising the emotional turmoil through which he was trying to work his way, she accepted the situation as it was. Their lovemaking was desperate and passionate, Mark seeking to slake his sexual thirst with mixed success, and Madeleine content to try and meet his needs, if only on a temporary basis. Afterwards, they would discuss the state of the Church and the world, and Mark would agonise over the contradictions so painfully present in his own life.

FIFTY FIVE

It could not last. Mark had not forgotten the warning he had received some weeks earlier in the anguish of the despair-filled small hours, and at the beginning of September, the crisis finally came.

This time, it happened in the full light of day. The waves of black despair suddenly hit him as he was processing out onto the altar for Mass. A kind of panic gripped him as he wondered desperately whether he would be able to get through the service without openly breaking down. Summoning his last reserves, he somehow managed, then hurrying to his room, he threw himself onto the bed and allowed the tears to come.

For some time he wept, deep groans forcing their way out of his aching chest, the tears drenching his pillow. His throat ached as the sobs tore at him, but eventually, the physical reaction subsided, and once more, he was able to regain control and begin to take stock of himself and his situation.

Things had fundamentally changed. He needed time to rest, time to think; time away from the parish and its myriad demands. He immediately thought of a friendly old priest for whom he had given a mission a couple of years previously. His parish was in a small south coast town, and Mark knew he would be welcome there. Hurrying along to the superior's room, he made his request for a few days break; he explained in general terms that he was tired, run down, and needed a little time off.

"We're all tired, father" his superior began a little stiffly.

"Look, father" Mark interrupted starkly, tears springing to his eyes, "I need time off, and I'm taking it, whether you like it or not. If I don't get away now, I won't answer for the consequences."

The older priest realised immediately that this was no ordinary request, and seeing Mark's state, hastily agreed. The necessary arrangements were quickly made, and Mark soon found himself on his way, a few belongings stuffed hurriedly into a suitcase.

"Let me know how things are after a day or two" his superior had requested, and Mark had agreed in a bemused sort of way, though communication with the powers was the last thing he wanted at that moment. Boarding the train, he sank into his seat with a sense of relief, and watched the grimy London suburbs slipping away. The regular, rattling motion of the train had a soothing effect on his jangled nerves, and he quickly began to relax, closing his eyes, letting his head rest against the rough padding of the old fashioned bench seat. He was wedged comfortably in the corner, and a sense of peace began to steal over him.

What was happening to him? He could as yet offer no answers, other than that he was exhausted; physically, mentally, emotionally and spiritually. But he knew that he had reached a turning point; things would never be the same again. He knew that he had to allow himself the freedom to rethink his whole life; he could take nothing for granted.

The days that followed afforded him ample leisure for this pursuit. His welcome had been warm, and he quickly settled in. He told the priest the bare bones of his story, and wisely, the old man gave him the privacy he needed by forbearing to question him. His days were spent in long walks round the town, along the sea front and even out into the surrounding countryside. Ten, fifteen, and soon even twenty miles were nothing to him as he walked, the September sunshine and the mellowing seasonal tints providing a comforting backdrop for the tumult within, which sought expression in the unrelenting physical demands he imposed upon himself.

At first he hardly dared think of it, but very quickly, he began to ask himself some ultimate questions. His life he saw as a shambles; celibacy he now admitted to himself had long since become an insupportable contradiction. In the early days as a student, it had been a present reality in his life, though even then it had never been joyfully embraced. Desires had been rigorously suppressed in the name of temptation, and he thought bitterly of the years of scruples, the torment of darker urges occasionally threatening to surface, and later the constant masturbation which made him feel soiled and disgusted with himself. Then there was his affair with Madeleine. He did not condemn himself for it rationally, but it crippled his conscience none the less.

The priesthood itself too he saw as another element in his nightmare burden. The Church exacted the last pound of flesh from her priests; they were the dogsbodies on whose unremitting toil the whole edifice rested. His sense of vocation had suddenly gone; drained by the years of service that the Church had demanded as a duty, without gratitude or appreciation. He now felt a need to be free.

Did he have to remain a priest? Others had taken the tremendous step of seeking laicisation; should he follow in their footsteps? He suddenly saw such a course as not only possible, but even as necessary, as his present life was so eminently unliveable.

He voiced these thoughts to his superior when reporting back to him, and the effect was to bring about a hasty visit. Mark's position was rapidly hardening; within the space of a few short days he had progressed from an appreciation of his need for a break from the burdens that had crushed him, through an initial recognition that a different form of life was a possibility, to a strongly burgeoning desire for such a life.

A course of counselling sessions in London was hurriedly arranged. He would travel to town once a week for his session, returning to his seaside retreat afterwards. He approached his first one somewhat dubiously, wondering whether he was being sent to a brainwashing centre as a last ditch effort to save his vocation, but he was quickly put at his ease. His counsellor was a nun, a few years older than himself, and she quickly overcame his initial prejudices. He soon realised that he could trust her, and that she was not trying to persuade him one way or the other. She understood that her role was to help him in his task of pondering on his life and seeking answers to the questions he needed to be able to ask himself. She helped him to see that he could be free; laicisation and even marriage were possibilities for him which he could allow himself to consider. The change of perspective was staggering: for as long as he could remember, from the distant days of childhood, marriage and an honourable fulfilment of emotional and sexual needs had been avenues closed to him. Suddenly, the bonds imposed by his deep sense of vocation had been loosened, and the possibilities opening up before him were breathtaking.

As the sessions progressed, he quickly began to realise that his initial sense of rejection of his pain and its causes had been healthy, and the way forward was going to be through a fundamental change in his whole life. Meanwhile, he realised that he had to keep people informed of what was happening to him. He wrote to Madeleine, a task of comparative ease, as she had known of the troubles facing him, and their theoretically possible outcome. His family was another question.

In the first instance, he wrote to Tony and Elizabeth, sensing that of all his family, they would be most likely to understand and sympathise. He recalled Tony's words of years before, when he had promised his help if ever things turned sour in the priesthood. His letter was stark, a bare presentation of the facts, and in it, Mark put plainly the course he was considering. As he wrote the words 'I am thinking of leaving the priesthood' their import awed him, yet filled him with a heady sense of freedom. Writing the words 'I want to be free to marry if I wish to,' he was filled with a deep sense of excitement at the physical and emotional fulfilment it could bring.

Sealing the letter, he quickly posted it, with the sense of taking an irrevocable step. The fat was in the fire now. But he need not have worried. Tony and Elizabeth's reaction was as he had hoped; total sympathy and understanding, an acceptance of him as their Mark; any other consideration was for them of very minor significance. They wrote back immediately, expressing their support and offering him a home with them for as long as he needed one.

"Mum and Brenda will take it hard, though" warned Tony, and Mark realised that this would be the case. Attitudes to priests leaving had moderated more recently, but still for many Catholics it was the ultimate disaster, the unforgivable sin, the final betrayal. This, he suspected, was how the rest of the family would see his actions.

He suddenly realised how far his decision making had gone; he was not only allowing himself the possibility of thinking about leaving the priesthood, but in a real sense, he knew that the decision was already made. He could not contemplate a backtracking, a picking up of his burdens and problems once again.

He felt like a newly released prisoner, blinking in the unaccustomed sunlight. The idea of turning his back and re-entering the cell from which he had just emerged was unthinkable. Yet part of him was afraid, and would have welcomed the security such a move would have given. He knew that enormous problems lay ahead. Some people would think of him as, and call him a Judas; perhaps his conscience would to an extent join their ranks. Also what would he do? He would have a living to earn, and he felt singularly unfitted for anything. Priests who left usually seemed to end up in teaching or social work, but Mark felt no desire for either of these vocations.

"But come what may" he vowed to himself, "I'll find something. I'd rather sweep the streets than go back to life as it was as a priest."

He told Neville, who as ever, took the news calmly enough. He phoned Mark one evening, and they talked for some time.

"You seem to have made up your mind, dear boy."

"Not yet; I'm just allowing myself to think about it" protested Mark, but he knew that Neville was right. His letter breaking the news had given Neville the basic facts, and his friend seemed generally sympathetic to his situation.

"I can't put myself in your shoes, my dear Mark, but it certainly seems as though needs must in your case. It will be a hard road that you will tread, leaving the priesthood; the Church does not forgive such a move easily. For a Church that prides herself on being the Church of sinners and the remission of sin, she tends to adopt a very pharisaical attitude in this regard."

He then added thoughtfully: "Every sin can be forgiven except this one; not that we are even talking about sin here. But even if she grants you laicisation, which she may, after a long wait, you will always be something of an outcast. You will become a non person in her eyes; someone whose existence she would prefer not to have to acknowledge. But of course you must always remember that I am your friend, for what it's worth, and my poor efforts will always be at your service if I can render assistance in any way."

Mark blinked back the tears at his friend's words; he wept frequently and easily at this time; a song, a word, the slightest stimulus seemed to be sufficient. He promised that he would always keep Neville informed of his plans, and quietly replaced the phone.

Peter was more robust in his reaction. He made a special journey to Mark's seaside haven to discuss the situation with him.

"I knew it would come to this" he groaned as he poured a generous libation of whisky into the glasses Mark had made ready. Peter, true to form, had produced the bottle as if from nowhere. In his eyes it was the indispensable accompaniment to deep discussion, and on this occasion Mark was grateful enough for its comfort.

"Bloody hell, though, Mark, I didn't know there was a woman in the case."

Mark had told his family and friends the broad outline of his position, though carefully concealing Madeleine's identity. He felt a loyalty to her that made him reluctant to disclose more than was absolutely necessary to explain his position.

"Imagine the earnest and sincere Mark having it off with a woman" he wondered. "I hope you had the sense to use a Johnny" he added crudely. "You wouldn't be the first priest to dip his wick, but the problems really start when the woman gets in the club. But seriously, Mark, you've got to think long and hard about what you're talking about doing. You don't have to chuck in the priesthood because of this sort of problem, you know. Many priests have problems regarding sex; I'm sure you realise as well as I do that lots of the blokes masturbate on occasion. I know I do; in fact meet the wife" he said, holding out his right hand, the temptation to his rather robust sense of humour irresistible, in spite of the deadly serious approach he was taking to the discussion they were having.

"Sometimes I feel that I'm about as pure as driven shit" he confessed, "but God forgives and strengthens us. Sinning is a part of human life as it's lived in the real world. In fact to be perfectly honest, I sometimes feel that a good screw to get it out of our systems would do none of us any harm. Have your fling discreetly, then get on with life - I don't say it's a good thing, but it can be a solution as far as I'm concerned."

"I'm sick of buggering about with double standards, Pete" protested Mark. "I can't live like that any longer. I've been kidding myself and living a lie as it is. I can't go on doing it in cold blood. As I see it, you're a priest and therefore more or less chaste; we can forgive and forget the occasional lapse; that's human weakness. But we're talking about something entirely different here. Celibacy for me has been a bloody shambles from day one, when I look back at my life. It's always been a major problem, and I'm sick and tired of trying to cope with a state I just don't want. I want love, I want a sex life if you like. I want it, and I need it. Trying to be celibate is destroying me. I have to be able to be at peace with myself and the only way to do that is to leave and get married."

"What about the 'thou art a priest for ever, according to the order of Melchisedec' idea, then? You're a priest, Mark; with the vocation comes the means to live it faithfully; no-one is tempted beyond his strength."

"It's too late for all that, Pete" replied Mark wearily. Maybe a saint could take on those sorts of burdens but I'm just speaking from a profound reflection on my life and experience as it's been. In some way, I'm in the wrong place in life. I can't explain it fully. I've always had a deep sense of vocation to the priesthood, but it's just proved impossible to live up to. There's the problem of sex, the most urgent and immediate, probably. But I've never been comfortable in the ecclesiastical world as such, either. I can't accept the priesthood as a superior caste in the Church. I feel totally stifled in a situation where I've got to dress differently from ordinary people, live a life that's essentially apart from theirs; subject myself in obedience to a system that forbids frank and honest discussion of problems. Oh, I know it's a lot better now than it used to be, but even you must admit that the Church does not allow freedom of discussion to her priests. She doesn't even allow them freedom of conscience. The Holy Office is alive and well, as many a priest and theologian knows to his cost."

Mark stared at the floor for moment before continuing.

"It's no good, Pete. I've been looking at myself and not liking what I see. I see a man whose life is falling apart. I can't live without some sort of sexual fulfilment, and so my life is full of all sorts of grubby substitutes for the personal realisation that most men take for granted. Maybe it's different for you; you perhaps have a celibate life that's marked by the occasional failure, or even the fairly frequent failure. But you accept the basic notion as a viable way of life for yourself. I can't look at it in that way. To me, the whole thing has become something hateful, that I resent with every fibre of my being. It's turning me into the sort of person I'd rather not be. I find myself becoming bitter, resenting the happiness of ordinary people. To me, that's a strong signal that it's time for a fundamental change."

Mark looked at his friend, who was toying with his empty glass, as if uncertain how to respond to his attempts at self-explanation.

"The whole situation is killing me, stifling me, Pete" Mark continued, "I've got to get out and save my sanity and self-respect. I suppose that sounds terrible to you, but I do accept the Church as Christ's Church. My faith is still fundamentally there. Maybe the system as it exists is basically O.K. too; all I'm saying is that I can't live with it any longer. Not that I'm not willing to live with it, even; I just find myself literally unable to, any more."

Peter stared in silence at his friend for a few moments, and then sighed deeply.

"I've been worried about you for two or three years now, Mark, and I can see I had good cause to be worried. God, what a bloody mess! Is there no way..."

He paused. "No, I suppose not," he brooded. "It's obviously gone too far for that. But you do realise what's down the road you're taking?"

Mark nodded dumbly. "I know, Pete, but it has to be; I know I'll be hurting people, they won't understand; motives and integrity will be questioned. But what else can I do? And don't suggest one of those ecclesiastical rehabilitation centres" he added hastily. "I don't need rehabilitating, I just need to find a way of life in which I can function as a person. I don't ask a lot out of life; a simple living so that I can pay my way; a woman to love and be loved by; maybe a couple of kids; and that's it."

"But what about your sense of vocation?" Peter protested.

"It's just gone; I can't explain it, but something within me just refuses to accept it any longer. Thinking about it, I suppose I could imagine living and working as a priest in a very different set-up to the past. If the Church came to accept weekend, married priests, if you like; men who did ordinary jobs and lived ordinary lives, who then ministered as priests to their local brethren in house Masses or the Sunday liturgy in church; that I could accept."

Peter snorted contemptuously.

"You're a bloody day-dreamer, Mark. You talk a right load of crap sometimes. God knows what sort of shocks you're in for out in the world. It's a rough and cruel place to be, you know. In the Order, you've been sheltered and looked after; you're in for a bloody rude awakening."

Mark sighed and shook his head sadly.

"You may well be right, Pete. I'm not expecting an easy time in the outside world, but can't you see," he pleaded, "that I'm doing what I feel is right, what I have to do? Don't you, my oldest and deepest friend, question my motives and integrity. At least allow me that much."

Peter softened somewhat. He had a fairly well developed emotional streak in his nature, though he would have described himself as being as hard as nails, but he was in many ways unable to put himself in anyone else's place. He could only see problems from his own stand point, and so could only see Mark's position as a betrayal and a ghastly mistake, but at least he could see his sincerity, and reluctantly, had admitted as much. He assured Mark of his friendship if not his support, but later, as Mark waved his farewells, watching Peter's train begin its return journey to London, he realised that Peter was leaving him in a more fundamental sense. He knew that something had gone from their relationship. A friendship that had started between two eleven year olds had altered; it would never be the same again. Peter could accept Mark's modern and way-out theories as long as they didn't affect him, but when they became more than theories, then that was another matter.

Their paths were diverging, probably for good, and God alone knew whether they would ever even meet again, let alone confide in one another with the easy camaraderie of yesterday.

The days passed, and Mark restlessly pounded the well-worn tracks of his established daily walks. His moods altered suddenly as his emotions ranged between guilt over the past, a wild elation caused by his new-found freedom, and a numbing sense of grief as his old life struggled in its death throes, and his new life pushed its way as painfully into the world.

He had been celebrating his daily Mass until this time, but now, suddenly, it became unthinkable. He realised this one morning as he was halfway through, and finishing the ceremony became something of a battle. As he removed the vestments, he knew it was for the last time. But the Mass was still important to him, and so he continued faithfully to attend Mass and receive Holy Communion.

The Vision was still a reality for him amid all the pain and confusion of those days, and would, he hoped, remain the mainspring of his life, but it had to be restated. God so often seemed far distant from him; he had known a sense of nearness to Christ on occasion; he thought back ruefully to the early days when penitential self-flagellation, now long since abandoned by the Order in its efforts at modernisation, had given him a real sense of closeness to the suffering Christ through a physical sharing in his pain. More recently, his celebrations of Mass had brought an experience of unity with his Lord, but it was as though these moments were mere islands in a vast sea of sterility as far as his relationship with Christ was concerned. The Vision had long excited him, and still had the power to move him, but was it merely an intellectual experience distilled from his appreciation of modern theology? He knew that the yawning gulf between the Christ of faith and the world of nuclear fission, the computer and the chip shop, Parliament and the public house, had to be bridged somehow.

The answer for some today seemed to lie in the puerile excesses of the Charismatic movement. Mark had come into contact with it on occasion, but it had always left him cold. The excitement that sometimes ran like a flame round a crowded room, filled with singing, swaying bodies, left him feeling a complete outsider.

Where did the answer lie?

As he walked and thought and prayed, the sea, sun and sand his only companions, the glimmerings of a possible way ahead began to form. The two keywords of his Vision were Incarnation and Resurrection.

"The Word was made flesh, and dwelt amongst us." Man's final and complete experience of God was based on the Incarnation, God becoming man. He suddenly realised that the Word had for too long: been formalised, imprisoned in the trappings of conventionally organised religion as surely as the host was looked in the tabernacle.

The Word had to be made flesh in this day and age; in his case, this meant in the concrete circumstances of ordinary secular living in twentieth century Britain. The flesh of the entwined bodies of man and woman, the flesh of factory and football match, the flesh of the blood, sweat and tears, the laughter and grief, the work and the enjoyment that made up the rich and varied banquet that we call human life. He knew that for too long he had tried to be content with the crumbs that fell from the table; now he had to take his seat with the other diners, and somehow not so much bring the Christ of his faith to the banquet, but rather, find that in faith, his Christ was already seated there with the other guests.

Slowly, his conscience came to grips with his new approach to life; nothing in the rules gave him any positive help, so he realised that he had to continue to rely on the basic moral imperative: good must be done, and evil avoided. He accepted his way forward as good, and the evils of his life heretofore seemed apparent. The Church may frown and condemn, but he could still pray and accept the basic commandment to love the Lord his God, and his neighbour as himself. In the months and years ahead, this had to be his guide as he sought Christ in, and brought Christ to, the secular world into which he knew he must plunge himself.

The decision was made. The theoretical possibility had rapidly developed into the dawning reality in his life. He was, in his own eyes at least, already an ex-priest. He communicated his decision to his superiors, who reluctantly agreed that at least on a temporary basis, he should spend some time in the outside world. Mark contacted Madeleine once again and arranged to go and see her. The thought of her sensuously feminine body soon gave him the familiar sense of churning desire in the pit of his stomach, and he realised that he had to possess her once again.

He caught the train to London, and impatiently sighed as the miles seemed to drag by, but eventually he reached his destination and hurriedly made his way to the familiar house, knocking at the door and almost pushing his way inside in his eagerness to hold her.

"Let's get married" he breathed as he seized her and hungrily kissed her. She made no attempt to resist his passion, but afterwards she discussed with him the major decisions he had been making.

"You are a free man now, my love. I know I have played my part in making you free... "And in making me a man" whispered Mark mischievously, unable to resist the impulse as he held her close to himself.

"But I want you to be free" Madeleine continued, trying vainly to release herself from his possessive embrace. "You have just loosened yourself from the Church's apron strings; you must not immediately try to tie yourself to me. Go into the world, find your feet, learn to live your new life; then we'll see."

"But I want you, my love; I need you" protested Mark.

"But do you love me for myself, my darling?" she questioned. "We both need time; I need time, but you need it far more. Go and settle down in your new life; we'll keep in touch with one another, and we shall see."

With this, Mark had to be content, and kissing him tenderly, she sent him on his way. She would have married him without hesitation, but her love for him was too great for that. His freedom was a tender young plant that she had seen slowly and painfully struggling into life. She would not take advantage of his innocence and naiveté; part of her hoped and prayed that he would come back to her; though in her heart of hearts she knew that when he settled down, he would realise that she had been able to be his teacher and guide, but he needed a wife nearer to him in age who could possibly give him children. However, time alone would tell.

Meanwhile Mark arranged to go and live with Tony and Elizabeth, as his first step into his new world. As foreseen, the rest of the family was stunned by the news of his decision; an uncomprehending bewilderment, a shocked sense of hurt was the immediate response. Mark's new-found life, his infant sense of freedom and sanity was madness to them. He could only plead for patience and trust in the integrity with which he had tried to reach his decision, and leave the rest to the healing effects of time and the mercy of God.

He wasted no time in making his preparations for departure from the monastery. He packed his few belongings into his battered suitcase, leaving his habit, clerical collar and the other accoutrements of his priesthood hanging forlornly in the rickety wardrobe that had housed his worldly goods for the past few years. There was no sense of regret; merely an impatient desire to cut himself off from the past, and immerse himself in his new life. He had to find a job, learn to be independent and support himself. He was consumed with a need to make a start.

Armed with the few pounds given him to meet his immediate needs for the next few days, he gripped the handle of his case, strode along the corridor for the last time, and opened the front door. The day was young and bright; his life was half over but just beginning, he thought to himself as he stepped outside and firmly closed the door behind him. The past was already yesterday, and his unknown tomorrow held out its arms to welcome him.

Printed in Great Britain by
Amazon.co.uk, Ltd.,
Marston Gate.